Overwhelmed by YOU

BOOK 2: TEAR ASUNDER

NASHODA ROSE

Overwhelmed by You
Published by Nashoda Rose
Copyright © 2014 by Nashoda Rose
Toronto, Canada

ISBN: 978-0-9937023-2-7

Copyright © 2014 Cover by Kari Ayasha, Cover to Cover Designs
Content Edited by Kristin Anders, The Romantic Editor
Formatting by Self Publishing Editing Service
Line Editing by The Polished Pen
Proof Reading by The Polished Pen

Warning: This book contains offensive language, violence, and sexual content.

ISBN: 978-0-9937023-3-4

Prologue

I swung the statue down onto his skull again and again.
The sound of crushing bone crackled throughout the room.
Blood splattered my green T-shirt like a mist of rain.
I didn't care. Not one bit.
He destroyed her.
He deserved this.
Images of the bruises on her arms, the puncture marks, blurred my vision.
She watched me kill him.
Sitting on the floor, dazed with a glassy look in her eyes.
This was my fault.
I let this happen to her. I didn't protect her.
I threw the statue aside. It made a loud thud as it hit the wood floor, and she jerked. I glanced at the needles on the bedside table.
The yellow elastic band.
I was glad he was dead.
I strode over to her, picked her frail, weightless body up, and ran.
Her beauty was wilting. My angel. I had done that.

Ream

"Babe … You're going to fuckin' kill me." Body tightening, I groaned as my dick jerked in her mouth. "Ahh, Christ." She withdrew then circled the tip with her tongue as her hand cupped my balls, only to slide a finger down further to caress between my butt cheeks. Holy fuck, I'd never been blowed like this before—ever. Shit, who was I kidding? I never let a woman have this kind of control over me. If I had … I didn't like to remember it.

The heat of her mouth surrounded me again, and she slowly took all of me until her lips touched my balls. I nearly came right then as I swore beneath my breath, my fingers fisting in her hair.

"Baby."

Her silky moisture felt like I was wrapped in velvet. She slowly slid back and my hands curled into the sheet as the pressure increased until I slipped from her mouth. She took a breath then swallowed me again. I was so turned on, I couldn't even think straight. Watching her take me like that … God, how the fuck did I ever get off before her?

Her head bobbed up and down faster, then harder, and all I could hear was her sweet mouth sucking my cock like it was her Popsicle.

I closed my eyes. Jesus, I never wanted it to end.

Harder. Suck me, harder.

My eyes flew open and I stiffened. No. Don't ruin this. Fuck.

But it always did.

Be good and it won't hurt.

I was breathing too hard. I was too tense. It would hurt more if I was tense.

Smack.

Ask me for more.

No. No, more.

Smack.

Ask me nicely.

2

Mo ... re. Plea ... se.

Fuck no. Jesus, why?

Because I hated this and I needed to end it and get the fuck out—fast. Letting her go down on me was a mistake. I never let a chick put her mouth me. Shit, what had I been thinking? I thought it might be different after spending two weeks with her. I liked her, damn it. But I couldn't do this.

I grabbed her by the shoulders. "Get off me."

Her magnetic blue eyes widened, and I felt her hand jerk on my cock. "What?"

"I said get the fuck off me." My hands tightened on her shoulders and I felt the familiar sickness rolling in my stomach. I had to get the hell out of here. I should've never done this with her. I didn't do sweet and slow; I did fast and hard and I was out of there before the bullshit barreled into me.

I went to roll out from under her, but she found my hand that had a death grip on the sheet. Her fingers slowly pried open my fist, and then she entwined them with mine and squeezed.

I looked down at her and for a moment I thought maybe I could … "No." I said the word, but didn't move.

She lowered her head, but kept her eyes on me while her tongue teased the head of my cock. She kissed it, gentle and tender, something I'd never had before. And I wanted it, but chicks sucking my cock was off limits. It was them having power that let the demons in.

I groaned as her tongue flicked over the sensitive tip. My fingers dug into her flesh and I fought the need to throw her away from me and, at the same time, push her head down on my cock, forcing her to take me deeper.

"I want to taste you. Come for me," she said.

I couldn't. Not like this. She had too much of me already. Fuck this. Screw all of it. I pushed her off me and her hand slipped from my cock as she fell to the side.

"Ream?"

I ignored her as I sat up and swung my legs over the side of the bed. I went to get up when her arms came around my neck.

"What do you need?"

"To leave." I reached down for my jeans lying on the floor. This was stupid. I should've never hooked up with her. She was my band-mate's girl's best friend.

I went to stand when she grabbed my arm and pulled me back until I lay on the bed. "Jesus. I don't want to fuck you, Kat." I knew it was a lie because I wanted to fuck this girl bad.

I'd spent two weeks with her at the farm waiting for news about Emily and Logan. We'd unpacked all the boxes, painted the rooms, fixed fences for the horse paddocks, even planted flowers in the gar-den. Okay, she did that, I watched while drinking a beer.

There was no question Kat was hot—long legs, blonde, beauti-ful bright blue eyes, and she had this angled jaw that made her look hard and intense, but Kat was … fun. Despite the emotional worry that we both felt for our friends, Kat wasn't a sobbing mess. Shit, I never once saw her cry.

When we'd met at the bar the night Emily was kidnapped, I'd seen her from the stage and my first thought was she looked like a snobby bitch. But she was hot, so I wanted to fuck her. Probably would've if shit hadn't hit the fan with Emily.

I'd found out over the next two weeks that Kat was nothing like I'd labelled her. Fuck, the girl had a strength inside her that sur-passed my own. And that made me want to fuck her more.

I was dragged back to the present when Kat leaned over me and our eyes locked. The corners of her lips slowly curved upwards with that sweet, sassy smile. "Bullshit," she said. Her hand found my pul-sating cock again and she stroked it once. "This," she squeezed and I groaned as the blood rushed to the head, "wants me. So, tell me what you need?"

I never had conversations in bed with chicks, let alone had time to discuss what the hell I needed, because I always just took what I needed and then left. Always quick, hard and done before there was time for the darkness to fuck with me.

But she'd already far surpassed my usual flings. I didn't do repeats and yet here I was fucking the same chick over and over again and, to top it off, I let her suck my cock. What had I been thinking? I hadn't been thinking, that's how it had gotten this far.

But Kat brought me back from my inner darkness that she didn't even know existed. She'd kept it away. That was until she'd gone down on me and then it all went to shit again.

For once, I wanted a girl ... and not just to get off. I had no qualms about kicking a woman from my bed and had done it so many times now that I was numb to the hurt I saw on their faces. It wasn't like I didn't tell them straight up what it was before they spread their legs. I was discreet about who I fucked and I didn't get emotionally attached; it was impossible for me. I was never meant to appreciate women. That was ruined for me a long time ago.

But Kat ... Kat was unexpected. She gave me what I needed. There was no clinging, no worshipping like the band's groupies. I hated that.

"I want you inside me again." Kat straddled me and as soon as she did I abruptly grabbed her around the waist, and she squealed as I tossed her onto her back then crawled on top, pinning her in place with my weight.

"You belong beneath me, beautiful." This is where it was safe. Beneath me. Where I could walk away if I wanted. Where I could control her. I needed control. I could have it no other way.

Kat laughed, her eyes sparkling like blue gems. I froze, staring at the woman trapped under me. Unfuckinexpected. We'd both decided that this was a one-nighter, although technically it had already become two. How did this happen? I asked myself this, but I knew how. It was like she fed a part of me that had lain dormant for years. Her honesty and ease, the way she moved without insecurity. Not self-absorption ... no, it was purity. Something I didn't have in any part of me anymore.

Fuck, it had been me who'd woken up this morning with my

arm slung over her waist. The shock that plowed into me had me do the only thing I could to get rid of it … I rolled her over, straddled her and sunk my cock in hard and abruptly.

She'd woken up moaning and arching her hips up to meet my thrusts. I came within seconds. She didn't and it was the first time I felt guilty for fucking a girl and not looking after her. But Kat kissed me and then got up and went into the bathroom where I heard the shower turn on.

I lay back and the first thought that came to mind was if I should go in there and join her. I imagined licking her pussy, making her beg me, tasting the sweetness and hearing her moan beneath my assault.

But I didn't. I needed distance, to get my control back of my emotions. Instead, I listen to the water and imagined her hands rubbing over her body until I fell back asleep.

That was when I woke to her sucking my cock.

"Belong?" Her brows rose and I wanted to kiss that sassy look right off her face.

I knew she wouldn't like that comment. There was no question we'd clash; her confidence and sassy mouth, my need to control every situation, something I lacked as a kid and now had to have in every part of my life. That's why the band trusted me to look after the negotiations. Nothing slid by me, I kept emotions out of business, and was never afraid to walk away if I didn't get what I wanted.

"Take it or leave it." Harsh, but it had to be this way. Better she know that now.

I narrowed my eyes as laughter trickled from her parted lips then she tried to slip away. I grasped her under the armpits. She thought I was teasing—I wasn't. "You belong where I say you do, and that's with me on top of you, sinking my cock deep inside that sweet, tight wetness. And make no mistake, it's begging for it, Kit-kat."

"Begging?" She licked her lips.

I leaned forward until my mouth was so close to hers that if I took a deep breath they'd touch. Her chest stopped rising.

Not yet, beautiful.

Anticipation was the tie to control. I could control it. I knew how to make a woman want a man so badly she'd do anything to stop the aching need. It wasn't something I was proud of, but I'd learned it and I'd use my skill to bend Kat to my will. If she understood that, then maybe I'd consider letting her stay in my bed a little longer.

Her breath was like a warm breeze heating my skin. I tilted my head to the side and let the two day growth of facial hair graze lightly across her skin. I grunted when I heard the sound … that distinct inhale of air and then the quivering of her body.

"Beg me." I was used to being the one forced to beg. Now … now I had to have it this way.

"Never," she retorted.

I could have her pliant in minutes, but the tightening in my chest was a reminder of what I tried to forget every fuckin' day of my life. I had to walk away from this.

Okay, one more time, and then I'd leave. She knew this wasn't anything more than satisfying both our needs. She'd be good with that. The question that pushed into me like a bull charging was— was I? I buried it hard and fast, just like I did my cock between a woman's legs.

"Oh, baby, wrong answer." Both my hands went to her wrists and I pulled her arms above her head and locked them there before she could protest. I may not get her to beg, because shit, I didn't have the time for that, but I could make her moan and writhe beneath me.

"Ream, let me go."

I knew my grip was bruising, but I needed her immobile. I needed her to submit to me, the nightmares were too close now to let her touch me. I shut her up by taking her mouth, my tongue pushing past her teeth and then sealing her words with my forceful, hard kiss.

She squiggled with protest, her lush body still damp from her shower. It was delectable how her lips moved over mine willingly, meeting the harshness with her own even though she was protesting. I pulled away. "Beg me."

"No," she breathed and struggled to free her hands. "Let me go."

Sweet fucking God, she was hot. Her breasts bounced and swayed while her body thrashed against me. The soft, heated glow in her cheeks made her look even more irresistible, and for a second I was the one who was losing control as the anticipation to sink inside her again outweighed winning.

Kat nearly clocked me in the fucking neck as I loosened my grip and her one arm freed. Her elbow swung in front of me, and I had to lurch back. "I don't beg. Ever."

My cock was throbbing between her legs and there was no chance I could let her go now. This wasn't just about me getting off anymore. This was about letting her win and still getting my way with her. The anchor holding me down in the darkness of my fucked up past was easing as she lay beneath me breathing hard, her eyes wide and almost … scared?

Fuck. What was I doing?

"I'll let you go, but new rules, don't touch me." I waited for her nod then I released her wrists. I suspected she'd have bruises there and a wave of guilt came over me. I hadn't meant to hurt her, but my control was slipping with Kat and I needed it back. This was the only way for me.

Her chest rose and fell, erect nipples grazing my chest with each inhale. "Ream, why did you—"

I cut her off before she had the chance to ask questions. Ones I'd never answer. This was why fucking a girl more than once was a mistake. Too close. Questions. Wanting to do more than just fuck fast and hard.

I crushed my mouth to hers and swallowed any further protests she might have had. Although, in the last forty-eight hours of us being in bed, Kat hadn't protested anything I'd done to her. And I thanked fuck for that.

She moaned beneath my assault, and her hands slipped into my hair. A cold shiver pushed past my desire and I froze.

"No! Grab the headboard." Her fingers uncurled from my hair and I put my full weight on top of her as I rubbed my aching cock between her legs.

She's just another fuck. Just another fuck.

Chicks were objects to me. I used them and they used me. I was always straight up about it and never had I let one stay the night. I'd never cuddled and never wanted to … until Kat.

The demons still lingered, but with her … it was more than a hot chick I was fucking to try and erase the past. For once it felt real, not a machine screwing to prove to myself that this was what I wanted.

As long as I could do it my way. If she could follow the rules then maybe the demons would stay away and we had a chance. I had a chance. Fuck, I wanted that with her.

After spending the last two weeks with her, before even touching her pussy, I knew this was different. Kat was different. She was strong and direct, and it was refreshing as hell. This wasn't some sappy chick hanging on every stroke of my guitar and then my dick. I'd been used all my life, but for once it didn't feel that way, and I wanted that feeling to last. I wasn't ready to let her go. I ran the tips of my fingers down the side of her face. "You're fuckin' mine, Kitkat."

Her eyes widened. Yeah, I shocked myself and hadn't realized it until the words slipped from my mouth. But I was taking this chick … at least until I was done with her.

"Babe?"

She hesitated and I tensed when I saw the flicker of uneasiness in her eyes, but it disappeared quickly and in its place was her smoldering, flirty blue eyes. "I'm not yours."

Yeah, I figured she'd say something like that. Despite the way she fucked, she was standoffish.

"But you can try your best to convince me," Kat said.

And I sure as hell could do that. I kissed her again—hard, unrelenting, as if trying to proving to myself that this was the usual fuck, but it wasn't. I knew that. I'd known that before I even kissed her.

When I pulled back, her eyes twinkled with desire. She wanted me—bad, and I fuckin' loved that I could do that to her. I suckled her nipple then kissed my way down her body, hesitating over her belly piercing, swirling the little diamond around my tongue. I stared down at her, eyes closed, muscles tense with anticipation to feel my tongue on her clit. And I couldn't wait to taste her again, have the power over her, make her scream with ecstasy. I rarely went down on a woman, that took too much time, but with Kat I'd tasted her twice already and watched her body writhe beneath my tongue.

Her hands came down on my shoulders, fingers sinking into my skin.

I stiffened. "Hands off."

Her eyelids flew open. "What's wrong?"

Her hands caressed my skin and the voices moved in like a thick black smog ready to blanket me and destroy this. "Don't. Touch." I pulled back, ready to leave when she slowly moved her hands away and grabbed the headboard again. "Ream?"

Christ, I loved how she said my name. It was like her tone lowered and the sound vibrated from her chest. I sighed feeling the tension leave my body. "Yeah, baby?"

"Ream … fuck me."

And that I could do. "I plan on it."

I stroked my finger over her shaved mound, wishing I could taste her again, but knowing it wasn't the time. Instead, I slipped my cock into the dampness between her thighs.

"Christ, you're wet."

She smiled and her tongue rolled over her upper lip. "Hmm. All for you. Now put it inside me."

I lifted her up by the hips, slid my hands beneath her ass, then drove all the way in hard and fast.

I pushed the paint roller up and down the wall, the rhythmic sound of the thrum back and forth. I hated painting, worse was painting in a farmhouse without any air-conditioning in the middle of summer. I glanced over at Kat, who was standing on the ladder, painting the trim around the window, well, she was supposed to be painting it. Instead I found her staring at me, her hand frozen in place, bristles of the brush squished against the window pane leaving a big yellow splotch.

It was cute. Shit, Kat was cute. Not in looks, no she'd be classified as regal, not cute. But her personality was cute. She had this honesty about her, not caring that she walked around with no make-up or was covered in dirt. Although, the night I met her at Avalanche she'd been dressed to the nines, looking sexy as hell with her flirty short dress, sassy smoky eyes, and full red lips.

When she moved to the farm, I'd come by to check in on her because ... well damn, her best friend was missing and her life had been uprooted by the lead singer of my band. I owed it to Logan to help out, but it became way more than that. I ended up staying to help out, not for Logan, but for Kat.

She was so determined and unruffled by what was happening. Damn, the girl even slipped under the tractor to do an oil change. She had no idea what she was doing, and it ended up me crawling beneath the filthy machine and showing her. I knew nothing about tractors, but I did know about cars and even though it was cute seeing Kat covered in streaks of grease, I didn't like the thought of her getting hurt. It was a strange feeling since I'd never cared about a chick in my life.

I tossed my roller in the tray, strode over to her, and then yanked my shirt hanging from my back pocket and used it to wipe the paint splotch off the window. She was still staring at me, but it wasn't at my naked chest, it was directly at my face as if she was seeing something she'd never seen before. I didn't know what the fuck it was about that moment, but shit changed.

I helped her off the ladder with one arm around her thighs, plucked her paint brush from her hand and dropped it onto the plastic sheet covering on the floor.

"Let's eat. I'm cooking." I took her hand and guided her downstairs to the kitchen. I sat her on a bar stool then started taking stuff out of the fridge and cupboards.

"I'll help." She was half-way to her feet when I glanced up at her while taking the chicken out of the packaging. I was getting that Kat was hands on; she wasn't some chick waiting for a guy to wait on her or be her protector. The thing was I was crazy protective of anyone I cared about.

Losing *her had done that to me. I wouldn't risk that ever happening again, so I kept chicks at a distance—until Kat.*

"Sit," I ordered. And I had an issue with getting my own way, probably because I lacked it as a kid and now I overcompensated. Not probably—it was.

Kat and I had an ease between us, we were good together, we clicked. I wanted to spend time with her, to see her smile, hear her laugh ... fuck what was I thinking? I'd never do a relationship. I couldn't even have sex with the same chick twice. And when I did have sex, the entire time I just wanted it to be over. Could the feelings be different with Kat? No. There was too much bullshit with my past.

Kat grabbed the cutting board from beside the microwave and put it on the counter beside where I was basting the chicken and then washed her hands, grabbed the veggies, and started chopping. I should've known she'd ignore me and maybe that's what I needed. A chick that could stand against my bullshit.

She softly started humming a Maroon 5 song and something swelled in me. And it wasn't between my legs. It was where I never expected, in my chest ... and shit it was fuckin' nice.

Bang.

I jolted awake at the sound of a door shutting. I turned over expecting to find the silky warmth of the body I'd just fucked for the last forty-eight hours and found nothing. I sat up then rubbed my hand over my head, thinking I'd drag her to the shower where I could have her again before breakfast. She certainly wasn't objecting to my tastes, so there was no harm in keeping her a while longer. Shit, the voices had only happened that once when I let her go down on me.

Instead, I saw her pulling on her jeans. "What the fuck? Where are you going?"

"I have plans." She pulled her shirt over her head then picked up her purse.

"Plans?" I repeated, frowning. "Were you going to wake me?"

"No. You can hang here. I'll be back in few hours. I have an appointment."

This was her brother Matt's condo and I had no intention of hanging here while Kat was gone. Matt stayed at his bar, Avalanche, most of the time, but it didn't mean he wouldn't pop in. Finding me lying naked in his sister's bed. Jesus, that was all I needed.

I threw my legs over the side of the bed and stalked toward her. She stood her ground while I looped my arm around her waist, picked her up, tossed her over my shoulder, and spanked her ass.

"Ream!" she screamed. Her purse fell to the floor as she grabbed my waist for balance.

"Cancel." I had to have her one more time. Then we could go our separate ways.

"Ream, I can't. It's important." Her voice went up an octave on the last word as I threw her onto the bed.

My dick hardened at the sight of her lying there, blonde hair messed, lips plush and shiny with pink gloss.

She scrambled to the side of the bed, but I caught her before she had a chance to escape. "I'm not done with you," I said. And suddenly I wasn't sure if I ever would be. Jesus, what the fuck? I'd known her for two weeks, and yet here I was contemplating starting some sort of relationship? A relationship I'd never had before. Never wanted or intended. I didn't want a chick, but Kat … was strong. She could handle my shit. And it was real bad shit.

Was it possible? Or would that sick, disgusted feeling catch up to me with her too?

"Ream, I'm serious. I can't miss this appointment."

If I let her slip away, would I lose the taste of what it was like to feel during sex? Would the unemotional coldness slam back into me like I was dead? Fuck, I couldn't. I didn't want that again, and I'd do anything to keep this feeling alive.

I lowered my naked body on top of hers, feeling the course material of her jeans on my dick. I had to get rid of her fuckin' clothes ASAP. "Reschedule."

She pushed at my chest as I undid her jeans. "I can't. Ream, seriously." She punched me in the shoulder, and this time I looked up, my hands pausing on her zipper.

I reached over to the nightstand and grabbed my phone. "I'll get you another appointment tomorrow. What's the number?" I figured it was a hair or nail appointment. Girls were funny about shit like that.

She rolled her eyes. "I'll be back in a couple of hours."

"No." I cupped her between the legs and half smiled when I heard her moan. But to my disappointment, it didn't last and she slid out from beneath me and got to her feet.

I fell back onto the bed, closing my eyes. "You and me. We aren't done, Kat." Fuck no. I didn't want that numb feeling of fucking some chick I didn't give two shits about.

"Umm … yeah." She paused and I heard her shuffling around. "I'll catch you later." Her voice was too high-pitched, and I sat up to find her on her hands and knees scrambling to put items back in her purse that must have fallen out when I threw her over my shoulder.

I swung my legs over the side of the bed to help her when I saw it.

I stared, a crushing disbelief blanketing me.

She froze.

Then at the same time, we both dove for it, but it was closer to me and I grabbed it first.

"What the fuckin' hell?" My heart pounded with fury and disappointment. *Fuck.* I knew she was too good to be true. Jesus. My fingers curled around the syringe as I glared at her. Jesus. Fuck. Why? Why did this shit have to be thrown back at me in every facet of my life?

"Ream, it's not what you think." She held out her hand. "Give it back."

"That's what they all say, isn't it?" I shoved past her. Fuck. What a Goddamn waste.

The sick feeling in the pit of my stomach whirled and tossed like a friggin' washing machine. Just looking at the needle made me want to throw up. It was like a slap in my face with the tip of a wet towel.

I felt her delicate hand curl around my bicep and I wrenched away as I pushed open the bathroom door.

She raised her voice. "Ream, no."

Panicked. Figures. A fuckin' junky that hates her stash being wasted. I didn't want or need this bullshit. Not a chance in hell was I going down this road again.

I pulled the lid off the syringe.

"Damn it, Ream. Don't you dare!" She made a grab for the syringe and knocked it from my hand as it slid across the ceramic tiles.

We both dove for it at the same time, Kat landing on top of me as my knees hit the floor. Her slight weight was nothing to me. I easily shoved her off and she fell backwards onto her butt.

I grabbed the syringe, got to my feet, then turned and glared at her, shaking my head. "Pathetic. Jesus." I removed the cap then pressed the plunger releasing the clear liquid into the toilet. After flushing, I replaced the cap and tossed the empty syringe onto the counter. God, I couldn't even look at her, it disgusted me. She disgusted me. "I don't fuckin' screw junkies. Period. I'm out of here." Fuck. How could I have missed this? I knew the signs but somehow I'd missed them with her.

"You bastard!"

I was taken aback by the fire in her eyes. Why the hell was she pissed at me? She was the one with the problem. Crazy bitch. Figures.

She scrambled to her feet then came at me shoving me in the chest several times, and I staggered back toward the wall. All I could do was take what she gave because I sure as shit wasn't into striking a woman, even one that was freakin' her shit on me over one hit.

No doubt her *appointment* was to meet her dealer.

"God, you're such a jerk." She pushed me so hard with both hands that I crashed into the bathroom wall. "Thanks for the fuck, asshole. Now get the hell out."

I didn't hesitate. I strode back to the bedroom, yanked on my jeans, grabbed my shirt, and pulled it on while heading to the front door.

Then I stopped. I ran my finger over the ink on my right arm, the butterfly. This is why I had to walk. Drugs. Fuck. The pain in my chest was agonizing, like a vise gripping around my heart so tight that it was going to explode at any minute. I needed air—fast. I was drowning in the memories of Haven, and if I didn't get out of here, I was going to throw up.

"Tell anyone and I'll castrate you."

I walked back toward her and I witnessed the flicker of panic in her eyes. Kat was fearless, at least that's what I'd thought. I grabbed her by the arms before she had the chance to escape.

"Why?" I shouted. I had to know. "Jesus, why?" Why did she have to ruin this?

And I wasn't letting her go until she told me. I needed to hear it from her lips. I think she must have known because she blurted it out.

I abruptly released her. She continued to speak, but my mind became black muddled sewage and I didn't hear any of it.

No. Fuck no.

Control was slipping and I had to get out of here—fast. I couldn't breathe. I was suffocating. I had no control and it would kill me. I couldn't stop the emotions from plowing into me. I never expected I'd give a shit, but at that moment I knew that Kat had been more than a forty-eight hour fuck.

Now … now that was shattered. Her words crushed the smidgeon of hope I had of pulling up the anchor and being set free.

Without saying anything, because I was seriously too fucked up to say anything, I walked out.

Kat

My hips swayed to the beat of the music, my hands above my head, and a pair of hands settled firm on my waist. It had been two days since I'd seen Ream, and I still felt sick to my stomach. I thought coming to Avalanche and dancing would help me forget him … instead, it helped me remember, so I medicated myself with shots of vodka.

I hated every second of the guy's hands on me, but it was my punishment, self-preservation to convince myself that Ream was just another guy. No big deal.

Every swallow was like I had an apple lodged in my throat. Every breath sucked me under a little farther until the vodka made it a dull, aching pain.

I'd never told anyone about the drugs. Not even Emily knew. Only Matt. And Ream just proved what I expected to happen if anyone found out … would happen.

The male voice whispered in my ear and cut through my thoughts. "Come back to my place tonight, sweetness."

I shivered and it wasn't good shivers. Feeling him rub against me was supposed to make me feel wanted; instead, it made me feel repulsed. Jesus, even my usual flirting took a kick to the stomach by Ream's rejection.

I normally thrived off attention. It didn't mean I acted on it. The men were all for show, a way to make myself feel desirable. And guys went for me—blonde, tall, long legs. I loved to flirt. I was confident with my looks, but inside … inside I was disintegrating.

But, I tried to live every single day with no regrets.

Until now.

Now I regretted.

Ream I regretted. Because before him no guy mattered enough to hurt me like he did. It was supposed to be a quick lay, but something had built between us in the time we'd hung out together at the farm. There'd been no sex and I think that's why this hurt more. We'd become friends and now that was gone.

For two weeks we were just ourselves, hurting and worried over our friends while supporting one another. There were no games, no sexual play, we were natural and at ease with one another. It was only when Emily returned that it changed. We'd planned on a one nighter, neither of us wanting more, but something happened between us. I thought Ream had felt it too. I was wrong. What was worse was that I missed just hanging out with Ream every day. That hurt more than the sex.

"Kat." His voice. Jesus, I still heard it in my head. What the hell was wrong with me? Why did it hurt so bad? The sex was good, I mean he was rough and I could tell he liked having control, and I was good with that. Actually, I realized that it was hot letting him take control. I had it in every other part of my life, so letting him take charge was refreshing. But it hadn't just been mind-blowing, life altering sex. I sensed his distance, the need to have it hard and fast and then that thing with not wanting me to finish the blow job … yeah, there was something—

"Kat."

Oh God. His voice was real. I stopped moving and looked over my shoulder at the man that had caused me to take a few more of the pills in my nightstand than I normally would.

"We need to talk."

Ream stood in the middle of the dance floor, his face tight, lips pursed together, and he wasn't looking at me, he was looking at the guy behind me. Shit, he was royally pissed off. The question was whether it was at me or the guy he was driving nails into with his stare.

"You had your chance, asshole. And second ones don't exist in my world." I grabbed my dance partner's hand and pulled him through the crowd toward the bar.

My heart pounded so goddamn fast it was painful.

"Screw off," Ream said to the guy, coming up beside us. There was no mistake that it wasn't a request.

"Jesus. You're an ass." I looked at my dance partner. "Give us a second?" He shrugged and walked off toward the restroom. I sat on the bar stool and nodded to Brett. He looked at me then at Ream, who stood behind me. There was a second of hesitation before Brett grabbed a Stella then flicked the cap off and slid it toward me. Brett looked at Ream, who gave a subtle shake of his head, then he moved away and Ream moved in closer so he was standing between me and the bar.

He didn't lean against the bar or look uncomfortable or even show a trace of remorse. Instead, he stood stiff and cold while looking directly at me.

I raised my brows. "Well, what do you want?"

"You hit me with some serious shit. And it took you two weeks to do it."

I grabbed my beer and chugged back a quarter of it then slammed it down on the bar. The foam rushed to the top and spilled over.

Ream continued, "I'm not often wrong about people."

"Hey, Brett, vodka?" I yelled as he served another client

halfway down the bar. "You done? I'm busy."

"Who's the guy?"

I shrugged. "Don't know his name. Nor do I care. His cock feels big. That's all I need to know for tonight." It was meant to hurt him, not that he'd really give a shit anyway, but it made me feel better saying it.

Silence. I didn't need to look at Ream to know he was seething. The air was so thick around us that I struggled to keep my breath even.

Brett put my vodka down in front of me. "You good, Kat?"

I nodded.

Ream's fingers curled around my wrist when I went to pick up the glass. My eyes shot to his. "Hands off, asshole."

He kept his hand locked on me, eyes delving into me and I shifted uncomfortably beneath his stare. It was unsettling and I rarely felt that way, but Ream … there was something inside him that scared me. Not like he'd physically hurt me, and emotionally he'd already done that, but it was something else. A darkness that lay hidden beneath the surface. Well, I didn't need his shit in my life; I had plenty of my own.

"You've had enough. I'm taking you to the condo. We'll talk there."

Maybe I had, but it wasn't any of his business and I sure as hell wasn't going anywhere with him. "There's nothing to talk about." No, he'd made damn sure of that. "We fucked. That's all it was. Now let me go."

"Ream." Brett's warning cut through the tension and Ream let me go, but I could see by the way his jaw twitched that he was trying to contain himself.

I picked up the shot glass and tossed it back, the liquid scorching my throat as it went down.

"We had two weeks before we fucked."

Yeah and that was gone too. "Get lost, Ream."

"Fine, we'll talk here," he said then leaned in so his hands settled on either side of me on the bar stool. "I needed time to take it in, Kat."

"I don't give a shit what you needed. It was a mistake. Now, why don't you go find one of your groupies to fawn over you so I don't lose my fuck for the night." I could see the guy I was dancing with emerging from the hallway where the bathrooms were.

"Not a chance, Kat. No fuckin' way are you going home with that dick."

"Oh, you'd rather I'd go home with some pussy? Never done it, but I'm up for anything tonight."

"Stop. You're not going with anyone except me."

"Hell no," I said, shaking my head. "That tugboat chugged its way into the Amazon and was dragged under by a python two days ago."

He grabbed me by the upper arms, and for a second I was a little leery of him. "You really going to fuck that guy, Kat?"

I put a hand on his chest, and the second I did, I regretted it. The butterflies lifted and the sweet ache between my legs rose. I pushed him back so I could get up, then snagged my beer off the bar. "Yeah. I am. Just like I fucked you. Now stay the hell away from me, Ream."

I walked away, weaving my way through the crowd, feeling the burn of Ream's gaze on my back. There was one second that I hesitated wondering if I was doing the right thing, but then it was gone. I grabbed the guy I'd been dancing with by the front of the shirt and pulled him into me. I tilted my head and kissed him.

Chapter One

Kat

Two years, eight months later.

The prickling down my legs and across my stomach really pissed me off. I knew the familiar sensations were a reaction to the impending arrival of the band after their eight month tour.

Well, it was only one band member that was the cause, and I hadn't seen the asshole since he brought some chick to my welcome home party from the hospital eight months ago—after being shot by a sex trafficking psycho who was after Emily. I think it was at that moment I realized Ream was my poison. The toxin flowing through my veins consumed all the fight I had left in me when it came to Ream Dedrick.

And that night I felt defeated by him. I had nothing left. I think he recognized that when he looked at me from across the table. The usual rage lingering within the depths of his eyes had been replaced with … concern. I couldn't figure out why, considering he'd never visited me in the hospital. No, the asshole took off the moment the doc said I was out of danger.

But even after that, my breath still hitched when I saw him. My stomach dropped like I was leaping off a cliff into a pool of water. When he looked at me it was all consuming, as if I was his marionette and he could do as he pleased with me. I kept my emotions on a short leash, but with Ream ... he set parts of me free. I'd imagined what it would have been like if he'd never found my needle; if I'd never told him.

But I did. And maybe it was better to discover he was an asshole before I got in deeper with him. Ha, deeper with Ream could've been one more night and then he'd have ended it anyway.

His attempt to talk to me again the night I arrived home from the hospital. Well, I was like a kid and ignored him, pretended he didn't exist. Ream didn't take well to being ignored and cornered me against the fridge when everyone was outside on the deck. Maybe I hadn't been completely defeated by him because I hauled off and slapped him across the face.

He'd been so shocked ... that look ... it was haunting.

For eight months now I'd lived with that look tiptoeing through my dreams like a dark shadow. Popping out when I least expected it. Month after month passed, and I kept thinking about it. Had I seen that look in his eyes before? Had I been so angry at him that I couldn't see past it until the moment I felt the impact of my hand against his cheek? It was like I'd struck myself. I cracked open and saw what I'd been missing all this time—his torment hidden beneath all that anger.

Ream walked out after that. The sting of my hand still burning. He never said another word. He just strode out the front door.

And now, eight months later, he was about to walk back in.

Emily texted me a few weeks ago letting me know the band was coming back to stay at the farm, including Ream. I thought it would be fine, that it wouldn't affect me, but the truth was that Ream would always affect me in some capacity.

No matter what other flavors of ice-cream were at your table, if your favorite sat among them, it was nearly impossible to avoid tasting. Your body controlled your reactions, and you couldn't do anything about it.

"So, Banana Cake, you decide what you're going to do about Ream?" Georgie took a bite out of her apple and juice slid from the corner of her mouth. Her tongue darted out and licked the remnants, then she winked at me. "There's some serious tension between you, and now with Lance … I vote sit on his face and make him lick you until he's begging for mercy and end this shit between you."

I shot her a nasty bitch glare. She knew damn well that mentioning Ream licking any part of me would awaken the dormant desire I'd buried for the last two years and eight months since we'd slept together. Well, tried to bury. I hadn't been able to go past first base with a single guy since Ream. Pathetic. Thank God Ream didn't know that, and I'd made sure he thought otherwise. I wouldn't be thought of as some weak, vulnerable chick he put his dick into.

I retorted, "Deck haul your drunk ass out of Avalanche lately?" Deck, scary JTF2 commando guy, constantly dragged Georgie out of her latest drinking incident. He protected her like she was some glass figurine. Georgie was anything but glass, more like rubber because she always bounced back from whatever shit she got herself into.

"Nope. Left three days ago, thank fuck. I was getting tired of buying batteries for my vibrator."

I choked on my soda water, and a fine spray escaped my mouth. "What? I didn't think you liked him? I mean—at all. You're always bitching about him."

Georgie took another bite then tossed the core into the disposal. "Don't need to like a guy to get off on him. You see what's between his legs?"

"Actually, no."

"Well, look next time. Besides, it's dry season. Haven't seen a hot, fuckable guy in months. Well, except maybe Lance and he's out of bounds, stupid girl-rule and all."

Like Georgie would ever try and shag a guy I was dating. Shit, I wasn't even sure Georgie had ever had sex with a guy. I mean she talked like she did, acted like she did, but she'd never had a boyfriend, and her mouthing off about sex was never anything but that … mouthing off. If she was sleeping with random guys, Emily and

I sure as hell didn't know about it.

"Your new guy is something edible, fuckable ... all of the above. But Deck is my go to man. Strictly fantasy of course."

"Of course." I nodded. I had enough fantasies of my own to write a book, and that book needed burning because it contained only one guy. "So why not sleep with him?" I saw the way Deck looked at her; there was something there besides his oath to her brother to watch over her. Riot, her brother's call name in the JTF2, had died years ago when he and Deck were on a mission in Afghanistan. Deck left JTF2, the Canadian counterterrorism unit, after that and started his own business. I wasn't sure what it entailed except that it was undercover and dangerous.

Georgie hesitated for a second, and I caught a brief flash of uncertainty. Then it was gone and she was all attitude again. "Because Deck is no fun. He's a fusspot for rules. I bet he has rules on how to fuck ... yeah, no thank you. Missionary isn't my thing. I'll stick to my fantasy Deck."

I wasn't so sure about that. Deck was intense, quiet, controlling, and mysterious. I was guessing the guy was the same way in bed, and that was hot. Ream was that way. He was all that and more.

It was a shock to discover and maybe that's what ruined me for all the other flavors because dammit, I still felt his body on top of mine, his cock inside of me, and the unrelenting sweetness of his mouth on my lips. I pictured him standing in the kitchen making dinner. I felt his hands around me as he dragged me out from beneath the tractor and remembered the look in his eyes, the frown on his face as if he'd been concerned for my safety.

Shit, I'd read so much into it, and I knew better. I should've never slept with him. He was a lead guitarist in a rock band; that was enough of a fluorescent warning sign. But I thought I could just do sex and go back to being friends. And it may have worked if it hadn't all blown up in my face.

I didn't need a friend like that anyway. The problem was I was constantly thrown in Ream's path and it was utterly pitiful. Because

Ream had hurt me. He ran out on me the moment he didn't like what he heard and then had the nerve to come back two days later to try and fix it … yeah, I didn't do fix. I had no time in my life for mending anything, and second chances didn't exist in my books.

Since then, we were constantly trying to hurt one another, and even if we had an entire army rebuilding the bridge between us, there wasn't enough foundation to hold it.

"They're here," Georgie squealed then grabbed my hand and pulled me toward the front door. "Come on, buckle up. Make him wish he could taste that pussy tonight." My nerves were going haywire and I couldn't get away with hiding the fact that I was unsteady, so I stopped at the doorway and leaned against the frame. Georgie scoffed. "Chicken." She made her brows do a happy dance. "I'm thinking Crisis might end my dry spell. A smart-assed, cocky cock between the legs—like yummy sour keys."

I knew Crisis wouldn't be stupid enough to fuck Georgie; that would be like going up to Deck and spitting in his face. Not happening unless you wanted to be beaten into the ground and live next to the slugs.

Dread hit me as the sound of gravel crunching beneath the weight of the sleek BMW grew louder. I felt like one of those tiny pebbles being shoved up into the treads of the tires and going round and round making the anxiety worse, squished and pounded into the ground with every breath as I waited for the car to stop.

Emily said the band would be staying for up to a year while they recorded an album. That meant Ream would be here. That meant I was finally going to have to deal with the shit between us. That was if Ream could be rational for five seconds. I'd prefer to stomp my feet, run to my room and lock the door. That option was negated as soon as I turned twenty a few years ago. There were limits on immaturity once you hit twenty.

I rubbed a bruise on my arm where I had shot the drug into an hour ago. I hated that I had to do it. The issue would be if Ream opened his big mouth and told anyone about my problem. He hadn't yet so chances were he'd keep it quiet. But him in my face, living in the same house, I didn't know if I could do it.

No, this was my home and Ream wasn't chasing me out of it. Christ, my income came from painting scenes of the horses, and I needed that income to eventually move out and buy my own place. The Havoc series of six paintings I did was getting a ton of attention at Lance's gallery. The gray horse was majestic with her long mane and contoured muscles, making my paintings of her an instant success. Lance had even set up my first solo show, planned in a few weeks.

I'd held out dating him for months but it hadn't been easy. The guy was persistent and yet not annoyingly so. I finally said yes, and part of me ... the part I kept dormant ... was doing it to make certain when Ream returned I had Lance to keep me from skipping down that path I promised never to revisit.

But Georgie skipped, and it was right down the porch steps and across the driveway, her pink tipped strands billowing out in every direction. She reminded me of a flamingo darting across the yard, just not as graceful.

My body was so revved with nerves, desire, anger, and uncertainty that I felt like I was under a ginormous magnifying glass in the boiling sun. I was frazzled seeing Ream again, and my body knew it. Frig, who was I kidding? It wasn't frazzled, it was completely freaking out.

I tried to look casual and undisturbed leaning against the door frame with one hand on my cocked hip, but inside my heart was trying to slow down as it pumped the rush of heated blood through my veins, blood that was laced with Ream-venom—and it was hungry for more.

Emily had the car door open before it even finished rolling to a stop, and I smiled as I heard Logan shouting at her to wait. She ignored him and jumped out, throwing her arms around Georgie. I smiled as I heard their excited chatter.

God, she looked happy. I hadn't seen Emily's eyes so bright and full of life in ... well, ever, and we'd been besties since we were ten years old. We bonded at a time when she lost her father to cancer and my brother Matt and I lost our parents to drunk driving—my dad unfortunately being the stupid ass drunk.

Logan got out of the driver's seat, his watchful gaze never leaving Emily. There was no question he was her shield from everything bad in the world. I still didn't know the details of what happened in Mexico after Emily was kidnapped, but it was enough to know that Logan did and would do anything for her.

When the back driver's side door opened and a long, lean leg emerged, my heart skipped a beat and my fingers dug into my hip. It was in slow motion as I watched his over-six-foot frame unfold out of the car and straighten. I stared, unable to help myself. Any girl would stare. It would be almost rude not to because Ream was the type of guy who stood out. Not because he had pink hair or shouted or was obnoxious. No, it was because he was the complete opposite. Subtle and dangerously quiet, the feeling like if he spoke you'd better hope he liked you because otherwise you'd be falling at his feet begging for mercy.

Of course, I'd never do that.

Ream remained motionless beside the car, stiff and impenetrable. He was friggin' sexy hot, and Georgie's words about licking hunted me down and shot me in the lungs stealing my breath away.

It took two seconds before his eyes found mine. There was nothing but possession in them. As if he was taking everything from me and making it his with that single look. It was a total soul gripping statement, and I was so not ready for it because gone was the rage and torment I'd last seen in his eyes. It was replaced with complete confidence.

What made it worse was the indifference lying beneath the surface, as if he didn't give a crap whether I walked away or not because he'd just keep coming. I squirmed under his stare, my poise faltering as my hand slipped off my hip.

He shut the car door and the sudden sound made me jump. He

saw it. "Shit," I mumbled beneath my breath.

I stood upright, mentally kicked myself in the ass, and dragged my gaze away from his and smiled broad, way broader than was characteristic for me, then jogged down to Emily.

I pushed Logan's arm away from its protective and annoyingly sweet residence on Emily's waist. He scowled. I smiled and winked at him then threw my arms around my bestie.

He shook his head and I heard the soft chuckle. "Kat. Nice to see you," he acknowledged.

"Sculpt." I knew he was rolling his eyes without having to look at him. His fans called him Sculpt. Well, we all did before we found out his real name. I continued to call him Sculpt because I knew it annoyed him now that we were friends. He'd changed a lot since he'd managed to win Emily back, and the one thing he insisted on was his friends calling him Logan. He kept Sculpt for the stage. But when I was brave enough or stupid enough, whichever, I liked to tease him just to try and get a reaction. Scowling Logan sucked, but getting a smile or laugh out of him was pretty damn magical.

"God, Emily, I missed you. Havoc's missed you. That horse has been pining for you like an oversized puppy dog. I swear her hooves are worn down from dragging her feet for the last eight months."

Emily laughed. "Missed you too. I'm glad to be back. Logan has promised no more traveling for a year." She lowered her voice and whispered in my ear, "And if he reneges, you should hear what I get to do to him."

I could only imagine. Emily said Logan was into the kinky, and I suspected bondage was on his list because well, a guy like Logan would want complete control.

I breathed in and Ream's dark, musky scent seeped into me. My body recognized it and reacted instantly. The twinge between my legs put my panties to the test, and the pins and needles were now in an all-out war.

Shit.

I was afraid to look up because I knew the second I did, I'd be face-to-face with Ream and I didn't know if I was ready for it. I hoped he'd walk past me and go to the house.

He didn't.

Instead, when I pulled back from Emily, there was nothing to block my view of him. His hand rested on the roof of the car, eyes driving into me, and he wasn't smiling or looking like he was happy about being back. Or happy about seeing me. Or happy about anything actually. He was just looking unhappy—period. But trying to read anything else in Ream was like putting a puzzle together without all the pieces—impossible. Maybe at one time I thought I knew him but now ...

Emily was going on about the tour and how crazy it was, the insane fans ... I really didn't hear much because Ream moved, and it was toward me, and I went to mush. Gah ... I hated mush. Most of all I hated mushiness when it came to guys.

I swallowed. Then I silently pleaded for him to disappear because he looked hot in his worn blue jeans and the knitted Asterisk hat that screamed sexiness and totally contradicted with the tats running the length of his arms.

He stopped an inch away from me and I swear it was on purpose. "Kat."

The sound of his husky voice saying my name sent a shiver of anticipation through my body. Jesus, it was like his voice just pranced across my skin then fucked me. I briefly thought of just fucking him again and getting him out of my system.

Of course that was out of the question. I was dating Lance, and even though it had only been a month and we hadn't done more than kiss, I'd never do it. Lance was my shield against my own weakness when it came to Ream. Besides, he was nice.

"Hey." Even a simple three letter word came out wobbly. What was my deal? Ream was blowing all my confidence out of proportion here.

It suddenly hit me why it felt different this time ... there was no anger in him. The constant barrage of arguing we'd done was because we were both holding onto some serious issues, and that was the change. I had nothing to fight with, to argue against.

I'd built myself back up over the last eight months after I'd felt completely defeated. I'd expected pissed-off Ream to come back, not overly-confident, self-assured, all-knowing Ream. Okay, he was those things all the time, but now it felt like it was directed straight at me and I had no recourse.

Ream looked over at Logan and I saw the odd exchange, but I didn't know what it meant. Ream threw his bag over his shoulder then shifted past me and strode to the house.

Emily took my hand and squeezed. "You going to be okay with this?"

I shrugged. "No biggie." I sure as hell didn't want Ream or anyone else thinking I couldn't handle living in the same house as him. We may have slept together and had history, but we could be civil … well, I could be. Ream I wasn't so sure about.

Logan put his hand on the back of Emily's neck. "Lying won't help anyone, Kat. Bury the shit between the two of you, or I'll do it for you. He know about the guy you're dating?"

I glanced at Emily. She bit her lip and looked guilty as hell. She told him.

"No."

"Fuck." Logan ran his hand down his face. "Then you need to bury it fast. Like today."

There was no discussion with Logan. He set down the law, and from Emily's eyes moving heavenward, I guessed they'd argued about whatever he considered "burying it" meant. What I didn't get was why Ream would give a crap if I was with Lance. He hated me, was disgusted at the sight of me.

Logan was already moving toward the house, Emily tucked into his side.

"And if I don't?"

He kept walking and Emily looked over her shoulder and mouthed, "Don't go there."

I yelled, "Logan! What do you mean you'll bury it?"

"He means he'll lock the two of you in a closet until you make up or kill one another, sugar." The corners of my lips curled up as I heard the familiar voice. "He's already pissed about the Ream scenario, thinks it will cause shit in the house, and he hates anything that might upset his Mouse. Now, where is that sweet ass I've missed groping for eight months?"

Crisis strode toward me with his boyish grin and bouncing blond curls. He picked me up in a bear hug, swung me around, then threw me over his shoulder, and slapped my ass. "Looking fuckin' hot. Damn I missed this ass."

"What about my ass?" Georgie yelled from the other side of the car where she was chatting with Kite, the drummer.

Crisis asked, "Deck around?" I shook my head and Crisis smiled and turned to Georgie. "Shit yeah, baby. Missed that one too." Georgie wiggled her butt, and Crisis groaned then spanked me hard, put me down, and kissed me right on the lips. No tongue, just hard and quick.

"Miss me?" he asked.

I did. Crisis and I may not be interested in one another sexually, but we had a strange connection. It was as if he could act completely himself with me and not worry I'd kick his ass for being an arrogant male chauvinist pig. Crisis may be a cocky smart-ass, but I understood him.

Georgie chatted enthusiastically with Kite, who was getting the bags out of the back of Crisis's car. "Hi, Kite."

"Kat," he called and winked. Kite was like the rest of the guys, over six feet, sexy, hot, and yet his personality was completely different. The pierced, tatted drummer was a sweetheart, a gentleman, and rarely got upset or mad at anyone. He kind of balanced out the band with his sweetness. "I'd wash your mouth out with bleach after letting that asshole kiss you."

I laughed and Crisis took the opportunity to try and kiss me again, but I shoved him back. He chuckled then grabbed me around the waist, and we started toward the house.

Chapter Two

"The Reamster has been the biggest prick. I swear he's had a boner for you since we left. You know what it's like having a boner for that long?" Crisis continued without letting me answer. "I swear if he doesn't get laid soon, I'm paying some chick to tie him down and screw him." He tugged me closer. "You up for it?"

I rolled my eyes, laughing, then quickly moved the conversation away from Ream, because really, I didn't want to imagine him screwing any chick. "Meet any nice girls to take home to mommy, pretty boy?" I knew full well he met plenty of girls as we'd texted a few times a week since he'd been gone. Crisis had told me that he had every intention of taking advantage of being the sexy blond bass guitarist.

"Fuck yeah. Some nice, some dirty …" Crisis clucked his tongue, his fingers squeezing my waist. "Damn, it's like getting your pick of your favorite model car every night and each one rides completely different. A few not so smooth and some need detailing and a fuckin' oil change."

I smacked his chest. "Gross."

Despite my apprehension on seeing Ream again, I was glad to have Emily and the boys back. It had been far too quiet in the house and I'd ended up staying a few nights a week down at my brother's condo just to be around people. Plus it was close to the gallery, and if Lance wanted to take me for dinner or lunch, then I was downtown already.

When we walked into the kitchen, Emily caught my eye and I knew exactly what she wanted … to talk away from the boys.

She kissed Logan then whispered something to him and pulled away. He snagged her hand before she managed two steps, yanked her back, hooked his arm around her waist, and kissed her again. There was no question the guy was smitten. I really never had any doubts, but even after eight months he still looked completely obsessed … and possessive … and in love.

Emily and I went to her and Logan's room and sat on the floor, our backs against the foot of the bed, shoulders touching, ankles crossed.

"So, tell me. What's happening between you and this Lance guy."

I shrugged. Lance had purchased the art gallery I had my work displayed in. I'd thought he'd ask me to remove my pieces, but instead he asked for more.

He said he owned two galleries in New York, although he knew little about art in my opinion. He was a martial artist, charming, a gentleman, and I liked him. Matt was on the fence about him, and Georgie thought he had a pickle up his ass, but since he was hot, that cancelled out the pickle … unless he sucked in bed. "You told Logan."

"Yeah. He knew something was up when I kept taking my calls behind closed doors. He doesn't like closed doors between us and secrets even less. I caved the second he called me on it. Sorry. I know you wanted to keep it quiet until you knew whether it was going anywhere. So, is it going anywhere?"

"I like him. I mean he has the potential for being Haagen Dazs quality and he's really nice."

"Nice? Kat, nice? You know what nice means."

We both said at the same time. "He lacks—Need. Infatuation. Craving. Excitement."

I sighed. "Yes. But I had that and look where it led me."

Emily nudged me with her shoulder. "What happened between you two?" All I'd told her was that Ream and I had become friends when she'd been down in Mexico but then we ruined it by sleeping together. "You guys have been at each other the second you're in shouting distance. Not today though. Something's different and I have to say it was nice you guys not throwing insults at one another." Yeah, Ream wasn't being an asshole. "Kat, he asked about you all the time when we were away. I'd catch him looking at me when I was talking to you." She took my hand and squeezed. "Is there a chance you guys can—"

I shook my head, interrupting her. "We're way past salvageable. Besides, I like N.I.C.E. It's stress free and I may not have the fire burning between my legs, but he treats me good." And my nerves aren't set off like live wires gone wrong. "So, enough about me and lack of mind blowing sex ... has Logan proved himself over the last eight months? Or does he need some tips?"

Her eyes lit up. "No tips required. I swear he has a book hidden somewhere on how to drive your woman wild. I thought I'd go crazy with all the girls at the concerts and stuff, Logan never looked at another woman."

"That's because he knows I'd chop off his balls if he did." He may have saved Emily from sicko Raul, but that didn't make him immune to my wrath if he ever hurt my bestie.

"He told me, Kat." Emily clasped her hands on her lap and wrung them together. "What happened to him after I left Mexico?"

Damn. I wasn't sure if I was ready to hear this.

"I had to know. I get that he was trying to protect me from it, but it's about trust and growing together. I think he understood that..." a slight smirk played at the corners of her lips "...after I tied him to the bed while he slept."

I laughed because seriously, imagining Logan tied up ... well, he'd have been pissed. Scary pissed and all the sexiness in the world wasn't going to cover up Logan's fury at being restrained.

Emily bit her lower lip. "Ah, yeah. It wasn't pretty. I stood on the far side of the room and was worried he'd escape the ropes with the way he yanked on them. When he stopped and became calm … well that freaked me out too." Her voice lowered and I saw her eyelids fill with tears. Emily went on to tell me what happened to Logan. I was shocked and disgusted, and by the end we held one another as she choked back sobs. Emily was good at being strong when she needed to be and could neatly tuck her emotions away inside a gift-wrapped parcel. She'd open it up eventually, though, not like me. I'd hide the present and whatever was inside would stay buried … except anger. I liked to tear that present wide open.

I pulled back and softly wiped her tears away with the pad of my thumb. "I should have known," she continued. "God, when he came back I hated him when I should've been giving him everything of myself."

"Emily. You didn't know. None of us did." Shit, if that happened to Logan I was afraid to find out what Emily had gone through in Mexico.

"Deck knew." Emily sniffled. "Logan made him swear to never tell me, but Deck warned me, Kat. I was more concerned about me. God, everything he did was to save me."

"You both suffered. What's important is that you found one another again. You're happy and you deserve it more than anyone."

"You know I watched him on stage and fell in love with him all over again every single day. Even after all that happened, I feel lucky. You know, I'd go through it again just to be with him. Is that crazy?"

Wow. "No. That's love. And love is a little crazy."

She bumped my shoulder. "I missed you like hell." We'd never been separated longer than a few weeks at a time since we were kids, and despite our texting and phone calls, it had been lonely without her here. "Now why the dark circles under your eyes?" I wasn't going to tell her that the lack of sleep was from thinking about the guy downstairs who tilted my world on its axis. "I saw the way he looked at you."

God, bestie's knew everything. And damn it, my heart started racing at the mere mention of his name … Ha, she hadn't even said his name, just alluded to it. Christ.

"Are you really going to be okay with him living here? He's said some real nasty things to you, Kat." Called me a bitch and a whore to be exact. "I hardly spoke to him the entire trip, you know. Okay, well, he seldom spoke to anyone when he was around, which was rarely. He'd take off all the time and not even Crisis knew where he went. But that bullshit he pulled with bringing that girl Lana to your coming home party … I swear the guy deserves a gold medal for best dick moves."

Yeah, he did.

Emily didn't say anything for a minute and neither did I.

"Still, if you weren't seeing Lance, I'd say just fuck him and get it out of both your systems."

I burst out laughing. Those were my exact words to her when I told her to fuck Logan. "So not happening. We detonate the second we touch."

"Yeah, in flames."

"No, into shrapnel."

Emily said quietly, "I never saw him with a girl. Well, I mean like romantically or sexually or … well, you know what I mean."

I hated that I felt elation at hearing that. "And you just said he disappeared all the time." Elation gone. What the hell was wrong with me?

"Listen, I don't know what he was doing, but I don't think he was off having sex with random chicks." Emily sighed. "You look like you haven't slept and you've lost weight. It's Ream, isn't it? I should've gotten to the bottom of the crap between you two before I left. I thought it would be over since you're seeing Lance, but it's not … for either of you. What's going on? What happened, Kat?"

"Mouse?" Logan's deep voice sounded outside the door. He didn't knock before he opened it and went straight to Emily, helped her off the floor, and wrapped his arms around her. He looked at me and I shifted uncomfortably under his intensity. "I'm saying this because it needs to be said and Emily won't … keep the shit between you and Ream under wraps."

"You said that already. Yeah, I got it. We're good."

He grunted. "From the way you both looked at one another … nothing's good." Jesus why was everyone saying that? We barely even made eye contact. "Sort the shit out. I told him the same thing."

"What did he say?"

Damn, something was up and she wasn't going to tell me. Although, I suspected she would if Logan hadn't threatened her somehow, probably sexually. Normally, I'd find that hilarious because from what she'd told me, Logan's dominant nature intensified in the bedroom.

Logan shrugged. Shit, he never shrugs.

I knew he was right though. Ream and I had to move past this. I needed to unearth the weed then destroy it. Only then could I move on and stop fighting him. No one ever said that pulling weeds was easy.

When I went back downstairs I was relieved that Ream wasn't there and after chatting for a while with Crisis, Georgie, and Kite, I went out to the barn to check on my horse Clifford and the abused horses that arrived a few days ago. The one thoroughbred was restless in the stall and fearful of his own shadow. We had yet to let him out with the herd as we were scared he'd bolt right through the fence, so Hank and I had been hand walking him and were hoping Emily could help the youngster.

The motion light near the barn flicked on and I stopped.

Ream was leaning up against the door, arms crossed and looking none too happy. I was going to walk straight past him when he grabbed my forearm and brought me to a halt.

"What?" Goose bumps sprinkled across my flesh, and I felt heat flood my cheeks.

"You've lost weight. What's going on with you?"

I yanked back, trying to dislodge his hand but he refused to give.

"Babe." His tone was curt and unrelenting.

"Yeah, I heard you," I shot back. "And don't call me that."

He stared at me and I was the one who had to look away first, and I didn't like it. Why did he make me feel so uncertain of myself? I hated that he knew about my problem. It made me feel delicate, and I hated feeling delicate.

His hand slid down my arm and my stomach dropped. He linked our fingers together. "Then answer me."

"I'm fine." My pulse picked up speed as his finger caressed back and forth on my wrist. I don't think he realized he was doing it.

"Not good enough, Kitkat."

His nickname for me falling from his lips sent quivers down my spine. "Listen, Ream. We've fought. We've agreed that we hate one another. So, let's just make it less awkward for everyone living here and just agree to ignore one another."

"I never agreed to hate you, far from it. And I'm not living in the same house as you and ignoring you. It's impossible. And I think you know that." He stepped closer and his other hand came up between us and cupped my chin. "God, I fuckin' need to kiss you."

"What?" I moved back a step and the gravel beneath my feet sounded like gunshots going off I was so hyperaware. Where the hell had this come from? We fought; we didn't talk about kissing. "You've got to be kidding." I made an awkward sound like a laugh-snort and cocked my hip as I stared at him with disbelief. Was he delusional? On drugs? Ha, like that would ever happen.

"Are you drunk?"

"Never been more sober."

"Kissing me is so far out of the realm of possibilities. Do orange juice and milk go together, Ream? No. They can sit beside one another and look good, but mix them up and it's complete anarchy. That's us."

"Orange Creamsicles."

"What?"

"It's milk and orange and they go damn good together."

I snorted and started to turn away when he yanked my arm and pulled me back around. I put my hands out to stop from banging into his chest, but as soon as my palms felt the muscles beneath his shirt, a liquid heat hit me between my thighs.

"I've never been the same."

My breath hitched. "What?"

"After we were together. Something changed in me and I'm not going back. I like the change. And I miss the woman who gave it to me. I'm not talking just about the sex, Kat. It was before that."

God, why the hell did he have to go and say shit like that? I was good. I could handle him pushing and me pushing back, but this … it was unsettling, and I didn't do well with unsettling.

"I want us back. And I'll take you any way I can have you. Even if it's just friends, Kat. I'll take it—for now of course. But the constant anger and pain we're causing one another is destroying our beginning, and our beginning was something fuckin' special."

It was. Ream and I supported one another when Logan and Emily were down in Mexico. We became friends, and now that was wrecked too.

"What happened with Lana?" I blurted out. It may have been eight months ago, but him bringing Lana to my coming home party still hurt. "Did you fuck her?"

"Shit." He ran his hand back and forth over his head like he always did when he was agitated. "I thought you knew. Matt didn't tell you?"

I placed my hands on my hips and raised my brows, waiting for him to explain something that was no doubt still inexcusable.

"I picked her up at Avalanche that night. She started talking and…"

God, I so didn't want to hear this, yet I had been the one stupid enough to ask.

"I told her about you and…"

Unfrigginbelievable.

"Jesus, Kat, I was drinking, had a few too many, and Lana—"

"Offered to suck your dick?"

His eyes narrowed and body stiffened. "You need to drop the fuckin' attitude. I never touched her and I sure as hell would never let her mouth near my dick."

"You know I can't figure it out. You're here trying to get me to listen to you after you did something so incredibly insensitive as bringing some chick to my homecoming. On the day I get back from the hospital after being *shot*." I pushed on his chest and tried to get him to back away but failed. "No, forget it, I don't care what excuse you come up with. Slime is slime, and it doesn't change its consistency."

Ream grabbed my wrists and locked them in place, so the palms of my hands were flat against his chest. "I hadn't planned on coming that night. I didn't want you to see how wrecked I'd been. Kat, you nearly died. Fuck. Fuck." His grip tightened and I winced. He noticed and loosened a fraction. "I was drunk and Lana offered to drive me. And you know why she did? Because she wanted to fuck your brother. I thought he would've told you."

"My brother doesn't tell me who he fucks, Ream."

He sighed. "This has to stop, Kat. The fighting."

"Fine. We'll ignore one another." And yet I knew that was impossible. I couldn't ignore him even when he wasn't in the same country. I was constantly bombarded with thoughts of him at the farm with me, of us making meals together, painting, when he wiped the grease off my neck with the tip of his finger after fixing the tractor. How he made certain he was the one getting the door when a delivery arrived. A rule he'd insisted on. He said it was important the delivery men knew a guy was living here. I remembered the first time I heard him chuckle. He'd walked in on me attempting to put a curtain rod up by myself and instead ended up on my ass with the white sheer material overtop of me.

I felt Ream's hand cup my chin and I met his brooding eyes. "That won't ever happen, Kat. And you need to get that, so I'm going to tell you something. Something no one knows, not even Crisis. I wanted to tell you that night at the bar, but that shit you pulled with the guy …" I bit the corner of my lip. He saw it and I immediately let it go. "I swear if Matt hadn't called security and got me out of there …" What? Shit, Matt would seriously have a hate on for him. "I'd have killed the guy." He took a deep breath as if trying to ease the anger over the memory. "What I feel isn't normal, Kat. It's fucked up because I'm fucked up. I certainly don't deserve you. But I've tried to forget you, and it's not happening. So we will do this another way. You need to hear why I'm like I am and why I left like I did."

I didn't like the sound of that because secrets were almost always bad. Mine were.

"What I'm telling you … goes nowhere. Understand?"

I nodded. Not sure why, maybe because I hadn't been the same either and I was searching for something to grab hold of. Was a truce possible for us?

"I had a sister."

Oh God. He said had. I could feel his heart racing beneath my palms and the tension in his hands.

"My twin. We were complete opposites physically, and yet we were one and the same. She'd often finish my sentences and knew how I felt without me saying a word. She was my angel, the light to my darkness. We balanced one another out."

He grunted then abruptly let me go and turned slamming his fist into the wooden barn door. I waited, not knowing what to say, if anything.

"She was only sixteen when she died." His ragged whisper was that of a broken, torn man fighting to keep control. He leaned his forehead against the barn, his arms outstretched, palms flat on the rough surface looking like a crucifix.

I didn't know what to say.

"It was my fault. It was my job to protect her and I didn't."

He was silent for a while, and I wasn't sure if he was waiting for me to say something. I realized that no matter what had gone down between us, he deserved to be listened to.

He stayed quiet. Unmoving.

"Ream." I moved toward him until I could feel the heat of his back seeping into my chest. Then I lay my hand on his shoulder and squeezed. "Ream."

His shoulders sagged. "I was in and out of the hospital constantly with her. Never knowing if she was coming out alive. It was the drugs that finally did her in." Shit. That was why he freaked when he'd seen mine. Was it why he'd left the hospital when I'd been shot? "I lost the only person I ever cared about. Until the band."

I closed my eyes as the wave of his words hit me. I knew the band was important to him. He took it really seriously and I was guessing that whatever happened in his childhood with his sister, the band had helped get him through that.

"I should've seen what was happening to her and stopped it. I could've found a way." When he turned back around, I was taken aback by the clear liquid pooling in his eyes. Ream's agony was written all over his features, the lines across his forehead, lowered brows and lips tight. He dragged a finger down his inner right arm over his tats then looked directly at me.

I avoided facing shit like this. But this … this was something I needed to talk to him about because it's what brought us to where we were now. "Why didn't you say anything?"

"Jesus, Kat. I saw the needle and it was my sister all over again. I freaked out." He sighed and ran his hand back and forth over his head. "You told me and … all I could think about was you dying like she did, trips to the hospital. I couldn't go through caring about someone only to lose them again. But, Kat, I freaked, got my head together, and I came to the bar to talk to you, to see if we could—"

"Could what? Work it out? You just said you couldn't go through it again." That morning I'd lost more than just Ream. I'd lost a part of me. He took what I feared the most and shoved it back in my face with his reaction. I hid it from everyone to protect me from his exact reaction. I felt dirty and worthless. He'd destroyed that and I'd been struggling to get it back ever since. I think I wouldn't have cared so much if we hadn't developed that friendship between us first. He ruined everything. I didn't have it in me to have him do it to me again no matter what his past had thrown at him.

His voice hardened. "Fuck, I don't have the answers, but I came to find you because I cared and I wanted to explain. We were friends, Kat."

"Yeah, we were. But friends don't run out on one another when they don't like hearing something."

His jaw tightened. "You were fucking another guy two days after we were together," he shouted.

"Not technically." It was meant to be sassy and flippant. It wasn't.

"Fuck, how could you do that?"

Because I'd been hurt and angry and needed my dignity back. I wanted to feel powerful and in control after Ream had stripped it away.

"It doesn't matter now." He sighed, lowering his head and shaking it back and forth. "You know, she was always laughing and bright. She trusted everyone. Once she was …" He stopped abruptly. "She got hooked on the drugs, and I couldn't get her back."

I asked the only thing I could, "What was her name?"

"Haven."

His half-broken words put a dent in the shield I had around me because I knew about devastation, about loss, the emptiness. The waking up every day and feeling like you're missing pieces of yourself. A twin … I couldn't fathom the connection they must have had and what it would mean to lose.

"What about your parents?"

I saw the moment the coldness guarding what he hid from everyone descended over him. It was like a dam had been opened then suddenly slammed shut with a loud bang.

He pursed his lips together in a tight line. "Don't know who my father is and my mother is dead to me."

"Ream …" I couldn't help myself as I felt the anguish mixed with anger pour through him. My fingertips brushed against the bare skin of his arm and I wanted to hold him, but I couldn't. I had to keep him at a distance. "I'm sorry about Haven."

"Me too." He looped his arm around my neck and dragged me into him. I was completely caught off guard by his sudden gentle display of affection and found myself snuggled up against his chest. He kissed the top of my head and then softly stroked my hair. The tips of his fingers touched my bare skin at the back of my neck, and I sucked in air from the intimacy of it.

"Baby." His voice was a low whisper, caressing my insides like a feather. "I fucked up. With my sister … with you. I'm all screwed up inside." I went to draw back so I could look up at him, but his arms tightened around me and he refused to let me go. "Not done yet." I sighed then rested my cheek against his chest and listened to his heart thump and his long drawn in breaths. "I can't take back the things I said to you over the last few years. Fuck. I was so angry at you for hooking up with that guy. Then the flirting shit with Crisis. Hearing you talk about fucking other guys like you did it all the time. And shit maybe you do, I don't know." His hand stroked my back. "What I do know is that you're all I've thought about." He tightened his hold. "I'm not letting you go, I can't do it anymore."

This time I used my palms against his abdomen and pushed. He loosened his hold, but just enough so I could meet his eyes. "Ream, it won't work. It's too late."

His eyes flashed with something that I didn't recognize. "This wasn't a discussion."

Whoa. What? "Ream—"

His head tilted then lowered, and I gasped just before his lips took mine. It was hard and unrelenting, and a tidal wave of desire shot through me. Tingling peppered across my skin and when his hand curled into my hair and yanked my head back, I sucked in air, taking his into my lungs.

When he pulled back, I knew my lips were swollen and red from his grueling kiss.

"Tell me you can walk away from that."

"I did before and I will again." Shit, I had to tell him about Lance.

Ream took both my hands in his. "No."

I huffed. "You can't force this, Ream."

His brows raised and the corners of his lips curved upwards. It was rare Ream ever smiled and I was a little uneasy as to what he was thinking. "Oh, baby, I won't need force." He kissed my forehead. "We'll see how long it lasts."

"How long what lasts?" My voice raised an octave as I watched his eyes flicker with amusement.

"It will be entertaining." He grinned and my pulse rate tripled at the rare sight.

I didn't like the sound of that. "What will be?"

"You denying us."

"Ream. There is no us. And I'm seeing—"

He cut me off. "Babe, there's been an us since the moment I saw you from the stage and wanted to fuck you. You need us being friends first? I can do that. But I'm making you mine again."

My voice rose. "Yours? Are you insane? You can't just make someone yours. Jesus, Ream, what the hell has gotten into you?"

"You."

"What?" Shit, was my voice cracking? It never cracked, but my heart pounded so hard and my insides were freaking out and in a war of melting mush and red-hot poker fury. I'd preferred it when he was shooting insults at me and losing his cool. This … this threw me off balance and he damn well knew it.

"You're in me and that isn't leaving. I've fought it long enough, and I'm not doing it anymore. I told you something I've never told anyone, but you needed to hear it to understand why I freaked when I did. Now, there is nothing stopping us." Any mild amusement left his expression as he continued, "I fucked up. I won't do it again.

You need help ... I'll be there for you. I won't run, Kat."

I stared up at him and even though every single blood vessel pumped "yes, yes, yes," I couldn't. He may have explained the freaking out over the needle, but it didn't make me trust him. I tried to live my life without stress, and Ream meant high-velocity tension.

"And what happens when I get rushed to the hospital like your sister had been, Ream? Are you going to freak again?"

"It won't happen." He ran his finger across my still pulsating lips.

I shoved his hand aside. "No, it won't. Because I'm seeing someone else."

He froze and it was such a scary look on his face that I nearly ran. I could feel the pulsating rage pumping through him. His jaw clenched and the lines between his brows were deep and scary. "Get rid of him."

"Are you freakin' insane?" Yeah, he was. I knew that already. We fought like we both were insane. "Seriously. You've been gone for eight months. Now I've met someone nice who treats me well. I'm not dumping him, and you have no right to tell me to do that."

Suddenly, everything changed in him like a switch was flicked, and he grinned. "We'll see."

Before I could find some sort of intellectual reply, he turned and walked back to the house.

Fuck.

Chapter Three

Her gentle voice whispered to me, "Are we staying here, Ream?"
"Yes."
"Do you think he'll feed us?"
I closed my eyes remembering the scraps we ate. Like a dog, I'd
scrounge through bins to try and find us something to fill our stom-
achs. Mom never cared. All she cared about were the drugs.
"Yeah, Angel. I think so."
"You won't leave me."
"No. I'll never leave you."
I'd do whatever it took to protect her.

Hank was in the barn when I finally went inside after managing
to tear my gaze away from Ream striding back to the house. He
looked up, a flake of hay in his hand. He'd heard. It was written all
over his face with his accentuated wrinkles pulled down on his forehead and his subtle hazel eyes filled with concern. Hank had come
with the purchase of the farm and was a godsend. He cared for the
horses with a gentle touch and soft words, exactly what the abused

horses needed. He tossed the flake into Gym's stall then came and put his hand on my shoulder and squeezed. Hank rarely said much, but that one gesture was all he needed to convey his support.

We took Clifford out and treated the deep lacerations around his fetlocks. He'd been left hobbled in a barren field starving for months. The big Appaloosa was a character, constantly undoing gate latches and escaping any place you put him. No doubt that was why the previous owner decided to hobble him instead of simply making a latch he couldn't open.

Clifford was the sweetest horse we'd ever had on the farm, and I'd decided the moment he arrived, starved and bleeding, that he was mine. He was one of the few that endured his ordeal without a broken spirit. He remained good-natured and trusting without a mean bone in his massive body. He had come with the name Axe, but I immediately changed it to Clifford because he had red spots and acted like a big loveable dog.

After Clifford we treated Gym, the Shetland pony that foundered and had severe thrush in the frogs of his feet from standing in a wet, unsanitary stall. I then spent some time quietly talking to the thoroughbred, Ice, offering him carrots, but the horse was so skittish he stood and trembled in the back corner of the stall. Hank came up beside me and I sighed, tossing the carrots into his feed bin.

"Emily will help him," Hank said.

I nodded. The media called Emily "a horse whisperer." Although she didn't really like putting a title on it. "I'll do night check after dinner."

"Sure thing, doll."

By the time I got back to the house, Ream's words were back spinning in my head. The feel of his lips on mine, the cocky grin, and twinkling eyes … that was exactly what I didn't want to see. *Damn it, Ream.* It was far easier resisting him when he was being a complete butthole.

"There you are. We ordered Chinese." Emily stood beside Logan at the kitchen counter. They were unpacking dishes from a brown paper bag. "Oww," Emily hissed as her fingers touched the bottom of one of the containers.

Logan quickly took it from her scowling. "Mouse, let me do it." He examined her finger before slipping it inside his mouth. When he withdrew it, he kissed the tip. "You good?"

She nodded and I noticed the flush to her cheeks.

"Damn, Logan. I haven't had any in a while. You mind keeping it to the bedroom." I'd need a few new toys living with these two. Logan's mouth twitched and Emily smiled. He was still a scary hot-ass, but Emily didn't see it. At least not anymore. She did for a while when he came back for her. It was that look in her eyes, a mixture of need and fear all whipped into one.

Then I noticed Ream standing in the doorway, his eyes watching me. Had he heard what I said? Did it matter if he did? Except now he'd know that I hadn't slept with Lance.

The heat in the kitchen went up a thousand degrees, and I breathed with my mouth open. I wanted to lick my dry lips but couldn't because all I was thinking about was Ream licking them for me. Having his eyes on me was like him running his tongue across my skin.

"You haven't slept with him yet?" Ream's voice was strung tight, and it was super sexy. I was attracted to his scariness and wanted to suck it right out of him.

I noticed the sudden silence as Emily and Logan stopped talking and unpacking containers and looked at Ream and me.

"I'll get the plates," I said, trying desperately to keep the quiver from my voice. What the hell was wrong with me? I never acted nervous, but Ream standing there with his deliciously tight ass in those jeans, his lips slightly parted—lips that had been hard against mine.

I reached up into the cupboard and my hands had just touched the plates when I felt him beside me. His scent caused a carnival to break out on my insides, and it was like I was riding a roller coaster in a haunted house.

He was standing so close that our arms brushed against one another. "I have them," he said as he picked up the plates.

I kept my voice low, so Emily and Logan wouldn't hear. "I'm capable of doing it myself. What do you think ... I'm going to drop them?"

His whispered words drifted like a warm breeze across my cheek. "Oh I know what you're ... capable of, Kitkat."

My hands fell from the edge of the plates as I stared at him, mouth agape. He quirked a half smile as he took the plates and walked into the dining room.

Fuck. The image of me on top of him was plastered in my head like a flashing billboard sign. Every emotion I felt back then was being catapulted into the forefront of my brain, and I wanted to knock it back to Forgottenland with a friggin' wrecking ball.

"Oh Chinese," Georgie said as she barged into the room. "I hope you ordered chicken balls, hot stuff." She nudged Logan with her hip and grabbed a piece of broccoli from one of the open containers then popped it into her mouth. Then she was jumping up and down with her mouth open yelling, "Hot, hot, hot."

Crisis came in after her and went straight to me, putting his hands on either side of my waist, palms resting on my hips. "You've lost weight, sexy. Were you pining for me?"

I laughed. "Yeah, must be that." Crisis was a touchy-feely guy, and I got that because I was too. He never pushed the boundaries, and not once had he asked me to sleep with him. We were strictly platonic, and yet for some reason Crisis was in the habit of flirting with me especially in front of Ream. Of course I didn't do anything to stop it because when a guy flirts with you, it makes you feel pretty damn good inside, and I had been missing that lately. So flirting back, I wiggled my hips and Crisis moaned, "Yeah, sugar. You still have it."

Ream didn't find it funny—at all. "And that shit ... ends now," Ream stated from the doorway.

Crisis laughed, but didn't let me go. We'd been through this before. Ream usually said his piece, we'd argue, then he'd storm off. This time he was looking like he was going to remove Crisis from my person if he didn't let me go.

"Ream," Logan's voice bit into the air.

Ream's eyes never left Crisis as he spoke to Logan, "I told you what was going to happen."

"And I told you to cut it loose if she doesn't want it."

"Not happening."

Crisis slowly stepped back from me. "About fuckin' time, shithead." Crisis turned to me with a broad grin. "Looks like it worked."

"What worked?"

"Sweetcakes, I love you. I love touching you, but Ream's my best friend. I'd never touch what's his. Now, he's *finally* picked up his balls and is claiming you."

"Claiming?" The voice that blurted the word was unrecognizable. "I'm not something to be claimed." And what happened to the friends thing? What was Ream playing at?

"Damn right you are. And looks like the other guy hasn't done it yet," Ream said as he strode into the room toward me. I felt trapped. He took up all the air in the kitchen, and I couldn't breathe properly, his words ringing in my head like a gong.

I heard Emily's breath hitch and Logan's grunt just before Ream reached me. I thought he was going to kiss me, and I backed up until my lower spine hit the kitchen cabinet. "Ream …"

He moved in until his chest was up against mine and then … he reached up and over my head into the cabinet and grabbed another plate. "Forgot one." He hesitated, the feel of his rock hard thighs pressing into me. He backed off achingly slow, and I locked eyes with him. He winked and I swear my stomach hit the floor. This Ream I was scared of. Terrified. Because my snarky sass couldn't beat him. I knew it and he had figured that out, and it was frightening to my resolve.

I breathed a heavy sigh as he disappeared back into the dining room. Oh my God. I was pathetic. What the hell was I doing? I was way better prepared to deal with Ream when we argued. This … this was wreaking havoc on my emotions, and I was losing the battle.

"Holy bajoodles," Georgie said as she grabbed a bunch of utensils from the drawer. The clang of them hitting each other felt like my insides sparking off. "That man is hazardous to the libido." She smacked her lips together. "Who's taking bets he has her in the sack by nightfall?"

"Georgie. You bitch," I gasped. She knew damn well I was seeing Lance.

"One week. Sugar is still fighting it," Crisis shouted. Georgie and Crisis followed Ream, arguing the wager as they went.

I looked over at Logan and Emily who both had their eyes on me. "I'm with someone else now."

No matter how much I was attracted to Ream and wanted our friendship back, there were no second chances. After what he'd told me about his sister, I understood why he freaked out. But trusting him not to do it again—impossible. Friends stuck by one another, he obviously couldn't do that. And that was the most important quality I needed in a relationship—any relationship. I'd rather be alone than with a guy who couldn't stand by me when things got rough.

"I know." Emily nodded toward the dining room. "He doesn't look like he's going to back off though." She looked up at Logan with narrowed eyes. "What are you going to do about it?"

He chuckled. "I love when you're demanding, Mouse. Try it in bed tonight, we'll see what happens." Logan chin lifted toward me. "He's out of here if you say the word. He knows that."

Shit. Ream was determined, but I was stubborn. And once I got something in my head, I didn't back down. The doctors said that was why I was still alive after the shooting; I was too damn stubborn to die. "Maybe it's time for me to look for my own place." I was saving my money to buy a house, but it would be a struggle to do it now. I'd rather wait a few more years, unless of course hiding my *issue* from everyone became a problem, then I'd have to leave. No way in hell was I risking anyone knowing. It was bad enough Ream knew.

Emily's eyes widened. "No. You love the horses. You've made your career painting them. If anyone has to move, Logan will tell Ream to." Emily let go of Logan's hand and walked over to me and gave a half smile. "Actually ..." She glanced back over her shoulder at Logan and he nodded. "Logan and I are moving out."

"What?"

"Yeah. I know it may not be practical at first. I'll still be here every day to help with the horses, but we found a place only twenty minutes away and it's gorgeous. Well, it looks gorgeous from the pictures the real estate agent sent. We're going to see it tomorrow." She reached out her hand behind her and Logan approached and took it in his.

"Oh." I was happy for her, but at the same time I didn't want her to leave.

"Logan ..." Emily paused and looked up at him and my eyes went to his as she looked for consent. He gave a subtle nod and a rare grin. "Logan wanted to tell his mother first, but ... he asked me to marry him."

"Holy shit!" I immediately threw my arms around her, knocking Logan away in the process. "Oh my God. When? Where's the ring? Who else have you told? When's the day? Oh my God, this is amazing. I suspected it wouldn't be long before he put a ring on your finger. Your boyfriend is crazy needy when it comes to you and this would be his ultimate seal the deal."

Logan grunted and frowned, although I saw the hint of a smile playing at the corners of his lips because he knew I was right.

She laughed and pulled back. "He asked me a week ago. He wanted to ask me while on stage at the end of his concert. I think it was so every single guy would know that he was making me his legally. Although, I think most of them know better than to try to steal me away from an ex-underground fighter. Anyway, he didn't ask me on stage because I would've killed him and instead it was ..."

"Babe." It was Logan's warning tone.

"Logan considers it unshareable info."

"Ah, so he tied you up and spanked you until you agreed to marry his sorry ass."

Emily laughed and a bright flush rose to her cheeks. "Something like that." She turned to Logan. "But he knows I'd have said yes no matter what he did."

I playfully hit her shoulder. "But a week? And you're telling me now?"

"I wanted to see your face when I told you." Emily leaned back into Logan's encompassing embrace. "We decided it might be a good idea if we had our own place too."

"Yeah. Of course. Wow. Grats to both of you." I really was excited for them; I mean they'd been to Hell and back, both of them suffering because of that monster Raul. I hugged them and it felt odd because Logan wasn't an easy guy to hug. Even though I knew he was completely smitten with Emily, Logan had this protective shield around him that still made him unapproachable.

"Hey, food's growing green hair. Kinda funky, let's eat it," Georgie yelled from the other room.

Emily lowered her voice. "We haven't told anyone yet, so …"

"Yeah, of course." I ran my fingers across my lips. "Zipped. But you're showing me the ring first."

Holy crap. With Emily gone that left me alone with Crisis, Kite, and Ream. Dangerous. And so not going to work.

I made it through dinner with Ream sitting beside me, which I tried to avoid, but he'd waited until I sat before he dropped down next to me. He even had the nerve to shift his chair a few inches closer to me, to which I glared at him and he ignored.

His thigh was so close to mine that I could feel the heat radiating off it. Every time he moved in his seat, a torch lit inside me anticipating his touch, yet he never did, even when he reached in front of me to grab the pepper. His body leaned across the invisible line of personal space, but only the fine hairs of my arms felt the brush of his skin.

When he sat back down, I expected him to look at me, knowing full well what he was doing, but he didn't. He merely started shaking the pepper onto his lemon chicken.

I ate a few spoonfuls of vegetables and steamed rice. It was all that I could have since I started this new diet. Considering I used to pig out on the spring rolls and beef lo mein, no one seemed to notice.

After we cleaned up, I snuck out the side door to do a final night check on the horses. I'd made it three steps before I heard the door click and the footsteps.

I didn't have to look behind me to know who it was; there was a confident rhythm to his step that I'd recognize anywhere. I closed my eyes for a brief second while I continued to walk toward the stables.

"You barely ate anything."

"I wasn't hungry."

His arm brushed up against me, and I pulled my arm in closer to my side. "What are you playing at, Ream?"

"I'm not playing."

I stopped dead in my tracks and spun around. "Bullshit." I was the one who flirted. I didn't like that Ream was making my heart jump out of my chest every time he leaned close. "Stop whatever it is you think you're doing."

Ream ignored me and kept walking to the barn. I watched him from behind for several seconds, admiring how his faded jeans clung to his ass and thighs. I rarely painted nudes, but the thought of painting Ream was playing in my mind.

He reached the barn door and swung it open. "Coming?"

Barn. Alone. With Ream. Shit. He thought he could play this game better than me, and I excelled at flirting. Well, I did until he screwed that up too. Now, it wasn't any fun.

I reached the barn door and his whispered words swept across my skin. "I missed you."

Oh God. I was used to being in control, and tonight he made me feel completely out of control, especially when he surprised me with saying shit like that. "Well, I didn't miss you."

Ream didn't say anything as he followed me into the barn. The five horses stuck their heads out over their Dutch doors and a few nickered at us, knowing they were getting their night hay.

I noticed Ream keeping his distance from them by staying in the center of the aisle so the horses' noses couldn't quite touch him. Clifford tried his very best, stretching his thick neck out as far as he could then nodding his head up and down lifting his lip and flapping it.

I laughed at my obnoxious horse, and Ream froze, eyes watching me. I tucked my hair behind my ear and his eyes followed that too. Heat blazed. That familiar belly drop hit hard and fast as I looked back at him, neither of us moving. God, I missed this. Us hanging at the farm together. The comforting presence of him at my side. Did I just think that? We *had* comfort, then we had anger. Now it was … well I didn't know what it was, but getting back to the ease between us was impossible.

I needed to get my mojo back and get control here. I chewed my lower lip, raised my brows, and cocked my hip. I excelled at this. I loved flirting. It gave power and I liked power, and I felt like Ream had it all right now so I needed to take some of it away.

When he began walking toward me, I decided that playing with Ream was a mistake. He obviously wasn't going to back off. I quickly turned and grabbed the scissors hanging on the wall and cut the binder twine on the bale of hay against the wall. The twine snapped just as Ream came up behind me. I jerked, the presence of him so close to putting my confidence to shame.

His breath wafted across my ear as he leaned in, never touching but so close that I could feel every inch of him. "Fire playing with fire only leads to an uncontrollable inferno. You ready for that, Kitkat?"

I pulled hard on the twine and my elbow shot back hitting him square in the chest. I smiled when I heard him grunt. "I'm not fire.

I'm the fire hose."

The sound of his laughter had me swinging around, needing to catch a glimpse of the easygoing Ream that I'd tried to eradicate from my mind. It was a mistake because the memories hit me like running into a brick wall.

A loud bang sounded and I jerked my eyes away from Ream to Clifford, who was nodding his head up and down while kicking his hoof into the stall door. "Coming, buddy." I picked up a flake of hay and passed it to Ream.

He backed away without taking the hay. "I don't do horses."

"What?"

He shook his head. "I'll wait outside for you."

"You're kidding, right? Just throw it in his stall." I pushed the hay into his chest and he had no choice but to take it or let it drop. "That guy over there." I pointed to Clifford, who was making the racket and was the only horse in the barn that would make Ream's job difficult. Clifford liked to nip playfully, and he had a big reach with that neck of his.

He hesitated and I smiled. It was cute. This hot, sexy guy who was all muscles, tattoos, and confident was nervous of a group of horses that were likely more terrified of him after the abuse they'd been through. Okay, except Clifford. He wanted attention and wasn't scared to demand it. Ha ... He and Ream should get along perfectly.

I threw hay to the other four horses before he even managed his one. He stood facing Clifford, who was sticking his neck out like a giraffe and trying to grab the hay from Ream's hands. Clifford was getting pissed off and kicking the stall door harder. It looked like Ream was contemplating how he was going to get close enough to throw the hay in without the horse attacking him. The funny thing was that Clifford would suffer to Hell and back, and had, and he still didn't have a mean bone in his body.

I was about to give in and take the hay from Ream before

Clifford kicked a hole through his door when Ream raised the hay over his head and tossed it like a basketball for the hoop. Clifford backed away just in time, and the hay disappeared into his stall. He snorted and began eating.

When Ream looked back at me, there was a determined expression on his face, confident and unwavering. Shit. There was nothing about Ream that was N.I.C.E.

"I made the mistake of not protecting Haven. I don't repeat mistakes." No, Ream contemplated all angles before he acted. Probably, another reason why he ran out on me as soon as he found out what he was dealing with. "Deny us all you want, Kat, but you're not pushing me away." He nodded toward Clifford. "I don't trust or like them. But you do. So, I'll learn."

Ah fuck. "I'm dating Lance. You may think otherwise, but I don't date or screw two guys at once." I was trying to act like his words meant nothing to me, but really I was melting into a puddle of heated butter at his feet.

I flicked off the lights and we left the barn, Ream close beside me.

"The arguing, fighting, and hurting one another—that's finished. We were friends first. I'm getting it back." We walked several feet before he added, "And this guy you're dating, he hurts you, that involves me, so he better watch his step."

"Ream, he's nice."

He grunted. "You don't like nice, Kat. Doesn't do anything for that sassy attitude of yours. You'll be bored with his nice, but try … and know when his nice doesn't do anything for you … I'll be waiting." He lowered his voice, "'But, baby, I know what makes you wet and it isn't nice."

I snorted. "Full of yourself, aren't you?" But he was right. He was on a whole other level than Lance. "It's not all about the sex, Ream. Maybe that's where you've gone off course."

He was quiet until we reached the side door where he grabbed my arm before I could slip inside. "Sex is primal. And it's ugly as fuckin' hell. I know that better than anyone. But with you … with you it's all beauty. You managed to obliterate the ugly, Kat."

The electricity in the air sparked off in every direction. I held my breath and he was so close that if I stood on my tiptoes and leaned an inch forward, our lips would meet. But I couldn't. No matter what my attraction was to Ream, I was trying to move forward and be with someone else.

"Nite," I mumbled and made a dash for my bedroom. When I slammed the door behind me, I leaned up against it, my breathing harsh and ragged.

I had no clue what I was going to do living under the same roof as Ream and with him acting like he was. It threw me off balance and into complete chaos. I couldn't let him back in. He may have kept my secret, but I didn't trust him to not hurt me again.

I changed and brushed my teeth while staring at myself in the mirror. Maybe he felt like he could save me after failing with his sister? But I didn't want that. Ream may think he can win me back with his games, but I wasn't a prize to be won. Hadn't Ream figured out yet that I couldn't be fixed?

I tossed and turned for hours in bed before I finally gave in to my festering thoughts and got up. I quietly opened my door, listening for anyone awake, but the house was silent. I padded down the hallway to the sunroom, which was off Logan's office. It was a small glass-enclosed room with one chair and ottoman and my easel and paints. I turned on the lights and stared at the painting I'd been working on over the last few weeks. It was an abstract of a herd of horses galloping head-on with dust kicked up and swirling around them.

I walked over to my easel, picked up the tubes of Payne's gray and titanium white, spurted blobs on my palette, then began mixing until I had the perfect shade. Then I painted until the wee hours of the morning.

Chapter Four

She was safe.
Nothing else mattered.
Nothing would touch her.
I swore to protect her at all costs.
But her beauty had emerged.
And he had noticed.
I had to protect her from him. From everyone.

Logan and Emily were gone by the time I rolled out of bed at nine. I never slept in but was unable to sleep due to the Ream-poison sloshing through my veins, so I was up painting until four in the morning before I managed to crash.

I felt the familiar signs of my body reacting to the stress and exhaustion, and I pulled out the little bottle in the back of my nightstand and slipped one of the green pills into my mouth. The needles did nothing to calm my nerves that shot off like jet speed sprinklers. But the pills did and I hoped it was enough to get me through the day.

There was a note on the fridge from Emily that she and Logan went to see the house with the real estate agent and then to visit Isabelle. She put a little winky face beside the xx. I knew exactly what they were doing, and I was really happy for them. Ream, Crisis, and Kite were no doubt still sleeping. I imagined their sleep schedules were all screwed up after touring.

I looked out the living room window on my way back to the sunroom with my coffee. I glanced out at the horse field hoping to catch a glimpse of Clifford. Hank usually turned them out around seven every morning.

My breath caught in my throat as I saw Ream standing at the fence line, his hand stroking Clifford's muzzle. I stared for a few minutes, watching him look vulnerable and uncertain, while Clifford pushed and insisted on being patted.

It was like us, I realized. Ream was confident and sure of what he wanted, insisting. Me … I didn't want to open myself up to the hurt again. I'd been destroyed when my parents died. A scar that never went away. To lose someone you loved so much … Ream knew what it was like, but for me it was more than just emotional. I felt it physically too. It was all about staying safe. No stress. Lance was safe. Ream was a threat.

I turned away from the window and continued into the sunroom, closing the door and shutting out the image of Ream.

It was several hours later when I heard the shouting and the swearing. I ran out into the living room to see Crisis, Kite, and Ream all sitting on the floor, their legs out, leaning up against the couch. Crisis and Ream had controllers in their hands and the shouting had been at the TV where cars were racing down a track.

"Sweetcakes, sit and watch me beat your boyfriend's ass," Crisis said, then groaned as his car went spinning out of control around a corner and Ream's went flying by.

"I'm seeing Lance now, Crisis."

"Yeah, whatever." He waved his hand in the air as if he didn't believe me.

I let it pass. After all, it was Crisis and he enjoyed stirring shit up. Although, Ream's face looked pretty damn pleased, most likely from the comment and not that he was now winning.

I went and sat on the arm of the couch. Ream held his controller like he did everything else, with confidence. There was no screwed up face like Crisis, who was currently sticking his tongue out, scrunching his nose, and moving the controller in the direction he was turning. "You know, it's amusing to watch, but you do realize that moving your body doesn't have any effect on what's happening on the screen in this game."

"He thinks it does. You should see him play the fighting games," Kite said then chuckled.

I hadn't noticed it before but Kite's laugh was hot. The kind that sunk into your bones, a rough, raspy sound … huh. I looked at Kite again, wondering why the hell he didn't have a girl. He was hot, covered in ink, and was a good guy. Okay, he had some serious piercings, but I imagined that the stud on his tongue might feel pretty damn hot in certain places. When I glanced back up, I saw Ream watching me watching Kite and he was scowling.

"Woot!" Crisis yelled and threw his arms in the air. "Busted. Next time, eyes on the road instead of the babe."

Ream and I both looked at the screen. His car had spun out on the grass just within sight of the finish line.

I laughed.

He stood.

My lips parted and heart raced, along with the horde of butterflies causing frenzy in my lower body. Then he did that subtle wink again. Ream winking at me was super sexy, and it left me breathless.

I was still uncertain about where we stood and if he was taking the friends idea seriously or if he was going to push for more. He held out his controller to me. "Play Kite, he'll take it easy on you, Kitkat. The loser plays me. Winner, Crisis."

I stood and walked over to him. That was my first mistake

because being in his space meant I could smell him, and it was good and my body remembered it being good. I grabbed the controller then frowned, holding it out in front of me with two fingers. "You want to grab me a cloth or something? This thing's all sweaty and gross."

Ream chuckled and it sent a wave of tingles through me, and it was all good tingles. Yep, his chuckle was hotter than Kite's. He leaned in and whispered, "I can bring you anything you want, beautiful. And I specifically remember you liking sweaty."

I sat on the floor. It was quick and ungraceful because my body was hyperaware and sparking off with desire. It was like little fairy hands were partying on my skin and reaching out for Ream, screaming his name.

Crisis hopped over the back of the couch. "We need beers for this race. Might want to take a piss before they start, Ream. You know how Kite plays … old grandpa driving. Kat, you could beat him on a scooter."

Ream smacked Kite on the shoulder. "Try and keep it on the pavement, buddy." Then he looked at me. "You any good, Kitkat? Need some tips?"

I shrugged. "I've played. I prefer the fantasy games. You know, using your brain to figure shit out. Driving in circles around a track doesn't really appeal to me."

"What does appeal to you?" Ream asked, and from his tone I knew he wasn't talking about games, but I decided with Ream it was better to ignore his innuendos. I was used to Ream being pissed off and getting angry, losing his shit. This … this reminded me of when we met and it was ramping up my uncertainty to a whole new territory.

"Men in tights mostly," I said. Kite burst out laughing. "You know like the superheroes."

"Oh, sweetcakes, I'll be your superhero any day. I can do wonders with my cock …" Crisis stopped mid-sentence, one leg over the couch, the other on the floor, and four beers in hand. He looked at

Ream, who didn't look happy—at all. The kind of mad that made you stop and stare then wonder if maybe you should run. Crisis didn't of course. "First Emily, now Kat. What the fuck? What chick am I supposed to flirt with now? Christ, Kite, man, we need another chick to move in."

Ream grabbed two beers from him and opened them, passing one to me. "Thanks." He nodded then tilted his head back and swallowed the ice cold liquid.

I couldn't tear my eyes away and was caught staring when he lowered his beer and our gazes collided.

Shit.

"Earth to dollop?" Crisis ruffled my hair.

"Dollop?"

Kite pointed to a blob of paint on the back of my hand then nodded to the TV. "Pick your car, lovely." Kite had a faint Irish accent, but it accentuated with the word lovely. He went on to suggest which car would be best for me and then gave me some pointers. Before long we were racing.

I forgot about Ream, well forgot is a strong word, I was always aware of him, but I pushed him to the far back corner of my mind. Shit that was a lie too; he was sitting beside me, long, lean legs stretched out in jeans. Not just any jeans, but ones worn out at the knees. Faded and just snug in all the right places. Our shoulders touched—okay, inches apart—but the magnetic pull I felt, it was like we were touching. Why couldn't I get him out of me? Why was he so hard to forget? Could we be friends again? No, there was too much sexual tension between us to just be friends. I couldn't imagine seeing him with another woman … Oh God, I hadn't thought of that.

"Kat, what the hell are you doing? Girls." Crisis slapped his knee and laughed.

I focused back on the screen, and I was going full throttle into a bridge, tires skidding and not going anywhere. Kite was laughing his ass off so hard that he rammed his car into a sign and did a one eighty. I reversed and started back on the track. Kite was half a lap ahead of me.

Ream's hand came down on my thigh and Jesus I was so surprised—and yes, ready to jump the asshole—that I dropped the controller and my car came to a dead stop in the middle of the track.

"Hands off, bucko." I glared at him and he put up his hands, but I saw the flicker of a smile tugging at the corners of his lips. He wanted me to lose ... cheater. "No touching the players. I'll call distraction."

Crisis looped his arm around Kite's throat and pulled him backwards. "Kat. Go. Go. Go. You can still beat this pussy."

I laughed and got down to business and made my way around the track, but Kite had managed to escape Crisis' hold and was nearing the finish line.

"You suck, sugar," Crisis said, shaking his head. "Give me the controller. I'm kicking some Kite butt." I passed it over and heard the roar of the engines as the boys waited for the countdown. "Eat my gas," Crisis yelled as he shot off ahead of Kite. "Fuckin' did that on the tour bus," Kite muttered. I couldn't stop the laugh-snort from emerging. "Kat, did Emily tell you about Logan banning Crisis from the bus in Minnesota?" I shook my head. "The pig was walking around naked, drunk, and with a chick, who was no shy screamer, in his bunk. Emily saw him and ... shit Ream ... didn't she say she puked a little at the sight of his naked ass?"

"Ha. More like wondering if she was in the wrong bed," Crisis said.

I laughed because there wasn't even the remotest chance that Emily would ever think that. Even if his cock was the size of a baseball bat.

"And at least I can make them scream." Crisis swung his arms out wide as he made a turn and nearly clocked Kite in the face. "That punk chick you fucked in the dressing room ... remember her?" Kite grunted. "Yeah you do, so does the whole fuckin' crew. Shit." Crisis's car crashed into a median and slowed as it hit the grass. Kite's car whizzed past.

"You're going to lose, dickbrain," Kite said, grinning.

"Fuck." Crisis focused on the TV and the story I wanted to hear was left unsaid.

Crisis ended up winning and Ream and I clanked beers with him. It was good to see them not at each other's throats. Guys were funny. They could beat the shit out of one another, call each other the worst names ever, and then be best buds drinking together the next minute.

I hated that the shit between Ream and me had caused conflict with Crisis and Ream. But it also seemed part of what they did, like brothers. Egging one another on, teasing, and that was what Crisis had been doing. Pushing the boundary with me in front of Ream.

"Ready?" Ream's voice was soft and gentle and at the same time had an edge to it that heated my lower region into a low boil. Fuck. I need to concentrate on not getting my ass kicked.

Kite passed me his controller, and I picked my car then paused. "How about we pick another track? Something a little more … challenging?"

Ream shrugged. "Whatever you like. Your choice, beautiful."

I loved when he called me that, and that's why I hated it so much. "Call me that again and I'll have to kick your ass and embarrass you in front of your buddies." I scrolled through until I found the off-roading.

Crisis started laughing hysterically, and Kite shook his head back and forth. He leaned close and nudged me with his shoulder. "That's Ream's specialty. You sure you want to pick that? 'Cause you're not kicking his ass on that track no matter what you do."

"It's just a game, boys. Not like I'm losing anything big."

"Bragging rights," Crisis muttered.

"Pride," Kite decreed.

I laughed.

Ream chuckled. "I'll take it easy on her. I love that you picked my favorite track, baby." He leaned closer and I held up my hand.

"No touching. Don't call me *baby* or *beautiful*, and if you manage those things, then maybe I'll take it easy on *you*."

"Oh I don't need you to take it easy on me, *beautiful*. Everyone already knows I'm king of off-roading. You see the score board?" He clicked a few times and up came the scores for the track. Ream's name was all over it. He lowered his voice. "I may even let you get your name up on the board if you let me kiss—"

I frowned. "Not a chance. I'm kicking your butt because I'm better than you."

He laughed, head thrown back exposing his throat again. A throat I'd nibbled on and suckled and ran my tongue across. Then I bit my tongue and jerked my head to the screen and buckled down.

Ream was good … no, he was great at off-roading, but I did grow up with an older brother and I omitted a little truth. Fantasy games were my favorite, but I excelled at car racing. Purposely losing the last game with Kite had been fun, beating Ream was better.

"The new love of my life," Crisis exclaimed as I tore through the finish line ahead of Ream by a fraction.

"Again," Ream nudged me with his shoulder, and I tried to control my giddiness. I expected him to be mad that he lost, but instead Ream was all playful and sweet, and I was melting.

We played for another hour and Ream beat me twice and I kicked Crisis' butt, which had him changing up the game to boxing.

"I'm out, boys." I passed my controller to Kite then got up and went to the kitchen to grab something to eat before I went back to painting. I never heard Ream follow me, but when I shut the pantry door he was right behind me.

"We're going for lunch." Ream took my hand before I could object and started walking to the door. He snagged keys from the hook on the wall. "Later, boys," he called out.

"Ream." He pulled me out on the porch. "Ream. Seriously, I'm dating someone else."

"So. We're friends going to grab food." He stopped at his car and held open the passenger door. "In." His brows rose at my hesitation. "I'm beginning to think you argue with me on purpose because it turns you on."

I opened my mouth to argue then slammed it shut. Then I got in and watched his sweet ass stride around the front of the car and slide in next to me.

He took me to a cute little pub in King Township. Emily and I had been numerous times since it had a live band on Friday and Saturday nights and was close to the farm when we didn't want to travel to the city. The pub also had food I could eat with my new diet so I ordered a cob salad and chicken sandwich toasted on rye.

I snagged a fry from Ream's plate, and he reached across and dug his fork into a baby carrot. When he bit into it, I imagined him biting me. Gah ... this was a bad idea. We'd never be able to just be friends.

We talked about Logan and Emily, the band, the tour and what it was like, and plans for the new album. He asked about Clifford and my upcoming art show at the gallery. I expected Ream to push about our relationship, but he didn't touch the subject and it felt like ... like we used to be. He was completely relaxed, even the usual intensity in his dark eyes was calm.

"So do you love it? The touring?" We'd talked about the concerts and how it was wild and crazy with a ton of people constantly around.

Ream stretched his legs out under the table and his calf rubbed up against mine sending goose bumps across my skin. "You cold?"

I cleared my throat and crossed my arms trying to hide the effect he had on me. There was a mischievous spark dancing in his eyes. I shook my head and took a sip of my coffee.

"I do. But I prefer it here. Quieter." He was watching me ... eyes lazy as he continued. "And there is something here I want."

That threw me completely off balance, and my coffee spilled on the table as I set it down too hard.

He shrugged. "But touring is a good time, too much drinking, too little sleep, and yes too many chicks. Although, Crisis would never admit to that."

It felt as if a lead weight crushed into my chest. So he had been with other women. Well, not that he wouldn't; there was no reason why he wouldn't. We weren't together then or now. Shit, we'd never been a couple. So why was I so upset about the thought of him being with another woman? Or more than likely women. Was that where he'd gone when Emily said he disappeared? To have sex with some chick?

He nudged my leg and I looked up at him. "What's up?"

My fake smile was good—I mean I could get it past Matt and Emily without being detected as a lie—but my smile faltered when he scowled back at me. "Nothing."

"Don't lie. You're thinking about something and it isn't good." He reached across the table and linked his fingers with mine. It passed the boundary of friendship, but I didn't pull away because I liked it—a lot. His thumb stroked back and forth, and it was intimate. Too intimate. I thought of Lance and quickly yanked back. What was I doing? Christ, I know Lance and I were just dating, but holding hands was past the friendship rule. "You going to tell me or am I going to have to embarrass you?"

I balked. "What?" There was no chance I'd tell him that I was upset he'd been with other women.

"Embarrassment it is."

I grabbed his hand but he easily slipped away and then slid out from the table. I don't know what I expected, but it wasn't to go talk to the bartender. After a short conversation he walked over to where the band had set up for tonight's performance. I should've snuck out right then, but I didn't embarrass easily and I was curious.

Ream slung the acoustic guitar over his shoulder and sat on the stool. When the music started I felt the heat rise in my body because his voice had a dynamic rippling effect on me that grabbed hold of my insides. There was no microphone, no electric guitar, no background music, just his magnetic voice and the strum of his fingers across the strings of the guitar.

Ream sang right to me, and as I looked around the bar, everyone smiled and looked between Ream and me. He thought it would embarrass me, but it didn't one bit. Ream had a gorgeous, deep voice that had a slight rasp to it, and listening to him was a gift no matter what was between us.

I slid out from the table and walked toward him. His eyes never left mine as I approached. I stopped a few steps away, closed my eyes, and started moving. Dancing was my thing and maybe he'd done this on purpose because he knew that. I'd dance anywhere if I could. After being shot, I'd had to keep my movements calm instead of my usual crazy-ass dancing or my legs would react.

It was a slow song and I moved unhurried and seductive, his voice urging me on as it spun a web around me and held me captive. Even with my eyes closed, I could feel him watching me and I knew if I opened them his heated gaze would make my knees shake and my belly drop. When his voice drifted off, I stopped and looked at him. His hand rested on the guitar, his body stiff, and there was that dark intensity back in his eyes.

"Kiss her," someone shouted as the patrons clapped and hooted and hollered.

Ream set the guitar aside then approached me. He looped his arm around my waist and brought me in close. The crowd went wild and yet I didn't really hear what they were yelling because all I could do was try and maintain some semblance of control when everything in me was screaming to jump him.

He leaned in. "You're not embarrassed."

"And you're not half bad."

He chuckled. "Thank you. I get by."

"Kiss that hot piece of ass before I come over and do it for you," a guy yelled from across the bar.

Ream stiffened and went to move toward whoever shouted. "No." I put my hand on his neck and curled my fingers in his hair. "Leave it. But, Ream, I can't kiss you."

"One kiss. For the crowd."

"Ream, I'm seeing someone."

"You guys serious?"

"Not exactly. But kissing another guy, one I've ... been with before ... wouldn't be fair."

"So it's fair that you're not giving me a chance?"

"Ream." There was no question we had chemistry, but it didn't start out that way. Actually, I specifically recalled him saying when we were lying in bed that when he first saw me, he thought I was one of those stuck-up, spoiled, know-it-all bitches.

A second chance was something I didn't give people because life was too short to waste it with a guy that got scared the second he saw my drugs. He even admitted that it reminded him of his sister and the hospital and his shitty past. He'd proved it to me twice already. He may have stayed at the hospital until I was out of critical condition after I was shot, but he still left me. Friends didn't do that. He said he cared, but actions spoke louder than words and his actions sucked ass.

"Fuck, man, kiss her," the same voice shouted, and before I could stop him, Ream leaned in and his mouth stole my words, my body, and my soul. His lips took and at first I sunk deep into him, the crowd's applause lost to me as I pressed in close, the familiar dance of his tongue, the warmth of his lips that were hard and yet pliant.

Oh God, what was I doing? I violently drew back, breathless and trembling. I stared at him and he was looking completely irresistible with his smoldering eyes and freshly kissed lips.

Then within a second it washed back out to sea as the waitress came over and asked for his autograph. Ream slipped out of my arms and took the pen and paper from the cute brunette. They chatted for a minute while I started back for the table. I didn't get far before his hand grabbed mine and tugged me back in beside him.

He gave the girl the paper and some bills for our tab and then started toward the door, keeping his hand tight in mine. As soon as we were outside, he stopped abruptly and I slammed into his back.

He was mad. Shit, what the hell? This guy had issues. I was the one who should be furious after he kissed me when I told him we couldn't.

"Don't walk away from me." I went to smart mouth him back, but he was quick, cupping my chin and placing a finger over my mouth. "I mean it, Kat. Friend, girlfriend, or my fuckin' wife. I don't want you walking away from me when some other chick is vying for my attention because no matter what we are … you are more important than them."

Not very often was I speechless, but Ream did it to me. There was no arguing, no smart-ass remark, no discussion; it just was a beautiful thing to say no matter what he was to me.

He made an abrupt nod of his head, as if satisfied that I got what he was saying and wasn't going to argue the point. Then he let me go and we went home where I escaped into the sunroom, away from Ream and what I was struggling to deny.

Chapter Five

Her hand stroked my back up and down like a yoyo.
Stop it.
I hated it. They always did that to me after they hurt me.
I gagged then threw up the last of my dinner into the toilet.
She flushed and I watched the water swirl around and around. It was me. It felt like me, helpless to do anything, but submit.
I blocked out her soft words telling me it would be okay. That it wouldn't be so bad.
I wanted to slam her head into the toilet. She had no clue what I faced week after week.
The shadow appeared in the door, and I spit into the fresh water staring back at me.
I stood.
She took my hand and my stomach cramped with disgust.
Then we followed the shadow to the basement.

It wasn't until dark that I heard the loud holler of Crisis and realized I'd been lost to the rainbow of colors all day.

I plopped my brush into the jar of murky gray water then went into the kitchen to see Crisis with Emily in his arms swinging her around. Logan stood close by, arms crossed, looking none too pleased that another man had his hands on his girl. I could see by the way his muscles twitched that he was barely tolerating it, and if Crisis didn't let her go soon, Logan was going to do something about it.

"Our girl is getting married," Crisis yelled to me as he placed Emily back on her feet.

I smiled at Emily and then caught a glimmer of the ring and gasped. "Damn, missy." I went running over and grabbed her hand, staring at the magnificent ring on her finger. It wasn't just a rock; this was a ring with two delicate horse shoes sprinkled with tiny diamonds. To connect them together sat a beautiful cut diamond. It was perfect for Emily. Subtle, but it held so much meaning. The abused horses healed Emily just as much as she healed them, and Logan had given that to her.

"It's perfect," I whispered. Then I glanced up at Logan who looked real proud of himself. "Fine. You did good, sexy. You can marry her."

Logan laughed and Emily looked up. I saw her body sag as she watched her soon to be husband. She really loved him. It was the most beautiful sight, watching the two of them. They read one another so well, as if Logan knew how Emily felt better than she did herself. He knew what she needed from him and he gave it to her.

"Avalanche," Crisis announced. "This calls for drinks. Where's Ream and Kite?" He took out his phone and started texting.

"I've got Georgie," I said and hugged Emily again before I fished out my phone and texted her. Then I called my brother and told him to save us the usual table, to which he groaned and complained that the band was too popular now and he'd need to call in more security for the night. Then I bitched and complained that he hadn't been to the farm in weeks to see me. He shut up.

I sent Lance a text too. We didn't have plans tonight, but he liked knowing what I was up to. I thought it was nice and it was, but nice ... well, nice was just nice. I told him we were going to Avalanche to celebrate Emily and Logan's engagement but didn't invite him, even though any normal girl dating some guy would. But with the way Ream was acting, throwing Lance into the mix was pulling the pin from the grenade and dealing with that on a night that was for Emily ... I wasn't taking the chance of it being ruined.

Ream's car was gone and Crisis complained that 'my boyfriend' wasn't responding to his texts. I smacked Crisis hard on the shoulder for the boyfriend wisecrack and was silently glad that Ream was AWOL. Alcohol ... emotions teetering on a tight rope and a volatile history ... well, it was safer Ream wasn't joining us.

We made our way through the crowd to our reserved table near the stage. It was busy as usual and I noticed Matt had a few security guys around I didn't recognize.

I stopped to chat with Molly, one of the waitresses who'd been at Avalanche for three months. Cute girl with bright red hair, obviously dyed since she had black roots. She had pale skin with freckles sprinkled across the bridge of her nose and brilliant blue eyes—too brilliant. I suspected she wore contacts. No one had eyes that blue.

Molly was twenty-four and I remember Matt nearly didn't hire her because she looked sixteen and he thought she was using fake ID. It was only when the tears fell and she begged that he decided to give her a chance. But first he took her driver's license and had it checked by the Ministry of Transportation to make sure it wasn't a phony.

A few weeks ago Brett told me Molly had escaped an abusive relationship and had moved here from Vancouver with nothing except the clothes on her back. She supposedly lived in a rundown house in a rough part of the city with a couple of unsavory roommates. Brett had offered to find her something a little safer, but she refused to take any help.

Kite smiled and winked at Molly on his way by. "Hey, lovey."

I smiled when I saw her hide her face in a curtain of hair like she usually did. She mumbled something back to him, although it was too soft to hear over the music. I didn't know how she managed getting through a night at Avalanche she was so shy and easily embarrassed, and the regulars were relentless with their teasing.

"Looking appetizing as usual." Crisis smacked Molly on the butt and sent her staggering forward. I had to help steady her and the tray of beers she held.

"Crisis," I chided.

He held up his hands. "What? She looks hot. Girl needs to hear it." Before I could say anything else, he was already weaving through the crowd.

We chatted a few minutes more before I saw her look over at the bar and then she quickly made her excuses, stumbling all over her words and darted off. I glanced at the bar and caught Brett watching Molly and he was frowning. Brett rarely frowned. I searched for Molly and saw her serving a bunch of guys, and one of them had his hand on her arm.

Interesting. Was Brett hot for Molly? I'd never seen him with a girl, and he took plenty of numbers from working Friday and Saturday nights. The guy was a mystery, a successful real estate tycoon, hot, charming, and rarely lost his cool. He could have any girl he wanted, but he chose to serve them drinks at a bar instead of spending his weekend nights taking them to fancy restaurants.

Maybe Molly would change that? I smiled to myself then made my way across the dance floor toward our table.

I stopped.

My breath hitched. Then I stared and it was me watching him without him noticing. For a brief flicker I set my emotions free, and it was like leaving the door to a bird's cage open. Hesitant to leave the protective cover at first, and then spreading its wings and experiencing the freedom. It was cathartic and I wanted to stay there and allow him in.

He was sitting with a beer in hand, slowly turning it in a circle, his head down. There was a hint of sadness, something cracking his confident all-encompassing attitude. I wouldn't have seen it if he knew I was looking at him. The slight defeat in his shoulders, the tension in his jaw line, and the longer than usual blink as if he wanted to close his eyes.

He had one arm slung over the back of the chair next to him, and it was then my eyes hit the petite brunette sitting in it. He wasn't touching her, and it wasn't that chick that sent my blood pressure on the rise. It was the other girl who walked up and was hanging over him, her hand resting on his shoulder as she leaned in whispering something to him. I knew the tactic; shit, I'd done it. Slight touch, nothing too much, voice low and sexy letting your breath whisper across his ear.

The cage door slammed shut.

Jesus, why did I care? We were done. This was good. Maybe he'd stop playing with my head if he hooked up with another chick. But the thought of Ream screwing the blonde was like a punch to the stomach. The combination of anger and feeling ill threatened my usual cool, and I had to look away for a minute to collect myself again.

"Kat?" Emily came up beside me. She looked at Ream then back at me. "It always happens. The girls around them. You get used to it."

I flicked my hair over my shoulder and pulled my shoulders back. "He can have any girl he wants. There's nothing between us. I'm dating Lance, Eme."

Emily nodded, although I knew she didn't believe me. Shit, I didn't believe me.

As I approached the table so did Crisis, and he slapped Ream on the back and drew his attention away from the girls. "Hey, buddy."

Ream nodded to him and said something I didn't catch. Crisis gave a curt nod, and I caught the quick look at me before he threw his arm around the blonde and carted her away. My eyes drifted to his tatted arms that were now flexed with tension then traveled back up to his face. He was watching me.

My lips parted as I took a few deep breaths and locked gazes with him. He never took his arm off the back of the chair with the brunette, and to anyone who didn't know him, they'd think nothing was wrong.

I knew though. I saw how his brows twitched and the twirling of his beer stopped. The slightest tightening of his grip on the bottle and then the shift of his legs so they were no longer crossed at the ankles, but rather ready to react. I felt like the rabbit caught coming out of the hole with the wolf lurking nearby.

"Sis." Matt came up beside me and pulled me into a hug, breaking my view of Ream.

Matt was lean, over six feet, with broad shoulders and dark blue eyes that were just like our mother's. He would've been a star quarterback if he hadn't had to stay with me when our parents died. Being eight years older than me, eighteen at the time, he gave up his scholarship at Western University in order to raise me. I was only ten and when he told me what had happened to our parents. I could remember begging over and over again to see my mom while Matt cradled me in his arms. But no matter how much I begged, I never saw her again.

"You've lost weight." He looked me up and down then leaned in keeping his voice low. "You okay? It's the fucking drugs, isn't it?"

Not really. And no, I wasn't okay. I was used to ignoring what I didn't want to face, and Ream wasn't allowing that. I was off-balance and my body reacted to it. I knew a pill would help, but I was trying to control the amount I took.

"Kat?" He squeezed my hand.

"Umm yeah?" What had he asked again?

"You've lost too much weight. What's going on?"

"It's fine. I'm just trying something different with my diet. There's an adjustment period."

He still didn't look satisfied by the way his lips pursed together. He pulled me a little farther away from the group. "You're too skinny, Sis. You want to try and eat healthier, we'll see a nutrition- ist."

"God, I'm not sixteen anymore. I'm fine."

"You don't look fine. And you're not sleeping." I tried to hide the black under my eyes with makeup. Guess I failed. He nodded toward the table. "It's Ream, isn't it? Fuckin' guy. I know shit went down between you two and it's obvious he hurt you. I don't like it. I don't like him." Ha ... if my brother knew Ream called me bitch and a whore, he wouldn't have been allowed inside Avalanche.

"We're fine."

"A lot of fines here, Kat."

I put my hand on his arm, and gave him my most annoyed look: lips pursed, eyes narrowed while giving an exasperated huff. "I love you, but clamp down on the overprotective brother for tonight. We're celebrating Logan and Emily's engagement." I eased up on the annoyed look when I got that he wasn't buying it. Gah ... big brothers were the best and the worst. I softened my tone and gave him a big fake smile. "Talk tomorrow? And I'll see a nutritionist, okay?" I kissed his cheek and that did it. He relented, although knowing Matt he'd be on the phone tomorrow looking for a nutri- tionist for me.

I sat in the farthest seat away from Ream, unfortunately it was also opposite him, so I had the pleasure of watching him talk to the brunette. Emily sat on my right and Kite on my left. Molly brought over a round of shots with two bottles of champagne—on the house. She chatted with Ream and I noticed his scowl and pensiveness as if he was trying to figure out something. I did my best to ignore Ream, and for the most part I did, except my body couldn't ignore him. It knew he was a few feet away and every time I heard his deep voice, goose bumps jazz stepped across my skin.

"Oh my God. Kat. Dance. Come on." Emily pecked Logan's cheek and went to get up and fell back down into Logan's lap. She giggled and he leaned in and whispered something in her ear which had her cheeks turning bright red. She went to stand back up and staggered a couple of steps. "Oops," she mumbled and the corner of Logan's mouth curved up as he took in his drunk soon-to-be wife. The way he looked at her it was as if he caressed every part of her with his eyes.

I stood and swayed for a second as the shots and champagne hit me. Having nothing to eat since lunch, everything went straight to my head. I caught Ream's watchful gaze, and he was scowling with a quiet intensity. It was the same look he gave me when he'd found me trying to fix a fence rail by myself. Protective and consuming. I quickly looked away, grabbed Emily's hand, and with my hips swaying, we walked to the dance floor.

Emily leaned into me and whispered, "Drunk sex tonight. Well, me drunk, Logan sober. It's the ultimate ice-cream." Emily twirled.

I did what I always did and let the music take hold of me and seductively came alive. I tried to take it slow, but the music was fast and soon pins and needles flared in my feet and then worked their way up to my thighs. I had to slow down or I was going to fall down.

"I'm going to go sit—"

"Oh my God, Coldplay," Emily screamed above the sound of the music and grabbed my hands.

Shit. Okay, I could do one more song. Well, I thought I could do one more song before the tingles became numbness.

I was wrong.

I made it through half the song before I stumbled, losing my balance. Damn it. I went to grab Emily for support but hands seized my hips and pulled me backwards, and I slammed into a solid chest.

"Relax. I got you." I stiffened when I heard Ream's low, gravelly voice next to my ear. His arm slid across my abdomen, and he took most of my weight onto him as he kept moving to the music. His rock hard thighs rubbed against mine, and his groin pressed into my ass while he kept me locked up against him. I could feel his heated breath on my neck next to my ear, and it wasn't only my legs

OVERWHELMED BY YOU

tingling, it was my entire body.

Emily noticed us and smiled with brows raised. Then she trounced off the dance floor, leaving me alone with Ream.

"We should go sit—"

"Shh," Ream ordered as he kept me glued to him.

"But—"

"Kat."

"I'm dating—"

"Babe."

"I don't want to dance with you."

"Shut it."

"I want to sit down."

"No you don't."

"What?" I tried to pull away from his arms, but he was like the locked bar on a roller coaster. "Ream," I ground out between my teeth.

"You try and walk back to the table yourself, you're going to fall. Your new boyfriend should be indebted to me for making sure you're looked after. So relax. We'll wait until your legs are better."

Oh God. He knew. He'd been watching and saw me struggling to keep up with Emily. The overwhelming feeling encompassing me was too debilitating to do anything other than lean back into his arms and seek the support he offered.

Ream's breath hit the spot just below my ear, and the fine hairs on my skin rose. His fingers touched my bare skin as my blouse shifted, and I swiftly inhaled. He hesitated when he heard me, and then his palm splayed flat on my abdomen, sending an animated need to pool between my thighs.

His hand moved upwards, slowly stroking, caressing, touching, until his thumb was just beneath my breast. Every time I exhaled, the tip would graze the underside of my breast and send a burning wave of heat through me.

I closed my eyes.

Then my head fell back onto his shoulder as I shuddered. I

83

couldn't control it. Ream was in me. No matter how much we fought or hurt one another, it was always the same when we touched. It was a want so powerful that it gripped the edges of my sanity and made me insane with need. Maybe that's why we had tried to hurt one another? Because we were both fighting so hard to hate when we felt the exact opposite.

But Ream wasn't fighting it any longer.

I wanted to let him in. God, just to be held in his arms again made me feel warm and safe and yet … it terrified me too. Because Ream could hurt me. He had once before, and I couldn't afford to waste a single day on a guy that had already proven to me that he would run as soon as things got rough. And things would get rough. I had no misconceptions that I could be in trouble at some point. Did he know that? Had he a clue what being with me would entail?

"Kitkat," he murmured into my ear then brushed his thumb over my nipple that strained against my lace bra.

Oh God, yes. His cock was hard and pressing into me, and I swallowed the tightness in my throat as I thought of him thrusting it inside me. His muscles contracting, sweat gleaming off his skin, hands locking my wrists as his weight pinned me down.

I was breathing fast, my chest rising and falling, as he continued to sway to the music. I wanted to whirl around in his arms and kiss him then drag him into the back of the bar and rip off his clothes and have him take me hard against the wall.

Ream groaned then nibbled on my neck. Shivers trickled across my skin, and I licked my dry lips. "I'll be there for you. He doesn't get you like I do."

I jerked at his words, stiffening. Lance. Fuck. What was I doing?

The tingling in my legs had faded, and I knew it was safe for me to go back to the table. I tried to yank myself from his arms, but he only tightened his grip. "Let me go."

"You're making this messy between us. Call the guy tonight. Tell him you're with me."

"What? I can't do that." I didn't do well with any guy telling me how it was going to be.

"Can't or won't."

"Both."

He spun me around, looped his hand around the back of my neck dragging me back in close, then took my hand and put it between us and pressed it up against his cock.

"You feel that?" He didn't wait for a reply. "It hasn't touched another fuckin' girl since it was deep inside you." His fingers tightened on my neck. "You know why? Because it wants no one else. I want no one else. We started something and it was good. No, it was fuckin' great. I've never had that, baby. Never thought I could."

Holy shit. He hadn't slept with anyone since me? I tried to think of something to say. I was good at hurtful remarks. Shit, I'd called his dick melting ice cream, but he threw me off my game and it took me a minute to pull myself back together and find my voice. "Could've fooled me. I seem to recall you saying..." I pushed hard on his cock "...it shrunk every time I was around."

"You're feelin' it right now, beautiful. Tell me if I lied."

Neither of us moved for several seconds, our eyes locked, my hand on his cock, his hand coiled around my neck. People around us danced and sang to the new Hedley song while we stood frozen in the middle of the dance floor.

"You getting shot was the second worst day of my life. And I've had some seriously fucked-up bad days. I spent eight months wishing I wasn't on tour so I could be with you. Now, I'm back and the only way I'm running again is toward you." He lowered his voice, and the gravelly, deep tone drummed into my chest. "Fight me all you want, Kat. I'm going to keep coming."

I thought of the only thing I could to try and get him to back off. "Shows you don't give a crap about me. The worst thing for me is to get stressed out and you're the cause."

Ream threw his head back and laughed. The reaction to my excuse was one I hadn't expected and I glared at him. "Oh, baby. That excuse won't work with me. You see, I know how you quiver beneath my touch. How your breath quickens. I know you're soaking wet right now. You're putting the stress on yourself by denying us."

"I may want to fuck you, but that's semantics. I have a perfectly good guy I'm dating that will look after my needs."

Ream's grin washed away instantly. "You said you haven't fucked him."

I didn't say anything, even though I wanted to lie and say Lance and I had screwed and it was amazing. But I wasn't stupid. Ream was hanging onto his cool by a thread, and I wasn't going to be the one to break it.

He suddenly let me go, turned, and headed back to the table without a single backwards glance. And damn it, I was hoping for one.

I was going to have to address the Lance issue. I needed a safe relationship and Lance could be that guy except … I was dating him while wanting someone else. I had to get over Ream and stop this constant need that flowed through every part of me. Was it even possible to stop the feelings?

I went and sat beside Crisis, and he looped his arm on the back of my chair and leaned in. "Brett's been watching you and Ream. You're a wanted woman, sweetcakes. I'd kiss you right now, just to make both of them jealous, but I think I've surpassed Ream's limitations." He nodded to Molly who was serving drinks at a table close by. "She was watching too. Wonder if she's interested in you or Ream?"

I smacked his shoulder, laughing. Then I sobered. "It was all on purpose, wasn't it?" From the corner of my eye I saw Ream signing some girl's stomach with a black marker. It appeared like now that Logan was taken, Ream got all the attention.

"He's my best friend. Moved in with my family when we were sixteen. Asshole is like a brother to me." Crisis lowered his voice further. "He was pretty fucked up. And a stubborn goddamn mule. We fought like a couple of testosterone driven mountain lions."

I hadn't known Ream moved in with Crisis. But I really didn't want to talk about Ream anymore tonight. What I wanted was a few more shots to numb out that shit on the dance floor, and Brett was serving. "You getting to the point?"

"Yeah, sugar. I know Ream better than anyone. I saw what he was like after the two of you hooked up. He was so pissed off all the time. He was hurting, Kat. You did something to him. Women are objects to him. He doesn't care about them, never has. Not one chick lured him into more than a basic sexual encounter, and trust me, they tried. But after you ... something changed." Ream had just said the same exact words to me. "Why do you think I pushed the flirting with you?"

"He nearly kicked your ass for it too. By the pool ... he was so furious." I had pushed Ream in the pool after he'd been arguing with Crisis about me. He'd retaliated by picking me up, throwing me over his shoulder, and jumping back into the pool.

Crisis chuckled. "Yeah. Fuckhead doesn't like me touching your fine ass, but, sugar, just so you know, I love touching your ass. It fuckin' rocks. And it sucks I can't do it anymore." I smiled. "Don't know what went down between you two, but I heard the shitty ass crap you've said to one another. If he didn't care about you, he'd have treated you like any other chick." He nodded to the dance floor. "He was practically fucking you from behind out there."

"And it was wrong. I'm seeing someone else."

"Sugar." Crisis' boyish smile dropped. "Don't know the guy, but you need to dump his ass then get some real fucking." He shrugged when I rolled my eyes. "Just saying."

"Well, don't. It doesn't suit you being a matchmaker." I pushed back my chair and stood. "I'm getting a drink." I turned and crashed right into Ream, my palms landing on his chest.

"Let's go."

I balked. "What?"

"You heard me. We're leaving."

Umm, I was thinking that maybe I missed something because

no one else looked like they were leaving. "I'm getting another drink."

"You've had enough."

"Excuse me? What are you my pimp?" From the corner of my eye, I saw Crisis grinning ear to ear. His chair squeaked as he leaned back, hands behind his head, watching.

Ream's expression tightened and his eyes narrowed. His voice was strained and controlled as he said, "Say that again and I will throw you over my knee and spank that ass of yours right in front of everyone."

It was a low move on my part to call him my pimp, but I was tipsy and angry and so friggin' sexually frustrated.

"Jesus," Ream swore beneath his breath shaking his head. "Babe, do you really want to start our shit right here?" A young girl, who looked too young to be in the bar, came up beside him and tried to pass him her pen. He shook his head and the devastation on her face nearly had me grabbing the pen from her and shoving it into Ream's hand, except that there was a trend happening. A number of girls hovered near the table now, and I suddenly got why Ream wanted to leave.

"Then leave. Alone."

Ream's fingers caressed down my arm until they settled around my hand. "Kat."

"Hey, Kat," Brett shouted. "Molly says this is yours." I pulled my hand out of his grasp and walked over to the bar. Brett pushed a shot glass of clear liquid toward me. "You and Ream an item now?"

I shook my head. "No. He's just having issues taking no for an answer."

Molly came up beside me, plopping her tray on the counter. "Tell your new guy. Maybe he'll get Ream to leave you alone."

I raised my shot glass to her in thanks for the drink, and she smiled.

"Another?" Brett asked.

I'd really had enough, and being stupid and drunk with Ream

around was just plain ... well, stupid. Brett stiffened and I noticed the easy, calm expression he always had about him vanish.

"Guess he might be able to look after the problem right now."

"Oh, he's here," Molly said.

"What do you mean? Who's here?" I looked in the direction Brett nodded and saw Lance walking toward me.

Chapter Six

Lance's long, lean body cut easily through the crowd. It was like everyone knew to get out of his way. It didn't help that he was the only one wearing a suit. Frig, this was so not going to be good. Ream was talking to Crisis with his back to the bar. Okay, I could diffuse this.

"I'll see you later, Molly, Brett. Tell Emily I got a ride with Lance."

"Sure thing," Brett said.

I met Lance halfway and his arm went around my shoulders and drew me in before he leaned down and kissed me. He tasted like he'd just brushed his teeth as his mouth, gentle and warm, slid over mine.

He was at least six foot two with an olive complexion, and I suspected he was part Asian. Smooth skin and defined, sculpted features with dark penetrating eyes. Definitely, he was in the hot category, and even more so that he was a master in Tae Kwon Do.

His kissed the tip of my nose while keeping his arm around me. "I thought I'd surprise you. I've wanted to meet your friends you've been talking so much about."

I couldn't recall talking about them that much. Actually, I'd probably mentioned Georgie and Emily and the band in general, but never the guys. "I was just heading to the condo."

"Then we'll be quick. One drink. Or are you trying to hide me from them?"

"Don't be silly." Okay, maybe this was good. Ream would have to get that we were over and I was seeing Lance now. "But you need to get that the band is close. Been friends for a long time. And I used to date … well sorta dated Ream, and he won't like you so don't take offense to—"

Lance chuckled. "I can look after myself, love. And I already know what you're trying to warn me about because I see his eyes on us right now."

I stiffened then glanced back over my shoulder to our table. Ream was standing beside Kite and Kite's hand was on his shoulder. It wasn't a friendly gesture; this was to hold Ream back. The fury in him made my stomach roll, and I didn't like seeing it. Instead, I had the instinct to soothe it. What was wrong with me? I seriously had issues. I'd always been the strong one, the girl who knew exactly what she wanted and went after it. Now, suddenly, Ream was throwing it all out of balance and I was floundering. I hated floundering.

"We should just go."

Lance looked down at me, put his finger under my chin, and kissed me again. This time it was hard and possessive as if he was making a point to everyone who was watching us. "You still interested in him, Kat?"

"No. It's just … complicated."

He kissed me lightly on the lips. "Kat, I like you. A lot. I want this to work between us, and I think you do too."

Oh God.

"Kat?"

Shit. I wanted nice, right? I liked Lance. He was a gentleman, and yeah, sure, he didn't know about the drugs or what came with them, but he was gentle and patient. He loved my art and had no drama in his life. No fans, no arguing, and no having to leave for months at a time. He was stress free and he'd be the guy who didn't run the second he heard something he didn't like. I needed that in a relationship. I had to have the rock that would stand by me no matter what.

"Precious. Whatever you need, okay? We'll keep it slow. Let's have one drink with your friends so we aren't rude, and then we'll go."

I nodded. But it felt as if fleas were biting my skin making me anxious and uncomfortable.

Lance kept his arm around my waist as he led me over to the table. I kept my chin up, my usual sway in my hips, and I tried to look like I wasn't ripping apart on the inside as Ream's face took us in. I saw the hurt flicker in his darkened eyes, the narrowing, and then something different, as if he was contemplating.

Lance was the perfect gentleman and shook hands with the band and then graciously nodded to Emily and Georgie. But when he went to shake hands with Ream, I swear each one of us held our breaths. There was a slight hesitation as Lance held his hand out and Ream didn't take it. Ream's eyes narrowed and he looked him up and down, as if he was trying to figure out whether Lance was worthy or something.

Then Ream chin-lifted and shook hands. It was only after their hands separated that Ream blew it. "Hurt her and I'll fuckin' kill you."

"Jesus, Ream." I expected Lance to grab me and walk out of there. Instead, he nodded to Ream and then sat and pulled me onto his lap. I knew it was done on purpose because I never sat on Lance's lap.

The tension broke except for mine. I was strung so tight my nerves acted up and I could do nothing about it except try and stay calm and hope they passed.

"Well, aren't you looking the hottie in an expensive suit," Georgie purred. "Why hasn't Kat brought you by my shop yet?" Georgie twirled a pink strand around her finger. "But just so you know, hotties don't get free passes in the in-gate." What was she talking about? "Hotties, still need to pass my test before they get in. Non-hotties don't get into the group—period." Oh God, Georgie was drunk and rambling. There was no test. She was making this up as she went. Where was Deck when you needed him?

Bringing Lance by Georgie's Perk Avenue coffee house meant Deck would be checking into Lance because Deck checked out everyone who came by the coffee shop. His security cameras made sure of it.

I squeezed Lance's leg to get his attention and leaned back into him and whispered, "We should go."

Lance grinned. "No. This is amusing. And if I need to pass a test to be with you, then I'm game."

Okay, Lance was sweet and nice—and brave.

Georgie propped her elbows up on the table and rested her head in her hands. "So, can you make a girl come multiple times? My girl here needs to know what she's getting into."

My mouth wasn't the only one that dropped open, and I glared at Georgie. "Shut it, Georgie. Jesus. I swear Deck needs to reel you in, strap you down, and teach you some manners."

She laughed and then chugged back her beer before slamming it down on the table. "Deck's not here—again. He's probably making some girl come multiple times right now." I thought she said Deck would suck in bed. "So, Mr. I-look-hot-in-a-suit. You *up* for an answer?"

I felt Ream's eyes on me, not on Lance or Georgie, and I squirmed on Lance's lap, which to my horror made something hard press into my butt and I immediately stilled. Lance looped his arm around my waist and pulled me back against him then whispered in my ear, "Yeah, better to stay still, princess." Then his voice rose so the table could hear, but his eyes remained on me. "Multiple doesn't seem like quite the right word. I'd use," he paused for effect, "copious."

Oh fuck. I knew it before it happened. Ream was controlled, calm, and had a head for business, but that all detonated when it came to me and him.

The scrape of his chair echoed as Ream violently pushed it back then grabbed the edge of the table and flipped it over on its side. Glass shattered as the drinks crashed to the floor. Emily and Crisis were covered in beer, and Georgie had fallen over backwards in her chair and was laughing hysterically on the floor.

I wanted to be mad at him, but I understood why he flipped the table. I couldn't imagine if I saw him with a chick on his lap and we were talking about orgasms. I might not flip the table, but I'd have freaked. Maybe dumped my drink all over the girl and Ream.

Logan, being the ex-underground fighter, took him down. He grabbed his arm when Ream came for Lance then threw him to the ground, bending Ream's arm behind his back at an odd angle. I didn't hear what was said between them, but Ream nodded, got up, and without a single glance at anyone, he went into the back of the pub. I saw Molly go after him and hoped she could calm him down, but a part of me wanted to be the one to go talk to him. Okay, fine, I was jealous that Molly was with Ream and I wasn't.

Georgie struggled to her feet, stumbled, then fell on her ass again. Crisis took her arm and pulled her drunk ass up and set her chair upright and shoved her down in it. "Well, so now we know how Ream's *really* feeling. Hope you're not lying about the copious, Lancey-baby."

Gah … everyone looked at me, and I grabbed Lance's hand. "Let's go. You can drop me at Matt's." I had no intention of going back to the farm and running into Ream tonight.

Lance politely nodded to everyone and said goodbye while I tapped my foot and tried to head for the door before Emily and Georgie could trap me in a snare of girl talk about Ream that I so wasn't ready to talk about. Not with Lance around.

Lance took me back to the condo, although he'd suggested his place and I knew why; I felt the why while sitting on his lap.

He escorted me to the door where he pulled me into his arms. With the tip of his finger, he pushed my hair out of my eye. "You want to tell me what that was about?"

I leaned up against the door. "I told you, we had a thing."

His brows rose. "Looked like more than a thing."

"Not really. He was there when I needed him, and then we hooked up for a couple of nights. That's it."

"But he doesn't think that's it."

I shrugged. "Ream's … intense." And I couldn't stop thinking about him. All I saw was his face when he flipped over the table, the devastation, the rage, the pain. I wanted to take it all away.

"Listen, Kat. I like you. And I'm not scared of some ex who isn't man enough to control his temper. But I'd like if we could step away from that to see if what we have is something more. After the gallery opening, I have a place in Vegas that I'd like to take you to for a few days."

"Lance." Shit, I hope he wasn't going to cancel my show. "I think it's better if we stop seeing one another. I like you, but I need to sort some stuff out."

His brows rose with surprise. Then he stepped back and scowled. It was the first time I'd seen him kind of pissed off, and it made me really uncomfortable. "With Ream." A shiver coursed down my spine at his tone, and I put my hand in my purse and searched for my keys. "That's not the best idea, Kat."

"Whatever I decide to do, it's my decision, not yours." God, why was I suddenly pissed off? Because Ream was fucking things up for me. I'd met a good guy and now I was breaking it off with him because why? … Because Ream couldn't let me go?

No, it was because I couldn't let Ream go and I needed to do that before I could be with Lance.

I found the keys and turned around putting them in the lock. Lance's hand came down on my shoulder. "You going back to him?"

I stiffened and my hand gripped the key hard, the metal pinching into my hand. "No, but what Ream and I do is none of your business."

He put his hands on my waist, and I wanted to shrug them off. "You are my business."

I turned to face him again and suddenly I didn't like him very much with the way he was confronting me. "Are you going to cancel my show?"

"No. But I wish you'd think about this before deciding. Do you really want to be with a man like him? Jealous. Uncontrollable. A rock star that has women all over him. He'll never be faithful. He'll cheat on you the second he goes out of town." I flinched at the thought. Seeing all the girls around him tonight had put that thought in my head. Cheating was a deal breaker. "You obviously aren't together for a reason." His eyes narrowed and his fingers dug into my side. "You choose this, you'll regret it."

"Wow, Lance. That sounded like a threat." I pushed his hands off my waist. "I'll see you at the show. And then I'll move my art to another gallery." I'd been wrong about Lance. He had a side to him I hadn't seen or anticipated. Maybe he wasn't so nice and safe after all.

"That's not necessary, Kat." He put his finger under my chin and stroked his thumb down my cheek. "You're face—gorgeous. I wish …" He sighed. "I really wanted this to work. Will you think about it? Take a couple of days?"

I shook my head. "No. I don't need time to think about things, Lance." Especially after what he'd just said.

"A real shame, princess." He turned and strode away.

I sagged against the door as I watched him walk past the elevators and push open the door to the stairwell. The door slammed shut behind him.

A part of me wanted to go running back to the bar, back to Ream, the part that still needed him like my next breath. But that meant a second chance at what could be a one way road to hurt and devastation. I had a life that didn't have a place or time for second chances. Shit, I was already internally self-destructing.

I was thankful I had the condo to myself until Matt got back after the bar closed in a few hours. Plan of attack to numb the emotions—grab a big comfy blanket, make popcorn, and curl up on the couch and watch a silly romantic comedy.

I woke to the door rattling and stretched from my cramped position on the couch. Glancing at my phone on the table, I saw it was two in the morning, Matt must have asked Brett to close the bar and came home early. The TV was still blaring; I'd put it up loud to drown out our neighbor Neville's music from next door. The guy loved classical and Friday and Saturday nights he let everyone know it. Matt never cared because he was at the bar late.

The door opened and I got up folding the blanket. "Bro, that crap that went down with Ream. Totally my fault, but I want it known before you go 'on the burner,' that I asked Lance to leave and he—"

A hand curled into the back of my neck and I tried to jerk away, but it happened so fast. The pressure increased and I was violently pressed forward. My head slammed into the wood coffee table. Agony tore through my head as I collapsed to the floor, my vision blurred and it felt like heated syrup dripped down my face. Hands grabbed me and I managed a half scream before I was picked up and thrown across the room. I hit the drywall hard, biting my tongue on impact. Blood filled my mouth then dripped from the corners of my lips.

Oh God. What the hell?

I held my hand to my head where the table hit and tried to get my bearings again. I looked up and saw a tall, lean figure striding toward me. He was wearing a balaclava with black dress pants and a long sleeved black shirt. His hands … Oh God he was wearing gloves.

Fear smothered my insides like thick tar, and for a second I couldn't move. I held out my hand and repeated "no" over and over again. As the large figure drew closer, I snapped out of the haze of frozen fear and scrambled toward the kitchen. I could hear his heavy thudded footsteps nearly upon me. My heart pounded so hard it hurt, and I was having trouble breathing.

My mind reeled with confusion, a mishmash of pain, fear, and anger. What the hell was happening?

I kept thinking I had to get to the cutlery drawer. It was within sight, if I could just … the booted foot struck me in the small of my back and I went flying into the island, hitting hard and then falling to the floor. His foot hoofed into my stomach and knocked the wind out of me, and I curled into a ball fighting to breathe.

He curled his hand into my hair and pulled me to my feet. I struggled against his grasp, swinging my arms and trying to kick out. My head was hammering with pain and my vision was distorted. I couldn't see anything but his black clothes.

Until I saw the knife.

I stopped fighting as he pressed the cold hard steel laid against my cheek. "I like a fighter. He fought me in the beginning. Just like you will." His voice was high pitched as if he was disguising it. I knew he was strong—big, but my vision was blurred and I couldn't see him clearly.

I was in severe pain and yet I couldn't control my outburst as the fury gripped me. "Only fucking cowards beat up women."

There was no warning at what he was going to do until the pain hit me as he dragged the knife down my cheek. I screamed and he shut me up by throwing me to the floor, booted me in the ribs, then came down on top of me. His hand clamped over my mouth.

"Now, I'm going to have what he had. Just the thought of it turns me on." The knife fell away from my face.

What the hell was he talking about? I heard the clang of his belt buckle being undone and then the distinct sound of a zipper. Oh God, no. No. I flailed against his massive weight, but I was like a mouse to a lion's paw. My screams were muffled by his large rubber-gloved palm that pressed down so hard on my mouth that I felt the pain in the back of my head as the hardwood pressed into my skull.

His other hand was on my pajamas and pushing them down. I could feel the stickiness of the rubber against my thighs and the invisible fine hairs on my legs stuck to the rubber and pulled. I heard a loud snap like … Oh God, the glove was gone and his sweaty warm fingers slid up my inner thigh.

I screamed and screamed, but nothing but muffled sounds came out. My body was tingling and reacting to the anxiety and soon I'd lose circulation in my limbs. I winced as I felt a slap against my inner thighs.

"Open them."

Oh God, I wanted Ream. He was all I could think about, and I wanted to cry for us, for what we'd lost. For the pain we'd caused one another. Whatever had happened between us, I knew Ream would protect me, he'd destroy this man for what he was doing to me.

The knife rose above me again, and the moonlight streaming in through the window hit it just right so that it shimmered. The blade sliced across my forehead, and my body tensed, back arching as my skin separated.

I stomped my feet into the floor as hard as I could, over and over again, hoping the neighbor below would hear and call security.

"You're making this worse than it has to be." His hand slid down my body, kneading my breasts and then pinching my nipples. My eyes widened at the excruciating pain and he chuckled and then did it harder.

I shook my head side to side so violently it wrenched my neck. His hand shifted partially off my mouth and it was what I needed. I bit down as hard as I could, tasting the rubber of his glove, then flesh, then the blood filtering into my mouth. He shouted and jerked back, and I screamed as loud as my lungs would allow.

Neville's classical music from next door stopped abruptly.

The intruder froze, stared at me, and I saw his dark brown eyes glaring. He suddenly leaped off me and darted from the condo. The door slammed.

I lay on the floor unable to move. The pain agonizing from where my head hit the table from the first blow and the cuts he sliced into my cheek and forehead.

Pounding on the door. More pounding.

Then ...

"Kat?"

I choked back the sob that I tried to keep contained, knowing if I let it in, I'd break and I couldn't. I had to stay strong. Weakness would kill me. I couldn't let it in or I'd crumble.

"Oh Christ. Kat." I heard his knees hit the floor beside me and then felt his hand on my head. "Open your eyes for me."

I winced as I did. Neville had turned on the light and the glare made my head burst with a sharp jab. "Sweet Jesus, baby girl. What happened? No, no, don't talk. I have to get my phone and call an ambulance. And ... we need to cover you up."

I heard his clothing rustle and his comforting touch disappeared. "No. Don't leave me." I grabbed for him and he took my hand and squeezed.

"Okay, okay. Where's your phone, sweetie?"

I started shaking violently and I wasn't sure if I was dying or what, but it felt like the heat had been zapped from my body and I was soaking in a tub of ice cubes. "You're going into shock." He shifted again, but kept talking. "I'm just walking over to get the blanket off the couch, okay. I need a phone ... never mind I see one." His footsteps ran back toward me, and I felt the weight of the blanket on my body. There was a beeping of my phone and then he was talking to someone, answering questions about me.

I heard him dialing again. "Matt. Yeah it's Neville ... yeah from next door. You need to get here—now. It's Kat." There was muffled shout echoing from the phone. "Yeah, real bad."

Neville held my hand while he talked to me, making me open my eyes every so often and then ordering me to squeeze his hand. My mind was all fuzzy and trying to comprehend everything he said was agonizing. I lay on the floor and shivered. My only comfort was that I wasn't going to die alone.

"They're coming. An ambulance is on its way. You have to stay awake for me though, okay. You have a nasty cut on your head. Do you know where you are?"

"Condo."

"And your name?"

"Kat, but ... you call me ... baby girl and I ... hate it."

Neville chuckled. "Okay, you're noggin' can't have been hurt that badly if you remember that."

"My ... face."

His hand flinched in mine and I knew it was bad.

"A few lacerations, nothing the doctors can't fix." His hand tightened. "Did he ... were you raped, Kat?"

No. But I still felt violated and my stomach churned when I thought about his hands on me. "No."

"Okay, hon. Just try to stay awake for me."

It became hard to distinguish his words, and I think I passed out for a while because next I felt him shaking me and calling my name over and over again. I could hear sirens and I moaned as the pain hit me again. I wanted to sink back into the darkness, but then Neville was shouting. "Who the hell are you?"

"Baby."

Oh God. Ream. The relief was so overwhelming that I wanted to cry, to finally let the tears escape their prison and sob in his arms. But they were trapped, and the key no longer fit the lock to open the door.

His hand came beneath my head and when I opened my eyes, he was leaning over me. "Jesus, baby. Talk to me. Who did this?"

I shook my head. "Ream. How did you ..." Was all I managed to get out.

But he seemed to know what I was asking. "Saw Matt running like hell out of the bar. I jumped in his car as he was pulling out. Only something to do with you could make him look that fuckin' scared."

That must have pissed Matt off.

Then suddenly my brother was holding my other hand and

talking to me. Everything else happened in a blur as I was lifted onto a stretcher and taken away.

I knew Ream never left me. I didn't have to open my eyes to know it was him holding my hand and him talking to me in the ambulance.

I woke briefly to a white room with a loud beeping sound. I saw a shadow of a man standing by the window, his shoulders stiff, arms crossed. I was still groggy and my vision blurry, but I knew who it was. I'd recognize Ream through a dense fog.

My throat was all scratchy as I spoke, "Don't you dare leave me this time, asshole." And then I fell back into obscurity.

Chapter Seven

It hurts. Please, no more.
It was a silent plea. They always liked it when I pleaded for them to stop. It made it worse.
Friday night. It was him. Always him. I hated him.
He pressed harder then groaned.
I screamed louder, but there was never any sound.
A silent scream for help that never came.

My eyes flashed open as I woke from the worst nightmare. But as the pain registered, I realized it hadn't been a nightmare. It had been real. The intruder. The pain. The violation of my body. I wiggled my fingers, feeling the weight of a hand in the cradle of my palm. But it wasn't the hand I wanted it to be.

"Sis. Hey." Matt stood and kissed me on the top of my head. "How are you feeling?"

"Like a bull hoofed me in the stomach then raked his horns across my face." Matt winced. "He left me alive and didn't …" I couldn't say the word, "so I'm happy dancing inside … quietly …

without moving, 'cause to move sucks. I'd still like to gut the bastard though. Did they catch him?"

Matt shifted and his face tightened. "The police want to talk to you. When you're up for it."

I was so disappointed in Ream. I ... God what was wrong with me? I knew he'd run. He'd told me he couldn't deal with hospitals after his sister was in and out of them all the time. I was fooling myself to believe he'd suddenly get over it.

For me, it was vital to have a guy who'd stick by me and be there when I need him. And Ream obviously wasn't capable of that.

Maybe I was jumping the gun here. He could be getting something to eat. Maybe he was in the washroom or went home for a shower. Shit, it was selfish of me to want him here when I woke up. Fuck, I was just being girlie-stupid over a guy. I was never girlie-stupid ... gah, this sucked. But the truth was I wanted Ream, I just didn't know if I could trust him to stay.

"Did you recognize the guy?"

I shook my head then winced. My head felt like an axe had cracked open my skull and someone was slowly chipping away at the bones with a chisel and hammer. And that was only my head. The throbbing in my ribs and abdomen produced a wave of nausea with every breath. Damn, men and their steel-toed shoes.

I told Matt what I remembered, which wasn't much. Lance walking me to the door, how I broke it off with him and then curled up on the couch and watched a silly chick flick. I'd woken to the door rattling and thought it had been him struggling with his key.

"The lock was picked. He knew what he was doing," Matt said. "Jesus, Kat if Neville hadn't heard your screams ... I can't even think about it. Fuck." Matt ran his hand over his head and then down his face.

"What is it?"

"The police think the guy knew you. Or of you, maybe followed you and Lance from the bar? This wasn't random." Matt's hand slid from mine and he cleared his throat and then sighed. "Listen, Sis.

There's something else. I don't like the guy and really I don't give a shit, but I know if I don't tell you someone else will and then you'll be pissed I never told you." He ran his hand through his hair and cleared his throat. "Ream was taken in for questioning last night. A person of interest they said."

"But … No he was with you. How could they even …"

"Calm down. It's fine. They just want to talk to him because he had that freak out at the bar."

My heart skipped a beat and I stopped breathing. I heard the heart monitor start beeping like crazy, and within seconds the nurse barged through the door. She pressed a few buttons and the beeping stopped. The older woman wore her gray hair in a bun. She had soft, plump features and looked sweet, but when her eyes narrowed and mouth tightened, she was fierce.

"Out. Now," she said to Matt. "I warned you … if you upset her, no visiting."

Matt swore beneath his breath, and I was silently freaking out wondering what the hell happened to Ream.

My stomach twisted and the nurse put her hand on my forehead and urged me back onto the plush pillow. "I need you to calm down." She fiddled with my intravenous and within minutes I couldn't keep my eyes open anymore. The last thing I heard was the door clicking shut.

The police asked me question after question. I told them I didn't get a look at the suspect, that he was wearing a balaclava. I gave them what I did know, that he was over six foot and had brown eyes.

"Brown? Are you sure?"

I nodded now remembering the haunting evil glare before he lowered the knife and sliced my cheek. I put my hand up and ran the tip of my finger over the stitches. There were five of them across my cheek and four on my forehead. The doctor explained that they were clean cuts therefore minimal scaring. But I knew the truth; every time I looked in the mirror I'd see the reminder.

"Anything else, miss?"

"The smell. I smelled something. It was his breath." But I couldn't place it. "Mint? Peppermint, maybe? I'm sorry, it happened so fast ..."

They asked a few more questions about the evening, any suspicious people I'd met at the bar, about Lance, and then they mentioned Ream and a warm then cold sick feeling came over me. What a contradiction, just like us.

"I understand he has a temper."

My eyes widened and I looked from one officer to the other. I started shaking my head back and forth. "No. God, no. Ream would never hurt me." Well, not physically at least. "Jesus. I'd recognize him anywhere."

"Miss, you need to calm down. We're not saying he's a suspect." The woman officer glanced at her partner, and I could hear the frantic beating of my monitor again. "We took him in for questioning. That's all. A witness claimed he was violent at the bar ..." She looked down at her notepad and flipped back a few pages. "Avalanche. Your brother's establishment. He was upset with you? Correct?"

"No. Well, yes. It's not what you think. Ream and I have—"

The door burst open.

"Get out!" Ream stood in the doorway, still wearing the same clothes as last night. His hair was a mess and there were smudges of blood on his shirt—my blood. I'd never seen him so haggard and completely well ... fucked up. He was pale with black circles under his eyes and hard lines marring his face. He looked scary. Really scary and still, I thought he was the best sight I'd ever seen.

The officers looked stunned at the demand, and then the female officer snapped her pad closed and was about to say something when my doctor appeared beside Ream. The doctor didn't have to say anything; the officers knew with his appearance that they were being asked to leave.

"Thank you, miss. We'll be in touch." They hesitated at the door, and I couldn't see their faces, but I could see Ream's and he got scarier looking. Then they pushed past and left.

Ream said something to the doctor, shook his hand, and then the doctor left too.

Ream's walk to the bed was the longest four seconds of my life. Just the sight of him was like being bundled up in my favorite child-hood blanket, every breath comforting as my lungs filled with warmth. He sat in the chair beside the bed, and while keeping his head bowed, he slid his hands into mine. Our fingers linked and curled around one another, then he leaned forward and rested his forehead on the bed beside my hip.

The muffled sound of his whispered voice swept over me like a sprinkle of rain. "Baby."

I closed my eyes, placing my free hand on his head, fingers weaving into his hair. We stayed like that for a long time with the only sounds our breathing and the steady beeping of the monitor.

It was how I fell asleep, Ream's hand in mine, leaned over, his face hidden in the nook of my side. When I woke he was gone and I thought I'd imagined him there until I saw the note in the palm of my hand. It read, *I'll never leave you.*

"Kat." I looked up and saw Georgie and Emily on the other side of the room by the bouquets of flowers. "You're awake. Oh my God, we thought you'd never wake up." Emily rushed over and hugged me, and I winced as the soft strands of her hair brushed against my cheek. She noticed and immediately pulled back. "Sorry, I just had to hug you."

"You're going to have to suck it up, 'cause I'm hugging you too, cupcake," Georgie said as she pushed Emily aside and moved in. "Jesus. Look what that pig bastard did to your face."

"Georgie!" Emily scolded.

I knew it couldn't look good, and I suddenly wondered what

Ream thought. I'd have scars on my face now; he couldn't call me beautiful anymore, that was for sure. I curled my fingers around the note.

"Thank fuck he didn't rape you. Christ, did he touch you?"

"Georgie," Emily abolished. "I'm sure Kat doesn't want to re-hash what happened right now."

Or ever. It made me cringe and sick to my stomach to think that his hands were on me intimately. I still heard the snap of his rubber glove coming off just before he touched me.

Georgie was animated as she talked, throwing her hands in the air and pacing back and forth. "When the police catch him, I'm going for his dick. And when I get ahold of it, I'm peeling it open like a goddamn banana."

Emily groaned.

We chatted, well Georgie and Emily chatted, and they told me Crisis was picking up nurses while Kite was going for the female doctors. They'd supposedly snuck in to see me a few hours ago when I was sleeping with Ream passed out beside me in the chair. Logan was at the police station with Matt giving statements and going through mug shots to see if anyone the police had on their list was seen at the bar and on the condos security cameras. The problem was that the condo only had cameras at the front doors, nothing at the back, so someone could've let them in. Emily also told me that Matt and Ream got into a big fight earlier today and that was when Logan took Matt with him to the police station.

"Lance is here." Emily put her hand on my shoulder and squeezed. "He's been asking to see you. But Ream ..." she half smiled. "He won't allow him even on the same floor as you."

"Where is he?"

"Suit-cake or rock star-cake?"

"Lance."

"Downstairs in the waiting room. He says he won't leave until he sees you."

I nodded. "Okay."

Georgie kissed me on the cheek. "I'll sneak him by Ream. That crazy-ass piece of hotness is a vigilante. If Kite and Crisis didn't lock him down, he'd have beaten the shit out of Lance for even showing his face here. He really doesn't like that guy."

Yeah, because Ream was a little crazy. But I realized that no matter how much I tried to stop him or deny it, 'he'd keep coming,' just like he promised.

"I'll take Ream to the cafeteria for something to eat. I swear the guy has paced ten pounds off his weight in the last twenty-four hours." Emily kissed my head then squeezed my hand. "You sure you're good to see Lance? Matt told us you broke up with him last night."

"Yeah." I wasn't sure, but his presence here showed he cared and was concerned about me.

Lance was completely distraught, blaming himself, saying that he should've stayed with me until Matt got home, thinking that it was a guy at the bar who followed us back to the condo. Both of us knew that no one was to blame and what he was saying was unreasonable.

He suggested delaying the show we had planned at the gallery in three weeks. For a second, I thought maybe he was saying that so that my scars had more time to heal and wouldn't scare the prospective buyers away. Lance wasn't like that though; at least I didn't think so.

Georgie popped her head in. "Copious-orgasm-Lance, off-his-rocker-Ream is on his way back up."

Lance nodded then turned back to me and ran his finger down my cheek, the one that didn't have the sutures. "Your face …" He sighed then continued, "I have contacts. They're looking into who did this."

I nodded, uncertain what he meant by contacts but too concerned about Ream finding Lance in here and freaking out. The last thing I wanted was a fight between the two, especially when Lance was a master black belt and Ream wouldn't give a shit.

Chapter Eight

Saturday night.
Anything was better than Friday nights.
Tonight was a young woman and she was pretty, like I'd have
wanted my mom to look like.
The woman was nice to me. It didn't hurt. She made me feel good.
"Anticipation. Make her wait." Her voice was sugary and sweet.
"Control. That's what you want. Take it."
I shouldn't like this, but I did. I liked her. I liked what she gave me.
Control.
And I was never letting it go.
I hope she comes back.

Ream didn't leave my bedside again until I left the hospital the next day, which was a bit of an issue with my brother. Actually, a big issue because Matt didn't want him around. He relented because well, Ream wasn't going anywhere unless he was "forcefully re-moved," his words. I knew about his sister and how being in a hos-pital brought back memories of it, so it was a big deal that he was here with me. I did notice that he disappeared into the washroom numerous times and when he came back the strands of hair around the edge of his face were all damp.

We didn't talk about us; actually we barely talked at all and it was … it was soothing. I was glad he never asked me the details of what the guy did to me, although I suspected he'd managed to get everything from the doctor. I mostly slept and he held my hand unless the nurse or doctor asked him to leave the room. His displeasure was made known with his grumbling about how he'd already seen everything. I hid my smile because the nurse had no fear of him or his attitude and shoved him out the door.

When they released me, Matt drove me back to the farm, despite the argument I heard between him and Ream outside my hospital room door. Matt won.

The first thing I did when I arrived home was inject myself. Then I went to the bathroom and looked at my face. It wasn't a pretty sight, actually it was horrifying to see all the stitches across my forehead and down my cheek. I winced as I touched my finger to the bruising around my wounds. I'd always been confident with my looks, but this was pretty messed up and I felt uneasy with this new me. It looked like my outside was now going to match my inside.

"Babe." Ream casually leaned up against the door frame. "You're the strongest woman I've ever known."

I turned away from the mirror and half-sat on the counter. "Yeah." But it was a half-ass reply because I didn't feel strong right now. I felt ruined and confused and like I was falling apart.

"Going to take you a week or so to get back on your feet."

"I'm on my feet just fine."

"And you're the most stubborn woman I know."

I huffed.

He pushed away from the door frame and strode toward me. A wave of need hit me and it wasn't the desire, it was the need for him to wrap me up in his arms and hold me. I held my breath as he raised his hand and cupped my chin. His body was inches from mine, thighs so close that if I took a deep breath they'd touch.

"I let him hurt you."

"I'm fine, Ream. It wasn't your fault." I knew Ream had inner demons, most likely from not protecting his sister, so it was just like him to blame himself for this.

"Are you fine, Kat? He touched—"

I cut him off. "Ream, I'm good. Really." Yeah, I still felt his hand on my breast, my nipple, but I knew how lucky I was. I'd survived him. That was what mattered. I still wanted him caught and castrated though.

He nodded. "Yeah." He looked down for a second as if to gather his thoughts and then met my eyes again. "I'm giving you a week. I want nothing more than to look after you and have you all to myself, but you need to be here with your friends. For now." His thumb stroked back and forth over the slight dip in my chin. "The doc said you need eight days then … things change."

"What's that supposed to mean?"

"It means, you need me, I'm here. But otherwise I'm backing off to give you what you think you need. Next week that changes."

I was speechless because one, he was leaning in close and I could smell him and two, because I didn't want to speak. I wanted him to kiss me.

But he didn't. Instead his hand dropped from my chin and he walked out.

I slept for two days straight and I knew Ream had come to check in on me because the note he'd given me at the hospital was now on my nightstand. I'd thought the nurses had thrown it out. The third night I dreamt that he held me while he caressed my hair. When I woke I saw the indent in the mattress and knew it hadn't been a dream.

Night after night I tried to stay awake to see if he'd come, but I was groggy from the meds and I always fell asleep. I suspected he slept beside me every night, but he never stayed, and when I asked him about it, he merely shrugged and walked away. He was quiet around me and it was so unlike Ream, and yet it was what I needed from him right now. The distance. The time to heal inwardly as well as physically. I still heard the snap of the rubber, but it was getting less and less.

For the last few days, Ream and the band were gone during the day to the recording studio, Emily was teaching a horse clinic, and I spent every waking moment painting. It had always been my way to deal with emotions. I was so good at avoiding them, and my outlet was to paint. That way I could remain hidden behind a veil of poise the rest of the time.

The cuts on my face were healing which meant they were itchy as hell, and I was glad when eight days passed, although I was also apprehensive at Ream's reference to things changing.

It was Friday afternoon when Matt took me to the doctor's to have them removed. He was worried about the pain killers I was on and didn't want me to drive myself. I didn't tell him I stopped taking the pain killers days ago. I was worried about them reacting with my other drugs. Matt dropped me off while I was getting my sutures removed so he could swing by the drug store to pick me up more vitamin D.

I walked out of the doctor's office to wait for Matt when I saw Ream leaning casually against his car, arms and ankles crossed, looking like a lion leisurely waiting on his cliff for his mate.

And it stole my breath away. He was so relaxed and yet still so full of intensity. I walked over to him with a sultry sway and his brows rose as he looked me up and down and then the corner of his mouth curved up which made me smile because witnessing Ream smile was like being handed the sun.

When I stopped in front of him, he did something unexpected … Ream cradled my chin in his hand then leaned forward and kissed up along the scar on my cheek and then across the one on my fore-head.

"I'll kill him if I ever get the chance. For these. For putting his hands on you." He moved to my lips and kissed me, slow and soft like the gentle touch of a feather. "You'll always be my beautiful. Nothing will ever change that. Inside and out, Kat."

He pulled away a few inches and then showed me his left arm. It was a butterfly like he had on his other arm, but on this one he had the word *Beautiful* curving over the top. "You make everything ugly inside me beautiful, Kat."

I stared at the ink, the skin still red and inflamed. The artist had captured the butterfly in flight, the shadow of its fluttering wings making it pop from his skin. The most intricate designs decorated the wings with black and a brilliant blue.

I looked up at him. I didn't have a chance to say anything as he lowered his mouth to mine, soft and gentle like a feather brushing up against my lips.

He hadn't attempted to kiss me since the attack. But it wasn't that; it was that Ream didn't do gentle kissing. He was passionate, hard, and insistent. He was trying to be tender as his lips roamed over mine sweet and warm, but I needed him to be rough and unforgiving. I needed Ream to be Ream.

"God, Ream, kiss me damn it."

"You just had your stitches—"

"If you don't kiss me like you mean it right now, I'm walking away." That was a lie and I suspected he knew that.

He groaned then flipped me around, and I staggered backwards until my spine was against the car. His mouth hit me hard, seeking, claiming, and finding me all at once. My hands slid up his chest to feel his heart hammering beneath my palms.

He pulled back for a second to look at me then tilted his head and his mouth slammed into mine again. It was two cars colliding, bent then broken now fusing together.

The ache between my legs vibrated as he pressed into me. I rubbed my thigh up against his and he grunted then slid his hands down my back to my ass and picked me up so I could curl my legs around him.

"Jesus, baby. I've missed you."

He didn't let me respond, and honestly I wanted to avoid all talk and just kiss him because I'd needed this for far too long. Now I was getting it and I didn't want it to end. It was one thing we never lost, the passion for one another.

His lips softened against mine and our frantic need slowed, but the urgency still claimed us as he held me pinned between him and the car. His fingers curled into my ass and I moaned. "I want you to trust me again, baby."

"Ream? Kat?"

A car door slammed.

Matt. And he didn't look happy—at all.

"What are you doing here, Ream?"

Ream didn't let me go but let me slide down his body until my feet hit the pavement. He half-turned toward my brother like a protective wall of muscle. I ducked under his arm and was going to ward off Matt, who looked ready to start a fight, but Ream grabbed my hand and pulled me back.

"Matt. It's fine," I said.

"What's your problem with me?"

"You're an ass. That's my problem," Matt retorted, still glaring at Ream.

"Says the guy who didn't tell his sister about Lana. Fuck man, why the hell wouldn't you say anything? You knew what your sister thought."

"Because she is better off thinking you're a piece of shit."

"Matt. Seriously?" I said. "That is so not cool."

"He shows up at my bar. You're drunk as hell with another guy and this asshole is saying shit about needing time. I saw you two leave together two nights before that. I'm not stupid, Sis." Shit, Brett must have overheard. "Then he loses his shit and I need to have his ass thrown out of my bar. No, Kat. You don't need a guy like him in your life. No stress remember?"

"Matt, stop."

Ream locked his arm around my waist and pulled me into him. "Baby, if your brother needs to say shit …"

"Fuckin' right I have shit to say to you." Matt stopped right in front of us and as Emily and I would say he was 'on the burner.' "You had your chance. You screwed up. You're not getting that again. And I don't care that you showed up at the hospital *this* time. I let it happen because Kat, for some reason, wanted you there. But hooking up with you again is a mistake and I'm not letting her make it twice."

"Matt. Let me—"

He turned toward me. "What's the deal, Kat? I thought you were done with him. He doesn't deserve you."

Ream's entire body went stiff and completely still. When he spoke it was with a hard, gruff tone that even I didn't want to mess with. "Maybe I don't. But this is between her and me—not you."

Matt's hands clenched and the pink of his cheek turned red. He was ready to blow a gasket.

The pins and needles in my legs sparked like fireworks. "Both of you. Stop it," I shouted.

Neither of them paid attention to me, and Ream let me go as he strode toward Matt, fists clenched, body tense. My legs weakened as the tingling turned to numbness and I staggered into the car, grabbing at the edge of the door for support. A slight yelp escaped me as I just about fell.

"Fuck." Ream dove for me, wrapped his arm around my waist. "Is it your legs?" I glanced up at Matt and saw the surprise in his face. "Babe, get in the car while I deal with this."

Matt's voice was suddenly calm and quiet as he stared at me with shock. "He knows?"

I nodded.

Ream tightened his hold around my waist and Matt's expression instantly changed from fury to concern. I couldn't blame him; he'd raised me, been through all the testing, and sat with me while the neurologist gave me the bad news that I had Multiple Sclerosis. I remember him reaching across the space between us and taking my hand. It was the most comforting gesture he could've ever done. No words. No anger for what I'd been dealt. Just support. I'd always remember that moment. I'd been sixteen and scared, not understanding what this meant for the rest of my life. But I knew I had Matt and that made everything a lot less scary.

"You need to sit," Ream whispered into my ear.

"I'm good. Just don't let me go for a minute." His arm around me was the only thing keeping me from landing on my ass. "Matt, I love you. But I can fight my own battles." He opened his mouth and I quickly continued, "Back off."

He glared at Ream. "Hurt her again and be ready to move to another country."

"I move anywhere, she's coming with me."

"Oh shit," I mumbled.

"Get in, beautiful."

"Do you even have a clue what MS is? My guess is you don't and—"

"Matt. No." Crap. Ream was not going to take any accusation lightly.

But Matt kept going. "She can't go anywhere. She's sick and her disease is eating away at the myelin on her nerves. Do you even have a clue what myelin is? Well, I fuckin' do, and she'll never be going on tour with you, did you think of that? Health insurance won't cover her MS out of the country. I bet you never thought that far ahead, did you? I wonder why? Because you're a crazy, fucked-up asshole, that's why. You'll use her then push her aside when things get rough for her. My advice ... walk away now before I have to kick your ass when you fuckin' hurt her—again."

Whoa. I was taken aback by Matt's words. He'd always been protective of me, and I loved him for it, but it also pissed me off because I hid my disease from everyone so I wasn't treated like he just treated me. Weak. Vulnerable. Incapable. I was none of those things and I fought real damn hard to make sure I wasn't.

Ream urged me into the front seat and then stepped back. I grabbed for his arm, but he avoided me and moved toward Matt. He didn't hesitate as he threw the first punch. Matt was ready though and at the last second dodged the blow and took it to the shoulder instead of the intended jaw. Matt tackled Ream to the pavement.

"Matt. Stop. Ream." I couldn't do anything but sit there and watch as they punched and rolled around on the ground. I winced when I heard a sharp crack as Matt's fist connected with Ream's cheek and then Ream elbowed Matt across the face.

"Stop it."

Ream jumped on top of Matt and pinned him with his arm to his neck, cutting into his air supply. "You don't fuckin' get it, do you? Her disease doesn't have ahold of her ... she has ahold of the disease with a goddamn iron glove. She hides it from those who mean the most to her because you protect her like she's fuckin' sick and she thinks everyone else will too ... but she's not. She's living. And I intend to be there for every second of it." His voice got quieter. "And if it takes leaving the band, then I will. But don't ever say I'm using her again."

My breath hitched at Ream's words. He stood up and his eyes immediately found mine. His words echoed in my head over and over again.

He understood.

He got it.

He knew how I felt.

And did he just say he'd leave the band for me?

For once I was speechless. Tantalizing warmth spread through my body as we stared at one another. I heard Matt climbing to his feet, but I couldn't tear my eyes away from Ream. Didn't I promise myself to live each day to the fullest? To take risks? Wasn't Ream a risk I was willing to take? There was no question I wanted him, but I still wasn't ready to jump in with both feet like he wanted. With Ream, it was proceed with caution and right now I had one foot in and one out.

"Baby," he said and held out his hand. It settled in mine and I wanted to sigh.

I looked at my brother. "Matt, no matter what happens ... I'm going to be okay."

"Kat ... Jesus." He glanced at Ream and we all were silent for a few seconds. Then Matt, with blood running from his nostril, held out his hand to Ream. "Okay, buddy." Buddy? It was buddy now? "Maybe you do have the balls to take on my sister and understand what it entails. And I'm not just talking about her MS. But I'm still watching and if you fuck up ... I'll roast your balls."

"Fair enough." Ream squeezed my hand. "We'll be back in a couple of days."

"What?" I looked up at him and he winked. It was sweet and cute and I loved when he showed that part of himself.

Matt frowned. "You have everything she needs? She has drugs that—"

Ream raised his brows. "Yeah, Matt. I got this."

Matt hesitated another second, and I saw the conflict on his face. He'd always worry about me, he'd made it his job, but he had to stop worrying and start living for himself. Sometimes, I wish he never knew about my MS. But living with this disease alone ... it was hard facing the mystery of it ... the unknown of what could happen to me. Despite my will to be strong and face this alone as much as I could, I needed my brother.

"Love you, Sis." Matt then strode back to his car.

"Ream? What do you mean a couple of days?"

"We're taking some time to sort shit out, you and I. No distractions."

And that was him wanting me to jump in with both feet. "Whoa, I don't think—"

"Yeah, don't think. Just do." Ream closed my door then went around to the other side and folded in. Within seconds we were moving.

"Ream?"

"Yeah, baby?"

"Thank you." For him saying what he did to Matt, for being at the hospital when I knew he had trouble staying there, for giving me time after the attack but still being there if I needed him. It was for all of it and I knew he got that.

He nodded and kept his eyes glued to the road. After several minutes he said, "This weekend we get back where we started from—our friendship."

I missed the Ream I'd known at the farm. And I wanted that back too, but I really didn't know if that could ever be built back up again.

"No sex."

"Excuse me?" Now, that was a surprise. Ream and I had passion in abundance and he wanted to go away for two days and not have any?

"This isn't about that. We need time to sort our shit out and sex makes it complicated."

"Well, maybe I want complicated." I didn't, far from it, but us alone … well if I had one foot in then it was to have sex with Ream. The friendship was high risk and there was a Slow Down Construction Ahead sign flashing.

"You're not getting it. Now put on your seat belt before I have to stop the car and do it for you."

I reached over my shoulder and brought the belt across me and clicked it in place. "I need my injections if we're going to be gone a couple of days."

"Taken care of."

I jerked my gaze to him and he briefly met my eyes. "You planned this?"

"Baby, why do you think I met you at the docs?"

"How do you know where my needles are?"

"That big smart-ass horse of yours told me."

I smiled, he chuckled and the sound sparked a flame inside me. "What if I said no?"

"I'd planned on throwing you in the car anyway."

"You can't just throw a person in a car and drive off. That's kidnapping."

His brows rose as he looked at me for a second. "I call it coercion."

I snorted.

"That drug you take is kept in the fridge. You keep a small one in your closet." Shit, he researched the drug I was on and knew it was kept in the fridge? It was safe to keep them at room temperature for a week at a time.

"Well, I hope you don't plan on going across the border because I need a letter to travel with those drugs."

"We're not going over the border."

"Okay, so where?"

Ream laughed and I loved how the tension he always had in his expression briefly relaxed in the moment he let the laughter in. Even when I saw him playing the guitar up on stage, looking sexy hot, he wasn't relaxed. He was intense and focused.

"You don't like surprises, do you?"

"Of course I do. I'm spontaneous."

It was his turn to snort.

"What?"

"You can believe that if you want, but we both know it's a lie. You pretend that's what you're doing, but what you do is try and control every aspect of your life."

"Well, you should know. You're the definition of control."

His lips twitched and damn it, I wanted to lean over and kiss them. "You're right. But you fucked that up from the moment we met." I opened my mouth then shut it again when I caught a glimpse of his scary scowl that sent shivers of desire and fear through me at the same time. "So, now I'm smoothing out the wrinkles."

"Do I have no say in any of this?"

He glanced at me and just the slide of his gaze running the length of me had me shifting uneasily in my seat. "No. That time has passed. I gave you time to pull your head out of your ass. You didn't. I get back from tour and you're with some prick who doesn't know how to look after his girl."

"What happened to me wasn't Lance's fault. And my head isn't in my ass."

Ream threw back his head and laughed. "I sure as fuck hope not. But still … you're doing what I want this weekend."

And I didn't like the sound of that. "I don't like being told what to do or being looked after."

"Yeah, I got that loud and clear, beautiful. But this weekend you're getting that." He raised his brows when I went to object. "I want two nights."

My heart pumped faster and faster as I began to be fully aware of what the situation was. "To what?"

"To have no arguments and give you what you need."

"How do you know what I need, Ream?" But despite what had gone on between us, I think he did know.

He looked completely at ease with his hand slung over the steering wheel and one leg bent. "Kat, it's a weekend of no arguing with me. A couple of days. Just us."

Words were easily forgotten; actions made the difference, and Ream's actions in the past were shit until recently … Could I let him have control, no arguing for two days?

"And if I say no? If I want you to take me home?" I was curious as to what he'd say. We were both stubborn and liked to get our own way, even if it was a way we didn't particularly want, but just wanted to win.

"You in my car?" I nodded, suspicious as to where he was going with this. "Do you know where we're going?" He knew full well I had no idea where we were going. "You had your chance to say no before you got in the car. Now, you're with me and I get my time. Then you can decide."

"Decide what?"

"Whether to let me in and give me all of you."

"You've got to be kidding." I laughed, shaking my head back and forth. When I looked at him he wasn't smiling, he was dead serious. Could I let him in completely? Would he do the same? He liked control and it wasn't just sexually. He had demons and yet, he'd told me little about them except his sister dying. I wasn't the only one hiding and for us to even have a chance, to build trust again, he'd have to let me in too.

He sped onto the highway and merged into traffic. "No sex until you agree to be mine."

"Yours? That sounds a little chauvinistic." More like the size of a killer whale chauvinistic.

He shrugged. "It is what it is, Kat. And it goes both ways. But I'm already yours, so that part is done."

I thought about what he wanted. It was so ridiculous that I couldn't wrap my mind around it. I mean, us together—alone—and no sex … that wasn't going to happen. But he wanted more than that. Ream wanted control over the next two days. No arguing with him, just trusting him to give me what I needed. The thought made me uneasy because I hated being taken care of and the thought of giving him that made my heart race and my stomach churn.

The only way this would work was if we had sex because being alone with Ream … well resisting him would be painful. "I want to have sex."

"No."

"Ream that's what there is between us now. We both know it." There was more, at least there had been. I just didn't know if it was possible to find that again. The thing was … hope was beginning to blossom.

"That's where you're wrong. We were friends first and we're getting back to that."

"I can't just be friends with you."

"We'll see."

"Ream."

"Kat."

I crossed my arms. Shit, he thought he could do this? Spend two days together and do nothing but what … talk? Ha. "Fine. You can have your weekend. No sex and no arguing."

He chuckled. "Wasn't asking, baby."

Gah … I so wanted to smack that arrogant smirk off his face, but then I wanted to kiss it and crawl on his lap and …

How hard could this be? I wasn't scared of much. He could be taking me bungee jumping and I'd be ecstatic. But I was apprehensive about the no arguing part, because … well, I was good at it.

I hoped he was taking us to a spa. Now that would be wicked, plus I could escape him by going into the ladies' room anytime I wanted. God, we clashed all the time. There was a history of hurtful words and anger and I felt like all we had left was this sexual chemistry and the rest was gone. That wasn't a foundation … that was quicksand.

"We're incompatible. You know that right?" We may want one another, but it didn't mean it could work.

"We're not incompatible, Kat. We've just lost our way."

"We're arguing right now."

"No. We're discussing. And do you really want to go there? Because I have you in my car, no one knows where we're going, and I confiscated your phone from your purse while you were kissing me."

"Shit," I grabbed my purse off the floor and started digging through it. No phone. "Why?"

"Because you're so focused on making certain no one is looking after you that you think every time they are, there's some underlying reason for it. You're hiding your MS because you're so goddamn scared everyone will think you're weak, but, Kat, it's backfiring. You're weak because your real emotions are locked up so tight that you don't let yourself do the one thing that you claim you're doing—living."

I snorted and tossed my purse on the floor. "You have no clue, Ream. No fucking clue. That's so not true."

"Did you cry over what that bastard did to you? He fuckin' touched you, Kat. He cut your face and beat you. Did you ever cry?"

I stiffened. "What?"

"You heard me? I was in the hospital with you and not once did I see you cry. A guy fuckin' did that to you and you didn't cry. A week at the farm … not once did you break down. You control everything about your emotions. You don't take one moment for yourself and let what you're feeling in." He looked over his shoulder as he changed lanes. "The only time I see you lose control is when you're angry. Tell me, Kat, when you were diagnosed, did you cry?" Oh God. "Did you feel sorry for yourself for five minutes? My guess is you didn't."

"I cried when Emily came home."

"That's exactly it. You cried for her. But never for yourself." He looked at me and I quickly looked out the side window. "I think it's great you're taking control over this disease, baby. But you still need to grieve. You need to tell the people that mean the most to you and stop trying to control what they will do if they knew."

I remained silent. I couldn't speak. I didn't want to hear it.

"So my advice, don't argue with me this weekend. If you do … then you'll find out what being turned on and not having release is."

Holy shit. "Are you kidding me? You can't do that?"

He nodded. "Sure I can."

Fuck, I didn't like the sound of that. Double fudge brownie cookie-dough fuck. What a bastard. "I hate you."

"We'll see."

I didn't like the sound of that either.

Chapter Nine

Why did she always have to wait for me?
I was so sick of her pity. Of her constant need to be around me.
She was standing at the top of the stairs, and I wanted to push her
down them. I hated that she knew where I went. It was almost like
she was glad I was trapped there.
I hated that she tried to comfort me.
There was no comfort.
I didn't want it.
I didn't want anything. Not from anyone.

Something nudged my shoulder, and I pushed the offending dis-turber away with a flick of my wrist. I rubbed my head against the hard glass trying to get comfortable again when suddenly my glass pillow was taken away.

I opened my eyes and saw Ream standing outside the car, his hand on the door, his faded blue jeans snug against his muscular thighs, and damn he was too delicious to resist with a sleepy head.

"Let's go, beautiful."

I unclicked the seat belt and it snapped back in place. He had a black bag thrown over his shoulder, and I hoped like hell he had packed my comfy pajamas. The ones they'd taken me to the hospital in, I'd asked Matt to burn. He stepped aside as I slid out of the car and took in the surroundings.

Shit. It wasn't a luxury spa. It wasn't even a hotel. It was a tiny cottage surrounded by ... I breathed in ... pine trees. The car door slammed behind me, and then I heard the crunch of snapping twigs under his feet as he walked toward the cottage—better description: shack.

"Really, Ream? If you were trying to win me over, this certainly isn't doing you any favors." I stayed by the car afraid to leave the luxury.

"Get your ass moving, Kitkat."

The three porch steps he stepped on creaked under his weight, and I imagined he'd fall right through them before the weekend was up. Why the hell would Ream bring me here? There was nothing quaint about the place. Shit, the place needed a coat of paint and ... he better not have brought me here to paint.

"Inside." He held the rickety screen door open for me, the metal hinges making a sharp shriek at the slightest movement.

I grumbled under my breath as I stepped past him.

Surprise lifted the dread of walking into a daddy long-leg sanctuary plagued with webs and dust. Instead, I was greeted with the aroma of fresh cut flowers, lavender, and fresh bread. The hardwood floors sparkled. The small but modern kitchen had a European feel with the stained glass backsplash tiles and dark mahogany cupboards. It opened up into a living room that had a big bay window looking out onto a deck which overlooked the lake.

"Okay, not as bad as I thought."

I shivered when he came up directly behind me, his hands resting on my hips. "Glad you semi-approve. Not that it matters if you did or didn't."

"Smart-ass," I retorted.

"Mmm," he murmured. His hands slipped away and he strode into one of the three rooms off the living area.

I could see a bed with a white duvet and soft beige throw pillows. There was a painting above the bed of a woman walking along the beach, the water coming in to glide over her feet.

"So whose place is this?" I asked, kicking off my shoes and plopping down on the bar stool at the narrow kitchen island that also doubled as a place to eat it seemed.

"A friend."

"Well, since I know most of your friends, then I must know who it is."

"You don't know this one."

Oh. "A girl?"

"Jealous?"

"No. Curious." He took clothes from the bag then placed them in an old dresser. Ream ran his finger slowly over the butterfly tat on his right arm, the one similar to the tat he just got for me. It looked like an unconscious gesture, and I'd seen him do it before. I thought of what he'd called his sister. His little angel.

"Why do you do that?" And curiosity can't kill the cat.

"Do what, babe?"

"Touch that tattoo all the time. The one on your upper right arm. Is it your sister?" He shut the dresser door and stood up straight watching me. I watched back. Then I grew uncomfortable under his gaze and went to explore when his voice stopped me.

"Now I have both of you on me." That was all he said. "Come here."

I really didn't want to. I mean I was feeling anxious and … yeah, completely turned on and keeping my distance was a damn good idea when there was a no sex rule. Why was it that you thought of something more when you knew you couldn't have it? "I'm going to go explore—"

"I said come here, Kat."

"Why?"

He wasn't smiling. He was serious and I finally realized what he meant by no arguing. Oh shit. I was so not good at following orders. It was like it set something off inside me telling me to rebel.

"Kat." His command—and it was a command—was stern and direct. I thought about it for a couple of seconds and then got up and walked toward him.

I stopped in the doorway. Why was my breathing faster? I shifted uneasily under his intense gaze, feeling as if he was undressing me with his eyes. Shit. The ache started in my belly and then the throbbing went lower and that tightness between my legs that made me want to say fuck this and jump him … yeah, it was screaming at me to do something.

"Get ready for bed. It's late."

I saw my little pink makeup bag but no pajamas. "Umm, did you forget something?"

He leaned back against the dresser and crossed his arms. "No."

"What am I supposed to sleep in? Nothing?"

He didn't say anything.

Shit. And he wanted to skip the sex part of the weekend. Who was he kidding? "Give me one of your shirts." I held out my hand, expecting he'd give in to my demand. Instead, he snagged my hand and pulled me into him until I was snug against his chest.

When I raised my head to glare at him, he was already looking at me and his eyes were smoldering. He cupped my chin, his thumb stroking my cheek slow and gentle like a pendulum. "No shirt. You can wear your panties to bed … if they're sexy."

If he hadn't been holding my jaw, it would have dropped. Instead, he lowered his head until our lips were so close that if I puckered they'd touch. "Never clothes in bed, baby."

I glared and then relented because it was he who'd be the one breaking his own rule. I could do this. "Fine." I easily stepped from his arms, well, easily meaning he chose to let me go.

I started unbuttoning my blouse, taking my time making sure he could see every inch of my skin being exposed bit by bit. When

I got to the last button, I let the blouse fall open and then slide down my arms to the floor.

His jaw clenched then unclenched, eyes watching, expression stoic, and yet I witnessed the swelling in his jeans. No sex rule, my ass. We were not lasting the first night. I undid my jeans and with a slow bend at my waist, I caressed my thighs with the denim as I sashayed them down and stepped out of them.

I thanked God I was wearing my turquoise lace thong with matching bra because damn I wanted to look and feel hot in the body department since my face was … well still on the mend.

I glanced back up at Ream. Big mistake. His eyes were swimming with so much desire that it swept me up and took hold of my insides and brought me into him. Damn. He hadn't even touched me and I wanted to touch myself to stop the ache that pulsated mercilessly. I had the control. I had it and now it was slipping through my grasp like sand.

I turned around to undo my bra.

"Face me," Ream ordered.

My bra unhooked and fell forward. I slowly turned, expecting his eyes to be on my breasts. They weren't. They were locked on my eyes. "Even just undressing, you're fighting the entire time to take the control. You're so intent on being strong that you're not letting go when you need to." Ream stepped toward me and I was breathing so fast that my chest heaved in and out. He stopped inches away, so close that I could feel the fibers of his clothes tickling my hairs that stood at attention. "When did you get the ink, baby?"

It was after he left for the tour. Everyone was gone and Georgie and I had decided a little pain was a good idea. It was my first one and I loved it, a tribal horse on my side over my ribs. He traced the ink with his finger and shivers caressed my skin.

I barely breathed as I roughly whispered, "No sex."

Ream grinned. "Oh, baby, I know the rules and I won't be breaking them either." He nodded to the bathroom. "Get ready for bed."

I took a deep breath about to argue when I realized there was nothing to argue. I picked up my pink travel bag and strode into the adjoining washroom and closed the door. It was only when I was alone that I let the emotions come down on me. I rested my hands on the edge of the counter and stared into the mirror and what I saw completely terrified me.

I felt vulnerable to the emotions creeping up on me. He was taking control ... No, he already had it and that meant he could open me up to emotions I didn't want to face. I wanted us to have a chance, but in order to do that I had to let him in—completely.

I abruptly turned away, brushed my teeth, relieved myself, then went and crawled into bed. Ream wasn't around and I was glad because if he saw my face, he'd know what I'd seen in the mirror.

I pulled the sheet up over my shoulders and nested it between my legs then fell into an exhausted sleep.

Chapter Ten

I woke up so friggin' hot and sticky, as if I was lying in a sauna. I tried to push the duvet aside, but it wasn't a duvet, it was Ream and he had his arm snug around my waist, his leg hooked on top of mine while the long length of his body pressed up against my side.

Shit, I was at the cottage-shack-cabin-thingamajig. Alone. With Ream. And I was in my panties and he had his leg thrown over my thighs—his naked muscular leg.

Holy damn. When did he crawl into bed? God, was he naked? Did he at least have boxer briefs on? I'd go with that. But my mind had already far surpassed that thought and was onto him being naked and his cock hard up against me while his lips were nestled against the base of my neck.

I had a choice: I could quietly turn and slip his cock inside me or quietly climb out of bed. I chose the second option because, really, I needed some control here and being stubborn, I wanted Ream to be the one to break his rule first.

I placed my hand on his wrist then gently tried to lift it from me. It was like lifting a barbell strapped to the floor. It wasn't moving.

"Go back to sleep, beautiful," he mumbled against my neck. The vibration of his lips sent a shiver of pleasure through me. I really needed to escape fast.

"You're breaking the rules."

"Since when is sleeping sex?"

"What? No. It's not, but you're naked and it's close enough."

He chuckled then nibbled on my shoulder. "Oh, baby, there'd be no question you'd know if I was inside you." Yeah I would. "Go back to sleep."

"I want to get up."

He sighed and pulled me in closer. "Do you ever stop fighting?" His voice was that rough, lazy morning voice, and it was making me wet. Who was I kidding? I was already wet. "Where's the fun laid-back chick I once knew? I want her back."

"Lost," I mumbled, not expecting him to hear me.

"Then we'll find her," he murmured against my shoulder where he was sprinkling kisses.

Shit. "I want to get up, Ream."

"You have to piss?"

"No."

"Then you're staying here. I'm not ready to get up, and you need to learn to relax and sleep in."

"I never sleep in."

"Bullshit. We spent two days in bed."

"Since when is sleeping sex?"

"Mmm."

He moved his leg up farther on my thigh, and his cock was there, unrestrained and ready. Nope. No boxer briefs—shit. I tried to shift away because seriously the throbbing between my legs was so close to diving off the cliff that if he touched me with one finger, I'd be screaming in ecstasy. He tightened his arm and tugged me back in. Then he had the nerve to chuckle.

"Go to sleep, Kitkat."

"I'm not tired."

"Then lie here and think of me fucking you."

"Ream, that's ridiculous."

"No, you're being ridiculous for not shutting your mouth and just enjoying cuddling."

"You're an ass."

"Never said I wasn't. Now close that sweet, fuckable mouth before I find another way to shut it."

"That's a form of sex," I retorted, although the thought of tasting him again made my breath quicken and my mouth water. Some men tasted like shit; Ream tasted like heaven, but I sure as hell wasn't telling him that.

"Oh, I wasn't thinking of that, beautiful. But it's nice to know that you are."

Gah.

His arm loosened and his fingers splayed across my abdomen, then with a slight feathered touch he caressed my skin. That was how I fell back asleep, wrapped in his arms, hot and bothered and Ream caressing me.

I moaned and pulled the pillow underneath my cheek then slowly opened my eyes. I was greeted with the sun blazing beams of light across the room. I bolted upright and listened for any noises. No Ream. It was quiet. Tranquil. It was … beautiful. I hadn't slept in this long since … well, since forever.

The farm could be quiet and serene when the guys weren't there, but there were always things to do, horses to look after, paintings to finish. This morning I had nothing to do.

Except deal with Ream.

And since there was no sign of him, I scrambled out of bed, threw on the shirt lying on the end of the bed, and quickly went to the washroom to freshen up. I froze as my gaze hit the cup by the sink. My pink toothbrush stood beside his blue toothbrush.

I didn't like it. Not at all. It made it feel … well, real. And that scared me because despite wanting this to work, I was ready for it not to. I had to prepare myself for the worst because the worst always knocked at my door. I knew how to handle it if I kept my emotions hidden. The problem was Ream knocked loud, and with Ream I was afraid he would bust right through. He was right, this wasn't about sex.

No sounds came from the kitchen, so I walked out the screen door and peered down at the dock. Ream sat with his feet in the water, a mug beside him. He hadn't noticed me yet, so I stood and watched as he swirled his feet back and forth leaning back on his elbows, his face tilted toward the sun.

Wow. There was nothing of the man I knew down there. Even when we had the two weeks at the farm, he had an edge to him. This was a part of Ream I'd never witnessed. He looked completely relaxed and content, and I suspected if I were closer, I'd be able to witness the tension gone from his face.

Was that why he brought me here? So I could see this side of him? Why did he look so … at peace?

I went back inside, careful to quietly close the door so he wouldn't know I was awake, then I went in search of my cell phone. It had to be here somewhere.

I went through the kitchen drawers and cupboards, then the dresser in the bedroom, messing up all the neat piles of clothes he'd placed there last night. Then I looked under the bed, in the nightstands, went through his pockets, and even searched the fridge, which surprisingly was full of food. He had someone come stock the place before we arrived? How long had he planned on bringing me here?

"Find what you're looking for?"

I bolted upright from looking in the bottom drawer of the oven and smashed my head on the corner of a cupboard I'd left open. "Oww. Shit." I rubbed the spot and then closed the offending cupboard door. "Where's my phone? I need to call, Emily."

"I already did. Next."

I clamped my jaw and glowered. "I need to know the time. There isn't a clock in this place."

"Where are you going that you need to know the time?"

I had no answer. I just wanted to know.

And Jesus, I really wish he'd put on a shirt. Ream watched me, the corners of his lips curved up. I pursed my lips together and glared back. He knew exactly what he was doing.

"I need to call Matt."

"Matt knows we went away."

"Yes, but he needs to know where we are."

"You mean you *need* to know where we are."

Shit.

"Babe, enough of the fuckin' *needs* and get your suit on and come down to the dock." He walked to the coffee maker and poured two cups. His tats glistened with sweat, and the ones over his shoulder blades expanded as he picked up the mugs. "And stop thinking about everyone else for a change." He paused then added, "Except me. You can think of me deep inside your pussy anytime." He hesitated and I saw a flicker of unease in his eyes as he said, "Or would you like to suck me off again?"

"You've got to be kidding."

He turned and leaned up against the counter, steaming coffees in hand, chest staring at me like a beacon for my fingers to trail over the contours of valleys and hills. He raised his mug and took a sip, his eyes never once leaving me. "Guess that's a no?"

"Yeah, it's a no. It's your stupid rule about the no sex."

He shrugged. "Haven't you ever broken the rules?" He paused then he did the sexiest move ever, eyes intense and smoldering, slightly lazy. He slowly trailed his gaze from the tips of my toes up to my mouth, hesitated, then locked on my eyes. "Mmm, you're right. We can't break the rules. Meet you down at the water, baby."

I noticed my fingers were pinching my arms, and I quickly let them fall to my sides as he nonchalantly brushed aside his obvious sexual perusal of my body. Christ, I needed a cold shower. I crossed my arms over my breasts where I knew my nipples were erect as shivers trickled across my skin. "I don't feel like putting on my bathing suit."

"You want to find out what happens if you don't?" The playful tone was gone and the scary, dominant ass returned. Shit, I couldn't figure out what turned me on more.

I glared and he met it head-on with his annoyingly hot, sexy expression of a man brooding.

"If you're not dressed in five minutes, I'm coming back up here." He strode to the sliding door and opened it with his foot. "Wear the red one."

I gawked. A red bathing suit? I didn't own a red bathing suit.

I wore my *white and gold* bathing suit that was packed along with a red one that I'd never seen before. I tossed it into the bathroom trash and then proceeded to tell myself that this was a good idea. Then I wrapped my soft white sheer wrap around me and made my way down to the water.

Ream stood on the edge of the dock, his tall lean form a picture of perfection. Suddenly, he threw his arms forward and dove into the water. I stopped dead in my tracks, my breath caught in my throat while I watched him surface and shake his head, water droplets dispersing into the air. He ran his hand down his face, and from the side profile I could see the usual tightness around his mouth was gone.

And I liked it. What was I doing? What were we doing? What we needed was to fuck and get it out of both our systems. This ridiculous idea of no sex was just that—ridiculous.

Ream disappeared beneath the surface again and reappeared several feet farther out. Then he began swimming, his muscular arms rhythmically pulling him through the water easily.

I started walking again, sitting down and placing my feet in the cool water once I reached the edge of the dock. I leaned back on my elbows like I'd seen Ream do and closed my eyes, letting the sun filter into my skin and take the slight chill of the breeze out of me. The sun was the best medicine for MS, vitamin D overload. I took five times the amount a normal person would take in a vitamin per day, along with Omega 3s and B12 injections every month, plus my daily injection to try and keep any flare ups away. The pills I took on occasion were to calm my nerves when they were acting up.

I was diagnosed when I was sixteen after an episode where I lay down and lost feeling in my arms. It was pretty terrifying waking up and not being able to feel my arms. It was like they weighed a thousand pounds. It took several months and three MRIs, but they finally made a diagnosis that I had MS after confirming lesions on my brain. I had to sleep sitting in a recliner for a couple of months. Even washing my hair had been a task; keeping my hands above shoulder level caused them to go numb. Eventually the symptom faded, and I felt pretty normal again.

When I turned eighteen I was allowed to start the daily injections. It wasn't a cure, but it was to try and keep the flare ups at bay.

The sun warmed my skin and I sighed as I relaxed. It had been a long time since I had done anything like this. After my parents died it took Matt and I years to get our lives back in order. Then when we finally felt comfortable, I was diagnosed and then the testing and uncertainty at what was going to happen to me began.

I sighed as the cloud moved away and the sun hit my face again.

The cold hand on my ankle jerked me from my stillness, and then I screamed as water rushed over my skin. My cry was quickly swallowed as my head went beneath the surface. I burst back up and heard Ream laughing.

"You dickhead." I went to hit him, but he was too quick and dove away from me making a huge splash.

"Careful, Kat."

"What are you going to do? Dunk me under."

He chuckled, eyes scintillating with amusement. "Oh, baby, you haven't seen anything yet."

My eyes narrowed as I bobbed up and down. I wasn't quite tall enough to stand and be above the water like Ream. "You're not into that whipping and shit are you?" The thought was a bit exciting, but I knew my body wouldn't deal well with any sort of physical abuse, sexually related or not.

"No," Ream replied, coming closer to me. "A different type of abuse."

I didn't like the sound of that. Then why did my stomach flip-flop? Nerves. Definitely nerves. "Yeah, well, I'm not into any kind of abuse."

"Oh you'll like it. Trust me."

"That's the issue, Ream. I don't trust you."

"You'll learn."

"It's earned, not learned, asshole."

He shrugged. "Semantics," he said, copying my very words.

"I'm going for a swim now that you got me all wet."

As soon as the words were out of my mouth I regretted them. His eyes gleamed and his lips parted. He came toward me and I started to back paddle.

"You wet for me, Kat?"

"You know what I mean." I kicked my legs out as I floated on my back, trying to get away as he waded through the water.

"You're lying again. That's okay, I'll check for myself."

"Don't you dare." I kicked my legs faster then reversed onto my stomach and started swimming.

I was completely mortified when a girlie scream escaped my mouth as he grabbed my ankle and yanked. I went under then sputtered and coughed when I came back up.

"Stay still."

"Fuck off."

"You going to argue with me?"

"I'm not arguing."

"You're arguing." It was a statement.

"We're having a discussion," I corrected, and he immediately laughed which I didn't like because, really, his laugh was so hot and I felt like sighing then swimming into his arms and begging ... no, no, no, never begging.

"Stop fighting me, Kat." He sounded really serious now. "Just relax and let me look after you for two days. Not much to ask, is it?"

Of course it was. I'd fought for so long to not have anyone look after me that to lose my grip on that control was like I was losing a part of me.

"Out of the water. I want to try something."

I didn't like the sound of that. Okay, maybe there was one molecule swimming around wanting to know, but it was one out of trillions. I swam over to the ladder and climbed out. Ream followed and I couldn't help but glance at his dripping wet skin as he approached.

He bent down and grabbed a towel then shook it out and laid it on the dock. "Lie down." He nodded to the towel.

I had no idea what he had planned, but since there was no sex and no whips, it couldn't be that bad. I lay on my back and he reached over to the side of the dock then came and knelt beside me, a thick white rope in hand. I bolted upright.

"Fuck no." But he was quick and wrapped it around my wrist so fast that I didn't even manage to get to my knees before he was done.

"I told you, I'm not into that," Ream reassured. "Okay, maybe some bondage if you're being rebellious, but that's not what this is about. It's just to stop you from touching me."

"What makes you think I want to touch you?"

His brows rose. Gah ... was it that obvious?

"Lie back," he gently urged, and I did, although my panic at not being able to move my wrists apart caused my breathing to run rampant. "Baby." He smoothed his hand over my head. "Take a deep breath. You're freakin' out. The last thing I want to do is get your symptoms riled up." I was getting that Ream knew more about my MS than reading a blurb about it online. He sat back on his heels and watched me for several minutes while I got my shit together.

"Then let me go."

"I want you to feel."

"I do feel. All the time. I'm feeling pissed off at you right now for making me do this."

Ream cracked a half smile. "No. Forget about everything else and just feel me."

"I did feel you. For years I felt the hurt from what happened that day."

His eyes darkened and he frowned. "You ever just think about what the fuck you're saying, Kat? Because it's really pissing me off. Been for a while now. You're holding shit over my head for what I've apologized for and explained why I walked out and needed time to process that shit. I'm not repeating myself. I hurt too, Kat. Don't think you were alone in that. You fucking another guy two days after me ... you think that didn't blast a hole through me?"

He straddled me and droplets of water from his body dripped and landed onto my skin. My hands tied above my head, the heat of the sun, both of us soaking wet and Ream leaning over me yet not touching a single spot on my body, it was maddening. I wanted to say fuck everything and fall under his magnetic spell. "You either forgive me and accept what I've said, or you don't. Which is it?"

I hated that he was right. "I didn't sleep with him," I whispered. He froze.

God, just the look on his face made me cave and tell him the truth. "I never planned on it. I just ... I was hurt you ran out. I thought you were disgusted with me and I ... I was trying to find a way to get my dignity back. So that ... so that it looked like you didn't matter."

"Kat." His voice was quiet. "You matter. We matter. Always have. But no more hurting one another. I want to hear you say the words."

"Ream." I took in a large inhale of air. "I ... I don't want us to hurt anymore."

"Me neither, baby."

Hands on either side of my head, knees straddling my pelvis, chest inches from my breasts, and all I could do was lie still, my breathing erratic and my lips dry and aching. Shit, could lips ache to be kissed? Because mine were and if I moved, I'd touch him and I wanted that desperately. "Your nipples are aching for me to touch them." He lifted his hand just above my right breast and I stopped breathing. "Do you want me too?"

My pride screamed no, but my body screamed "hell yes." I

arched my back and he moved his hand away. I made a low growl with frustration.

"Ream? What are you playing at?"

"Not playing at ... playing with." He leaned closer, his lips hovering over mine. Water drops slipped down his strands of hair and sprinkled my face. "You didn't follow instructions."

"What?"

He looked briefly at my breasts. "The red suit. What did you do? Have a hissy and throw it out?"

I averted my eyes. "Yeah, well I don't follow instructions very well."

"Oh, beautiful, I know that. And we're going to take the next couple of days to make certain you do."

"I'm not a fucking dog, Ream."

He chuckled and I felt the vibrations in the dock penetrate into my body. "We going to have issues?"

I glared.

"Yeah. I see we are." He suddenly got up and grabbed the towel lying next to me and wrapped it around his waist. Then he leaned down, undid the rope, and started walking back to the cottage. "Let's eat."

What? He was walking away? He ties me up, straddles me, teases me, and then he casually gets up and walks away?

I was so livid and turned on at the same time that I couldn't even begin to understand the emotions playing havoc on my body. I'd wanted him to grab me and kiss me then sink his cock into me so hard and fast. Jesus, I can't believe he had the nerve to walk away? Just because I didn't put on the red suit he bought me?

I scrambled to my feet and dove into the water. Just before I went beneath the surface, I heard him chuckle.

Chapter Eleven

By the time I came back to the cottage, the aroma of bacon, burnt toast, and eggs flooded the air. I hesitated at the screen door, peering in, seeing Ream with his shirt off, shoulder blades reflecting each movement as he shoveled around eggs in the frying pan.

As if sensing me watching him, he glanced over his shoulder. "Eggs are nearly done. I burned the toast. Put some more on, would you?"

I slid the screen door open, walked in, then set the mugs on the counter. If I moved a few steps closer, my body would be up against his, hands able to stroke every contour of his back. I quickly looked away.

The scrape of the spatula on the aluminum pan reminded me of fingernails skating down skin—Ream's skin. I couldn't do this. I was on fire and I was going to combust. How could he calmly stand there flipping eggs when ten minutes ago he'd been on top of me with my hands tied?

I jerked as he slid the pan off the burner then turned. "Toast?"

"Umm, yeah." I slid past him and grabbed the bag of bread and pulled out four pieces, which I plopped in the toaster. I pressed the lever down and stood staring at it, palms flat on the counter.

I jumped when I felt his hands on my hips. I could feel every pad of his fingertips through my sheer cover up. Suddenly I wished I'd gone and put something thicker on ... like a snowsuit. He moved in closer and his naked chest pressed into my back.

Oh Jesus. My throat was dry and I swear any willpower I thought I had just got machine gunned and lay in a pool of blood on the kitchen floor.

His hands slid up my sides and then back down again, and it felt like he left a trail of electricity behind. I closed my eyes, my stomach dropped, and a swish of desire settled in deep. I couldn't do this.

He won. I admit it. My stubborn resolve was splattered across the heated frying pan and I was letting him win.

I swung around so fast that I think I startled him, and he fell back a step. I grabbed him on either side of his head and yanked him in—hard.

The kiss was unrelenting, harsh, and without mercy. Denied sexual need drove both of us into a wild frenzy. His arm wrapped around me and caged me against him, his cock pressing into my abdomen while his other hand grabbed my hair and tilted my head to give him better access to my mouth.

I moaned as he caged me into the counter. All I could think about was him inside me, the ache between my legs a throbbing pain-pleasure that had been deprived for years.

"Baby, you taste so fuckin' good." Ream pulled my head back farther and it hurt, but I didn't care. I wanted it to hurt. I wanted Ream to take me right then. I'd figure out the other shit later, but for now I wanted him.

He kissed my neck, tongue swirling where he bit me. I winced then moaned.

"Ream." I pressed my hand down between us feeling his pulsating cock that I wanted to free from its confines and push inside me. "Now."

The smell of burning penetrated my nostrils.

"Fuck." Ream pulled away then reached beside me and pressed the lever up on the toaster.

I was leaning back on the counter, my body betraying every single ounce of denial I had and Ream ... Ream was looking as if he had complete control, not even breathing hard.

"That's all you get. Next time, don't throw out the bathing suit I buy you." He nudged the tip of my nose with his finger then went and grabbed plates from the cupboard and proceeded to pile on the eggs and slices of bacon. "Get the door for me, beautiful."

Shit. I was still standing completely stunned at what just happened, and he was at the screen door, holding both our plates without even a flush to his cheeks.

Holy shit. How the hell was I going to survive another night? Why was he so insistent that we not have sex? But I did know. He wanted to prove to me that we were more than just sex. That all the fighting was just us trying to find our way back to our beginning.

We ate out on the deck in crappy, orange striped folding chairs and a table that looked like it had permanent dirt embedded into it. I ate the eggs and avoided the bacon, although I was dying to eat it. There was something about the smell of bacon that made my mouth water, although I suspected my mouth was watering more from the frustrating male specimen sitting across from me.

"You a vegetarian now?" Ream nodded to the uneaten bacon.

"No. Well, not by choice." I shifted my plate around and he took the hint and grabbed the three slices.

"What's that mean?" He bit into the bacon and I watched, wishing it was me he was biting into.

Then I picked up my melted pride that was still splattered on the kitchen floor and tried to get some of my self-worth back by sitting up straight and meeting his intense, direct gaze. "I'm trying a new diet. It doesn't allow meat for the first year."

He tossed the half-eaten piece of bacon on his plate, his brows knitted low over his eyes. "You're not going on a goddamn diet. You're already way skinnier than when I last had you in my arms."

"It's not like I have a choice, Ream. It's for my MS."

He sighed and shifted the bacon around on his plate. "I know the diet. Talked to a few neurologists about it. How long have you been on it?"

"You talked to neurologists?"

"Baby, you think I just forgot about you?" Well, kind of yeah I had. "Lots of great doctors have ideas about treating MS, Kat. Some believe in this no fat thing, others don't. It makes a lot of sense to me, but not if you're losing weight. Now, how long have you been on it?"

"When?"

"When what?"

"When did you talk to neurologists?"

"When I was on tour. I set up appointments in the cities before we left."

Oh my God. The disappearing all the time. He hadn't been having sex with women, he'd been meeting with neurologists. I was speechless, emotions whirling through me, churning.

"How long?"

I jerked from my thoughts. "Umm, yeah, a few weeks maybe."

He grunted. "We'll figure something else out. See a nutritionist. You can't keep doing it like you are. Fuck that."

"Ream—"

He shoved his plate aside. "No arguments. You lose any more weight ... this disease will take the rest of you. Not happening."

I wasn't used to anyone contesting what I did with my body. I mean, Matt tried to but he relented to my judgment. After getting shot, Matt became a little more persistent in asking me about my symptoms, but he didn't interfere in how I managed day to day.

"That's not your decision," I said, quietly. And I really had to get out of here before my emotions took over completely. I could feel the walls crumbling like cracked plaster.

I picked up my plate and started for the door but turned back around at the sound of his chair legs scraping on the wood deck. He was standing right there, his expression dark and scary again. He grabbed my plate, tossed it on the table, and the loud clang echoed across the lake.

Whoa.

"I've researched this disease since the day you told me what the fuck was happening to you. I'm not a doctor, but I know when my girl is too skinny beneath my hands." He cupped my chin and forced me to look him directly in the eyes. "You and I are doing something about this. We are working it out, and we fight this disease together."

I pulled back. "Did they tell you what can happen to me? Do you realize that I may have trouble speaking, go blind, or end up in a wheelchair? Are you forgetting those parts? Because that is the reality of this disease, Ream."

Ream kicked the chair and it flipped over on its side. "Of course I fuckin' know. Didn't you hear me? And I know that you can be okay too, that it may not get worse."

"So you're okay with that part."

"Jesus. You think everyone is going to leave you if you get worse, don't you? Is that what bullshit is wreaking havoc with your head, Kat? Is that why you refuse to tell anyone? Are you scared they will fuck off on you? Not want to help you? Care for you?"

I did think that. I'd be a burden and I never wanted that. I was fighting it with everything I had.

"Are you fighting us because you don't trust me or because you are afraid you'll ruin my life? Because that's what it's looking like here, Kat." He grabbed me by both shoulders. "Christ. You give me far more than I could ever give you. If you only knew ... Babe, you're ruining me by not being with me."

I swallowed back the tears. I wouldn't cry. I never cried. I tried to turn away and run back inside, but Ream refused to let me.

"No." He tugged me back. "You've pushed me away enough. This time you don't get to do it. You're the one fuckin' running, Kat, not me, and you have to stop."

"I'm not running. I'm trying to get away from your assholish-ness."

He sighed. "You're running."

I felt the burning in my eyes and knew if I didn't escape, I'd be a mess of tears. I yanked against his hold. But he pulled me in closer until I was snug against his chest, my face on his shoulder as he stroked my hair.

"Baby, stop pushing me away and let me in."

I wanted to. God, I wanted to give him all of myself. Everything he said was true and I was running because I was afraid to hear it.

"Jesus, Kat," Ream murmured as he hugged me to him, his whispered words vibrating against the top of my head. "It won't take control of you. Let yourself grieve. Be scared. Stop running from yourself. Let others care about you."

I slowly stopped fighting him—it was a pointless battle anyway—and sagged against him. My hands curled into his chest as he held me to him, his mouth resting on my head, arms around me.

There was a lock around my emotions and I didn't have the key, or if I did somewhere, it was too damaged to fit anymore. The reality was … I was terrified of what was in store for my future and I didn't want anyone to know. If I let that in, I may never be able to get back to being strong again.

He sighed and slowly withdrew then leaned down and kissed me. Then he let me go and went and picked up the plates. "Get changed. We're going racing. And this time I'm winning."

Chapter Twelve

When he said racing I hadn't expected go-karts. I thought he had packed a gaming console so he could get a rematch. This was so much better. The seriousness was gone and I was thankful that Ream let the conversation go and he was back to being playful, which I liked big-time.

I had to bite my lip to stop from laughing when he folded his six foot two frame into the tiny little cart with the red racing stripes. Then I did laugh when he had trouble fitting his other leg into the small space.

"You won't be laughing when I beat your pretty ass." He raised his brows. "Care for a wager?"

I could never resist a bet, and I'd been go-karting numerous times. My parents used to take Matt and me when we were little, and I'd sit in front of my dad until I was old enough to drive one by myself. I considered myself a natural so I had no doubt I could kick his ass. "Sure. How about I win, we go home." And then his little no sex rule would be over. Although I had to admit, I enjoyed being here with Ream even though it was sexually frustrating.

He laughed, his head thrown back, eyes sparkling. God, he looked hot when he laughed. I wondered why he rarely did it. It was like he was afraid to let himself enjoy, but right now he was so re-laxed ... Yeah, it was beautiful. He was beautiful. I saw it even more now than ever after what he'd said at breakfast.

His face went dead serious and I noticed that blanket of darkness shield over his expression, contradicting his next words. "How about a blow job? It's not sex."

I laughed. "You're such a pig." Although, the thought of going down on Ream was really tempting. I'd never had the chance to finish before he'd stopped me the first time.

"Anal?" I knew his words were meant to be teasing, but there was still the hint of … discomfort.

"Bah," I barked out, trying to lighten whatever was bothering him, and Ream's grin was back.

"Fine, I'll take a kiss. Anywhere. Anytime for the rest of the day. No pushing me away."

I thought about it. I wanted him to kiss me and knowing Ream, he'd take it regardless of whether or not I agreed to the bet, so I was better off to say yes and set the terms.

"Okay. And I get my phone back." At least then I could call Emily and get some girl feedback.

"No."

"Why not?"

"Because I want you all to myself. I'll give you one call."

Oh. Well, I wasn't expecting that answer. I shrugged. "Then one kiss."

Ream's hands tightened on the steering wheel. "Fine. You get your phone for the night if you win. If I do, I get as many kisses as I want with no complaint."

It was a stupid bet on his part. Because he could kiss me anytime he wanted anyway. Okay, I guess the no complaining thing was something because I would complain and not because I didn't want his kiss, but because I wanted more.

"Done," I proclaimed just as the attendant came over and started my go-kart. As soon as I heard the peppering of the engine, I smiled at Ream. "And I'm not above cheating." I pressed down on the gas and took off before the attendant had the chance to start Ream's.

I couldn't hear him swearing, but I knew he was, and most

likely scowling, and I laughed as I went full speed down the straight-away. Matt and I raced a number of times as kids, and he taught me how to take the corners without spinning out.

I glanced back over my shoulder after the fifth curve, braking before the turn then speeding out of it. "Shit." Ream was on my ass.

I swerved to the outside of the corner as he tried to take me and our karts collided. We looked at one another and I played dirty be-cause ... well, I liked to win ... so yeah, I took my hand off the wheel, licked my finger, then ran it around my nipple.

His mouth dropped open, eyes glazed over, and then he crashed straight into a pile of tires. I laughed my ass off the entire next lap as I cruised around the course, Ream far behind me. By the final lap though, he was behind me again, and this time when he came up beside me on the straightaway, he didn't even look at me.

A sharp corner was coming up and I slowed.

So did he.

My kart bounced off the tires on the inside of the track as I tried to keep my lead and I skidded as I came out of the corner.

That gave Ream enough of a chance to come up on my right as we sped down the straightaway. The engines were at full speed, and I was sure neither of us would let up into the final corner. It was give it or lose it, and I wasn't one to lose.

Suddenly, Ream fell back behind me and I looked over my shoulder.

Mistake.

He came up on the inside and pushed me wide into the corner, taking a huge lead as we sped down the straightaway.

He was waiting for me when I stopped my kart, and despite los-ing, I still smiled. Ream eased out of his kart and tossed his helmet to the attendant then strode to me and unclipped the strap under my chin. He pulled it off, tossed it in the kart, then looped his arm around my waist and I stumbled into his arms.

"Nice race, Kitkat. But no chance was I giving this up." He tilted his head and claimed my mouth. And it was claiming. There was no other way to explain what it was like. When Ream kissed me, he took and I crumbled. Maybe that was part of the issue. With Ream I felt like I lost my strength. I became his.

My belly swirled with pretty little butterflies, and my knees weakened as his lips melded with mine, tongue tasting like velvet sweetness.

"Hey, buddy," the attendant said.

Ream nipped my bottom lip and a jolt went through my body. He squeezed my butt then pulled away but didn't let me go as he snagged my hand. Ream reached into his jean pocket, pulled out some bills, and shook the attendant's hand.

I looked at the young guy and he winked at me, shoved the money into his jean pocket, and strode off. Ream guided me toward his car as my head reeled with memories of go-karting with Matt and my dad. I was really young and may have missed it, but I never recalled my dad giving the attendant a tip. Nor did Matt when we'd gone a few times.

Ream pulled out of the parking lot, the tires skidding on the gravel. He looked pleased with himself—too pleased.

"You gave the guy a tip?"

Ream's hand stopped tapping on the steering wheel. "Yeah. Good guy."

Silence. He turned up the tunes and Avicii played. I turned it back down.

"Why?"

"Why what?"

"Why did that guy get a tip and none of the other guys?"

"'Cause he got us the karts, baby."

I saw the twitch in his cheek and the tightening of his mouth. There was no anger either; he was trying to hold back a smile. "Asshole!" I punched his shoulder. "You cheated. You paid him for a faster kart," I yelled. "You sneaky bastard." Shit, he totally played me. I should've known that normally he wouldn't have ever been able to catch me with the head start I had and then again after he crashed his kart. They had speed limits—except for a souped-up attendant's kart. "Shit."

Ream grinned and rubbed his arm where I'd hit him. "Not above cheating, Kitkat. Not for a chance at those lips."

"Mmm," I mumbled, and yet inside I was a little giddy because Ream had unlimited access to my lips and I liked that.

I turned the music back up and started singing the chorus. Okay, I had fun. I couldn't remember laughing as hard as I did when I saw Ream slam his kart into the tires. The look on his face just before he crashed … priceless.

"What are you smirking about?"

"I'm not smirking. Only men smirk."

"Bullshit. You smirk. Seen it a number of times, although not often enough."

"Oh, like when?"

"The first time I saw you from on stage. The night Emily was taken."

"What?" I'd seen him for like twenty seconds when he came on stage and I had been gaping not smirking.

"Babe, I saw you. You were standing with your beer and looking right at me all bitchy and full of yourself. You were wearing that way too short ass black dress that showed every fuckin' curve of your body. You knew it too. You knew I saw you and you smirked."

Shit. "Fine. I may have mildly smiled at you."

"You wanted me. And if that shit hadn't gone down with Emily and Logan, you would've been all over me."

"Bah." I scoffed. "I may flirt and I don't have any shyness about showing off my body, but I'll tell you right now, the most you would've got from me was the chance to buy me drink."

Ream parked the car at the front of the cottage and put it in park. "So what were you smirking at?"

I thought we were off that. "Just your face."

He looked in the rearview mirror and I laughed.

"No. Your face when you crashed."

"You thought that was funny, did you?" He threw his wallet and phone on the dashboard then undid his seatbelt and without saying a word climbed out of the car. He went around and opened my door.

I smiled as I unclipped my belt. That died real fast when he reached in and grabbed me and threw me over his shoulder.

"Ream!" I pounded my fists into his back. "Ream. What are you doing? Put me down."

He ignored my pleas and kept walking. He weaved his way through the bush, up a steep hill, to a small clearing where he finally set me down. Then he proceeded to kiss me and I forgot about everything except his mouth and hands running up and down my sides.

He broke away groaning. "Jesus, I don't think I thought this weekend through enough." Before I had the chance to respond, and what I was going to suggest was say screw his stupid rule of no sex, he reached up and grabbed a yellow rope that looked frayed and a hundred years old.

"Don't you dare." I tried to escape, but he hooked his arm around my waist and lifted me off my feet. "Ream!"

"Hold on, beautiful." And without any further warning he went running to the edge of the cliff and we swung out into the air, then he let go.

My stomach dropped as we fell plunging into the depths of the cool lake. Ream still had his arm around me as we surfaced, and this time it was him laughing and my mouth open spitting out water.

He brushed aside the hair in front of my eyes with the tip of his finger. He looked all serious as he stared at me, lips slightly parted.

"Fuck, I love you wet." Ream didn't give me a chance to do anything but take half a breath before he kissed me again.

He was a great kisser, hard then soft then sweet until I was putty in his arms.

"Bed," I managed to mumble beneath his mouth.

"No."

"Ream, come on." I would never beg, but I could do sweet. I nipped his lower lip then kissed his neck, my hands beneath the water, running up his chest to his nipples.

He cupped my chin, his thumb caressing my lower lip. "My cock sinks inside you again … it's just me. No other cock. No other lips. The flirting stops, Kat."

"God, Ream. It's just sex."

His expression got dark and I saw the anger simmering beneath the surface. "I hate just sex. I abhor just sex." That was so not a guy thing to say. What wasn't he telling me? I remembered how he tried to leave after I went down on him, how he pushed me aside, the way his body was stiff and cold. At the time, I didn't think much of it, but with these words I knew something was off. "So, no … this isn't just sex, Kat. With you … it's something else entirely. That is not how it's playing out."

I remember Crisis saying woman were just objects to Ream. Had he never had a relationship? Had he never cared or loved a woman?

"And if I say no?" I wasn't. I knew that.

"Then I'm going inside and jerking off in the shower."

Damn, I was getting tingly just thinking about his hand gripping his cock and jerking up and down.

His fingers tightened on my chin and his eyes flashed dark. Yeah, the teasing he was so not going to tolerate on this. "You telling me you're going to keep up with the flirting, Kat?"

"I like flirting."

"I don't." He leaned closer. "But I'll let you flirt with me."

I liked that idea. "I would like to see you jerk off. So what if I say no just so I can get that?"

His arm tightened around me. "Oh baby, you can watch me jerk off any day. All you need to do is ask. Come on. By the time we reach the dock, you need to tell me that you'll give all of you to me. Only then do we get back the sex." He began swimming and I followed thinking the entire time that Ream was going to be inside me in less than five minutes. There was sex and then there was Ream sex, and I wanted Ream sex—bad. Because the truth was … I wanted Ream.

As I swam, the familiar tingling started in my legs. I slowed the kicking and fell behind Ream. I hadn't swam since the new symptom after the shooting, and the movement was obviously too much for my legs.

Jesus. First dancing which I loved to do, now swimming. So far the horseback riding had been fine, actually my legs felt better after riding. The nerves worked in extraordinary complex ways.

By the time I reached the dock, my legs were in full-blown electricity zinging haywire. Not numb, but every movement sent a spark through me. It was like a wire that was short-circuiting in my body.

Ream took hold of my arm and pulled me to the ladder. "What's up?"

"Nothing." I just needed a minute to rest and then I'd be good.

"Bullshit. I see it in your eyes. Something's off." Realization hit and he frowned. "Too much swimming. Fuck. I should've known. It's like the dancing."

"Ream, seriously, why the hell should you know? I didn't know. It was just too far. I swam this morning and it was okay."

He ran his hand over his head and then down his face. "Jesus, Kat. You have to tell me this shit." He slammed his fist into the water. "We did too much today. Fuck."

"Ream—"

"Out." He helped me onto the ladder and was right behind me, his one arm wrapping around my waist. "We'll go lie down."

I stepped onto the dock and tried to whirl around to tell him I was fine when he picked me up into his arms. "Ream!"

"Shut it. You're so fuckin' stubborn, Kat. If I didn't notice, you'd have tried to walk up to the cottage. Just like you kept dancing when you should've sat down. No. This ends now. I want full disclosure."

"Full disclosure?" I wanted to laugh and instead it came out as a huff-laugh because he was looking scary again and laughing in his face would not help my cause.

"Yeah." I had my arms linked around his neck as he carried me up the path. His face was stern, unrelenting. He was completely serious. "Hold on," he warned as he held me with one arm and opened the screen door then proceeded to the bedroom.

He plopped me down on the bed. "Give me a sec." He walked into the bathroom and came back with a towel. "Strip."

I hesitated because I was in shock. Ream was really serious and I was realizing that no matter how much I fought others looking after me, Ream would do it anyway and … it was sweet and I felt like I wasn't alone in this. His brows rose when I failed to move and he reached for me.

I did a girlie squeal, to my utter horror, and then he lifted my soaking wet top up over my head and tossed it toward the bathroom.

"Bra."

Ream was my ultimate cookie-dough Haagen Dazs, and I wanted to taste him again. He was more concerned about my health right now than kissing me and I needed to change that. Biting my lower lip and tilting my head slightly to the side, letting my wet strands of hair fall forward as I reached behind my back to fiddle with my bra. It took me a while. A long while and I could feel Ream's eyes on me. I didn't have to look to know his eyes smoldered.

"Do you mind?" I asked and half turned. "It's all wet and I can't get it."

I didn't dare look at him because I'd be ripping off my bra so fast I'd probably hurt myself.

The moment his fingers touched my cool skin, shivers went through me in a domino effect. I closed my eyes as his fingers slid down my back to my bra. Then in one movement he had it undone, the straps slipping down my shoulders as it fell.

His fingers trailed up my spine and over my shoulders. He slowly pushed the straps lower until they caught on my elbows. I stopped breathing.

He didn't move. Hands resting on the nook of my arms, straps between his fingers, and my bra no longer covering anything as it hung just below my breasts.

I closed my eyes as I finally inhaled a shaky breath, the edges of my control beginning to teeter as he paused.

And then … Oh God. He leaned in and his lips touched the back of my neck. It was a stroke of velvet and moisture clinging to my skin. "Ream," I whispered.

He kissed up the side of my neck to my ear then took the lobe into his mouth and suckled. It was long and slow, a languished taste. His teeth grazed and sent tremors up my spine. Then he bit down and I gasped in pain. He licked the sensitive spot and I sighed exposing my throat and leaning back into him.

"This is a bad idea." He went to move away and I panicked, spinning around, reaching up and grabbing his head on either side.

"No. You're not leaving me like this."

"I'm not leaving you. I'll never fuckin' leave you, Kitkat."

Oh God. My heart cracked and so did my voice as I said, "I didn't mean it that way."

I turned into him and looked up. He was staring at me, with a narrowed gaze as if assessing the situation. Ream was cautious, I knew that. He didn't jump until he knew where he'd land.

But his coping skills sucked. There was a good chance I'd be in and out of hospitals at some point. Ream had a past with needles, with hospitals, then someone he loved and tried to protect died and he blamed himself. Then there was the uncertainty I often saw in him, a darkness hovering over him. Everything was stacked against us for this to work. But I wanted it to. I had hope that it could.

He showed a side of himself I hadn't expected bringing me to the cabin. He was spontaneous and I was getting that it was a part of himself he rarely showed others unless he … unless he trusted them. Him talking to doctors about my MS, that was something I'd never expected. It showed he cared and knew exactly what he was getting into.

He was frowning and I guessed he was calculating whether it

was the right move to fuck me or not. I wasn't sure why.

"Ream." I grabbed the front of his soaking wet shirt and put my other hand on the bulge of his jeans. He groaned. I smiled then slowly undid his pants.

He grabbed my hands. "When we leave here, you're mine."

"Ream—"

In one sudden movement he had me on the bed and straddled me, my hands locked in his above our heads.

"Ream, the bed. You're getting it all wet." Who was I kidding? I was happier than hell he was on top of me. There was something about the feel of a guy on top that felt so dominant and hot. It was his power and control and that was all Ream.

"We get back ... we're together—entirely. We change my room back into your art studio and I sleep in your bed." Before the band moved into the farm, my art studio had been Ream's bedroom. I went to open my mouth when he said, "Not done yet." I shut it because I really wanted to get this over with so he'd kiss me. "Crisis ... him grabbing your ass ... that does not happen." He leaned closer, his mouth so close that if I inched my tongue out I'd touch his lower lip. "Dancing with other guys ... does not happen." His weight leaned into me, and I felt his cock pressing into my pelvis. What did he just say, something about dancing? All I wanted him to do was shut up and kiss me. "I've had one woman to look after in my life and I fucked it up. That does not happen again. I don't make the same mistake twice—ever. That means I make certain you're looked after."

That got my attention. "I don't need looking after." Jesus, I didn't want to be babysat. The ache between my legs got a hard kick and plummeted off the edge of senselessness into the depths of cold reality.

"Kat, I'd say the exact same thing if you didn't have MS. Looking after you means I'll be there for you. Protect you. Care for you because your mine. I hope you'd do the same for me. Except for the protecting. I don't want you anywhere near dangerous shit. That's my job for the both of us."

Okay, maybe I could do that.

"No bullshit this time, Kat. I'm possessive and I don't take chances with your safety. I check every angle before I make a decision. You know that first hand." He grabbed my chin and forced me to look at him. "My past … it screwed me up. Once I'm in, I won't let go. I can't. It's who I am and it's too late to change. You have to get that. I need you to get that, Kat. So, you need to be damn sure."

I wanted to scream yes. But Ream was serious and there was something else in his eyes that I thought looked like … uneasiness. I didn't say anything at first because this was the second time he mentioned his past being screwed up. I was starting to put the pieces together and I didn't like where they were fitting. Something happened to him and his sister. She'd died of a drug overdose, they didn't have a father, and his mother he said was dead to him. What happened to Ream? Why was he responsible for caring for his sister? How did she get on drugs?

I knew Ream had a temper and that he was overbearing and needed control. Did that all stem from what he'd been through as a child?

The thing was, I felt like I balanced him out. I didn't break down at his overbearing attitude. I held my own and he held his own against my bullshit.

Ream moved off me then climbed from the bed and ran his hand back and forth over the top of his head. I sat up as he peeled off his shirt then his wet jeans. He had no qualms about letting me see his cock hard and ready.

I bit my lower lip as my gaze ran the length of him. "Ream." My whispered word was breathless as I stared, wanting, needing and maybe finally believing that this man who stood in front of me would stand by me no matter what happened.

Suddenly, he turned and walked into the bathroom and shut the door.

I sat stunned as I heard the shower turn on then the shower

curtain on the metal rings. What the hell just happened?

Chapter Thirteen

I scooted off the bed and stormed into the bathroom, thanking God that he didn't lock it as I banged into the door.

I jerked the curtain aside and then everything I was ready to spurt spiraled down the drain as I stared at Ream naked and gleaming, his hand on his cock, his face tight with tension, almost as if he was in pain.

His eyes flashed open and locked with mine.

"I need you to be sure, Kat. I can't have you once then lose you again."

Yes. Whatever damaged key he used, Ream was already inside me and it fit. We fit.

I nodded. "Yeah. I'm sure."

He grabbed me under the arms and pulled me into the tub then backed me into the tiled wall. His palms slapped up against the tiles making a loud whack. "Tell me you trust me. That you'll be mine."

"I do. I am." As I said the words, I felt a wave of relief fall over me because I did and I was. He gave me that.

Then he kissed me.

It was raw and gritty, something overflowing with so much emotional abandon that I swear it was almost painful the way his mouth took mine. We were uncontrolled, like we often were together, our heated passion boiling over into a danger zone that I should've been leery of, but instead I wanted to embrace it.

He unlocked everything.

His hands were rough as he kneaded my breast then pinched my nipple. I arched into him and moaned, the desire so frantic that I was afraid I would come before he even got inside me.

"Jeans, baby."

Shit. Right. I still had on my jeans. With one hand he undid them then tugged them down and I stepped out.

"Fuck you're beautiful." He ran his hands over my abdomen then between my legs, his finger slipping between the folds then hesitating at the opening. "And wet."

I ran my hand up his chest to his shoulder then curled my fingers in his hair. I remember I couldn't do that before; he'd had it too short. I liked it longer though.

His mouth slammed into mine again and it was so hard my head hit the tiled wall. There was a mumbled apology, but I didn't care. I'd wanted this man for nearly three years. I knew what I was getting into, Ream was crazy possessive and maybe that shit did stem from whatever happened with his sister. We were going to clash, I knew that, and I suspected he did too, but we clashed together and that was all that mattered. And right now, all I could think about was the sweetness of him filling me again.

"Condoms," I murmured under his mouth.

"Shit." He groaned. "I didn't bring any."

Oh. My. God. "What?"

His hand stilled between my legs, and I gasped as he slipped two fingers inside me. "The plan was no sex this weekend, so I didn't bring any."

I closed my eyes and moaned partially from complete and utter disappointment at not getting his cock and also from the pure pleasure of his fingers inside me.

"You on the pill?"

Fuck. "No." Goddamn it. Really? And I was mid-cycle, but maybe if he pulled out then—

He knew what I was thinking. "No. Not taking that chance, Kat.

165

Us—we are too important to fuck this up over something neither of us want right now. Besides, I don't want to share you for a long while." He kissed me again, long and hard, until I was moaning beneath his mouth. "I'd have them with you, beautiful. Never cared to before. But with you … I would if it's something you wanted. But only if it's safe. We don't take chances with your health."

Kids? He was talking kids? How crazy was that? The doctor said I could have kids. Studies showed that pregnancy was no different for someone with MS than someone without. The issue would be chasing after a two year old.

He hooked his arm under my leg and brought it up onto his hip. His thumb began to slowly caress my clit in circles. The party in my sex became a riot of warmth and tingles, and Jesus, I was going to come … and it was too fast. And I wanted this to last forever. "Ream," I whispered.

"That's it, baby." He kissed me again and the swirling tornado that was building started to teeter on edge.

"God, Ream. Harder."

His movements stopped.

I inhaled sharply, my eyes flying open. He was so still, his eyes wide open and staring, but he wasn't staring at me. It was as if he was somewhere else. "Ream?" He didn't move and I felt the tremble shift through his body. "Ream?" I said louder.

"Kat?" He suddenly shook his head as if he was clearing it from whatever place he'd been, and then it was like nothing happened and the desire swam in his eyes.

"Baby, where did you—"

"Grab my cock." His jaw was clenched and his tone was gruff as if he was in pain.

"Ream—"

"Now, Kat." He cut me off again while taking my hand. He wrapped it around his cock and squeezed. I saw the deep grooves between his eyes as if he was fighting something. "We're coming together."

My fingers curled around his length and the throbbing heat of him jerked. "Fuck. That's it." He groaned as I tightened my grip and then moved up and down before stopping and stroking farther down to cup his balls then back up again.

His pushed two fingers inside me again and I forgot all about the look on his face.

I pumped then caressed until I felt the tension in him rising. "Christ," he said as he started stroking me with his thumb again. "Oh God. You close, baby?"

I nodded because honestly words were not in my realm of capability right now.

"Faster," he ordered.

I did and he did, just before I felt that sweet tightening in my belly and then the slam of a tidal wave over me like a wall of heat. His cock shuddered in my hand, jerked, then I felt liquid heat spill onto my skin, only to be quickly washed away by the water.

I was still tingling and sensitive as he pulled his fingers out of me and let my leg slide back down. I leaned against the wall, eyes closed, deep breaths, as I took in what just happened.

When he kissed me again, this time slow and soft, the plush velvet touch of his lips against mine, tongue exploring and tender. He held me on either side of my head as he did it, and it was sweet, not something I expected from Ream. He was all intensity when he argued with me, with his kisses, with everything. But I'd seen way more to him this weekend. I saw the side of him I'd forgotten about from when we'd first met.

We didn't say anything as he gently washed me everywhere, his hands caressing over my body as if I was a precious gem he was afraid to break. A complete contrast to what we'd done five minutes ago.

When I went to wash him, he stiffened and moved away. Ream shut off the water and helped me out of the tub.

He wrapped me in a towel then proceeded to dry me with another. Even taking each foot and going between my toes. It was silly but I thanked God that I had on fancy red nail polish with silver swirls on my big toes. He ruffled my hair with the towel then tossed it on the counter before pulling me into his arms.

"My ice cream good enough for you, baby."

I burst out laughing and then he smothered it with a sweet soul claiming kiss.

Ream and I spent the next several hours making dinner and drinking wine and sitting out on the deck watching the sun go down. It was quiet and calm over the water, and I hadn't felt so relaxed with Ream—ever. There was still the sexual tension of a guitar string being pulled taut, but the small touches and Ream's kisses were sweet and I soaked it up.

When he pulled his phone from his pocket and slid it across the table to me, I was surprised because I'd lost the wager. Besides, I really hadn't even thought of calling Emily or Matt.

He stood. "She's called three times. I'll do the dishes."

I reached for his hand and the familiar sparks scintillated through me as our fingers touched. "Thank you." I squeezed his hand. "For bringing me here."

He nodded then picked up our plates and went inside.

I called Emily and wasn't surprised when I heard Logan's voice instead, since it was Ream's phone I was using.

"Where are you? You missed recording." Logan skipped any niceties and went directly to the point.

"It's me."

He grunted, then there was silence, and then Emily's voice on the other end.

"Kat. What the hell? Where are you? Matt says Ream took off with you. Then I get a message from Ream that you're with him, but he doesn't say where. Are you okay?"

"Yeah we are—"

"When are you coming back? Is he being—"

"Emily. I'm fine. We're fine."

"You are?" I heard her muffled words to Logan, the arguing, and then I heard Crisis shouting something in the background that I thought was "I told you so."

"Yeah. We're good. Ream and I had some shit to work out ... as you know. Tell Logan it's buried." I heard her tell him and then his gruff response, "about fuckin' time."

"We just had dinner and we'll be back tomorrow."

"You just had dinner?"

"Well yeah." I looked over my shoulder to make certain Ream was still inside and then whispered, "And, Eme, never told you this before but ... he shaves. And it rocks."

"What?" Then. "Oh my God."

I laughed. "Listen, can you call Matt and let him know I'm okay."

"Umm, yeah of course. But Kat ..." I heard the hesitation as she cleared her throat. "Are you sure this is what you want? Whatever you decide, I'm there behind you a hundred percent. I'm just asking because you ... well, you were really pissed at him."

I was sure. I had no clue if this was right or wrong or if there was such a thing as right or wrong when it came to ... love?

"Babe." Ream's hand came down on my shoulders and I looked up at him. Did I love this man? Is that why everything had hurt so much because I loved him?

"Is that him?" Emily asked. "Logan wants to talk to him."

Before I had the chance to say yes or no, Logan's voice came on, "Give him the phone, Kat."

I held the phone up to Ream. "Logan wants to talk to you and he sounds scary."

The corner of Ream's lips lifted before he took the phone then walked away. I watched as he listened to whatever Logan spewed, and I could only imagine that it wasn't good. Although, Ream looked pretty relaxed about it. He said a few curt words and the only sentence he said was, "I'll be there." I was guessing they were talking about something to do with the band.

He didn't say goodbye, merely slipped the phone in his back pocket and headed straight for me. I picked up my glass of red wine and wet my lips as I swallowed, because watching Ream stand under the moonlight wearing a snug black T-shirt and worn jeans ... I was letting him in and I probably loved him. No, not probably, I did. This wasn't something new. I'd known that for a long time. I'd hurt so much because I did love him.

He reached me, leaned down putting his hands on the armrests caging me in. "Ready."

"For what? More sex without the actual sex because someone didn't bring condoms?"

He quirked a smile and shit, it was adorable. You'd think someone like Ream couldn't ever be adorable, but when he did that cute smile where the corners of his mouth partially curve up with those sparkling eyes ... well, it was super-hot and I was betting he knew it. I felt like I was handed a part of Ream that few ever experienced.

He took my glass then helped me up.

"Where are we going?"

"I have this thing." He let my hand go as he tagged the wine bottle and his glass. "Addiction you could say."

"Well, I know it's not drugs."

He chuckled and I was glad that we could laugh about it now. "Real estate."

"Huh?"

I opened the screen door and stopped dead. Ream had not only done the dishes, he'd put out candles, and the coffee table had been shoved aside and instead a pile of pillows were laid out. In the center of them sat a board game.

I looked back at him then walked over. "Monopoly? You like Monopoly?"

He brought the wine and set it down on a side table. "No. I love Monopoly. You ever play?"

"Well, yeah, of course. But I'm not very good at it."

"Just like you're not very good at go-karting? And gaming?"

Ream asked, brows rising.

Okay, maybe I wasn't going to fool him this time. Matt, Emily, and I played a lot when we were in our teens. I was more of a "spend everything and buy anything you land on type" while Matt was cautious and saved his money for the big properties. Emily could go either way, a wild card. She also never won.

I sat on a pillow and Ream passed me my wine. "I'm going to kick your ass. And this time if I win the stakes are high." I slowly smiled and he frowned immediately, suspicious. "I give you a blow job." I did it for two reasons, I wanted to give him one and because I wanted to see how he'd react.

Ream studied me for several seconds before muttering, "Fuck."

And maybe I had read too much into it. Ream had desire swirling in the depths of his eyes. Well, now he'd just have to decide what was more important, winning or a blow job. Either way, I won and he'd have to sit there thinking about me sucking on his cock for the next two hours.

Ream sunk to the pillows looking rather defeated, and I grabbed the dice and rolled. "Ready? I have a feeling this is going to be a long, long game."

Ream scowled. I laughed to myself. Although, I was beginning to think that he wasn't the only one who would be tortured for the next couple of hours.

Chapter Fourteen

I could see the conflict on his face. He didn't like losing.

He tossed down his last dollar onto the center of the board, eyes on me. I squirmed a little because, really, being under the gaze of a guy like Ream sent a parade of emotions through me. It was like the clash of a tambourine, the thumping of the bass drums, and the gentle stroke of a guitar all at the same time. My body didn't know how to feel.

I glanced at his crotch then back up.

He wasn't smiling. Not even a little bit. Was he that much of a sore loser? Kind of turned me off. Okay, not really, but I was disappointed. I thought he'd take it better.

"Kat." His voice was rough.

"Ream."

"Good game."

"Did you lose on purpose?"

He hesitated. "Do you think I'd lose on purpose in order to get a blow job?"

I laughed. "All guys would."

He remained quiet.

I continued, "But you …" I suspected Ream would do whatever it took to win his game, regardless of whether losing brought a desirable outcome for him. He was the most stubborn man I'd ever met. He surpassed Logan and that guy was a badger when he refused to give up on Emily. I also thought sex wasn't as important to Ream as it was with most guys. "Never."

Ream's eyes widened as if surprised by my words. Maybe I had lumped Ream in a category of rock star bastard after what happened between us, but now … now I knew there was a hell of a lot more to him than any of us knew. And also a part I still didn't know. I hoped that he'd open up to me now that I was opening up to him. With Ream, it was about tactical moves and if I pushed like he pushed me, I'd get nothing. Maybe it was nothing. No, he'd said numerous times his past was fucked up.

I got on my hands and knees and crawled toward him. He waited until I was about to put my hand on his button fly when he said, "The bet was a blow job."

I sat back on my heels. "And that's what I'm about to do." So much for the sexiness and allure of crawling toward him. Damn, I thought I excelled at being tempting.

"But you never specified to whom."

"What? Yes, I did. I said I'd give *you* a blow job if I won." I recognized the playful expression on his face. It was the same before we raced, then again before we jumped off the cliff.

"Semantics …" He made a dive for me, sending me backwards, then grabbed my legs out from under me.

"Ream!" I screamed as he landed on top of me, hands pinning my wrists on the floor, spread eagle. "What are you doing?"

"A blow job."

"But I want to give you one." There was a nit biting at me wondering if he was avoiding me giving him one. But what guy didn't want a woman to go down on him?

"Babe, I've been dreaming about tasting you again for fuckin' two years, eight months, three weeks, and a day. I'm not waiting another minute. You have a problem with that?"

Shit. No. I was rarely speechless, but Ream talking about tasting me … well, I was on broil and so turned on that it zapped any argument about me winning and getting to decide who got the blow job. Arguing with Ream when he was on top, his cock pressed into my

thigh, mouth inches from mine, and his unrelenting expression …
yeah, I was shutting up.

"I see how I'm going to win arguments with you."

Shit. I liked winning just as much as he did, but for this … I
might just lose an argument.

It took seconds for him to pull off my jeans. Then his fingers
hooked into the top of my pink lace thong and slowly dragged down-
ward. The tips of his fingers followed the material all the way to my
calves and then over my feet. My eyes never left his as he took in
my body with a gaze that made me ache in places I never knew could
ache.

"Beautiful." He opened my legs and ran his finger from between my breasts to my pierced belly button then trailed down farther until I arched and moaned for him to reach the warmth of my
center.

I put my hands in his hair, and the second I did I felt the change
in him. I slowly released him.

He looked up at me, his eyes a mixture of desire and a fleck of
torment. "No touching. Let me look after you."

I nodded. I knew something lay beneath the surface with Ream
and it wasn't good. It scared me to think of why he got that glazed
look sometimes.

"You're fuckin' mine now." He lowered his head and his
tongue touched my belly piercing then he nibbled and sucked.

I opened my legs wider and he teased lower. I gasped as wave
of heat washed over me and then a trembling began in my legs. He
held my thighs to steady them or to make certain they stayed as wide
as he wanted them. I didn't know or care which.

I shuddered as his tongue flicked lightly over me several times.
Then he sucked and just the sound alone almost had me coming. I
arched into him and relaxed, letting the feelings pour through me
like the sweetness of heated syrup.

Suddenly, his fingers plunged inside me and I groaned in shock,
every muscle tensing around him and giving into the assault to be

replaced by pure pleasure.

The pressure inside me built and climbed until I didn't think I could take any more. Ream refused to give, even the littlest bit, instead he took and finally I gave to him, screaming his name, every muscle tense, every molecule throbbing. I trembled and shuddered as wave after wave hit my body.

I lay panting and completely spent. But he wasn't done as he teased my sensitive sex with light pressure on his mouth while his finger arched inside me.

"Ream?"

It was a weird feeling after I'd already come, but he continued to play and I felt the urgency building again. Oh God. He must have felt it, because his finger on my sex moved faster and then he pushed three fingers inside me and that was it.

It hit me hard and I screamed out as I came again, my body jerking and shuddering as wave after wave pounded into me even harder than the last. Holy fuck. I'd never ... Jesus, I never had that before. I thought it was all talk, and I was always so sensitive after the first one that I didn't think it was possible for me.

"Babe." He moved up my body until his lips met mine, and I could taste me on him and it was good. No, it was hot and I wanted it to last forever.

He fell to the side, pulled a pillow over so he could prop his head up, then grabbed me and curled me into his arms so my back was up against his chest.

He kissed my forehead then reached for the remote control on the coffee table behind him and flicked on the TV. He surfed through channels until he found a movie then pulled me closer so we were spooned, the heat of his body surrounding me.

"What about you?" I wanted to give him pleasure, to make him groan.

His body tensed up as he said, "I had you. That's all I need, baby."

"But I want to."

"No."

It was a sharp tone and I got that he wasn't allowing it and that bothered me—a lot. Because Ream surrounded me. He was part of me, and if I ever let go again, I'd fall and never find my way back up.

I woke to a ringing phone and it wasn't mine. That and I'd yet to see mine since we arrived. I was beginning to wonder if he'd ditched it in the lake.

I was in bed, snuggled into his side, my arm lying across his waist and my head nested on his chest. His one arm was behind me, locking me up against him while his hand rested on top of mine, our fingers linked.

I don't know why but there was something about interlocking fingers that was incredibly intimate. It was like chain link fused together, unable to be separated by anything. That was how it felt—fused together.

Ream's phone kept ringing and I heard him groan. His hand left mine and I thought he was going to answer it, but instead he cupped my chin, leaned close, and kissed me. It was a gentle, lazy kiss that left me wanting more. But I didn't get more as he reached over to the nightstand for his phone.

Without even looking at who was calling he said, "Better be fuckin' good."

He listened for a minute, stiffened, then swung his legs over the side of the bed. "Are you for fuckin' real? No, you don't get to know that," he shouted. He paused for a second and his grip on the phone tightened. "I'd never cheat on her. Who the hell—" He stopped abruptly then threw the phone across the room and it smashed against the wall.

I crawled up behind him, placing my arms around his waist then lowering my head and kissing the side of his neck along the ink. I kept going when he didn't make me stop like he usually did. I kissed farther down, loving the taste of his salty skin on the tip of my tongue. I caressed his inked shoulders then ran my hands down his arms while pressing my breasts against him.

The tension slowly eased out of his muscles as I explored his body from behind, taking my time. This was the first time he let me do this and I wanted to take care of him like he did me. These couple of nights, they were more than just Ream getting me back. It was me finding a part of myself that I'd lost. He'd seen that. He recognized that I was hiding from myself as much as I was from him and everyone else. I'd always thought I was stronger facing this disease without anyone knowing. But I was stronger with Ream. I'd be stronger still when I told Emily. Strength came from believing in yourself, not hiding from yourself.

Ream looped his arm around my neck and dragged me onto his lap where he proceeded to kiss me. It was the kind of kiss that made me proud to be his, to want him to take care of me. Not because I was weak or couldn't do it myself, but because he cared about me.

"You're not going to ask me?"

Yeah, I wanted to know who was on the phone. I had to bite my tongue to stop myself from asking, but I trusted him. He needed that from me. "No."

He nodded and stayed silent as I sat with my legs straddling him, his hand weaving through the strands of my hair. It was comforting and sweet and even though we had so much intensity between us, this moment was just the opposite and I reveled in being able to share it with him.

"When I'm with you, it feels like I've been given a second chance at living. I never thought I'd get that." He lowered his head for a brief second, his fingers splayed over my back stroking with the slightest touch. "I can breathe easily with you. When we were apart …" His finger slid over my lower lip back and forth. "You ever feel like you're body is silently screaming? Like you're constantly missing something, but you can't figure out what?" Yeah, all the time, but I'd never admit that to anyone. "For almost three fuckin' years, I felt like that. I didn't know at first, but then when I figured out it was you I was missing all the time, Jesus, the scream-ing, it stopped, Kat. And it became tranquil and beautiful.

"You think I brought you here for you? I'm not that nice of a guy, Kat. I brought you here for me. So I could glue you back to me." He leaned forward and kissed me then whispered against my lips, "It's permanent glue, baby."

Holy shit. I didn't know what to say. My heart pounded so fast with my lips parted, my breath was hesitant and uncontrolled.

"I'll do anything to keep you. You have to get that, Kat. Your MS I can't stop or control, but I'll fuckin' try. I may not deserve you, Christ, I know I don't deserve you, but I'm taking you anyway and when we go back, I'm making sure everyone knows it."

Wow.

He cupped my chin and made me look at him. "We won't ever be done."

"You know that sounds crazy, Ream. Relationships don't work that way."

"They do with me." He kissed the tip of my nose.

I was silent. What he was saying was what I knew already. Somewhere I knew that whatever happened with his sister made him this way. He warned me. I did know what I was getting into with Ream, but I also knew that he'd never physically hurt me. He'd pro-tect me with everything he had and I did want that. I wanted every part of Ream.

"Kat." His tone was rough and tweaked with a hint of frustrated warning.

I slipped my arms around his neck and kissed him. He groaned and I felt the smile on my mouth as I gave him what he needed: my acceptance of the man he'd become.

"I'm moving into your bed."

This wasn't a question. It was a statement and I rolled my eyes. "Then you're buying a bigger bed."

It was a tight chuckle, but still a chuckle. I desired every part of this man, his smile, his laugh, how he looked at me and made me feel ... he made me feel whole.

"We need to get back." Then he kissed me and it made my insides all mushy and wishing he'd brought condoms. He stroked the side of my face, and I noticed the tension in his expression. "The phone call was Lance."

"What? Why the hell would he call your phone?"

"Because you're not answering yours."

"Shit. What a douche." Stupid. Did Lance not see the overturned table at the bar or forget that Ream tried to beat him up at the hospital? "What did he want?"

"To know where you are."

If Ream hadn't looked so serious I would've laughed at Lance's stupidity, but I sobered when I thought of what Ream had said on the phone. "Why did you say cheat? What did he ask you?"

"It was nothing, baby. He was just saying shit to get me riled." Ream got to his feet bringing me with him, his hands now on my ass. "Kiss me." It wasn't him asking.

And I did. Because no matter how much I wanted to think I was strong, I wasn't strong enough to ever deny Ream and I didn't want to.

I was his.

Chapter Fifteen

We didn't make it to the farm, at least not right away. I made him pull over at the drug store and came out with condoms. Ream thought I meant for later. I meant for now and I wasn't waiting.

Ream pulled out of the parking lot and headed back to the highway. I blared the music and bounced along to it. He tried to turn it down. I slapped his hand then undid my seat belt.

"What are you—" He frowned and it was cute because his eyes narrowed, and I saw the heated desire as I wiggled out of my jeans.

The car slowed. His hands clenched the steering wheel, and he had trouble keeping his eyes on the road. The bass drum vibrated through me, and I moved my body to it as I shimmied out of my shirt, leaving only my pink bra and matching undies.

I put my fingers under the edges of my panties and snapped the elastic.

"Jesus, Kat. I'm driving."

I raised my brows and licked my lower lip while I crawled up onto my seat and leaned across the gear shift. "Hey, baby?" I whispered right next to his ear so my heated breath hit the spot just below. "Can I ride you while you drive?" Then I reached down and placed my hand on his hard cock.

"Fuck." Ream looked over his shoulder then cut off a car as he swerved to the exit ramp then made a sharp right then another and skidded onto the shoulder.

I had already grabbed a condom and had it unwrapped before he slammed the car into park. I yanked down his zipper, pulled out his cock, and rolled it on.

He grabbed me around the waist and dragged me on top of him, the steering wheel pressed rigid into my back.

"I need you."

"No shit." He hooked his fingers around the elastic of my panties, and with one swift pull ripped them from my body. I don't know where they ended up; all I knew was that I had his cock in my hand and was sliding it through my wetness then sinking down on top it.

"Oh God," I cried as I drove deep. Then I sighed at the familiar comfort of him … settled inside me where he belonged.

It was finding all of him as I gave all of me.

I kissed him with urgency, my hands on either side of his head, fingers curled in his hair, as I pressed my knees into the leather seat and he slowly slipped out of me to the tip. When I felt his hips arching up, I pushed down as he sunk inside me again.

Over and over.

I put my hands on the headrest, the crinkling of leather beneath the pressure of fingers digging into the material. He met my thrusts with the same urgency, and I moaned throwing my head back. Pushing. Straining. Needing.

His finger caressed the puckered sensitive spot in the crease of my ass, and it sent waves of desire to another level. He moved away and I was … disappointed.

"No, I want you to." I grabbed his wrist and pulled it back to my butt.

He hesitated and then he trailed his finger through my wetness then came back and circled the spot again. He began pushing slow but insistently against the tension.

"Push out, baby. Let me in."

I closed my eyes and then did what he asked. My back arched at the strange, erotic feeling as his finger went inside my virgin ass. It was hot and incredible and I wanted more. When I opened my eyes, he was watching me and wasn't moving. His eyes were glazed over and it was like ... like he wasn't there with me—again.

I stroked his cheek then tilted forward and kissed him. "Come back to me, baby." At first he didn't respond. Then suddenly he groaned and was kissing me back, harsh and unyielding. His finger slipped in and out of my ass, matching my rhythm as I moved up and down on him.

I didn't know exactly what happened next. It was like we both locked in on one another, his finger in my ass, his cock deep, the music pounding through the speakers, our bodies interlocked. I drove him into me with a wild abandon. Up and down as hard and fast as I could, the steering wheel rubbing into my back, his eyes watching me until we both collided, crashed, and came together. I screamed and he groaned at the same time, bodies tensing and gripping one another as if we were afraid to let go.

I collapsed, my head on his shoulder, breathing raspy and heart pounding. I began to hear the cars speeding by and the odd horn beeping at us and realized anyone looking could see me sitting on top of him only in my bra.

And it didn't matter.

He cradled my chin in his palm and brought my mouth in close to his where he kissed me all sweet and gentle. "That was hot." He kissed my shoulder then my neck and up to my lips again.

"You left me for a bit. Where did you go?" That emotionless, almost cold, expression he'd had for a few seconds.

"My cock inside you?"

I gave him a duh look, eyes wide, brows raised, and lips pouting.

"My finger in your ass?"

"Yeah, Ream."

"Then I wasn't anywhere but in you."

Fine, he didn't want to talk about it, and I wasn't ruining great car sex by pushing it. "You owe me new panties." I slipped off of him and fell back in my seat and put my clothes back on minus the underwear. "And I like expensive ones."

"I'll buy you the whole goddamn store, beautiful."

I realized I really liked it when he called me beautiful. The scars I had … they'd always be there looking back at me in the mirror. They were now a part of my story.

So was my MS.

And it was time my story was told.

When we arrived at the farm it was noon and no one was there. Logan left a note on the fridge that was in his usual direct tone. "Get to the studio. You're late. I told you to be back by nine."

Shit, that must have been what he told Ream on the phone last night after I spoke to Emily. Ream didn't look too concerned though as he crumpled the note, tossed it in the garbage then snagged me around the waist and brought me up against him. "I'm in your bed tonight."

Having a say in the matter wasn't really any option, he was stating a fact, and Ream stating a fact meant it was happening. And I wasn't going to argue because I wanted him in my bed so I nodded. He kissed me and I melted into him, unable to resist the way his mouth moved over mine and sent my stomach into an all-out party.

"You painting today?"

I nodded, wondering how on earth I would concentrate when all I could think about was Ream sleeping in my bed tonight and what that entailed. I thought I might paint my first nude today. It wasn't like I needed Ream to model—his body was etched in me. I slid my hand down between us and placed my hand on his cock. It jerked then swelled under my touch.

He groaned, his hands tightening in my hair.

"Do we have time?"

"No," he said and I pouted. "And the next time I sink inside you, it's not going to be quick." He stared at me, eyes intense. "For once I'm taking my sweet ass time."

The thought made my cheeks feel like they were burning up because spending days in bed with him again … shit, I had an entire day to ponder that thought.

He chuckled and I think I fell a little bit more for him. "Is my Kat blushing? Oh, baby, you just sealed yourself to me."

"I didn't. I'm not. I don't blush. It's summer and it's hot."

"And we're in an air-conditioned house. You're hot and wet thinking about me sinking deep inside you again." Fine, I was and I really wanted to tear open another condom right now. "Have to go. Be good and no playing."

My mouth dropped open.

"Yeah. Only I get to get you off today. No playing until I get back."

Shit.

"I'm not into whips and shit, but I am into anticipation. And I'll know if you do. That lazy look in your eyes … Don't think you can hide it from me, Kitkat."

I guess painting a nude of Ream was out of the question. I'd never last the afternoon.

Ream kissed me again then let me go and was gone.

I was left standing with a throbbing clit and wondering if he could really tell if I pulled out my bunny. I hopped in the shower, a cold shower that was really quick before I changed my mind and said screw Ream's no-play order. But taking the chance he'd find out then making me wait for the long sweet ass sex … not worth it.

I texted Emily and found out she was helping Robert with a new racehorse. I suspected Logan didn't know she was, because no matter how tight they were, there wasn't a chance in hell he'd let her go to that developer's place alone. I'd heard Robert had hit on her right in front of Logan the first time they met.

I could only imagine what he did. Logan had this unemotional expression that was super scary. I may tease him, but I wasn't stupid enough to screw with that expression. My guess was Robert would find that out if he even looked at Emily the wrong way.

I painted the rest of the day, working on an abstract of Clifford from a photo I'd taken of him rolling, all four legs straight up in the air, the sun beaming down on his red and white barrel. I'd decided to do another series since my Havoc one did so well, this one of Clifford. It would be more abstract and fun than Havoc's with the theme of colors linking them together.

I hadn't forgotten about Lance's phone call and the mention of cheating. It also bothered me about Ream's sudden detachment during sex and his avoidance of me going down on him. The thoughts were pesky little flies that I kept swatting aside.

I heard the door then footsteps. Emily strolled into the sunroom wearing her tight black breeches and off white V-neck T-shirt, hair tied in a messy pony tail.

"Details. What happened between you two? Logan was so pissed at Ream. He was worried about you and even called Matt to find out what the deal was. Then he was furious because Ream is supposed to be the business head in the band and they had a new song to record this weekend. I don't know how many times I heard him say he was irresponsible." Whoops. Getting on Logan's bad side was never a good idea. "Don't worry I calmed him down with the sweetness of my mouth." We laughed and I plopped my brush into the jar of murky water. "I want to know everything."

"Well, I'm not giving you everything."

"What? You always do."

"This is different."

Emily raised her brows. "Really? Like how different?"

"He wants to move into my bedroom."

Emily laughed. "Wants or is?"

I snorted. "Yeah, you get it." Then I told her about jumping off the cliff, go-karting, and Monopoly.

"Jesus, Ream can have fun. He's always so serious or raving mad. Well, he was lunatic mad whenever he saw Crisis flirting with you. So are you ever going to tell me what drove you to piss him off so bad with that guy at the bar? Trust me, I get the not wanting to share part, but I'm here, Kat. No judgments. You know that, right?"

I nodded. I did. Emily was the type of girlfriend you wanted on your side of the court. She had this subtle strength about her, resolute, honest, and unshakeable. But sharing this part of myself had never been about her, it had been about me and how I saw myself.

"We need a bottle of wine. Maybe two ... or three." Because it was time I let her in.

It was midnight. We were smashed after three bottles of wine and a whole water trough of tears on her part after I told her. At first she was shocked and a little pissed off I kept something so serious from her, but Emily was Emily. She got it. She understood why I didn't want anyone to know.

Then she told me ... after the second bottle ... what happened in Mexico. Alfonzo, the waterboarding, the public sex with Logan. She cried and we held one another, a new chapter born between us. We both saw strength in the other for what we had gone through except mine ... well, mine was still unknown. No one knew what would happen. But it wasn't as scary suddenly. I never thought I'd say it, but I felt stronger with her knowing. Ream was right; hiding it had been doing the opposite of what I thought it was doing.

We ended up blasting the music and dancing. I had to stop a few times when my legs began to get the pins and needles, but I'd never give up something I loved. I figured if I went slow and moved my upper body rather than my lower I could manage the dancing. It was sexy as hell, at least that's what Emily said.

We were dancing slow and seductive to Joshua Radin when the boys came home. I was sliding my hands down my sides and Emily had her hands in her hair, her hips moving as she spun.

When we noticed them, all four stood in a line at the edge of the living room. Crisis smiled ear to ear while Kite tried to hide his grin by looking at his feet because Logan looked at both of them, scowling.

"Geez, it's late." Kite looked at his non-existent watch and vanished.

"Sugars, looks like you girls need some man company." Crisis wasn't so smart and started walking toward us. Ream grabbed his arm and I saw Crisis wink at me before he put up his hand. "I get it. No touch."

"Disappear," Logan said, and Crisis chuckled then left. Yep, always the shit disturber. "Upstairs." It was all Logan had to say and Emily was giggling as he stalked from the room.

Then we both said at the same time, "Drunk sex."

Emily walked, or rather tried to walk, more like stumbled over to Ream and stopped. He looked down at her frowning. Then she stood on her tiptoes and kissed his cheek. "I get it now. Look after her."

His eyes widened for a second. Then he looked at me and Emily was gone. "You told her?"

I nodded. Him standing there looking at me like he wanted to devour every inch of my body ... the tingles were good ones, and I was throbbing and drunk and needing him to walk toward me and kiss me.

Then he did.

And it was so hot. Confident, sexy, and badass because Ream had that darkness in his eyes that was mysterious. You were never really sure what he was up to, and that was a total turn on. He made me feel so feminine and desired, and my body screamed at him to get to me faster.

There was no hesitation when he reached me. His hand cupped the back of my neck, and with one pull, I was up against him as he looked down at me.

"You're too drunk for lazy slow sex," Ream drawled, and I felt his fingers curling in my hair, making the goose bumps I already had scurrying down my spine, scurry faster and call all their friends to join them until my body was covered in them.

I gave a half smile. "Yeah." 'Cause I was and I'd be asleep or passed out before he got to tasting me if we didn't get to where I wanted him fast.

Ream's other hand was at the small of my back, pressing me against him. "You going to remember this in the morning?"

I squished my lips together and thought about it then shook my head.

"Then I'll wait 'til morning to tell you how much I love you." He didn't wait for a response as he grabbed my hand and started striding through the house, me stumbling behind.

Floored by his words, it took me a few seconds, probably longer because my mind was swimming in red wine, to comprehend that Ream just told me he loved me. And he was going to tell me again in the morning when he was sure I'd remember him telling me.

But really we only made it to the kitchen and then he stopped. I banged into his back and he grunted before picking me up in his arms and carrying me the rest of the way.

He wasn't smiling, but I wasn't sure if it was because there was no lazy slow sex tonight, because I couldn't walk in a straight line, or because well, it was Ream.

He slammed my door shut with the heel of his foot then walked to the bed and tossed me on it. I bounced twice then settled and got up on my elbows as I watched Ream undress. It was methodical and concise and the whole time he kept his eyes locked on me.

He folded his clothes and placed them on the top of the dresser, and by then my anticipation was shot so high that I was afraid the second he touched me I'd come, but I wanted him inside me when I did. I wanted to clench around his cock and have his finger in my ass.

"Ream?" I was breathing so hard just thinking about it that by the time he was naked, his body straddling me, I was hyperaware of everything. Nothing was foggy or desensitized. Having a man like Ream on top of you brought sober to a whole new level.

He waited for me to talk, his finger hooked in my black yoga pants.

"I'm going to remember."

He still didn't grin. Instead, he gave a subtle nod. "Good. But I'll say it again in the morning anyway."

"Okay. Now stop fucking around and take my pants off."

That got a twitch of a grin, and then he yanked them down taking my panties with them. And there was no folding of my clothes. No, Ream threw them on the floor and then he kissed me.

Emily was right, drunk sex was hot.

Chapter Sixteen

I woke to the velvet touch of his tongue circling my nipple and arched my back, moaning. Ream's teeth grazed the sensitive spot. Then he swirled his tongue around it again before he took it in his mouth and suckled long and hard.

"Oh God." I was fully awake now, and Ream hovered over me. All I could see was the top of his head. I curled my fingers in his hair as he moved to the other nipple and sucked that one too then surprised me when he bit down. I cried out in pain then moaned when he soothed it with his heated tongue again. "Slow, lazy, sex?"

"Yeah, baby," he murmured with my nipple still in his mouth, and the vibration of his voice sent shivers across the surface of my skin.

He trailed kisses between my breasts then down farther to my piercing where his tongue fiddled with the silver. "This is hot. I love this." He lingered there a long while then moved where I had my tattoo. "And this is hot." He kissed the ink and moved down farther. "And this …" He looked up at me and I held my breath because he was hovering so close and yet not touching where I needed him to. He watched me as his finger slid from the base of my ribs to my belly button, hesitating, then glided into the wetness. I sharply inhaled. "This …" The pad of his thumb pressed on my clit and I squirmed. "Stay still." His voice was demanding and raspy, and I immediately stopped moving, my desire heightening. "Good girl."

Jesus. I was burning up and ready to come just from his words. The pressure on my clit remained steady, and I wanted him to move his finger back and forth. I was aching for him to do it, but he didn't. He kept pressure there while two fingers circled my opening. "This … is beautiful. It belongs to me now. It won't ever feel another."

His thumb made a slight movement and a jolt of pleasure hit me. I needed more. I had to have more. It was too slow. I didn't like it. I was impatient and I wanted his cock inside me now. "Ream."

He pushed two fingers inside and I stiffened and arched toward him, gasping. He stayed completely still, and when I opened my eyes again, I saw his face and it was magnetic. He stared at me and it was like he was wide open. Nothing hidden behind those dark eyes, no frown, no grin, just pure, raw honesty in his expression.

I ran my finger across his relaxed jaw, and despite the raging yearning that pulsated through me, I wanted this moment to last forever. "I belong with you. I belong to you. And I love you." The words easily slipped from my mouth, and I saw the flicker of disbelief on his face; then it was all confident and self-assured again.

"No matter what." He was demanding, as if he needed the confirmation that no matter what I'd always love him. I didn't believe love could be stopped. You could run from it, hide, and cover it up with other emotions, but love didn't give you a choice.

He pulled his fingers out and pushed them back inside. "No matter what, Kat."

I smiled. Then I did what he always did to me and cupped his jaw in my hand. "Yeah, Ream. That's what love is. Unconditional."

The look that washed over him was relief, and he suddenly looked so vulnerable. I'd never seen it before. He was always strong and self-assured, knowing what he wanted and taking it. But it was there, hidden behind his dark eyes, an exposed Ream that trusted me to give him the words I just spoke.

I traced his lips with the tip of my finger. "Ream. Love doesn't come with strings attached. It just is." His fingers were still inside me, connected to me. "We're going to collide. We'll fight and argue and then we'll have great make-up sex." That managed a raise of his brows. But he was so serious and I didn't get why. It was like he was afraid that now that he had me I was suddenly going to disappear. "That's us. And I love us. You push me and make me face what I hide from. I trust you to give me that because it's what I need. Baby, I love you for you. And I love who I am with you."

He stared at me for several seconds then bent down and kissed my abdomen. "I don't deserve you." His words were quiet as he continued to sprinkle tiny kisses across my skin. "But I'm too selfish to let you go."

I whispered, "Then don't."

There were no more words as his thumb started moving back and forth and I couldn't speak even if I wanted to. He kissed and suckled and his satin tongue tasted every inch of me while I remained on the cusp, Ream not allowing me to break. Building me up then slowly bringing me back down again.

By the time he slid the condom on, I was panting heavily and so turned on that I was afraid I'd come the second he entered me.

But he took his time, his mouth against mine, lazy and sweet, while I caught my breath and came back down again. He sucked on my tongue at the same time he entered my body and I gasped beneath him, stiffening at the feel of the sudden fullness. His hips jerked forward and he sank deeper while he groaned against my mouth.

His hand locked my wrists together above our heads while his other flicked and pinched my nipple, then slow and soft on top only to pinch it again and send a shooting pleasure-pain from my nipple straight to where he moved inside me, slow and deep.

He kissed me, made love to me, kept me needing more, until we both couldn't last any longer. Then he held my thigh around his waist as he pumped into me.

His back arched and his fingers dug into my leg while my hands, now free, were able to touch the hard hills and valleys of his body.

"No touching," he growled.

"But—"

"Please."

I saw the torment in his eyes and I wanted to take it away, so I put my arms above my head again and his eyes closed. He pushed into me, harder and harder. I moaned, the pillow clenched in my hands as I felt the pleasure swirl and then dive over the edge into a pool of heat.

Ream groaned, his body stiffening and then he thrust twice more into me.

His eyes flashed open and our gazes locked. Just like we were. Us. There was no longer a separation; we belonged and whatever happened, there was no key. Our lock was broken, just like we were. The thing was, I still didn't know why he was broken.

It took us half the day to get out of bed. When we finally did it was to shower, and we did it together making love against the wet tiled wall. Then Ream carried me back to bed where he tasted me all over again. I noticed he fell into that glazed look a couple of times, and once when I touched his ass, he shoved my hand away so violently that I was shocked.

I asked him about it, but he evaded the question again and quickly had me thinking about other things. It bothered me that whatever it was, he didn't trust me enough to talk about it.

It was Logan who forced us out of our bedroom. "Ream. I'm not telling you again." It had been the fourth time he'd knocked on the door and told Ream to get up. Now he pounded on the door and his booming voice had me throwing the covers over my head and trying to smother my laughter. Pissed off Logan hearing me laugh at him was not a good idea, even if I did have Ream here to protect me. And I had no doubt Ream would. He'd never let anyone hurt me, and I think that was why I saw that moment of vulnerability in him. Because he knew that he'd never be able to protect me from my disease. It was something out of his control and no matter what angle he tried to look at it … there was no cure.

"Get your ass out here, Ream. We're leaving for the studio in five." Logan's voice was hard and unrelenting, but then I heard him chuckle and Emily squeal. Okay, he wasn't that mad.

Crisis shouted in the background. "Aren't you satisfied by now, buddy? Jesus, I heard you all night long. Didn't hear her though. Guess you're not that good after all."

That got a reaction out of Ream and he was off the bed and out the door, unconcerned about his nudity as he went after Crisis. I heard a fuck and a door slamming then Logan laughed.

Ream came back in the room and shut the door in Logan's face. His body language was all tension and angry, but the corner of his lips curved up and his eyes danced with playfulness.

He walked straight for the bed, grabbed me around the waist, and yanked me to the edge so my legs were on either side of him. He cupped the nape of my neck, tilted my head, and then he kissed me and there was nothing lazy and sweet about it. It was one of those epic kisses that I never wanted to end.

"Got to go, baby." He let me go and I fell back onto the bed, the sheet swirling around me, caught between my thighs. I pulled the material up farther so there was tension on my sex.

Then I started moaning—loud.

I wasn't sure what Ream was doing because my eyes were closed, but I rolled around on the bed, the sheet between my legs as I moaned louder and louder. "Oh God, Ream." I screamed as loud as I could while still sounding breathless. "Yes. Oh God. Yes. That's it."

I did a long drawn out moan-scream then stopped, propping up on my elbow and smiling.

He shook his head, grinning, his jeans in his hand. I winked and he threw his jeans aside and dove onto the bed.

Within minutes I was screaming for real.

During the day, Ream recorded with the band while I helped Hank with the horses and painted. In the evenings Ream would come with me to the barn and we'd groom Clifford. Well, I'd groom and Ream would watch ... from a distance. I had to give him credit though. He did try feeding him carrots, and after a week he got close enough to stroke Clifford's neck.

The sweetest moment was yesterday evening because it was so unexpected and beautiful. Ream didn't even know I was watching him since I had gone into the tack room to put the brushes away. I realized I'd forgotten the curry on the hay bale, and when I came back out and saw Ream, I stopped and stared.

He was talking softly to Clifford, his hand resting on his thick neck and Clifford was arching around with his head tilted as if he was listening to him.

It was so unusual for Clifford to not nip and play and nudge. He just curled around Ream with his neck, head low, lips lazy, and ears flopping out to the side listening. I knew it was a moment I wanted to capture in a painting. I'd hang it across from my bed so I could wake up to it every morning. My two men.

Ream took me out for dinner nearly every night, and he admitted it was selfish because he wanted me all to himself. He came with me to my nutritionist appointment Matt had set up. Ream did most of the talking, adamant that the diet was doing more detriment than good by the way I was eating. He went on about needing more proteins and different ways to get more weight on me without compromising the specific diet of very little fats. I sat back silently listening because really it was amusing and I was getting a kick out of it.

I was thankful the woman wasn't a push over under Ream's badgering, and she smiled at me kindly before she put him in his place and told him he'd be uninvited to the next appointment if he refused to tone down his attitude and be quiet.

I laughed, which made Ream scowl and had the nutritionist looking at both of us like we were crazy. Then Ream listened while the nutritionist and I figured out a plan where I would hopefully stop losing weight, but still keep the fat content to a minimum.

Finally, it was the night of my gallery showing and I was excited, nervous, and a little apprehensive at seeing Lance again with Ream there. Okay, very apprehensive. I'd spoken to Lance a few times, although always when Ream was at the recording studio, and he was cool about everything and nothing was awkward between us. Although when I asked him about why he called Ream when we were at the cottage, all he said was that he was looking for me to discuss a sale. The thing was, the sale never came through. Lance said the guy changed his mind.

I finished putting on my lip gloss then stood up straight. The reflection staring back at me was the same, except for the two scars that were fading but still visible even with cover-up. But it wasn't that which made me look different, it was the lightness in my eyes. I felt it. Telling Emily had lifted a huge heaviness off me, even more so when nothing changed between us. And Ream … Ream was sweet, but most of the time he was bossy and possessive. I thought I'd get annoyed at all his texts, but when I heard my phone beep, I smiled and couldn't wait to see what he wrote.

"Jesus."

I spun around in my six inch red heels and black low backed dress. Ream stopped in the doorway to our washroom and stared. It made me feel beautiful; shit, he made me feel that way.

"Baby, you look fuckin' hot." He strode over to me, his hands on my hips as he yanked me into him so we both faced the mirror. He bent his head and kissed the naked spot just between my neckline and my shoulder. "God, I love you."

Tingles sprinkled my skin at his raspy whisper. His hands ran up my sides to my ribs and back down again to settle on my hips. He nibbled my ear, taking the pearl earring into his mouth. "I can't wait to strip you out of this tonight. Keep on the heels though, hot stuff. I want to fuck you wearing those."

I clamped my legs together because I wasn't wearing panties

and I so didn't want to have to get changed after hearing what he wanted to do to me. The no panties was a surprise for later.

His hand reached down lower and I could feel the edge of my dress inching up. I grabbed his hand before he discovered the no panties and had me up on the counter and forgetting that I had a show to get to before the guests arrived.

"I have to go. I need to make sure everything is set up." I turned around in his arms and he groaned with frustration before he kissed me. His mouth fused over mine, tongue pushing past my teeth and tasting of toothpaste and apple. I sagged against him for a few moments, melting in his arms, feeling like I could just stay here forever and be kissed by him. When his hand went down between my legs again, I smacked him on the chest, pulling away.

He chuckled and I loved the sound of it. It made me giddy that I could do that to him because Ream was too serious most of the time. I loved that we could play and laugh, and I suspected I was the only one who really got to witness that as often as I did.

"I'd love nothing more than for you to go down on me and have me screaming your name ..." He chuckled again because we both knew it wouldn't be that. It would be him inside me and taking me on the counter against the mirror. "But I'm meeting the caterers in a half hour."

"Lance going to be there?" His body went stiff and the playful look vanished. "I don't like the idea of you being alone with that fuckhead."

"No, he's coming later. But he knows I'm with you. He was cool at the hospital. And I talked to him the other—"

His eyes narrowed. "You saw him at the hospital?" Ream's lips tightened.

I sighed, running my fingers through his hair. "Baby, he just wanted to make sure I was okay. It was no big deal." Ream's face relaxed as I continued to stroke his hair and the back of his neck. "You have nothing to worry about. I'm with you."

"Who helped him get into your room?"

Gah … this was where we collided. Ream was protective and I got that. He lost his twin sister—the only family he had—to really bad shit. He wanted to keep any bad shit away from me, and he saw Lance as bad shit. I wondered if whatever that phone call was about was way more than Ream admitted.

"It doesn't matter. He just wanted to make sure I was okay. It was like five minutes. I need to go. I'll see you there." I tried to slip out of his arms but he held tight.

"I don't like him, Kat." Shit, it was Kat, not Kitkat or babe or beautiful. "I'll come with you. Give me ten minutes."

I linked our hands before he had a chance to go change. "Ream, you have to trust me." I squeezed his hand. "You need to meet your manager. Logan will have a fit if you bail." I curled my hand around his neck and pulled his head lower so I could reach his lips. My mouth moved over his trying to get a response and after a few seconds with my tongue in his mouth and my hands on his ass, he complied and kissed me back.

"I'm moving my art from his gallery after the show."

I felt the stiffness instantly ease from his muscles as he whispered in my ear, "Thank you, baby."

"I have to go. Love you."

He reluctantly let me go. "You going to be okay in those heels?"

And he was still concerned about my legs. It was sweet, adorable, and I got that despite being controlling and over the top possessive Ream did it because he cared.

I ran a finger down his cheek then across to his mouth where he grabbed it with his teeth and sucked it inside the warmth of his velvet mouth. Heat swirled between my legs, and I quickly pulled away as desire flooded between my thighs.

He yanked me back. "What's wrong?"

"Getting turned on before I go isn't a good idea."

"Why not? I like you turned on and I want you thinking of me."

I smiled and then leaned in close and whispered in his ear. "Because, panties ruin the line of this dress, so …"

"Fuck." Ream swore then his hand shot underneath my dress as I squirmed to get away.

"Hands off the merchandise, sexy." I darted under his arm, laughing, and he dove for me, his fingers just grazing my shoulder. "I'll see you there." I made a dash for the door and slammed it in his stunned face.

Before I managed to escape the house, Ream caught me. "You do that for me or the dress?"

Shit, I couldn't lie. "You." Because I loved the idea of Ream knowing I was naked underneath it.

Ream kissed me and it was heated but gentle and warm and made me a puddle of goo at his feet. I think he knew it too because he winked and then smacked me on the butt then told me to drive safe.

I arrived at the gallery two hours before the show. I made sure everything was ready, the caterer, the wine. The waitress was Molly from Avalanche, who Lance suggested we ask serve, and I thought it was a great idea. Molly needed the cash and Lance said he'd pay her well.

I fiddled with my art, making sure they were hung perfectly, and then when everything was done, I helped myself to a glass of wine. Molly arrived early too and we chatted for a while. Or rather I chatted; Molly listened with her head down, always staring at her feet. I needed to break her out of her shell or give her to Georgie for a night.

Some of the most prominent men and women in the city packed the gallery, thanks to Lance, Emily, and Brett. Emily shared invitations in the horse community and Brett to his real estate connections. I really had no idea who Lance's connections were, but I was thrilled at the turnout. A young man and his wife, who had a breeding farm of Gypsy Vanners, bought the set of Havoc paintings, which would set me up well for an entire year and help with a down payment for my own place.

Being most of my work was of horses, a good deal of the

thoroughbred racing community was there, including Richard, the developer Emily was currently talking with. She was smart to chat with him now before Logan arrived.

Georgie was currently on the arm of some mystery guy who wore a suit and didn't look like he'd be with someone that had pink highlights, a smart-ass mouth, and drank too much. She'd whispered to me earlier that he kissed with the sweetness of syrup and the bite of a candy apple. I'm guessing that meant he kissed damn good.

Logan and Ream planned to arrive after the meeting with their manager. Crisis and Kite popped in for a few minutes to show their support, but mingling with this type of stuffy crowd was not their thing. Within a half hour of arriving they made excuses and headed to Avalanche.

I swallowed the last of my champagne and was weaving my way over to Emily when I felt a touch on my hip. I smiled, assuming it was Ream as he always touched my hips. But when I turned I was looking up at Lance.

He took my hand and lifted it to his mouth and kissed the back of it. "Beautiful. Congratulations. A great turn out."

I pulled my hand from him. I know he was just being polite, but it made me uncomfortable when he held it longer than what was polite. I also didn't like him calling me beautiful, that was Ream's and suddenly I was wondering what I ever saw in this guy. "Lance. Thank you for this. The turnout is incredible."

"That's all you. All I did was send out invitations. Your work is what brought them here." He looked briefly around. "Where is your bodyguard?"

My smile was tight at the reference to Ream. "He should be here any minute. He had a meeting with his manager."

"Ah, yes, the rock star." I flinched and was about to excuse my-self when he ran a finger across the scar on my cheek. "My men haven't been able to come up with anything. A random burglary gone wrong it seems."

I raised my brows. "Actually, the police don't think there was anything random about it and whoever it was knew exactly how to avoid the security cameras in the condo." I caught Emily's eye, and she got the hint and started through the crowd toward me. "Listen, Lance, I better go mingle—"

Lance took my hand before I could escape and guided me to the back of the gallery. I didn't want to make a scene, so I forced a smile as I followed him, my back stiff and my teeth grinding. He led me to the small alcove where I had my largest painting of Havoc hanging. "Lance, I should go—"

He stopped in front of the six foot canvas of Havoc rearing up, dust swirling around her coat and fading from her hooves. "Your best piece. I understand it is of a horse that was shot."

"Yes. Havoc. But I think—"

He cut me off again and I felt more and more uncomfortable and put my hand on his chest to push him back when he said, "A survivor. Like you."

My eyes shot to his, not liking the reference to me.

He chuckled, a deep resonating sound that sent shivers through me, and they were nervous shivers. "Yes. I know all about you, Kat."

I certainly didn't like the sound of that. "I'll be moving my pieces out tomorrow morning."

He didn't seem at all surprised or concerned. Instead, he stepped toward me and I backed away until I was caught against the wall.

I pushed hard on his chest, not caring that a few patrons saw me do it, then slid out from where he tried to trap me. His hand snaked out and grabbed my arm. "Do you know everything about your boyfriend? 'Cause I don't think you do. I think he hasn't told you a single thing about what he was." I gaped at him then yanked harder, but he kept talking. "I have a hard time believing a beautiful woman like you would be with someone as … soiled as him."

I gasped, shocked at his insult, and then the rage erupted. I didn't care if I never sold another piece of art and he blacklisted me. This bastard had no right to say what he just did. I raised my hand and slapped him hard across the face. The sting in my palm felt damn good, and I wanted to do it again when my assault failed to wipe the malicious smirk off his face.

"You bastard." I raised my arm, but he grabbed my wrist.

I didn't have to look in order to know he was there. It was so distinct as if every molecule in my body awakened to his presence. And I was glad. I wanted Ream to beat the crap out of him.

Ream's voice was a low contained anger. "Get your fuckin' hand off her." Lance let go putting his hands in the air, smiling. Ream pulled me behind him where Emily stood looking nervous. Logan came to stand beside Ream. They both must have seen me slap Lance, and I suspected from their faces, they heard exactly what Lance said.

"I never fuckin' liked you. And I certainly don't like walking in to see you holding my girl while saying shit about me." Ream's voice was scarily controlled. "I especially don't like that she had to slap you to get your hand off her." Ream was toe-to-toe with Lance "You never deserved her for a fuckin' second. Her art leaves your gallery tonight."

Lance didn't seem at all affected by my scary boyfriend and smiled. But it wasn't his usual debonair, charming smile. This was tainted. "Deserve? Interesting you should use that word."

Logan stepped in and grabbed Ream's shoulder. "Not here. Let it go. This is your girl's show. Don't ruin it for her."

I piped up, "Oh, I don't give a crap about my show. I just want this bastard's face—"

"Kat, not the place," Emily whispered into my ear.

Yeah, she was right. This wasn't just about me; her clients were here, as well as Brett's.

Ream suddenly turned, grabbed my hand, linked our fingers, and started pulling me through the patrons. He stopped. "Washroom?"

I pointed to the right and he didn't say anything as he headed for the hallway.

I glanced over my shoulder and a cool shiver went through me as I caught Lance watching us. And it wasn't a friendly watch. Then I saw Molly staring at us with a tray of champagne in her hands. Her face wasn't hidden by her hair, and I saw her eyes narrow and lips pulled tight. She'd obviously heard or seen the exchange between Lance and me. Maybe that girl had some backbone after all.

I tripped in my high heels and Ream steadied me with a hand around my waist, but he didn't let up until we were locked behind the closed door of the bathroom.

He backed me into the wall, grabbed my chin in a bruising grip, then before I could take another breath, he kissed me. No, it wasn't a kiss; it was a possession that spun out of control. And God it was hot. He groaned as he gripped my hair and tilted my head back to deepen his kiss.

His body slammed me into the wall, and I gasped at his roughness, but a jolt of pleasure encompassed me. I lifted my leg to rub up against his thigh, and he grabbed my ass and lifted me up so I could wrap both my legs around him. I could feel my skirt stretching across the bridge between us, and all I wanted was to rip it off and have Ream sink inside me.

"Baby," Ream growled against my mouth causing a sweet vibration.

"You nearly lost it."

"I didn't."

"But I wanted you to."

He stopped kissing me, grabbed my chin, and we looked eyes. "You did?"

"Yeah. I wanted to see his douche bag ass on the floor."

"Fuck, Kat. Marry me." I gasped. "It doesn't have to be now, but promise me one day, you'll marry me."

It was my turn to freeze and it was like a whale's tail had just slammed into my chest and if I wasn't against the wall, I'd have staggered back. He wanted to marry me?

"Don't look so shocked." I cried out when he nipped my neck— hard and then tenderly licked and suckled. That would leave a mark and my guess was that was what he intended. "Where did you think this was leading? I want you to be my wife more than anything. I was waiting to ask you when I knew for certain you'd say yes."

I raised my brows. "So now you're certain I'll say yes?"

"Fuck yeah. You stuck up for me, then slapped that slimeball across the face. It was the most amazing sight I've ever seen. Even though I was pissed off as fuck that you had to do that, I was so turned on and proud of you all at the same time." He kissed me again and this time it was so tender it made my knees weak. "I can't wait to make you my wife, and yeah, I trust that you're going to say yes." He paused and made sure I looked at him before he continued, "I'm fucked up, baby. My past is shit and even though you don't know all of it, you get that. I've been dead for all these years and you've cracked through the shell. I can't ever go back into that darkness."

"Is that where you go sometimes?"

He flinched and I waited. "Yeah."

"You going to tell me at some point?"

"Yeah, baby."

"Okay." It was enough for now. At least he admitted that there was something.

Then it was my turn to kiss him and moan and feel the emotions sinking into me. It was deep and real and raw—it was us.

I let my legs slide down until my feet touched the floor. Then he yanked my dress up to my waist as I undid his pants and pulled a condom from his pocket and slipped it on him. Then he lifted me up again, his hands squeezing my ass, as he sunk deep in one thrust.

I groaned in pain-pleasure at the sudden intrusion. Then he moved inside me and I kissed him, forgetting all about Lance, the gallery, and all the guests outside the door.

It was fast and hot and it was Ream making it known I was his, but he didn't need to prove it anymore. I was his. He was a little screwed up, but so was I, and he was mine.

Neither of us said anything as he straightened my dress, and I zipped up his pants. Then I smiled, meeting his eyes that still burned with desire. "Yes."

He grinned. "Fuck, yeah."

Chapter Seventeen

He stroked my head, slow caresses that made me want to vomit.
But I'd done that already. I had nothing left in my stomach.
"You know what to do." He touched himself and it jerked.
I did. It had been eight months and I'd learned what was expected
of me.
I slid down and lay like I was supposed to.
Then I did what he wanted while he held my head making certain I
didn't pull away.

It was three days after the gallery incident and Ream invited me to the recording studio. Emily was going too because the boys had a new song and they wanted us to hear it. Logan was pretty damn hot singing—shit, he was mesmerizing—but Ream … Ream was serious and intense and he became the music, as if his guitar was a part of him. The day he'd sung to me at the pub was something special, and I'd take that over him singing with the band any day. But this was exciting too, and I couldn't wait to hear what they were recording.

Emily and I met them there around six before they wrapped up for the evening, and we were introduced to Dan, the sound guy, who patiently explained to us what he was doing; although all I saw were thousands of buttons and switches.

The band went on the other side of the glass, and after ten minutes Dan asked if they were ready. Logan nodded.

I sat beside Emily on one of the high stools, and we tapped our feet to the music. It had a slow feel to it, except when it came to the chorus and then the guys' voices got all raspy and deep sending goose bumps across my skin. My eyes never left Ream, and I didn't think it was possible to fall in love with him any more, but I did. And I got what Emily had been saying about falling in love with Logan all over again every night while on tour.

Ream ... There was something about him when he sang, there was that hint of unsteady darkness he always had lingering.

Okay, he was also super-hot. Tats, guitar ... I got why the women were all over him. I'd have to deal with that because despite trusting him, I knew I'd be jealous.

The song was magnetic and touching, the words hauntingly beautiful, about a woman broken and torn and her fight to find her way back. Then a man who will never give up on her, how pieces of him die every time she cries. How they find one another and heal. It wasn't like anything I'd heard before. When I looked at Emily she was crying.

"Our guys did good." I reached over and wiped away the tears with the pad of my finger.

"He wrote it for our wedding," Emily said.

"Damn, missy. That's hot." I looked back through the window and Logan stood at the microphone, his hands wrapped around it while Ream talked to him, but his eyes were on Emily.

Then Ream looked at me and I smiled giving him a thumb's up and mouthing, "You're mine." He must have got it because he half grinned then winked.

When Ream came out he grabbed me by the ass and picked me

up off the stool. I had to wrap my legs around his waist and my arms around his neck in order to stay balanced. Then he kissed me and I didn't care that Crisis was hooting and hollering and Kite was laughing. All I cared about was kissing Ream.

Afterwards we went to Avalanche and it wasn't busy being so early on a Friday night. Usually the crowd started rolling in around eleven, plus Matt didn't have a live band tonight. We ate and drank and I loved how Ream's hand rarely left my leg. I noticed it tighten a few times and he'd stiffen, but as soon as I looked at him, he'd kiss me and I'd forget all about what was unsettling him.

"I'll be back, beautiful." Ream got up and left the table. I saw him head to the bar and say something to Brett, and then they both disappeared in the back. It was odd; Brett and Ream weren't close or anything.

Emily drew my attention away from Ream and Brett when she mentioned Raven, a girl who'd been trapped in the sex trafficking in Mexico with Emily. "Her real name is London Westbrook."

Yeah that made sense. I didn't know much about sex trafficking, but I bet real names didn't exist once you were brought into that hell. "Did he tell you how she's doing?"

"She's disappeared."

"What?" The last I'd heard, Deck had taken her home to her parents in New York. "When?"

"Been gone a few weeks. It looks like she ran away. Deck called Logan a couple of days ago and wants us to keep an eye out for her. He says she may try and come back here." I didn't think so. The girl held a gun on Emily. "Deck's working on something big and has all his men with him except one."

"And that one is on Georgie," I said. Because Deck would never leave Georgie without one of his men watching her. I didn't know what he thought would ever happen to her, but it was so usual now that it was no longer unusual.

Ream slipped in beside me again and then dragged me onto his lap. Well, it wasn't really dragging because I went willingly. I think he partially did it because there were a few girls who recognized the band and started to hang around. Ream nuzzled my neck and I leaned back into him, loving how his one palm splayed underneath my shirt against my skin.

"What did you talk to Brett about?"

I shivered as his fingers caressed my abdomen with a feathered touch. "Nothing, baby."

I reached around behind him and curled my hand into his hair. "That answer isn't cutting it, hot stuff. Spill it."

It was Crisis who saved him from my inquisition as he started singing and tapping his hands on the table to the beat of the song playing. Everyone laughed and Kite joined in, picking up a spoon and a knife and drumming on the table.

It was a good night and it was even better that Ream was with me, holding me, and I knew we'd be going home soon ... and having drunk sex.

I swallowed the rest of my beer and noticed Molly was busy so I slipped from Ream's arms, who was chatting with Logan about the album, and headed for the bar. Okay, so I was still curious about what went down between Ream and Brett.

"Brett." I smiled at him and he nodded while he served a girl, who then slipped him a card to which he took and placed in his jean pocket.

He walked over and slammed a palm down in front of me. "Vodka?"

Whoa, where was his usual banter? His scintillating blue eyes settled on me and there was no wink, no smile. "You not get laid last night or something?"

He ignored the comment and poured me a shot. "Just one?"

I nodded. "Brett. What's up?"

He looked up and then I knew. I didn't have to turn around to see; it was the familiar shift in my body like a negative finding its positive. Ream's hands settled on my hips and he pressed into my back then leaned in, his mouth kissing my collarbone.

Shivers, heat, dampness, yeah, it all peppered my body. "Beautiful," he whispered and I sagged against him.

Brett put another shot down on the bar then looked at Ream. "Threaten me again and you won't like what happens." With that he walked away.

Whoa. What? I stiffened swiveling around on my stool. "What did you do?"

Ream didn't even look chagrinned; he merely shrugged and said, "He's been watching you for years. I just made it clear that it stops."

"What? Are you for real? Ream, Brett and I are friends. He's not interested, never has been."

"You a guy?"

"What?"

"You a guy, Kat?"

"Well, no, of course not."

"Then you don't know. Only a guy knows when another guy is hot for his woman. And anytime I'm here, Brett's watching you."

"Yeah, because he's like a brother. He's looking out for me. Matt is in his office most of the night so Brett steps up to the plate."

"A brother doesn't look his sister up and down while she dances."

"Oh. My. God. He so doesn't do that."

He kept his voice low but Brett was at the other end of the bar so he probably couldn't hear us. I did notice him glance our way. "Babe, he does. He was watching you the night you were dancing with that schmuck."

"Ream, seriously, that was almost three years ago."

"Yeah, and he's still doing it. He was watching you the night we danced. That isn't a guy who thinks of a chick as his sister."

"Well, Molly watches you and you don't see me threatening her." Because she was harmless. Ream was hot, I got that.

His brows rose as if my comment was ridiculous in comparison. Maybe it was because Molly was shy and looked at Ream while hiding under a veil of hair, but still, I was pissed that he thought it was funny.

I crossed my arms and cocked my hip. "What did you say to him?"

Ream's hands splayed my waist. "That if he looks at you like that again, he'll see my fist."

I snorted. "Jesus, Ream." But I shouldn't be surprised. That is exactly the response I should've expected.

"Kat, why would he always be watching you? He's never asked you out, but whenever I'm here I see his eyes on you."

"It's meaningless, just like Molly looking at you."

Ream's hands tightened on my waist. "I don't fuckin' like it. Men watching chicks lead to shit and I'm not taking the chance."

"What? God, Ream. This is going overboard. Brett's been around since Avalanche opened. He's Matt's friend. God, you know him. What's next? You going to say I can't be friends with Crisis and Kite? That we can't live with them anymore because you saw Kite looking at me?"

"No." Ream's face hardened and he was really agitated. "That's different. Brett has never been my friend and he's never hung out with us, has he?"

"Well, no but—"

"The guy has more money than he knows what to do with. Can have any chick he wants and yet he works here looking at my fuckin' girl. It stops." Ream cupped my chin and kissed me, right there in front of Brett. It was a deep, claiming kiss that made my knees weak and my pissed off attitude seeped into the unknown land of forgetting my name after that kiss.

But this was too far. Ream was going to alienate our friends if he continued down this road. I pushed on his chest. "No." He looked a little startled, and when I put my hand up, he went to move in again, his brows lowered dangerously over his eyes. "You need to apologize to him. You stepped over the line this time, Ream."

His back stiffened at the word apologize. "Not happening."

I put my hands on my hips. "God, you're such an ass."

"Yeah, but I'm yours."

"No. Not if you're going to act like this."

His eyes narrowed. "You threatening me, Kat?"

"Not a threat. A promise." I would not be putting up with him threatening my friends. I got that he had issues, I accepted that, but there was a line and he just broke it.

"This is fuckin' bullshit," Ream shouted.

"Bullshit? Ream, this is crazy. Can't you see that?"

"Maybe it is, but I'm not apologizing for it. Bad shit happens when guys watch a girl."

"Does this have something to do with your past? Because if it does maybe it's time you told me."

He stared at me for several seconds, stiff and unyielding then said, "Let it go, Kat."

"Are you kidding me? Give me something here, Ream. I'm trying to give you time, but acting like this for no reason won't cut it."

"I have my reasons."

"Then tell me."

"I can't." He went to take my hand and I pulled back. "This is who I am, I told you that."

"Yeah, and I accepted it, but I let you in. I gave you all of me and you're still holding back from me. Why? I need to understand."

"Back off."

I huffed and crossed my arms. "Wow, I really don't like you right now." It was more to myself than him, but he heard me and flinched.

I felt someone's hand on my arm and turned. It was Emily and she looked worried. I saw the guys sitting at the table and watching us.

"Kat, maybe we should go. I'll drive us back to the farm. I've only had one beer." Emily squeezed my hand and then tugged, whispering, "Let's go before you both say something you'll regret."

Shit. Maybe she was right. I needed to cool off and so did Ream.

I nodded then followed after her.

"Kat." Ream's voice cut into me. It was pissed off and quiet like I'd imagine the silence after the pin on a grenade is pulled. But I didn't turn around because Ream had to get that this went over the line. Then his voice changed and it was haggard. "If I tell you I might lose you."

I stopped, but I didn't turn around. "You'll lose me if you don't."

We both needed to settle down before we had a collision. Ream would get what I was saying. We both were just so stubborn that stepping away from our fights was sometimes the best course of action.

"Drunk make-up sex is amazing," Emily whispered in my ear. Yeah, I hoped I'd get that tonight. We both just needed to cool off. "And make him beg a little."

Hmm, my guy begging. I might never do it, but he sure could. That sounded like great make-up sex. And then maybe I could persuade him to give me a part of what he was hiding.

But I didn't get the begging or amazing make-up sex because Ream didn't come home. I lay awake most of the night, and when I couldn't resist anymore, I texted him. After a half hour passed and it was now three in the morning, I called and it went straight to voice mail. I knew he was pissed off, and Ream liked to think things through, so I thought maybe he'd taken off to that cottage to think it over. Where else would he go?

He probably crashed at Matt's condo. I was overthinking. Besides, I had walked away from him last night.

I texted again then got out of bed and went into the sunroom and painted until I finally saw the sun rise. My phone never rang, dinged, or vibrated.

I went into the kitchen and made coffee.

By the time I got to my third coffee, my heart was racing and my hands trembled so bad that I had to keep them steady by inter-locking them around my mug.

Fear and uneasiness started to sink into me. It was a combina-tion of mistrust of Ream not being able to cope with what I needed from him and the memory of the morning the police officer knocked on our door. The two were colliding. One was the dread that some-thing had happened to Ream and I was worried about him, and the other was scared he'd taken off and I was furious with him.

I was ten years old when the police officer told us they were gone. That my father had been drunk and killed them both instantly. The begging, the crying, the praying … I'd done it all. None of it worked. I wouldn't get a second chance at telling them I loved them. They were just gone one day. I'd cried for so many days that I couldn't even remember what it was like not to cry. And then when I finally stopped, I knew I'd never do it again because all it did was make me feel worse and never changed the outcome.

And now Ream hadn't come home. We'd been out drinking just like my parents had. Was he dead or dying somewhere? Or had he left me? Jesus, I was being stupid. We had a fight and he was prob-ably passed out in Matt's office or condo. I picked up my phone again to call him when a text from Ream's phone came through.

Kat, it's Molly. I saw his phone and that you called and texted numerous times. Ream's here with me. I'm so sorry, Kat.

The sick feeling that came over me was crushing, like I'd been teased with a lifeline when the text came through that Ream was okay and then the lifeline was ripped from my hands and I was drowning. I stared at my phone reading the words over and over again, wondering if I had misinterpreted them. Texts were misinter-preted all the time.

He was with Molly? *With* Molly? No, I was overthinking it. It couldn't be true. Don't let it be true.

I ran upstairs and without knocking, barged in Crisis's room. "What happened to Ream last night?"

Crisis groaned. He had his arms above his head gripping the headboard and his face was contorted as if in pain and then I saw the blankets move. "Ahh, sugar, I was so close." The sheet flung back and a girl popped her head up.

I didn't apologize. I didn't give a shit that he was getting sucked off and I'd ruined it. All I wanted to know was why Molly was texting me that Ream was with her. "Why didn't he come home with you? Did he leave with Molly? Why is Molly saying Ream's with her?"

Crisis threw the covers back and I caught full view of the naked woman lying on top of him. He smacked her butt. "Get out of here." He reached for his jeans on the floor and pulled out a wad of bills. "Call a cab." The girl had no shame and crawled out of bed, grabbed her clothes, and disappeared into the washroom.

I turned away as Crisis threw his legs over the side of the bed, not caring that he was naked and I was standing a few feet away. I heard the rustling of material and him jumping a couple of times as he pulled on his jeans. A drawer opened and shut then he was next to me.

"Okay, let's go."

I turned and banged right into him, not expecting him to be right there. "Where?"

"To get him."

"We can't just go get him."

"Why not?"

"I don't know where Molly lives." And I was terrified to go. My head was reeling as I imagined the worst case scenario.

"Matt does." Yeah, he had to have it for employment records. "Kat, I know what you're thinking. But it would never happen. That guy is crazy about you. He probably just crashed there."

"Why would she say she's sorry?"

He shrugged. "You're a chick. Molly's shy, insecure. She probably feels bad you guys fought or something. I'm going to kick his ass for fucking up my morning BJ though."

"Just like that? We go there?"

Crisis shrugged. "Listen, sugar. Why wait around worrying? By the looks of you, you did that all night." He leaned over and snagged his keys from the dresser. "He needs a ride back here anyway. Fucker is probably feeling like his ass is on fire and his throat is like sandpaper after the shit he drank last night."

I started to breathe a little easier. Crisis was right. Molly took him back to her place because he was drunk and she was saying sorry because she saw Ream's phone and how worried I was. The idea of Ream ever cheating on me was ridiculous.

But I ate my words the moment I saw Molly when she answered the door. It was all over her face. The guilt, the way she avoided looking at me, how she shifted uncomfortably. Crisis must have seen it too because he shoved the palm of his hand into the door and forced his way in.

"Stay here."

But I didn't. I couldn't and I followed him as he took the stairs two at a time then started opening doors. It was the third door he flung open that he stopped.

I came up behind him and he blocked me with his broad shoulders then slammed the door shut again. He grabbed me around the waist and pulled me back. "Kat, you need to wait downstairs. Better yet, wait for us in the car."

"Crisis, no. What did you see? Is he okay?" Panic blanketed me as I started running scenarios through my head. Molly was here, so it wasn't like he was fucking her or anything. But had he? Had she just crawled out of bed with him? She looked guilty and Crisis wouldn't let me in the room.

"I'll get his shit together and we'll meet you at the car." Crisis wasn't often very forceful, but his tone was sharp and stern and he wasn't taking no for an answer.

"No. Fuck no." I pushed at his hands on my waist and tried to get him to let me go. "I need to see. Let me see."

"No, Kat. I can't let you do that, for both your sakes."

What the hell did that mean? Oh God. That wasn't good. Both our sakes? Ream and me? He called me Kat, not sugar. He was being insistent. It was bad. Whatever was behind the door was bad and I couldn't let that go.

I struggled to get away. "Damn it let me go."

He picked me up off my feet and started carrying me away from the door. Molly was at the top of the stairs, her eyes wide and her fist held to her mouth as she watched.

"Put me down." I kicked with both legs and heard him grunt. My nerves shot off like rockets and the pins and needles played dominos on my legs. I knew within minutes if I didn't slow down and calm down, they'd go numb.

But I had to know. If I didn't see for myself, I'd always wonder why Crisis wouldn't let me in that door. Somewhere inside me I already knew what I'd see. The emotional upheaval was ripping at my insides with a rusted jagged knife. Because I knew. I knew Ream was in bed with another woman. I felt it. Crisis wouldn't be so adamant about me leaving unless it was something so devastating.

And I had to know for sure. I had to see with my own eyes. Because I couldn't believe that Ream would ever do that to me.

He wouldn't do that.

He can't destroy us.

Oh God, Ream.

Don't break us.

I jammed my elbow back into Crisis's face, and he cursed as his arm released me. I stumbled back toward the room, my hand on the banister for support. He yelled for me to stop as he came running after me.

I threw open the door.

It was like I was watching a scene in slow motion and I was in it. The long drawn in breath that caught on the gagging fish hook in my throat. A hook that had pierced through my heart and was slowly being dragged from my body.

I was choking.

Unable to breathe.

Unable to move.

The agony ripping me apart, and all I could do was stand there and look at him.

Ream didn't just break us.

Ream executed us.

Chapter Eighteen

My half sob, half scream was like a tortured cat in the dead of night.

Ream lay on his stomach, his face turned away from me. On his right arm I saw the butterfly tattoo and maybe if I hadn't, I would've tried to find a way to believe it was some other man lying naked with a woman beside him.

But it was Ream, and the girl was curled into him, her hand in his hair as she leaned on her elbow watching me. I stared frozen, unable to move, as I met her brilliant green eyes that were filled with a cocky, knowing gleam.

The stark white sheets were tossed aside, and it was from the guy with the lean, hard body lying on Ream's other side. I choked on my gasp as I saw the young guy's hand on Ream's ass, gently stroking. He caught my eye and then squeezed and ran his finger down the crack.

No. Oh God, no.

The guy chuckled and the lanky blonde girl shifted, snuggling into him further, her head lowering. It was obvious she was kissing him, although Ream never moved even when the guy began to crawl on top of Ream.

I put my hand over my mouth and staggered backwards, my spine hitting the railing, eyes wide and filled with horror. I was shaking so bad I couldn't stand anymore and collapsed. Crisis grabbed me before I fell and gently lowered me to the floor where he held me in his arms.

"No." I repeated the words over and over in my head like a broken record. My stomach sloshed and careened, and I was unable to hold down the coffee I had and leaned over, vomiting on the rug. "Why?" I felt the wetness of tears on my face. They were real and I couldn't stop them from falling as the image of what was behind the door hit me over and over again.

"Jesus." Crisis held my hair away from my face and stroked my back. "Let's get you out of here."

My legs were numb and the devastation was so overpowering that I couldn't move. I wanted to tear into the room and rip him apart. I wanted to yell and scream and fight him with everything I had. But none of that could happen with my nerves reacting and sparking off. I was falling apart. I felt the pieces of myself crumbling to the floor and like dust, disintegrating.

Tears trailed down my cheeks and I sobbed so hard that I was having trouble taking in air. I'd never get the image out of my head. I wouldn't survive this. I'd given him all of me, every single piece, and I had nothing left.

There was no key. We'd been locked together and now … now I had no way of getting myself back after this.

"Please, Kat. You need to breathe here. Deep breaths okay. I'm sure this is not what it looks like."

His words caused me to snap. "He was naked in bed with a guy touching his ass and a woman lying next to him. Not what it looks like?" I screamed and couldn't stop. "How else do you want me to take that, Crisis? Tell me." I slammed my fists into his chest. "Tell me, goddamn it. I need to know. 'Cause if you don't tell me, I'm going to drown here." I started punching and punching until he wrapped me up in his arms and I buckled like a limp doll into his shirt.

"Oh, sweetie, I don't know. Jesus, I fuckin' don't know."

I had nothing left. Ream had all of me in him and now it was destroyed. "He was my sanctuary. My home. I loved him." I didn't even recognize my own voice as the choked words fell from my lips. "He burnt it to the ground." And all that was left were ashes of me being separated and blown apart in different directions.

Ream undid me.

Crisis picked me up in his arms and carried me out to the car.

The unfamiliar tears became familiar again as they kept spilling down my cheeks like a torrential downpour. I didn't have the energy to wipe them away any longer as I curled into a ball on my bed in the darkness. The curtains drawn, the door locked, and the insistent knocking of Emily now gone after several hours.

Words had been strangled from my throat. I was unraveling. A shred of paper lifted up in the breeze then pushed around, never knowing where I'd land. Confused and … God, the hurt was so overwhelming that my insides were cramped.

The worst part … the most horrific, agonizing part of it was that I wanted Ream to hold me and take this all away. It was fucked up and yet … the comfort of his arms … but then it hurt more because I knew he'd taken that away and I'd never get it back.

My mind screamed over and over again—why. Why would he do that to me … to us? He wanted to marry me.

But why? Why fight for me then throw it away?

I heard running footsteps and a loud bang then a ruckus as if fighting.

"Don't you fuckin' dare, asshole," Crisis shouted. "Leave."

"Get out of the way." Ream's voice was laced with a husky sound, as if he'd been shouting too much and it was dry and torn.

"Ream, please. Give her time. She doesn't want to see you right now," Emily said, and I could hear the crackled tone. She'd been crying and she'd never left, sitting outside my door for hours.

I heard a scuffle and wrapped the sheet around me and ran into the bathroom and locked the door. I got into the bathtub, closed the shower curtain, and sat with the sheet up over my head.

This … everything I was and am at this very moment … it was what I'd been hiding from my entire life. The feeling of no control. Of being weak and vulnerable. Powerless to stop the pain.

I hid behind my flirting, my smiles, and my avoidance of telling anyone about my disease so I never had to feel like this.

Now that had all been ripped and frayed apart … I'd become the person I hated and never wanted to be. I became weak and helpless to the emotions.

"Kat!" Ream's voice wasn't weak or vulnerable. No, he was merciless as he yelled my name over and over. "Kat. Open the fuckin' door."

I cringed when the pounding on the door started. They were loud hard thuds, and I knew he was trying to kick down the door.

"Kat!" A scuffle. "Get the fuck back, asshole. I have to talk to her." I heard more wrestling and then the door banged again.

And again.

And again.

I heard the second it gave way to the pressure, the wood splitting and the door hitting the opposite wall. Then footsteps.

I jumped when the knocking started on the bathroom door, but it wasn't pounding and forceful. It was soft and gentle and that made it worse.

"Baby. Please. Talk to me." His voice was quiet and yet still threaded with tension. "I swear. What you saw … Jesus, baby, that wasn't real." I heard a low curse and his fist hit the door. "It was real, but it wasn't me. Let me explain."

I heard a slight thump and it was either his forehead against the door or his palm. I held my knees tighter to my chest, willing all of it to go away. Begging it not to be true, just like I had when I was ten years old. But it had been true. Just like it was now.

Ream cheated on me. He'd lied to me, he fought to open me up, and when he did, it was beautiful. And then he ripped apart the beautiful and made it ugly.

"Christ. I love you. I can't lose you. Please. We need to talk about this. I'll tell you, baby."

His words struck me. It was as if he'd been right in front of me and slapped me across the face. I threw the sheet aside and stormed to my feet. Fury encased me. Love wasn't lies and broken promises. It wasn't opening someone up and bringing them into your heart and then tearing their heart out.

The anger burned so deep that when I opened the door and faced him, it was with a red haze of blurred tears. I curled my hand into a fist then swung, cuffing him as hard as I could across the jaw. His head tilted back at the force, but he didn't move. His hands were braced on either side of the door frame and I could see Emily and Crisis a few feet behind him.

"Did you fuck Molly too?"

He flinched then reached for me. I heard Crisis move toward us and then Ream stepped to the side and slammed the door, blocking out Crisis and Emily. The lock clicked.

"Ream. Open the goddamn door, buddy, or I'll break it down."

"Crisis, give me five minutes. Five fuckin' minutes. You know I'd never hurt her," Ream shouted back.

A thump on the door. "Sugar? You good with that? If not, I'm breaking down this door."

Was I? Not really, but Ream standing in front of me looking haphazard, eyes wild, and … yes, there was fear there. I needed to hear this, not to find an excuse to forgive him, but to find more reasons to hate him. "Five minutes." I heard Crisis walk away, but he swore the entire time.

Ream stepped toward me and I held out my hand. "Don't you dare fucking touch me."

He nodded then stepped back until he was against the door. His eyes were glassy and red, he reeked of alcohol, and his T-shirt was on backwards and inside out. The tormented look on his face …

guilt. Well, he could rot in that guilt for the rest of his life.

He rubbed his hand back and forth on top of his head like he always did when he was agitated. "Baby—"

"Call me that again and this conversation is over."

His face contorted as if he'd just been whipped by my words. Then he straightened his shoulders and met my eyes. There was a sudden hardness there and it was dark and cold, and it made me want to escape.

"When I was a teenager … I was a prostitute."

His words hit me like I'd been punched in the stomach with a battering ram, and I fell backwards until I hit the wall, my eyes wide with shock. The wave of pins and needles that already plagued my body tripled, and I slid down the wall until my butt hit the floor. It was either that or I was collapsing.

Oh God, what? How? Why? He'd cheated on me for money? He ruined us for money? No. No. It didn't make sense. Ream didn't need the money. Why would he do that? How could he hide something so … so totally fucked up?

"Bab—Kat, it was a long time ago when I was a kid. Jesus …" He exhaled a long breath of air. "It was to pay off a debt. I didn't … Christ, Kat, I'm not proud of what I did."

"So, what? You're doing it again?" God, I couldn't even talk about this. What he'd done didn't make me sick; it was that he was doing it now. That … that he hid it from me after I let him in. I picked up the small stainless steel garbage can and threw it at him. It missed, but it made a loud crash as it hit the wall. "Fuuuckkk. I let you in! I gave you all of me!"

He put his hands on either side of his head and curled his fingers around the short strands before slowly sliding down the door until he sat on the bathroom floor, his knees bent and his head in his hands. "No. Fuck no. Last night …" He looked up at me and there was confusion and bewilderment in his eyes, like he was lost in a nightmare of memories. Like me. "I don't know what happened last night. I can't remember shit. I left the bar earlier than the guys. I wanted to get back to you. I planned on cabbing it back to the farm and then I saw Molly outside and we shared a cab. Her place was on the way, but then ..." He closed his eyes, brows lowered as if he was thinking. "She was crying about her ex-boyfriend being back, and she was scared he was in her place. So I went inside to make sure he wasn't there." He looked up at me. "Kat, I can't remember anything after that. I swear. We may have had a drink together, fuck." He hit his head with the heel of his hand. "Maybe I said I'd stay a while because she was scared."

"So you were too drunk to know that you were fucking another guy and a woman?"

"They were her roommates, Kat. I don't know shit. I can't fuckin' remember shit. I woke up an hour ago and Molly told me you and Crisis had been there."

An ice cold hand gripped my chest and yanked—hard. Lies. To save himself after he ruined me. "Bullshit. Did you fuck Molly first? Who else, Ream? How many other men and women have you fucked since we've been together? Were you lying when you told me you hadn't been with anyone since we were the first time? Drinking too much doesn't cut it. And you say you used to do it for money? Well that doesn't get you a fucking pass to cheat on me now. Thank fuck we used condoms because you're a rotten piece of shit and I want nothing of you left inside me. Ever."

He didn't say anything for a long time and I was huddled with my knees to my chest, afraid to look at him, not wanting a single reminder of who he was. I wanted to erase him from me.

"Yeah. I am."

His husky whispered words made me look up and it was a mistake. I witnessed the tear teeter on the edge of his right eyelid then in slow motion, it dropped onto his cheek. The debilitating ache in my chest tore a scream from my throat, and I scrambled to my feet.

I needed out of here. I had to get out of here now. "Let me out. I want out."

Ream slowly stood and the devastation was clear on his face, the pursed lips, the drooping eyes, the trembling in his hands as he raised his arm to run his hand through his hair.

He moved to the side and I approached, weary and afraid he'd touch me. Because I couldn't handle him touching me again, the last pieces of me tentatively held together would crack. Who was I kidding? I'd already cracked.

I turned the doorknob and his whispered words hit me. "You always did deserve better than me, beautiful."

I don't know why his words hit me so hard, because I did deserve better than a guy who cheated on me. But it was more than that. He'd always said that to me. He never thought he was good enough for me and now I knew why.

If he hadn't cheated on me, if he'd told me of his past … I knew with everything in my heart that I would've loved him still. I'd have accepted that part of him because it made him who he was today. I understood why he'd said women were always just objects to him. It made sense. He used them; it had been a job. Had? No, it was.

I walked straight into Emily's arms, and she wrapped me in her warmth as she led me away. I don't know where we went, just that she held me for a really long time until I finally slept.

Chapter Nineteen

Days went by in a haze of grief stricken pain. Matt stayed at the farm the first few days leaving the bar to Brett to look after. Between him, Emily, and the guys I was forced to get out of bed every day and function. Georgie even came over and slept in my bed with me for two nights, holding me in her arms and never saying anything— so unlike her. Somehow she knew the silence was what I needed.

Ream disappeared. He'd even left his new phone on the kitchen counter. Everyone knew what had happened, that he cheated on me, but I didn't mention what Ream said about his past. Maybe it was because I owed him for keeping my secret.

My symptoms were bad, the pins and needles affecting my hands and sprinkling across my stomach as well as my legs. I woke up every morning uncertain whether I'd be able to wash my hair because I'd lost feeling in my arms if I held them above my heart for too long.

I took the pills in my nightstand, the valium to help settle my nerves. Some people took marijuana to help calm the symptoms, but the few times I tried it my heart started racing like mad and I didn't like it. The small amount of valium was enough to calm the tingles and relax the nerves that were short-circuiting.

After a week Logan asked if I knew where Ream was. I asked him if he'd checked Molly's. It was a sassy remark and Logan wasn't impressed, although he let it slide. I think he got what I was going through because he ended up pulling me into his arms and hugging me.

I was hurting and knew I would for a really long time. The only reason I even stuck around and didn't move to Matt's condo to get away from everyone was because of Clifford. He was the only one I could talk to and often at night I'd slip out of bed and go into his stall and sit and cry where no one would hear me. There was no judgment. Clifford just nudged me with his nose or stood and quietly munched on his hay.

It was three weeks and still no one had heard from Ream, and even I was getting concerned. I hated him for what he did, but love didn't die in a moment's reckoning. Love was too powerful to just vanish.

I heard the creak of the barn door and then the soft footfalls on the cobblestone coming toward me. I didn't have to look up to know it was Emily.

"Kat, it's been three weeks." Emily put her hand on Clifford's shoulder and he curled his neck around so he could nibble on her shirt. "No one's heard from him. Please. If you have any idea where he might be …"

I continued to brush Clifford's barrel then moved to his red dappled rump. Emily yelped and I knew Clifford had nipped her. My horse stomped his foot when she shoved his muzzle away.

"I wouldn't ask you if it wasn't important, but … if he's in trouble we need to help him. He's an asshole. A low piece of shit for what he did, but he left here all fucked up and … Kat, we're worried."

Worried about him? I was going crazy without him. Insane. Hurt. I wanted to find him so I could hit him again. I wanted to find him so I could look at him and know without a shadow of a doubt that I hated him. That I did the right thing. Every single day it hurt to open my eyes and face another day without him. Knowing what he did to destroy us … for what? An unemotional fuck?

"I gave him everything of me. He took it and I can't get it back.

Do you know what that's like? Waking up every morning and being faced with hating the man you swore to love for the rest of your life." I leaned my forehead on Clifford's flank, and his sides quivered like a butterfly's wings against my skin.

Emily rested her hand on my arm. "Yeah, Kat, I do."

I looked up at her and saw the tears in her eyes. Yeah, she did. She knew exactly what I was feeling right now because she'd hated Logan at one time.

"What he did was wrong. I hate that he did that to you. Christ, I want him to come back just so I can beat on him. But Crisis is his best friend and he says he's never taken off like this before. It's been too long, Kat."

"Why do you think I'd know where he is?" But I suspected. It wasn't like I knew exactly where it was, but the cottage was the only place I could think of that he'd go.

"You do, don't you?"

I hid my face in Clifford's shoulder and nodded. "He was in me, Eme. Now ... God, I feel ... I feel so empty and alone. He made me weak, and I hate that he did that to me."

"Oh, sweetie." Emily folded me into her embrace, her hands stroking my back. "You're never alone. And you're the strongest woman I know. You lost your parents, then given this disease, living every single day never knowing what will happen to you ... you've never complained. Never felt sorry for yourself. Just because you're hurting over what Ream did to you doesn't make you weak, it makes you human."

I'd become his. I was his and yeah a part of me would always be his. But I wanted me back. He didn't get to keep a part of me.

Footsteps entered the barn and I pulled away from Emily and put up my wall again.

Emily squeezed my arm then I heard her whisper, "Sorry, Georgie called him."

Before I had the chance to reply, she escaped. When I turned around, I saw Deck striding toward me. Guess he was back. And he looked like shit.

The barn door shut behind Emily.

He stopped across from Clifford and leaned against the stall door, arms crossed and his stance ... yeah, impenetrable. Shit. His eyes were weary and tired with black circles beneath. His clothes were wrinkled and his usual shaved head was no longer. He had at least a week's growth of hair on his face, and he still appeared hot with his lean muscular body and tats peeking out from the sleeves of his shirt. He was all darkness, brows, eyes, and personality. I was used to his scariness, but today ... Deck looked murderous.

"What's up, Deck?" I tried to act like I always did and put my hands on my hips but that didn't feel right under his direct gaze, so I turned away from him and picked up a curry and started to brush Clifford with it. "How's Georgie? Carry her out of any bars recently?"

"Came straight here from the airport. And you know exactly why I had to come straight here, so cut the crap. I have more shit than I know how to deal with right now."

I fumbled with the brush and it landed with a thud on the cobblestones. Shit, he was seriously pissed off and it was directed at me. "Ream?"

"That should be a statement, not a question, Kat." God, he was in a foul mood. Deck usually had a smidgen of sympathy in him, and yet he had none for me. Well, I didn't want his pity anyway. I just wanted him to get lost. "Now drop the attitude. I have forty-eight hours to get back to my men."

"Then I guess you better stop talking to me and go do whatever Georgie called you here for." Yeah, I knew Deck wouldn't have come back just for Ream's sake; he came back because Georgie asked him to.

Deck didn't move and from the corner of my eye. I cautiously watched him. I knew he killed people, and I knew he could do it easily without a second thought at ending a life.

"Ever seen your best friend blown up right in front of you?" The brush dropped from my hand. "It's not fuckin' pretty. Being too far away to do anything. Having to run for cover instead of running toward your friend to see if there is even the slightest possibility of saving him. But you can't because bullets are like sideways rain and you have seven other men who need you." I steadied my hands on Clifford, and the horse must have felt my nervousness because he started shifting his weight. "Then when you do manage to go back, his body is unrecognizable. Ashes. Not even dog tags to take back to his family." I looked up at him, fingers curled into Clifford's mane. I knew who he was talking about—Riot, Georgie's brother and his best friend. He watched me, his gaze unwavering.

"Why? Why are you telling me this?" I tried to hold back, but my throat was tight and I trembled at the thought of that happening. Of watching your friend blow up right in front of you and unable to stop it. Jesus, my shit seemed so trivial now.

"Because I was there. I saw it with my own eyes. I even heard the ding when the grenade hit the metal at the back of the Jeep he was in. I watched it explode. I thought I saw my friend burn to a crisp."

I sniffled and jerked as his words resonated in me.

He knew I heard right and he nodded. "Yes, I thought. It happened in front of my eyes and yet I was wrong."

I choked, eyes widening. "What?"

"And now you're wrong."

Oh god.

"You think you saw something, it was real to your eyes, but sometimes what you see isn't always the truth."

I swallowed. "Is ... is Riot alive?"

He shrugged. "Don't know that yet. But he didn't die in that explosion."

Oh Georgie. Hope. After all these years there was hope that her brother was out there somewhere. That was squashed when Deck said, "Probably dead by now, but I'm working on finding out. Do you get what I'm telling you, Kat?"

I nodded. That seeing Ream in bed with another man and woman may not be what I really saw. That maybe … maybe there was a chance I missed seeing the truth.

"I know Ream. Been around him since Crisis' parents took him in. Ten years ago to be exact. Know his story too. He doesn't know I know, but I always make it my business to know everyone's story. Even yours."

I felt the color drain from my face.

"Not too hard to figure out when you have two thousand dollars draining from your trust fund every month to a drug company. A few phone calls later and I have your neurologist's name."

"Deck—"

He shook his head. "Not my business. Not why I'm here. I'm here because Ream's past is dark and fucked up. He tell you?"

The churning in my stomach violently shifted as Deck's words ripped through me like a shredder as I thought about what Ream told me. "That he had sex for money?"

Deck's brows rose. "That's all he told you?"

"Yeah, Deck. I just saw him with another man and woman. I wasn't into listening much."

"You *saw.*" It was a statement.

How could I be wrong though? Crisis saw it too. There was nothing clearer than seeing Ream's butterfly tattoo on his arm, the tat on his back. It was him. He admitted it was him.

"Ream would never cheat on you."

"I saw him. A guy was naked with him. He was naked and …" My voice heightened as the flash of scene repeated and I felt ill.

"Heard that from Georgie. Doubt it's the truth."

Deck pushed away from the stall and stalked toward me. Clifford looked at Deck, his lips wobbling and ready to nibble on him. Then he snorted and lowered his head. Smart horse.

Deck was really unnerving. I mean Ream and Logan were too, but Deck surpassed them by far. It was like he didn't give a shit whether he hurt your feelings or if you died at his feet. He was steady and calm and subtle and that was damn terrifying.

"He's been gone three weeks." Another statement. "And I suspect you know where he is."

"Why would I ..." I shut my mouth because Deck tensed and then I nodded. "Maybe."

"Where?"

"You seem to know everything else, why don't—"

"Don't have time for this shit, Kat!"

I looked up at him. "I can't say." His scowl deepened and I hurried. "When we drove there it was dark and when we left I just remember Stephenson Road was the cut off of Hwy 11. It was about a two and a half hour drive." I thought of the twenty minutes we'd pulled over to have sex and my stomach churned with a combination of everything. "Maybe more like two hours."

His expression never faltered as he continued, "Let's go."

"What? I can't." I couldn't. I felt sick to my stomach at the mere thought of seeing Ream. I had nothing left to give him.

"You love him?"

Now that was a surprising question coming from Deck. I didn't think he would even know about the emotion love. "He cheated on me."

"Harsh for a girl who cheated her best friend the truth for seven years."

"What?" Clifford started shifting his feet and pulling on the crossties. "What the hell, Deck. This isn't my problem. I didn't promise to love someone, care for them, protect them, and then shit all over them. That wasn't me. He did this. Don't you dare turn this around on me." Screw his scariness and the way his jaw clenched. Screw all of this. I went to walk past him, but he grabbed my arm and pulled me back around.

"I didn't tell you that fuckin' story for the hell of it. No one knows that fuckin' story. No one except you now. He didn't cheat on you." I jerked, but it only pissed him off more and tightened his grip as he repeated, "He didn't cheat on you."

"I saw—"

"I don't give a fuck what you saw. Ream would never cheat on you. It's not in his makeup."

"Well, maybe, Deck … you think a little too highly of yourself to really know what the truth is this time."

"Probably do, but even if we bet on that *point* one percent chance I'm wrong, you owe it to him. You know why? Because he gave you more than he has anyone, and after his fucked up past, that was damn hard for him to do. Now you're going to save him because I have no doubt he needs saving right now. He should've crumbled down a real bad path a long time ago, but he didn't. For some reason he came back from that shit and found you. I'm not wrong, he'd never ruin that."

"You don't know that."

"Damn right I do." His harsh voice hit me—hard. "Let's go."

"Now?"

"I have men in the fuckin' desert waiting on me to get back so we can go in and kill some motherfucker who tortures innocent women and children. So, yeah. Now. Car in five minutes."

He strode out of the barn.

Shit.

Chapter Twenty

We made a few wrong turns trying to find the side road, but we finally turned down a road I thought I recognized. Deck drove slow as I tried to remember which driveway it was. I knew you couldn't see the cottage from the road and that it wasn't a real driveway, more like a grass path.

"There." I pointed to the right and Deck turned.

My heart was pumped so fast I was afraid I'd start hyperventilating. My emotions were all jumbled like they were the little numbered balls being spun around and around in the lottery machine. I didn't know which emotion would be picked when I saw him again. What I did know was that my nerves were freaking out and I had needles jet-setting through my legs.

Ream's car sat in front of the cottage.

Deck stopped and shut off the engine. We sat for a minute. Nothing was said and I was thankful he gave me a few minutes to get my shit together. I really didn't think any amount of time would help, but I appreciated it anyway.

He opened his door and it was like he cracked open a part of me because what I'd managed to hold onto all the way here was quickly decomposing.

Deck started walking up to the cottage. I got out of the car and Deck must have heard me because he paused on the steps and waited. I was a little slow because my leg nerves were in an all-out war and I was afraid of losing my balance.

Then Deck did something very unlike him. He cupped my chin and ran his thumb over the scar on my cheek. It was gentle and yet everything in his eyes read pissed off, like it was his fault my face was now flawed.

Then I thought of how Ream kissed my scars, his lips gentle as he made me feel like the most beautiful woman in the world—scars, diseased and coiled up inside myself so tight that I couldn't even cry anymore.

Until he ripped me apart.

Deck's hand fell away from my face, and he turned the knob and opened the door. The second it did, I was hit with the smell of alcohol, and I put my hand over my mouth and nose. Deck, of course, walked straight in, hesitating while he scanned the place, as if taking recon, then strode across the living room to the closed bedroom door.

Without knocking he threw it open. He stood rock still. I couldn't see past him, but Deck's entire body stiffened then he turned to look at me. "Make some coffee." He walked into the room and I saw him crouch down.

I ignored his order and walked to the bedroom and what I saw destroyed all the anger and replaced it with fear. I hated Ream for what he did to me, but I still cared about him. Deck had known that.

"Ream," I whispered in a hoarse cry.

He was lying on the floor naked and shivering, his fists bleeding and a broken bottle of rye beside him. I ran to him, falling to my knees, panic encroaching as I watched for breathing. Deck had his hand on my arm, but I didn't even notice it as I waited for his chest to move to tell he was still alive. All sensibility disappeared as everything crashed around me; the key turned and released the tears like a waterfall of blood.

"Go make coffee, Kat."

I looked up at him briefly, hearing his words, but not really comprehending. Coffee. He was alive if he wanted me to make coffee. The wetness slipped down my cheeks as I held Ream's cold, lifeless hand.

"I need to get him in a hot shower. You don't want to make coffee, go turn on the shower."

I choked on another sob. "He's going to make ..." Oh God, I couldn't say it.

"Yeah, he's out cold. Dehydrated as shit. Most likely been drunk for three weeks straight. Shower, Kat."

I nodded scrambling to my feet and running into the bathroom and turning on the water. Deck came in with Ream over his shoulder. "Take my phone and wallet out of my back pocket."

I quickly did as he ordered and then Deck pushed the shower curtain aside and went under the warm spray. I stood staring, my insides feeling like they were being torn out of me, stomped on, then shoved back inside greased with wreckage.

Deck propped Ream up against the back wall then directed the spray on him. He glanced at me. "Now will you make coffee?"

I stared, tears streaming down my face, praying Ream would open his eyes, that I'd hear his voice. He just looked so ... not Ream. As if he'd been drained of his strength and all that was left was a shell of a body.

I looked at Deck again, soaking wet, his olive green cargo pants now dark green, his face dripping with water. I finally nodded and left the bathroom, my nerves spiking to a whole other level of screwed-up. I swallowed back the tears, trying to fit the key back in and lock the emotions away again, but it wouldn't fit. I dropped the coffee can into the sink and brown granules spilled out all over the place. With trembling hands, I filled the coffee maker with water and put a filter in and cleaned up the granules.

There were empty bottles all over the place. No dishes, which meant he hadn't been eating. As I turned the coffee maker on I realized the state of the cottage: overturned couch, coffee table smashed, the game board ... Oh God, it was torn into pieces with the money thrown all over the place.

I couldn't take it all in. If I did, I'd fall apart. I knew Ream had issues. He told me he was fucked up, but I thought it stemmed from his twin sister. It was way more than that. He prostituted himself for money. Why? What pushed him to do that?

Why would he cheat on me if he knew it would end us? Why put himself in that position? Ream thought about everything before he did anything. He'd had to have thought of the consequences if I'd found out. Could he have been so drunk that he had no clue what he was doing? Was I trying desperately to find any excuse for something that was inexcusable?

I sank down onto the floor, knees up to my chest, arms wrapped around them, as fresh tears stained my cheeks. It felt weird crying, like I was that little girl again, all alone and scared. I hated the feeling, I hated that Ream made me feel like this again and brought me to this point of emotional agony.

I cried so hard it hurt my chest; my throat became raw and gritty. I don't know how long I sat there before I heard the shower turn off. I climbed to my feet and walked back into the bathroom.

I stopped at the door, hands gripping one side of it for support as I saw Ream standing there, a towel wrapped around his waist, his hands holding either side of his head. Yeah, I was guessing it hurt like hell.

Deck grabbed a towel off the rack and then without a word strode out. I heard the front door open and shut.

"Why are you here?" Well, those weren't the first words I expected out of Ream's mouth after we last saw one another. He looked down. "Why did you come, Kat?"

I had no qualms about telling the truth. "Deck made me."

He turned away, resting his hands on the lip of the sink, shoulders slumped, and everything in him read defeat. It didn't suit him. Seeing him this way, the man who never gave up on us, who brought me here to win me back, who sat with me at the hospital, who swore to love me no matter what happened with my disease.

I never expected to be standing here looking at him and

wondering who he was. Who was this man I fell in love with. A man I couldn't forgive for what he did. I wanted to, God, I wanted to run into his arms and have him hold me and take away all the pain I was feeling. I wanted Deck to be right and the truth wasn't what I saw.

"Why did you do it, Ream?"

He was silent for a long time, not looking at me, head bowed, hands clenching the sink. When he raised his head it was to meet my eyes in the reflection of the mirror.

"Guess I fell back into old habits. Sex is meaningless to me. I told you that."

Thank God I was holding the doorway for support because I would've fallen. His words stabbed right through me. Not because they hurt me, but because I heard the coldness in his voice. There was shame, indignity, pain. I saw it all staring back at me in the mirror. It's what he thought of himself.

"Not with us." I knew it wasn't. It meant something to both of us, and he could stand there and say sex meant nothing to him, but I'd never believe it was nothing when we were together. He'd told me that it was meaningless until me.

He turned and then walked past me into the bedroom. I heard the rustle of clothing. By the time I was brave enough to turn around, Ream was dressed and leaning up against the dresser. He looked like he was waiting for me to either say something or get out. I did neither.

"Go home, Kat."

I shook my head. I didn't know why, but I needed more. This wasn't just us breaking up because he cheated on me. Ream was a different person. He was cold and unfeeling. When he looked at me, it was right through me. There was more to this.

"If you're waiting for answers about why I did it, well, you're not getting them because I don't even fuckin' know what happened." He shrugged. "Doesn't matter anyway. We're better apart."

"Ream."

He kicked a glass bottle and it slid under the bed. "When I told you I didn't deserve you, I meant it."

"That's not true."

"Yes it is!" He shouted so loud it felt as if the room vibrated.

Then the rage died and he was looking at me, but it felt like he wasn't seeing me at all. "I was paid to sleep with women … men." Oh God. "It gave me a roof over my head and kept my sister safe from the same thing. That's who I am, Kat. It's not fuckin' changing because I don't do it anymore." He huffed. "Or maybe I do."

"What do you mean? Why?"

"It doesn't matter. None of this does anymore. And I want you to leave."

"You owe me!" I shouted. "You fucking tell me. You owe me that, damn it."

His expression never changed, even when I yelled. It terrified me because nothing of the Ream I loved stood before me. "Tell me."

Then he lowered his eyes from mine and shifted, but it was the smallest movement. "Then you'll leave?"

My breath hitched. He wanted me to leave and that hurt more because it should've been me wanting to leave. I nodded and it was like I was saying yes to my own demise.

It was several minutes before he spoke again and when he did his tone was detached. "It was survival. A way of life. I got through it by being numb to what I did. It became easy after a while. I mean easy in that I could do it without throwing up anymore. The men … that was never easy."

Oh God, Ream. I couldn't even imagine Ream subjecting himself to that. He was so strong and confident like nothing could touch him.

"I was fourteen. Old enough to know what I was doing and still young enough to be wanted by the sick bastards. There was one in particular …" His voice trailed off and then stopped. I put my hand over my mouth as my stomach violently churned. "It wasn't so bad though. My sister and I were looked after. Fed, clothed, went to school. It was just on Friday and Saturday nights I went into the basement. He said it was either me or my sister."

"Your mom?"

He snorted and kicked the empty beer bottle, and I jumped when it hit the bed post and made a loud crackle as it shattered. "How do you think we ended up there? My mom owed the guy money for her drugs. You know what my sister Haven was named after? It sure as fuck wasn't a sanctuary … Haven Dust—cocaine." He shook his head making a huff with his breath. "We were her payment." Ream shrugged. "He kept his word though. My sister never had to prostitute herself and I paid off our mom's debt. Two years later it stopped. I didn't have to do it anymore, but Lenny, the pimp, let us stay there anyway. We lived with him and his daughter. Ate together like a normal fuckin' family, at least as normal as could be with a low-life drug dealer. I thought it was going to be okay, that maybe it wasn't so bad after all."

"You were forced to have sex with men and women, Ream."

"No. Coerced. Not forced."

"Same difference," I muttered. Sudden realization dawned. "That's why you had to stop. Why you froze when we were having sex? Why you … you don't like my mouth on you?"

He nodded. "Sometimes the voices … I still hear them. It's worse when I don't have control and a woman down on me …"

"Has the control," I finished.

He nodded. "A lot of times, I never made it through the sex … it was always ugly for me. But with you … you could stop them. Christ you did. Told you from the beginning that you changed something in me. Never liked having sex until you."

I was drowning in confusion. I wanted to wrap him up in my arms and hold the boy who had suffered such a horrific circumstance, to bring the Ream I knew back from the cold darkness he was now living in.

"It was when Lenny died that things went to shit and I knew we had to get out of there. But we had no place to go and no money. Lenny's friend Olaf moved in with us and I didn't trust him not to

... I was afraid he'd make Haven and I work downstairs ... and I couldn't do it anymore.

"And Haven, Christ we were sixteen and she was too fuckin' pretty. There was one guy who used to come around and buy drugs from Lenny all the time. He'd watch her, it was really creepy, but he never did anything except watch her." My heart started beating faster and cold shivers raced down my spine. "But when Lenny died ... he stopped watching. He raped her. I didn't know about it for months. Shit, I knew something was wrong with her. She was in her room all the time, barely ate, but she never told me until I saw the track marks on her arm one day. I went ballistic. She told me what happened, fuck what was still happening. The guy came to her room for months and I never knew. I never fuckin' knew. He gave her the drugs. He fucked her up so bad that ... I went after him. Killed him with a marble statue over his head."

I gasped and my body was screaming to go to him as I listened with horror.

"It felt good. And I'd do it again in a second. I hit him over and over again until his skull was crushed and his face was unrecognizable. And to this day ... I don't regret it. That is the type of man I am."

My throat was so tight that swallowing was painful. Haven. His twin. Raped over and over again. The drugs. Why he'd freaked over Brett watching me. My pain over Ream cheating seemed so inconsequential now.

"I knew we'd have to leave. Escape before anyone saw the body. Well, his daughter saw what I did but I didn't care about her. We ran and lived on the streets, scared as shit that we'd be found and killed. Everyone knew everyone on the streets. An old woman found us sleeping in her shed one morning when we over slept. We always left before the sun rose; it was safer that way. But Urma saw us when she was getting her gardening tools, and she just smiled and asked if we were hungry. We stayed in the shed for a few months. I don't know why she never called social services, but she didn't. She even offered a place in her house, but I was scared that if Urma got involved in our lives she'd be in danger too.

Haven ... yeah, Haven never got over what happened to her. I saw it in her haunted face every single fuckin' day. She'd find the drugs no matter how much I tried to stop it. She was desperate to have them and she'd do anything to get them. The drugs were her escape, I guess, and she kept getting fucked up. Five times I took her to the hospital for overdosing. I'd have to get her out of there the moment she was well enough before social services picked us up. The last time ... I was in the waiting room an hour before the doctor came out and told me she was gone. I didn't believe him. She hadn't been that bad. She'd been fucked up way worse before. Why would she die this time? I freaked out. They had to sedate me and when I woke up I was in children's aid care.

"There was no funeral for Haven. I tried to find out where she was buried, but they had no record of her. Just another dead kid lost in the system. A few months later, I was lucky to be fostered by Crisis' parents." Ream looked at me, his eyes still unemotional as if he had to be that way in order to tell me all this. "You see, Kat, I am a piece shit, and you were right to get out while you could."

"Ream, I was angry. I don't ... Ream I didn't mean what I said."

He huffed. "Sure you did, beautiful. I just needed to hear it to remember."

"Ream, no." Oh God. No. No matter what I saw, what broke us apart, he wasn't undeserving. He protected his sister, let his body be used instead of hers. He tried to get her out of that life. I understood why he was crazy protective of me. Possessive. Maybe I understood it about him all along. I accepted it without even knowing this part of him. I didn't need to know because I'd loved him anyway.

"Women have always meant nothing to me. Even when I escaped that life, being with a woman made me ill. I felt soiled and disgusted by the way they fawned all over me. Even now, being in the band ... the women treat me like an object, something to brag about to their friends."

I was desperate to say no, but it was true. To them he was an object, a rock star. I wanted to hold him in my arms, but I stood silent and still, listening to his haunting words.

"Until you."

I met his eyes and had to look away or I knew I'd falter.

"You never groveled over me or made me feel like I was being used." He sighed and put his head down. "The first woman I slept with who I wanted to curl up with and wake up next to in the morning."

I choked back the sob that clogged my throat. I couldn't listen to him anymore. I didn't want to hear this. Where was the anger? I wanted it back. I needed to lock the tears away again and be strong. I had to remember despite his horrific story, he still cheated on me.

"No child should ever have to live what you and your sister did. I wish …" What? That I could erase that from him? Maybe the pain and hurt, but not who it made him. But the worst was that no matter how much I wanted to forgive him, I couldn't. "I can't forgive you, Ream."

His voice was hard as he said, "Never asked you to."

I flinched and then started for the bedroom door. I needed to leave before I did something stupid as fall back into his arms. "Did you love me?"

Ream's head jerked in my direction and his face tightened. "It's over, Kat. And I don't ever want your pity."

I nodded. "Yeah." I understood that better than anyone. And then I walked out.

Chapter Twenty-One

I was numb to it now. My body separated from my mind.
I could go off into another place where no one could touch me.
He didn't like it.
He made me ask for mercy. I did, just to please him.
I had to please him or it would be worse. He could always make it
worse.
I was a toy.
Unfeeling. Cold. Indifferent.
And broken.

It was another two days before I saw him again. Deck had told me or rather ordered me to take his car back home while he stayed with Ream. I stayed locked to my easel and painted away my emotions.

Deck's words continued to haunt me. That cheating wasn't in Ream's makeup. That what you see is not always what it is. I wanted so badly to believe that he didn't cheat and I kept running the scene over and over in my head but every time it broke me down a little more.

I couldn't let it go. I even asked Crisis if Ream had ever been so drunk that he didn't remember what he did the night before. Crisis said no.

Then I went back further. What happened that night? Ream had gone into the back of the bar to talk to Brett … to threaten him. It made sense why he did it. How that guy used to watch his sister all the time. The guy who ended up raping her at the first opportunity. I saw the haunted look in his eyes when he told me. Brett wasn't some low-life drug dealer, but Ream was vigilant and he had every right to be. He needed to make sure he never made the same mistake, and if it took warning Brett to stay away from me, then he'd do it.

When Ream walked into the house a week later, his eyes were dark and sunken like he wasn't sleeping, but behind the restlessness I saw the same cold darkness I'd seen at the cottage. Maybe Deck was right and he wouldn't come back from this, and that terrified me because I saw who Ream could be and that man I missed like hell.

Georgie was over since Emily and Logan had gone to sign papers for their new house, and I suspected Emily had asked her to come by and keep me company. I stopped fighting their need to care for me, and accepted it.

"What are you doing here?" Georgie attacked Ream the second he walked in the door, and I put my hand on her not wanting a fight.

"Georgie. Please."

"Just getting my stuff." His voice was stiff … monotone.

She huffed and flipped her now purple strands over her shoulder and grabbed my hand. "You're a piece of shit, you know that. No more cupcake for you, asshole."

I flinched. Ream didn't.

He did look at me though, and I felt goose bumps scatter across my skin; it was from fear and dread at what I saw in him. Ream's hard look was something that I knew could make him slip away from all of us. I wanted to hold out my hand and save him, bring back the man I'd seen laugh and tease me, but it was too late for that.

"Come on, Kat." Georgie tried to pull me away. We were taking a few of my paintings to the new gallery. I dragged my feet, stumbling as my arm brushed against his as we passed. My breath stopped, my heart pumped crazily, and every molecule was pulling at me to turn around and go back to him.

I just couldn't understand. He'd been so possessive of me. He loved me. God, he spoke to several neurologists when he'd been on tour. Why would he turn around and cheat on me? It made even less sense now that I knew about his past. If he hated sex so much, why would he risk everything to do it?

He never made a move to stop me. Touch me. Nothing. He just let me walk away and why shouldn't he?

"Kat, get in." I didn't realize that I stood at the passenger door with it wide open and Georgie had already started the engine.

Georgie jabbered about pretty much nothing except the hot guys that had been in her coffee shop this week and how Deck hadn't even stopped in to see her when he'd been here for two days. I never told her what Deck said about her brother. It would've been stupid to give her hope only to have it taken away.

We unloaded my paintings at the new gallery. Then I stayed to help the owner set them up while Georgie went to check up on her coffee shop.

I couldn't get the image out of my head of how Ream looked, dead and cold. I imagined that was how he was when he was a kid, trying to make it through one more night in order to pay off a debt. It made me so angry, at Molly and her roommates, at myself. Yeah, I was mad at myself for missing that piece of Ream that was so broken and damaged. I'd seen that dark, haunted look in his eyes, but I thought it had been from the loss of his sister. I never imagined the abuse he suffered.

I had to talk to Molly. She was the last person I wanted to see, but I had to find out what led Ream to do something that disgusted him. It didn't make sense. Or maybe it did. Christ, what did I know?

Ream. I knew Ream and he wouldn't do this to me. Somewhere

inside I believed that, and I held onto to the thread of hope with the last of my determination.

"Shit," I jumped up and down then grabbed my hair and leaned over, making a low growling sound. "Shit. Shit. Shit." Then I grabbed my purse and called out to the gallery owner, Marie. "I have to go do something, I'll be back later."

I darted out the door, glancing at my phone. It was still early, plenty of time before Georgie got back. I hailed a cab and told him the address. The entire way there I wrung my hands together, my heart pounding, nerves on edge.

But I had to do this. I'd promised myself to not be afraid to live; well, this was part of living. Finding the truth. Facing the truth head on.

When I got out of the cab, I swayed as the blinding pain of what transpired here hit me. I wanted to run as fast as I could, but I'd run long enough.

I went to knock on the door when it swung open and Molly stood there. "Kat? What are you doing here?" She stepped out onto the porch and closed the door behind her. "Everything okay? Does Matt need me at the bar early? Did Ream come back? I heard he took off after … well, you know."

Yeah, I did fucking know. "Yeah, he's back." I thought it strange she didn't invite me in and instead closed me out. "I came to talk to you about what happened that night."

"Oh?" She avoided looking at me, and it was nothing unusual for her. She was always shy and insecure. Shit, a slap on the ass from Crisis made her blush. That was the other thing that didn't make sense; I couldn't imagine her asking Ream to stay and have a drink with her. But how did her roommates get involved? "Listen, Molly. Why was Ream here? What happened that night?"

She shifted her feet from side to side and her hair fell in front of her eyes so I couldn't even see her expression. "I was scared. My ex had been harassing me and—"

"I thought your ex was in Vancouver?"

She softly moved the rickety wood chair next to her. "Yeah, he is. Well, he was. Now he's here."

"Why didn't you tell Matt? You know he'd help you out. Send one of his bouncers home with you. Or Brett. I'm sure he'd have helped too." I was screaming inside. *Why Ream? Why did you choose Ream?* It wasn't fair, but it wasn't her fault. They'd been leaving at the same time. He chose to share a cab, and then like tumbleweed, it rolled into everything else.

Molly didn't say anything and she kept her head down, but I noticed her body stiffen and her fingers curl into fists then uncurl.

"Molly. I'm just trying to figure out why I found my boyfriend in bed with your two roommates. It just seems so ..." Yeah, it was unlike him. "Ream's not like that." Because he was forced as a teenager to have sex with adults. The more I thought about it, the less it made sense. Ream choosing to randomly have sex with two strangers? Why? To get off? But he wouldn't get off on that, he said so himself. That sex was meaningless until me.

Until me.

"Maybe you don't know him as well as you think."

My eyes widened at her thoughtless retort, and there was an edge in her voice. She peered up at me and for a brief second I saw the corners of her lips curl up, but then it was gone so fast I thought I imagined it.

"I'm sorry. God, Kat. I'm just not getting along with my roommates after that stuff with Ream and with my ex back ... I've been uptight."

I nodded. "Yeah." What I wanted to say was "try being in my shoes bitch." Because despite always liking Molly, I suddenly hated her. She destroyed everything. Ream was locked inside himself, hating who he was and thinking he wasn't worth anything. I was living on edge, afraid to wake up in the morning and not feel him next to me.

"Listen, I better get ready for work." She turned to the door, her hand on the knob, then she said, "Maybe you should just leave him alone. Forget him."

Whoa. Did Molly want Ream for herself? "Did you fuck him too, Molly? Or did you just let your friends take advantage of a drunk rock star so they could brag about it?" The anger in my voice tightened. "Because he was mine, damn it. Mine." I don't know why I said it. Pissed off. Feeling like I was falling apart again after seeing Ream at the farm. Whatever it was, it made Molly react. She swung around and hit me across the face so hard I went falling backwards and stumbled down the steps until I landed on my ass.

I held my hand to my cheek in complete shock. Holy shit. What the hell?

The door opened.

Confusion, then sudden panic grabbed hold.

"Do I have to clean up your mess again, Alexa?" My breath hitched as I recognized Lance's voice.

Alexa? Molly was … who was Alexa?

Lance strode toward me and I scuttled back on my butt then tried to turn around and get my footing, but his arm looped around my waist and he picked me off the ground. I started screaming, but his hand plastered over my mouth and muffled the sound.

I inhaled frantically through my nose, the scent of his cologne churning my stomach. He picked me up and carried my flailing body into the house.

Chapter Twenty-Two

I was dumped in the foyer and my knees hit the hard unforgiving wood floor. I started to scramble away when I heard the distinct click of a gun. Shit, I'd never forget that sound for the rest of my life.

"You move again, I'll blow off your leg." Molly gripped the gun casually with one hand as she pointed at me. "It'll be messy, so I'd prefer if you stayed quiet and behaved yourself."

"What do you want to do with her?" Lance asked, casually leaning against the door as if this was a conversation about the weather.

"We can't leave her here. She'll have to come with us."

"Molly? Why?" Her hand was steady as a rock and there wasn't a single part of her that I recognized. Her shoulders were back and her eyes met mine, hard and fierce. She sneered at me like she wanted to kill me with her bare hands. I wasn't stupid enough to give her attitude because there was no doubt in my mind she'd shoot me. This wasn't Molly at all; this woman was Alexa, whoever the hell that was.

"Meet us out back." I glanced up at Lance on the phone to someone. This was a man I'd kissed, dated, and let into my life.

He put his phone back in his pocket and then strode into the other room and came back with a coiled yellow rope. "Hands, princess." I started to back away and he chuckled. "Alexa, she thinks she can get away."

He grabbed my hands and pulled them together in front of me then tightly wrapped the rope around them. Then he leaned in close and seized the bottom of my blouse. I panicked and started fighting, kicking and screaming, trying to crawl away with my hands tied in front of me. I felt like a seal out of water attempting to escape.

His hand came down on the back of my neck. Then he pulled and there was a loud tearing sound. He gripped a handful of my hair, yanked backwards, then straddled me and gagged me with the piece of material he'd torn from my blouse. He picked me up and threw me over his shoulder and walked down a hallway out the back door and then through a wooden gate into a back alley.

Lance tossed me into the backseat of a rusted old car with tinted windows and jumped in after me. I made a dive for the other door, but Molly was there with the gun pointed at me. She got in and then I heard the locks click as the driver pulled away.

"You best behave, princess."

"I'm not a goddamn princess, fuckhead," I muffled under the gag.

Lance's brows rose. "Perhaps not … anymore." A cold shiver ran over me as I saw his eyes pause on the scar on my cheek. Then he looked at Molly. "I think you overestimated Ben." Who the hell was Ben? "He fucked it up. Her face should've been a lot worse."

Oh my God. Lance knew who attacked me? Had he helped the intruder get in the building? Maybe that's why the security cameras never caught the guy because Lance had let him in the back door. And if Molly was in on it then the perpetrator could've been kept informed as to when Matt was coming home. I shook with fury. They did this. All of this. But why?

"He was supposed to rape her so Ream wouldn't want her. The scars were your gift. Now look at what we've had to do." Molly flung her hair back over her shoulder and crossed her legs, the gun resting on her thigh. "I didn't want this problem. Now we're going to have issues with that military guy. I don't like issues."

Lance scowled and tapped his fingers on the armrest while he stared at me. "We'll deal with it. It will be fine."

"How so? Kat vanishes and Deck will hunt us down."

So what were they planning? To take Ream? Deck would come for him too. How did she think she'd get away with this?

"Listen, Alexa, I wasn't the one who struck her. You're the one who lost your cool over your little obsession."

I figured she had to be some psychotic fan of Ream's. Found out where he hung out and got a job at Avalanche and was waiting for him to come back from tour. Shit, maybe this bitch had been following Ream for years. The bad news was I was a threat to her.

She picked up her gun and pointed it at my head. My heart started pounding unsteadily and the gag was all wet from my saliva. I breathed so hard it made a slurping sound with every breath.

"Alexa, don't be stupid." He put his hand on her arm.

I heard the hammer cock.

"Alexa. You want issues, then killing her will give you them," Lance warned.

"This is your fault, Lance. You were supposed to have her fall for you. Keep her out of the picture until I got him back." She turned to me and the gun wavered as she spoke. "And you. Dancing provocatively right in front of him—repulsive slut. He had to get up and hold you, didn't he?" At Avalanche. Oh God, she'd been watching us. "Didn't he," she screeched.

She was insane. I stared back at her; the rage teetering on edge as my mind whirled at what she'd done. The hurt Ream and I had been through, the betrayal. My brother took her in. We trusted her. I wanted to wrap my hands around her fragile neck and squeeze the life out of her.

"Didn't he?" she yelled.

I slowly nodded, my eyes watching her finger on the trigger. Not that I could do anything if she pressed it. At the moment I was more concerned about what else they had planned because whatever it was involved Ream and it made me ill thinking that he'd be subjected to this crazy bitch after all he'd been through in his life.

She lowered the gun and started rambling to Lance about what it was like having to be nice to everyone at the bar pretending she liked us. "I waited too long for this to have *her* screw it up."

"Alexa," Lance soothed. "You'll have him back. Calm down."

Back? What did he mean *back*? Had Ream slept with this crazy ass chick? He told me he hadn't slept with anyone since the first time he'd been with me. Was it before that? But then he'd remember her even if it was years ago. Okay, guys drank and slept with random chicks and maybe didn't remember much in the morning, but Ream … Ream I knew without a doubt wouldn't do that. Oh God, why didn't I see the truth? Why didn't he? He'd never cheat on me no matter how fucked up he was.

She nodded, her eyes gleaming wild. "Yes. Yes. He should've never left me. Now, look what I've had to do."

I had no clue what they were talking about, but I wasn't putting up with the saliva dripping from the corners of my mouth any longer. I turned my head to the side and used my shoulder to roll the gag from my mouth, not caring if they saw me do it. I wasn't sitting here drooling like some dog, and I suspected if they wanted me dead they'd have easily done it by now.

Neither of them said anything, and I suspected because wherever we were no one would hear me scream anyway.

"He'll cause problems for you, Alexa. He's not like how you remember him. It's been a long time and you were just kids. He's not going to do whatever you say."

A slow smile formed and her eyes gleamed as she looked at me. "Oh, I think he will. We may be able to use her as an … extra insurance policy."

"We have insurance. We don't need her to get to Ream." Lance kicked the back of the vinyl seat. "I say, dump her, get Ream on the phone, and play our ace card. Then let's get the hell out of here before we have that bastard Deck and his cop friends on our ass."

"We have time. That guy is in the Middle East and I'm paying you to shut the fuck up and do what I say, not for advice."

"If we have Deck coming after us, you're not paying me enough."

I hated her perfect white teeth, and I wanted to kick them out and watch her smile with a blood-filled mouth. "Kat, did he tell you about his colorful childhood? How he used to kneel in front of the toilet and throw up every Friday night. Do you know where he went? Or was that too much for your princess ears."

"Fuck you, Molly."

"Alexa," she corrected.

"What-the-fuck-ever, bitch."

I had nowhere to go as she hauled off and slapped me. Fuck. My cheek was going to have welts from this woman.

"What did Ream ever do to you?" And then it hit me so hard it felt like she slapped me across the face again.

She knew about his past.

She knew where he'd been forced to go every Friday and Saturday night.

Matt said she was twenty-four. I remember because he had her driver's license checked. She must have had her name changed or was using her middle name.

She laughed and the sound made me gag. "He did tell you? Fascinating. Yes, I think this will turn out better, after all." She clucked her tongue and sighed. "Poor Ream. But he will have me now."

"He was forced to—"

She cut me off in an abrupt angry tone. "I took care of him. He was mine. He is mine."

Oh God. No. Ream. The girl. Ream told me Lenny had a child. A girl. She'd been a couple of years younger than him.

"So he told you about me? I see it on your face. Yes, I'm Lenny's daughter Alexandria Molly Reynolds." She tapped her foot on the floor, her thigh shaking with the movement. "Ream and his pathetic innocent sister left me all alone. I had no one. He promised to never leave me. But he lied. He left me in that disgusting house with Uncle Olaf." Her voice got louder, the tone higher-pitched. "He ruined everything when he killed Gerard. Just because the guy was having some fun with Ream's precious little angel." She tsked, shaking her head back and forth. "I convinced Olaf to let him go, you know. He found out they were staying in some old lady's shed and wanted to kill him, but I couldn't let that happen, so I told him I saw Haven smash the statue down on Gerard and kill him. I don't think he believed me but, Olaf liked me and I was good at making him … happy." She shrugged. "It was Haven's fault anyway. She should've kept her mouth shut. She had to pay for her mistake."

My eyes widened as her words washed a cold fear over me.

"I was going to be his angel, not her." Oh God, no. Alexa smiled. "Yes, of course it was me. She wouldn't be so precious after the drugs and Gerard, would she? I'd be his angel. Me." Haven. God, the poor girl already abandoned by her mother and then Alexa's jealousy and wanting to destroy her. "I set it up for Gerard. I saw him watching her every time he came over. I knew he'd do anything to have her, and I gave him the drugs from Olaf's stash to help him with her." Her voice crackled and broke. "I was the one who looked out for Ream. I soothed him when he was sick. I waited for him at the top of the basement stairs every Sunday. That was me."

I put my hand over my mouth and looked around frantically for something to throw up in. I managed to grab a plastic grocery bag from the floor, even with my wrists tied in front of me. Lance held out his handkerchief when I finished emptying the contents of my stomach and I shoved his hand away.

Alexa was laughing and took great pleasure in all of this.

"He didn't sleep with your roommates or whoever the hell they were, did he? They were hired pieces of shit." I didn't have to ask because I already knew. Working at the bar to watch us, becoming our friend, Lance. The gallery. Oh God, the gallery.

I turned to Lance. "You don't own two galleries in New York, do you?"

"No. I don't know shit about art. Rented the gallery after the previous owner had an … untimely accident." Oh God. They did it so Lance could get close to me so I'd stay away from Ream when he came back from tour. He'd had me hire Molly for my art show, he asked me to get Brett and Emily to invite their friends because Lance didn't have any connections except maybe street druggies.

But Alexa's plan to keep Ream and I apart didn't work so she went further. She tried to have me raped. She scarred my face, hoping Ream would not want me. But none of it worked, so she set him up. Convinced him to come inside her house, pretending she was scared, then gave him a drink, drugged no doubt. In the morning, she texted me that Ream was there so I would catch him cheating. But he hadn't been cheating had he?

Oh God, Ream. I felt like curling up in a ball and crying for us and at the same time screaming my head off and diving on top of Alexa and ripping her apart with my fingernails.

The car jerked to a stop. "Oh here we are. Ready for some fun, Kat." Alexa bounced out of the car like she was going to an amusement park.

"Out. Now," Lance ordered when I remained seated trying to calm my body for what I was about to do.

I stepped out of the car and instantly gagged on the scent of rotten garbage. We were parked in a driveway with a broken down picket fence on the right that led up to an old run down house. The windows were all boarded up with plywood and there were bars on the basement windows. Holy Christ. I had to get out of here. If I walked into that house I had a feeling I'd never walk out again. I'd rather be shot than live my final days in that place.

A guy, I assumed the driver, grabbed my arm and yanked me forward. I stumbled and went down on one knee. As soon as he leaned over to pull me up, I bolted upright and jerked my knee into his face at the same time. I felt the crunch of his nose hitting my knee cap. He swore and I ran.

I hadn't run since the new symptom of my legs acting up, and I didn't know how far I could make it, but I wasn't going to be some chicken lured into a crazy-ass bitch's haunted house of horrors.

My legs had other ideas and the exertion was too much. I fell face first into the pavement, and my legs had a total freak out. I screamed as a hand fisted my hair and yanked me upwards. I tried to gain my feet, but they wouldn't support me, and I was off balance.

He pulled hard. "Get up."

"I can't you bastard."

"Bitch, you're going to fucking walk." He kicked me in the ribs and it felt like one of the bones broke and punctured my lung as agony tore through me. "Get up." He kicked me again and I tried tearing my hair from his grip, but it wouldn't give. He hooved me in the stomach, and I hung in his grasp as I choked for air.

"Stop. Pick her up. Don't be a lazy bastard, Greg," Lance said. "We have to..." he looked at me "...tie up some things."

Chapter Twenty-Three

The tying up was me.

I was stripped of my clothes except for my underwear and bra, and it wasn't an easy task. I fought the bastard Greg with everything I had. Even with my hands tied, I managed a sweet-ass kick to his solar plexus, which left him gasping for air, then I spit in his face. He cuffed me across the head, and it hurt like hell, but it was worth it to watch my saliva hit him in the eye.

Lance stood by and watched, merely looking amused at my pointless struggle. Alexa vanished somewhere inside the run-down house.

Was this where Ream and Haven spent two years of their youth?

We had bypassed a filthy kitchen with dishes piled high in the sink and what looked like tomato sauce splattered all over the smoke-stained white walls. We'd gone down a set of wooden stairs and into a dark, dusty basement. Shudders tiptoed over my body as the ominous feeling grew like a drum quietly beating then thumping louder and louder. God, this had to be where Ream was taken every Friday and Saturday night. I couldn't even begin to comprehend the terror a young boy must have endured walking down here.

Greg opened a door then dumped me on the cement floor. I was about to scramble away when he grabbed me by the hair and dragged me across the rough surface. I frantically grabbed at his wrists, trying to relieve the pressure on my scalp, then pushed back with my feet.

"Stop. I can walk. You bastard. Stop."

He let me go briefly and I looked around, my heart pounding faster and faster as I took in the canopy bed with the sheer white curtain pulled back. Then I noticed the chains attached to the bedposts and the stone wall with the array of contraptions. There was something that reminded me of a vaulting beam gymnasts used in the corner. It had a red pad on top and then padded cuffs attached to the foot of it.

Fear skipped across my body like pebbles being thrown at me. It was painful to breathe, my lungs gasping for air as I realized that this ... this place was where Ream had come every Friday and Saturday night.

He'd said downstairs. In the basement.

Ream. No. No. I couldn't even begin to imagine what it was like as a fourteen your old boy coming down here. To have to ... "Oh God." I violently shuddered and then crawled over to the bin beside the bed and vomited.

"Fuck," Greg muttered. "Stupid bitch." He waited until my stomach stopped heaving and then hauled me up and threw me on the bed.

I tried to scramble off the other side, but he snagged my ankle, yanked me back, then put a cold metal clamp around it that was attached to a bedpost.

"No. Fuck no," I screamed as I tugged and yanked on it to get free while Greg grabbed my wrists and untied them. As soon as they were free I pulled frantically on the manacles around my ankles. He grabbed a wrist and repeated the process until I was laying spread eagle on my back, heaving and writhing, chains clanking against the bedposts as I fought their hold.

"I'd save your strength. Your first client should be here within the hour, and he enjoys a good tussle." Greg laughed and then I heard the door slam shut.

There was no point in screaming. But I did anyway. There was no point in trying to escape the manacles—but I did anyway. And I did until I was bleeding and my throat was so raw that when I screamed I had a coughing attack.

No one came.

And I lay shivering on the bed, dried blood on my wrists and ankles from fighting the manacles. I constantly listened for footsteps, for the door opening, and perpetual fear that I was soon going to be raped.

But the door never opened for hours.

Then it did.

Chapter Twenty-Four

"What did I tell you?"
He was mad again. I made him mad because I tried to get away.
I couldn't help it. I hated him so much. It hurt so badly. The
women never hurt me; they took care of me. It didn't hurt. He hurt
me.
I had to protect her.
"Please, Uncle Ben. I didn't mean to." I never had an Uncle.
Don't even know if I had any relatives. Ben insisted I call him that.
He liked it.
He stared at me long and hard, his eyes glaring at me but lust
filled. I wanted to run and vomit. My stomach cramped.
"Be a good boy then. Turn over and let me do this."
I closed my eyes and took my mind to somewhere nice like the park
where Haven and I went after school the other day. It was fun. I
laughed, so did Haven.
I put my face in the pillow, my fingers clenching around the
material.
Then I went far away.

I couldn't see who was approaching the bed as the chains were too tight for me to sit up. My lips stuck together from the dryness, and it felt as if my eyelids had weights glued onto them. I'd been terrified to fall asleep, but my body fought me, the mental and physical exhaustion trying to make me slip into darkness.

When the girl came into view holding a water bottle, I just about begged. But I didn't have to; she cracked the plastic lid and then held it between my lips and tipped the bottle.

The cool liquid easily slid down my throat, and I sucked it back so fast that the bottle started crackling as the air left it. She pulled it away and I yanked upward on the chains trying to get it back.

She merely waited until the bottle's shape came back and then placed it to my lips again. I chugged it back until I sucked it dry. The girl pulled it away and then stared down at me. I stared back wondering if she was a prostitute. If she was, then she'd have a lot of business because she was stunning. Soft features, frail and subtle to match her eyes that were the oddest color—gray with a hint of pale green speckled within the depths. They were the same shape as Ream's, drooping slightly but vivid and with so much expression. I recognized the torment like I had in Ream.

Her hair flowed past her shoulders in long lazy curls, and pale flawless skin matched her blonde hair. It wasn't bright blonde; it was a quiet blonde that didn't scream at you when you saw the color, matching everything else about her.

But with all her beauty it was something else that caught my attention, the mark on her inner wrist. I only saw it for a second when she reached forward to give me the water the second time and then the sleeve of her silk white dress slipped over the top of it again.

It looked like a … a branding. Scorched words burned into her skin. She started to walk away taking the empty bottle with her when I called out. "What will happen to me?"

When she turned it was graceful and flowing, the silk dress floating around her legs as she moved then settling next to her slim thighs. I wanted to beg her to help me, to let me go, but begging never helped. It only made you appear weak, and I knew this girl wouldn't set me free. No one would.

"You'll die if she has her way." Even though her words tore through me like a knife, her voice was sweet and soft, perfectly matching everything else about her, except the emptiness in her eyes. I didn't see hope or laughter or even anger. They were just eyes watching and seeing, not reacting, yet hidden there was a familiar torment.

"Why?"

She didn't say anything.

"Why did you bring me water if I'm going to die anyway? Do you get off on seeing a girl in chains? What's next … you going to whip me? Are you going to ruin your pretty silk dress with my blood?" I knew I should keep my mouth shut, but if I was going to die, then I was going to do it fighting. "I'll never beg. You can whip me until I die, but I'll never beg you to stop."

"I was afraid of that," she said in a quiet, husky whisper. "They're always watching."

"What do you mean?" She walked toward the door and opened it. "What do you mean?" I screamed.

The door shut.

Greg escorted me to the washroom. My arms and legs were so cramped that I didn't have the ability to fight him. He kept his eyes locked on me as I lowered my panties and sat on the toilet. It took a few minutes before I could finally go; stage fright took on a whole other meaning.

I washed my hands and face and then his heated fingers coiled around my arm as he led me back to the bed. I hesitated and he yanked on me so hard I slammed into his chest. His dark brows lowered over his beady shit-brown eyes. His matching shit-brown hair hung like greasy strands of thread over his forehead. His fingers tightened into a bruising grip as he thrust me toward the bed.

I shook my head back and forth, instinct fighting me as we drew closer to what had become my cage. A cage of comfort and deceptive beauty, and yet it was anything but. This was sacrificial no matter how I looked at it. I was going to die here. Used until I died. Driven to beg, but I wouldn't, and I knew that would make it worse for me.

Greg tossed me face first on the bed, and then he was on top, his thighs on either side of my pelvis.

"Get the hell off me." I freaked, my heart slamming into my chest and my pulse racing wildly as I tried to get away. I flailed wildly and knocked both of us off balance. I landed on the cement floors, my right knee hitting so hard I was screaming in pain.

Greg had no mercy as he picked me up in a bruising grip and forced me face down on the bed again. Soon I was chained, but worse I was lying on my stomach. The panic of being unable to move rushed through me, and I pulled at the chains, my back arching, my cheeks pressed into the pillow.

"It won't be long now," Greg said and then strolled casually from the room as if this was nothing to him—that a woman kidnapped and chained to a bed was a usual occurrence.

"Good! Tell that bitch I'm waiting for her." I don't know if he heard all of it since halfway through my shouting the door slammed.

I must have fallen asleep because when I opened my eyes the gray-eyed girl stood beside the bed, another water bottle in hand. She crackled the plastic casing and the lid fell to the floor. I lifted my head as much as I could, and she poured the water into my mouth. Although half of it slipped out the side and soaked into the pillow. She placed her finger under my chin to assist me and poured the cool liquid slower so I could swallow easier.

"How long have I been here?" I asked when the water was finished.

"A day and a half." She stared at me for several seconds, her delicate thin brows lowered over her eyes. She tilted her head forward so her hair swung forward and hid her face. "He's here, being forced to watch you," she whispered, and then she spun on her heel and I heard the door open and close.

I jerked on the chains. What? What did she mean? Oh God, please don't let it be Ream. I'd rather die here alone, starving, and breaking until … I no longer existed. An empty shell with nothing left inside to love, to give to anyone, to feel.

Was that what Ream had meant? How he'd felt all his life—until me.

Baby. It was his voice in my head that would save me now.

Beautiful. He was all I had left, and when I died it would be with his arms around me.

I love you, Kat.

I closed my eyes and listened to his voice over and over in my head. And then after a while, I sighed as my mind took me … gave me him and I slept in his arms.

I woke to something heavy on top of me. An arm curled around my waist, tugging me upward so the chains were taut and manacles dug into my flesh.

Cold lips on my neck.

No. No.

The naked heated skin on top of me smelled of mint … Oh God it was him. My stomach revolted and I swallowed, trying to keep the water down as the heavy body pulled me in tight against him.

It was his whisper against my ear that sent me wild. "This time we have lots of time and no one to hear you scream."

I screamed anyway. As loud as I could. Fighting. My arms straining against the immoveable chains. He was too strong, and I was like a tied-up rag doll, pathetic and weak. Unable to get free. Unable to do more than cause him to get more turned on by fighting.

I felt his cock swell and jerk as he rubbed it up against my ass. His thighs pinned me between his legs like tree trunks. "Oh, Jesus, yes, you're better than Alexa promised. A real fighter." He kissed the back of my neck, his tongue sliding down my flesh to my shoulder. He circled and kissed the spot and then bit down hard.

I yelled as the agony of his teeth tore into my skin, my body straining with tension.

"You know I fucked your boyfriend in this same bed. He screamed too." I gagged on the bile that rose in my throat and stuck my face into the pillow. "He fought like you, at least he did the first few months. And then ... then I think he enjoyed it. He especially loved it when I went down on him. Of course that was after he took care of me."

No. Ream. No. That was why. Oh God.

I love you.

I love you, Ream.

"You'll stop fighting me too. And then we will have to try some new ... things." He nibbled on my ear, his breath heavy as if his weight caused him to have trouble breathing.

The loud crash had both of us jerking, except I had nowhere to go and I couldn't see the cause of it, but I heard it.

"Get the fuck off her." Ream's voice was laced with so much rage that it was barely recognizable.

The weight lifted. "Who the fuck are ... Jesus, you're the boy. Look at you, all grown up."

"Yeah, and you're Uncle fuckin' Ben, the bastard who is going to die begging *me* for mercy this time."

The elation and fear hit me like a parade of fireworks. It was relief at him being here and then terror that if he was here then maybe he was a prisoner too.

"The key. In the drawer of the nightstand. Undo her manacles." I couldn't see him, but the laced venom in his voice would've made anyone do as he said, even if he didn't have any weapon. "Now!" I heard the door slam shut.

The cutting metal fell from my ankles and then my wrists, and the first thing I did was curl up in a ball, my knees to my chest and my arms wrapped around them. It was protective and instinctive, like my body needed to feel itself after being forced apart for two days.

"Kat. You need to get up." I closed my eyes, letting his voice trickle over me like cool water. "Kat. Do it now, baby. Go to the bathroom and shut the door," Ream ordered.

Silence.

No one moved.

Then I uncurled and lifted my head and searched the room for him.

It was my strangled sob ripping from my throat that broke through the silence. Standing with nothing but a knife held in his hand at his side and a deadly darkness in his blood shot eyes. And it was terrifying. He was terrifying and beautiful all at the same time.

There was nothing in his eyes except coldness, an iciness emanating from every part of his body as he slowly scanned mine. It was like his hands were running over my skin and goose bumps rose from his cool gaze.

"Go in the bathroom and don't come out until I tell you."

I nodded and slipped off the side of the bed and backed slowly away from Ben, at least that was what everyone called him, and I suspected no one used their real names in this place.

Ream's eyes were locked on the fifty-year-old, naked piece of shit. There was a look in his eyes that was filled with hatred for Ben. It was encompassing. Driven. It was like a dam had broken and all the pain he'd suffered at the hands of this man was revealed in his eyes.

Hatred. Pure hatred so deep that it could only go one way.

I stood in the doorway, afraid to leave Ream, afraid to close the door and have him disappear.

He didn't even look at me as he said, "Run all the taps."

His stone-cold voice still managed to flutter across my skin like butterfly wings. "Ream." His eyes remained glued to Ben. "I love you. No matter what happens."

I saw the slightest ease in his stance, nothing anyone would notice, except I did. I could. And I knew exactly what he was going to do to Ben and it didn't matter. He needed to know that. Ben deserved the consequences for what he'd done to Ream and how many others over the years.

"You love this man-whore?" Ben laughed, but it was an uneasy sound with a slight quiver to it. He was scared of Ream. As he should be. "That's all he is. A whore. And he liked it. He screamed my name when it—"

"Close the fuckin door, Kat," Ream shouted.

I slammed it shut then turned on the taps full blast. I sat on the floor as far away from the door as I could.

"I'm going to rip you apart, you little fuck."

"And I'm going to let you try. But know that you're going to die for what you did to me and to Kat." Ream's voice was steady and slow, each word pronounced with obvious threat.

When the screams started I put my hands over my ears.

Chapter Twenty-Five

It was a long time before Ben's cries became moans of begging before finally the silence. Not moving, I was curled up with my head between my legs, arms wrapped around my body.

I felt his hands on my arms, his scent surrounding me, comforting me as I breathed in. And then he was all around me.

"Baby."

That was all it took. That familiar gentle voice that sunk into me. I violently threw my arms around him. "Ream. Oh God. Ream."

He stroked my head and burrowed his face in my neck. I'd never felt like I was home until that moment. It wasn't about the place, it was the person that made the home. And I had no doubt Ream was mine.

"I'm sorry. I thought … I should've known. I should've trusted you." All the pain I caused us for not believing in him.

"Shh." He pulled back and I didn't want him to. I wanted him to keep me in his arms forever. He insisted though and quickly pulled off his T-shirt and slipped it over my head. Then he held my head between his hands to make sure I was coherent and listening because I was sobbing uncontrollably now.

"The evidence was pretty damning, baby." He caressed my cheek with his thumb. "I didn't trust myself. I knew I'd never do that to you, but … waking up like that. Not remembering. All the fucked up memories from this place … it slammed me and I couldn't think straight. It made me sick to think I did that to you."

I kissed his lips, his nose, his cheeks. "You didn't, Ream. God, I love you. And I want to get out of here and show you how much. Maybe we can go to the cottage for a while and—"

"No. Not yet. Okay?" He pulled my head into his chest and kissed the top of it. "We can't go yet. A while longer."

"Ream, we have to get out of here." I wanted to look up at him, but he kept my head tucked against his chest and I listened to the steady rhythm of his heartbeat. It was soothing, like I was cocooned in my favorite blanket.

He slipped his hand in mine and gave a light squeeze. "We have time. How are you feeling? Your legs okay?"

"They're fine, not much exertion lying on a bed for nearly two days." I tried to make light of it, but Ream's body stiffened and his arms tightened around me. "Who is ... was he?" I knew without a shadow of a doubt that Ben was dead.

"Just a sick fuck that needs fear to make him get off. It's over now, baby." Ream had to live all these years knowing this man was walking around free, hurting others. Incarceration wasn't enough for someone like that. Ream had been so young ...Ben deserved whatever Ream had done to him.

"Alexa ... she's insane, Ream."

He nodded. "As a child she was obsessive and cruel. I suspect she was the reason many of the animals in the neighborhood disappeared. But she tried to protect me, even at twelve years old. She stood up to her father and begged him not to take me downstairs." He paused. "She'd hold my hand all the way to the door leading down here. Her father wouldn't let her come any farther and then she'd kiss my cheek and squeeze my hand and tell me it would be okay." He shook his head and sighed. "Never was okay. Even when she stood waiting for me when I came back, sometimes so beaten down that I had to be carried. Lenny was adamant about his clients not leaving scars. He wanted to maintain my look of innocence he said. Paid more." I choked on my sob wanting him to stop, but knowing he needed this. "Alexandria would nurse me back to health and by Monday I'd be back at school and everything would be normal again. Week after week the same thing, until it finally stopped. Alexa thought it was her begging, but the truth was my mother's debt was paid off and Lenny surprisingly kept his word."

I nodded. It didn't make him a good person though. He pimped out a kid for two years.

"She was fourteen then, and it was no longer a little girl trying to save her hero, it was a girl wanting to make her hero hers." His arms tightened around me and he took several deep breaths. "I was never a fuckin' hero, least of all hers. I hated her for what she did. I didn't want her help.

"She had it rough too. We barely had enough to eat, but with all the druggies that came to the house, Lenny never let anyone touch her. But she was insanely jealous of Haven. She pretended not to be, but I saw her always trying to keep us apart, blaming Haven for anything that went wrong." He grunted.

I was quiet a second then I said, "I love you, Ream."

He looked up at me and I saw the coldness lingering. "I'll get you out of here."

"Us."

"Baby." He leaned in then started kissing the tear stains away. "It won't work that way. Not this time."

His words hit me so hard it knocked the breath out of me. "No." He tried to kiss me again and I yanked back. "No. Ream. No."

He sighed stroking the side of my face along the edge of my scar then kissed it, the velvet tip of his tongue caressing the raised surface. When he pulled back there was so much regret in his eyes. "I did this."

"What?"

"All of this is my fault."

"No, it's Alexa's. It's your mother's for selling her children to Lenny for drug money. I don't care how many scars I get as long as you're with me. I can fight anything if I know you're beside me." I put my hands on either side of his. "Ream. No. I won't leave here without you."

He groaned.

"No. Promise me."

"Baby—"

I was trembling and shaking my head back and forth. "No." I tried to get up, but he leaned back against the wall and dragged me with him. "We have to go."

My back was snug against his chest and his arms were around me, fingers linked. He kept me locked against him as I fought to get free. To take us away from here.

"Kat, I need you to stop. Stop fighting me."

I pounded my fist into his thigh, and he kissed the top of my head. "We need to leave." But this time my voice was a whisper because I was realizing that this ... Ream being here with me had more to it than what I'd first thought.

"Alexa's mind is warped." Ream stroked my arms slow and casual, as if we were sitting on the dock and he was telling me a story. "She grew up surrounded by druggies. Her mother ... she ran away when Alexa was two years old, at least that's what the rumor was. Most likely she overdosed." He lowered his voice. "There is only one thing she wants."

My heart slammed into my chest. "She can't have you. You're mine. I'm not letting her have you."

His mouth was in my hair and I felt the curve of his lips. "Oh, baby, I love hearing that more than anything. Those words from your lips ... I love you, Kat." I heard the hesitation and my breath hitched. "But I can't let anything happen to you, you know that, right? I told you." Fear plowed into me like a Mac truck, and I tried to turn around but he held tight.

I couldn't. I wouldn't. He was going to do something stupidly brave or just plain stupid, and I wouldn't let him. "No."

"Kitkat." His tone was strong and fierce, but I knew no matter what he said, I'd never leave him behind.

"No, you promised to marry me." I felt him stop breathing, his body stiffen, and then it was like he let it all go and brought the warmth around me and took me into him.

"Even after knowing … what I was?"

I yanked from his arms and swung around and grabbed him by the cheeks. "Yes. Don't even question that. Ever. I fell in love with you, and that's all of you. What happened here is part of who you are now, and that is the man I love."

He stared at me for several seconds then a low growl emerged from his throat and he kissed me. It was hard and unyielding, like the rush of a wild river. Despite where we were, the circumstances, it didn't matter because we had one another. His tongue sought mine, and the sweetness swarmed me bringing me into him, our lips locking together like smoldering links of metal being welded together.

He was first to pull away, and I felt his body sag into mine and it scared me because it felt like defeat.

"Ream? Why can't we leave?" This … sitting here waiting … but for what? It wasn't right. Something was off and my stomach felt like a tide crashing into jagged rocks over and over again.

He sighed and lowered his eyes.

No. No. I knew something was off. We should be running for our lives, and we were sitting here in the bathroom. "Ream. No."

"Kat—"

I felt the tears, foreign tears that now weren't so foreign anymore. "No, don't say it. I won't leave without you." I tried to get up again, but he held me to him. "Ream, let's go. We can make it."

"No, baby. We can't."

I choked back my sob and yanked myself from his arms, scrambling to my feet. "The door, it was never locked, we can get out of here." Ream sat on the floor, knees bent, watching me. The fear was like a spider weaving its web around me. "Get up, damn it."

He was so calm. Too calm. Resignation. Oh God. No. But it made sense. How he found me. How he just walked right in here and no one did a thing. How there was no rush to leave. And then I did what I swore never to do again. "Please ... Ream ... please, we can try. Please."

He got to his feet and walked over to me and then cradled me in his arms as I begged through my tears. He stroked my back and wiped away my tears with the pad of his thumb, slow and gentle, his eyes filled with concern—for me. And it was maddening. I wanted to shake him and yell and beg and then run from this place with his fingers locked with mine.

"Alexa ... called me. Made me a deal. It was the only way to get to you fast enough before Ben ...." Oh God, I didn't want to hear the rest. I just wanted to take him and run. "Baby, look at me." I closed my eyes when he tilted my head up. "I need you to look at me." I didn't want to because I knew what I'd see ... the acceptance of what this was. Of what was going to happen here. He kissed each eyelid. "Open them, beautiful."

I did and everything inside me was screaming. "Deck. Deck will come."

He shook his head. "Deck's not coming. No one knows where we are."

My breath hitched. "But he'll figure it out. Georgie will call him and he'll find us."

He caressed the side of my face and I leaned into it. "Deck's in Afghanistan. Even if Georgie can reach him again ... I won't risk your life, Kat."

"You're telling me you came here without telling anyone? Jesus, Ream, why?"

"Because I want you to live. I won't risk your life. She'll let you go and this will end." He leaned in close and kissed my cheek. "I'll get out. I'll come back to you."

"No." I pushed away from him and shoved him backwards. I turned and started walking out of the bathroom then stopped dead when I saw the body. Ben was spread eagle lying on the bed, the manacles on him. There were welts and blood all over his body like

… I looked back over my shoulder at Ream and he stared back, a cold, indifferent expression in his eyes. He knew exactly what he did and there wasn't a flicker of remorse.

Ben had damaged Ream for two years. Whatever happened in this room had been horrific for Ream. He didn't have to tell me any of it; I saw all of it in that body lying motionless.

Suddenly the door opened.

I staggered backwards until I hit Ream's chest and felt his hands on my arms holding me steady. Alexa strode in with Greg and Lance, her knowing smile brilliant as she glanced at the bed and then at us.

"Well done, Ream." She gestured to Ben's lifeless body. "And deserving, I imagine. I knew you'd like your gift from me. Ben was all giddy about being able to fuck your girlfriend here. Didn't take much to convince him to come here." She tilted her head to Lance and Greg, and they started toward us.

"No. Wait." All the hope I felt when Ream walked through that door was gone.

Ream's fingers squeezed my arms and I felt his breath against my ear as he spoke, "She'll let you go. You walk away alive."

"You trust her? You think she'll let me go?" I broke free of his grip and whirled around in his arms. "It's not over. What are you saying? Ream, damn it. You can't …" I couldn't even get the words past my lips. How could he even consider staying with Alexa. For what … my freedom? My life? How could I live every day knowing he was with her. Forced to stay.

"Kat, listen to me." He glanced up and his eyes narrowed, and I suspected Lance and Greg were moving in on us. "Go home. And you won't say one word to anyone about what happened to me. We will disappear from here and it will end. This isn't a request."

I trembled so badly that I thought I'd collapse. He couldn't mean that. Deck and his men, they did this kind of thing … he got Emily out Mexico. He'd help—

"She's been planning this for years." He grabbed my arms and shook me like he knew exactly what was going through my head. "Kat—years. She's thought of every contingency ... fuck, she had years to think of every contingency plan. We end this now. All of this ends right now."

I stared up at him for a while, at least it seemed like a while and probably was because I could hear Alexa clearing her throat and the click of her high heels as she strolled toward us.

"And what makes you think she'll just let me live? That she won't kill me the second you're out of sight."

"'Cause she gives me proof, and if she doesn't, I will never be hers."

I wanted to scream that he wasn't. That he was mine, but the words were locked in my throat. I was stubborn and I'd fight for us with my last breath, but I wasn't stupid. Ream and I wouldn't escape past Greg and Lance.

"One more thing," Alexa's words sent a chill straight through me.

Ream jerked. "Alexa. Our deal."

She smiled. "Oh, it's just a little reminder to the little princess as to whom you belong now. And what will happen if she ever opens that luscious mouth of hers. I promise, she won't be hurt and then I'll have Greg drive her back to the city."

My heart pounded so fast I felt as if it would break through my ribs. The gleam in her eyes sparkled with pleasure at whatever she had planned.

Greg walked up and took my arm; I instantly reacted, trying to break free, feeling as if a noose was tightening around my neck.

"Go with him, Kat." Ream's words tore open my insides. There was nothing in his voice that was alive. It was like a frost had settled over him and numbed the blood running through his veins.

But I did what he asked and walked quietly beside Gregg, with Ream and Lance behind me, and Alexa's stiletto heels clicking, leading the way.

Chapter Twenty-Six

I writhed. I struggled. Fought. I shouted and I even resorted to begging. I knew it wouldn't stop what was about to happen. Nothing would and yet, remaining silent … I couldn't do it.

But Ream never fought. His face stoic and emotionless as Lance secured him to the wooden post, hands cuffed to a ring above his head.

Greg had his arm locked around my waist and his other hand was clamped around my wrists so tight I could no longer feel my hands.

Alexa strolled around the post like a cat stalking her prey, her long graceful strides, nothing like the girl Molly who she had pretended to be. "This is for her, Ream. To protect her. I'd hate to have to have her killed. She'll see the truth in my words once we are done here."

"I won't fucking say anything, damn it. I swear." But as I said the words, I knew they were a lie. Alexa saw it too. She knew what Ream meant to me. She knew what I was like; she'd been watching me and everyone else for months. There was no question I was lying because I'd hunt her down and kill her myself if I had to. I'd never leave Ream, and I'd do whatever it took to get him back.

"I suspect you will the first chance you get. You'll call Deck and then maybe the police, but I will show you what will happen if you do."

She walked over to the far side of the room, and Lance pulled a string which flicked on a light bulb above his head. It felt as if I'd been hit in the stomach as the air left me, and I choked back my horror at the array of weapons that hung on the wall. "No. Please. Don't do that to him." I sagged in Greg's arms as the devastation at what Alexa was going to do tore a hole through my stomach.

"We'll start light, shall we, Ream? To warm you up to the idea. Doesn't matter about scars now, does it? I don't mind them. It will be a reminder as to who you belong to." Alexa plucked a long coiled whip off the wall and walked back toward Ream. She ran her fingers along his tattooed back then down his spine to his jeans. She leaned close so her breasts were up against him, and I saw her whisper something in his ear.

Ream never moved. He didn't flinch. He didn't react. Nothing.

She laughed and then walked away a few feet before she turned and the leather whip uncoiled and sliced into Ream's back.

I screamed, fighting against Greg's relentless hold. "Ream," I choked out. "No. Please, I swear I won't say anything. Please."

There wasn't even a glance my way as my words went ignored and Alexa brought down the whip again. Then harder again. And again. He never moved. His back muscles flexed when the whip hit, almost as if they were trying to run away, but the muscles bounced back only to have it repeat over and over again.

Alexa nodded to Lance and my eyes widened in horror as he walked over to the wall and grabbed another weapon. It had several feet of long strands and at the end of each one was something shiny. Shudders racked through me as I watched Alexa take the weapon from Lance.

"You see, Ream came here knowing full well he was exchanging his life for yours." She walked around the post, the whip dragging along the cement floor behind her. "And he wouldn't risk your life by telling anyone or coming in here guns blazing. You know why, princess ... because I have extra insurance."

She raised the whip over her head, and this time Ream did flinch as the weapon launched across his back. His fingers curled into the wood and his body stiffened, and I heard a controlled groan escape his mouth. Blood dripped down his back from whatever was on the ends of the strands of the whip.

"Alexa, I swear I'll never say anything," I sobbed. And now I meant the words. She loved Ream, in her own sick, disgusting way, and she was abusing him, hurting him just to prove a point. To make certain I'd never forget the images of this in my mind.

And she was right. I wouldn't. She engraved them in me.

Alexa raised her arm and the sound of the whip hitting his flesh echoed in the room. It was as if I could hear his skin splitting open.

It came down on him again and again until he collapsed. All his weight hanging from his arms secured to the ring on the post.

Ream. Oh God. Ream. No.

My eyes tore away from Ream as Alexa stepped in front of me. I hadn't even noticed her. But when she held out her hand holding the whip with Ream's blood dripping off the strands I couldn't stop myself as I raised my head and glared at her.

"Fuck you, bitch." I spit in her face.

Suddenly Greg's arms released me and I saw Alexa's arm rise with the whip ready to hit me with it.

"Do it, and I'll never be yours." Ream's voice tore through the room in a loud bellow. I didn't even think he was capable of talking after what she'd just done to him.

Alexa lowered her arm and before Greg could grab me again I ran to Ream.

"Get her," Alexa said, her tone as if I was a pesky rodent who'd escaped her trap.

I banged into the post, my trembling limbs barely able to support me as I used the structure to hold me up.

"Ream." I was careful not to touch his shredded back as I cupped his head in my hands. Choked sobs and fresh tears streamed down my face. I could smell the copper scent of his blood and the perspiration of his ravaged body.

"Go, Kat." His voice was broken and raspy, as if it hurt him just to speak two words.

"I love you, baby," I cried then pressed my mouth to his quivering lips. They just touched before I was suddenly torn away.

Greg's arm looped around my waist, lifting me off the ground, and then he headed for the door.

"Ream!" I screamed. "Please. No." I didn't give a crap about looking weak or if I begged. Nothing mattered except that I was being torn away from Ream.

Greg's hand reached out for the doorknob just as it flung open and hit him square in the face. He staggered back and dropped me. I fell to the floor and went to scramble back to Ream when I looked up at the gun pointed at … I turned my head. Pointed at Alexa.

"My love. I told you to wait in my room. You'd see him soon enough." Alexa's voice held a slight uneasiness to it as she slowly started walking toward the door. "Do not act foolishly. You know what will happen."

"Don't move." The girl with the gray eyes held the gun with one hand, steadily pointed at Alexa.

"Sweetie. What are you doing? I've cared for you. Given you everything you've ever wanted. We have been like … sisters."

I heard the shuffle of feet and saw Greg make his move. I jerked when the gun went off and Greg fell to the floor, blood seeping from the wound in his chest.

When I looked back at Alexa, she didn't even seem affected by Greg's death. She confidently took another step forward and reached out her hand. "Give me the gun. We will talk about this."

The girl shook her head, and her blonde strands flowed back and forth over her shoulders. "No. You lied to me. You told me you'd never go after him if I stayed with you. You promised me. I did everything you wanted. Everything. Not once did I go against you and for what? So you could plan all along to go after my brother?"

I heard the clang of the ring hit the post and then Ream's ragged voice. "Haven?"

I gasped. Haven. His sister? But she died … in the hospital.

"He belongs to me," Alexa shouted.

The gun went off again and this time the bullet hit the floor next to Alexa. "Haven. You'd be dead in the street by now if Olaf hadn't taken you from the hospital. Ream couldn't look after you. We did. You're family. Both of you are. And now we will have Ream back, don't you see? We'll all be together again. I did this for us."

My gaze shot back to Haven and I expected to see her faltering under Alexa's persuasion, but her gray eyes remained unwavering and fixed on her. "Maybe I would be dead by now. But that would've been my choice. Do you think I wanted to live with you? To live in a disgusting house where I was terrorized then raped. To be fed drugs like candy so I'd have to rely on Olaf for my next fix. To have to beg him for it. And you … you wanted to keep me like a pet in a cage—"

"No. That's not true," Alexa said, her voice now beginning to quake.

"And now you want to do the same thing to Ream. No, Alexa. I will kill him before I will allow you to torture him like you've done to me all these years."

"Haven, I love you." Alexa's voice broke and I saw the realization in her eyes just before Haven said, "And you can die knowing I've always hated you."

The gun went off.

I watched as if in slow motion as Alexa's eyes widened and her hands went to her chest and then pulled away as she stared down at the blood. Her blood. She looked back up at Haven, her mouth opening like she was going to say something. Then she crumpled to the floor.

I didn't wait any longer as I staggered to my feet and went running to Ream. I'd forgotten about Lance and he dove for me. He was agile and quick, but Haven, whoever she'd become over the years, didn't hesitate as she pulled the trigger again, and Lance's hand just hit my shoulder as he fell.

Haven walked toward us, the gun still pointed at Lance now lying on the floor writhing in pain. Then she stood over him, and I saw him reach out his hand. She never said a word as the gun went off again; Lance's body jerked then went still.

Haven crouched down and searched in his pockets then pulled out a key which she tossed to me. "Get him down."

I didn't pay much attention to her as I quickly ran the rest of the way to Ream. I stood on my tiptoes as I put the key in the cuffs that were latched to the ring in the post.

"Baby." He was barely able to breathe from the pain. In shock, his flesh pale and body shaking violently.

As soon as his hands were free, he buckled into my arms, dragging me to the floor with him. "Haven." I couldn't carry him. I'd need her help to get him out of here.

When I looked up, she was walking back into the room carrying a red plastic gasoline container. She started pouring the liquid all over the place, the fumes so pungent I started coughing.

"Ream. Ream, we have to get out of here. Get up. You have to get up." I wrapped my arm around his waist and felt him stiffen as the material from my shirt brushed up against his wounds. "Ream, damn it. Get. Up," I yelled.

I tried to get to my feet, but my legs were weak and I didn't have the strength to pick him up from the floor. Suddenly, Haven was on the other side of him and she looped her arm around him and we both hauled him to his feet.

"Haven." His eyes were closed, but he knew she was there saving him. She was his twin, his other half, his angel.

She never said a word.

We half dragged, half carried him to the door. Then Haven stopped. She didn't even look at me as she passed me her gun then reached into her pocket, pulled out a match, and struck it against the doorframe. It sizzled as it caught flame, the bright orange illuminating her indifferent expression. Then she threw it over her shoulder into a pool of gasoline.

"Let's go."

The smoke was thick by the time we reached the side door. The crackle of wood as it burned sounded like gunfire, and I cringed every time, afraid someone was going to come up behind us and stop us, take us back, or kill us.

But soon I was sucking in fresh air, coughing, and spitting up the ash that was in my lungs. Ream hung between us as Haven pushed us farther, not stopping until we reached a fence line. She kicked at a couple of wood boards and they sprung free.

Then she hauled off and slapped Ream in the face. I gasped, but she ignored me and grabbed him by the chin. "Ream." He flinched and I saw his eyes flicker open, glazed over and bloodshot. He was nearly unconscious from the pain. "Get on your knees. You need to crawl through that hole. You hear me, Ream." When she let go of his face, I could see the imprint left from her fingers.

"Let him go," Haven ordered.

"But he'll—"

I didn't finish the sentence because Haven grabbed Ream from me and he crashed to his knees, his back arching at the pain jolting through him. I stared up at her in horror, my mouth hanging open.

"Pain drives the body to do more than you'd think possible." It was a statement and I had a feeling she knew that statement better than anyone. Then I thought of the branding I'd seen on her inner wrist.

Haven held the boards up and Ream agonizingly crawled through and then we followed. My legs reacted to the exertion, the pins and needles running rampant, but I didn't have the nervousness to accompany it, and that was how I figured I lasted so long. I was calm.

Ream was beside me. We were alive.

Just as the boards slammed shut behind us I heard the loud bang of something blowing up and instinctively covered Ream's body with my own. Haven wasn't waiting for anything though and grabbed my arm. "Move it. The police will be here any minute."

"But they can help ..." My voice trailed off as she picked up Ream, ignoring me. I scrambled to help and then we were running down the street. I noticed the street lights weren't working and wondered if that was coincidence or not. Five right in a row and one above the blue nondescript car she was currently unlocking.

I went to get in the backseat with Ream, but Haven pulled me back and pressed the keys into my hand. I looked up at her confused.

"I don't know how to drive," she stated, and then she went in the back seat with Ream and slammed the door.

I started driving; although I had no idea where we were and the car was really old and didn't have GPS. But Haven directed me to the highway, and after we passed the first sign, I knew where we were and pressed my foot down on the pedal.

The hospital wasn't that far away. I started to take the exit ramp that had the blue sign with the big H. A hand clamped down on my shoulder. "No hospital."

"But—"

I looked at her face in the rearview mirror and she shook her head. "No. I just blew up a house ... killed Alexa, and two men. Olaf. That filthy lowlife is still alive. If we go to the hospital and there is a report ... he'll find out we're alive. Our best hope is he thinks we all died in that blaze."

"Okay." Holy shit. There was no question this Olaf would look into what happened. "Okay, we'll go to the farm."

I saw her nod and then she leaned back in the seat, Ream's head in her lap. For a second when I looked in the mirror, I saw the cold, hard expression in her face falter when she looked down at him. I had a feeling the sister Ream once knew had died in that hospital and this woman ... the one who didn't even flinch when she killed three people … she wasn't his little angel anymore.

We arrived at the farm and I honked the horn all the way up the driveway. By the time I pulled the car to a stop, Logan, Emily, Crisis, and Kite were all there. No questions were asked as to who Haven was or what happened or where I'd been for nearly two days. I don't think words were necessary when they saw Ream's back.

Logan and Kite lifted him out of the car while Emily pulled me into a crushing hug.

"When Georgie showed up at the gallery and you weren't there … Then Ream disappeared … Georgie finally got a hold of Deck. He's on a flight here now." Emily's tears soaked into Ream's shirt I was still wearing.

"Ream. I need to see Ream." I didn't want to talk about anything right now; all I wanted to do was hold Ream.

Emily pulled away. "Yeah. Oh my God, yeah."

We started to walk to the house when a car door shut. Haven. Shit.

She was leaning against the side of the car, her body stiff and unyielding, blood all over her white dress. She held the gun clenched in her hand at her side, eyes narrowed on Crisis who stood in front of her staring.

"Fuck, you're his twin. You're Haven."

Crisis knew about her? I waited for her reaction, if she was going to give any at all. Her piercing gray eyes met Crisis's and she stared at him.

Then her rigid expression wavered, the gun fell from her grasp, and she collapsed to the ground.

Epilogue

Two months later

"Baby, get your ass over here." Ream had the frayed yellow rope in his hand.

I rolled my eyes then cocked my hip and placed my hand on it. "Pumpkin." He hated when I called him that. "I'm not doing it. Told you that. But you can come over here and kiss my ass."

Ream laughed. It was a real laugh, one that started deep in the stomach and went all the way up through the chest with a deep vibration. I bit my bottom lip as I watched, wanting to say screw this and run back to the cottage while everyone was here and have him do more than kiss my ass.

"He looks … relaxed," Emily leaned into me and whispered. "There was always something in him that was … I don't know, sad and dark. I could never put my finger on it." Emily nodded to Haven who was leaning up against a tree, arms crossed and staring off into the distance. She hadn't wanted to come with us, but Ream told her if she didn't come, then he was staying and if he stayed no one could go. She came. "That girl is seriously hurting."

I nodded. She'd woken up three days after she collapsed in the driveway. Deck found us a doctor willing to keep quiet—with cash of course. There'd been nothing wrong with her—exhaustion. Ream on the other hand had weeks of bandage changes and two rounds of antibiotics.

Like me, he'd live with the scars of Alexa and her madness, but it only made us stronger. She would've been pissed to know that.

"I can't get her to talk. Ream's tried so many times but she just … it's like she's staring right through him, not even taking in what he's saying." Ream had that look once, and now I knew where it came from. He'd told me from the beginning he had a fucked-up past; well, fucked-up didn't even begin to describe it.

"I'm sure the therapist I saw would be happy to see her. She was really nice, didn't push me—much."

I nodded. But I suspected Haven wouldn't take any help offered. Maybe not for a long time … if ever.

Logan and Emily had moved into their new place, a ten acre "fuck-nest" as Crisis liked to call it. It was quaint with an old eighteenth century house up on a hill overlooking a pond. It was also far from the road and had iron gates across the driveway. Logan had a security system put in, top of the line with cameras around the property. Emily came home last week with a German Shepherd puppy to which Logan said "no way." The puppy was named Tear. Emily said he was named after the band. Logan said it was because the dog tears everything to pieces. Tear was at the farm with Hank while we were here.

Haven moved into the farm, although we rarely saw her as she spent most of her time outside somewhere … None of us really knew where she went. Ream was frustrated and I suspected hurt because Haven refused to let him in. Maybe in time she would. I hoped she would. I knew she cared about him, I'd seen her face in the car, althhough that look had never crossed her face again.

They'd both sacrificed for one another. Ream gave up his innocence in order to protect hers, only to have it broken by her rapist. Then Haven gave herself to Alexa and Olaf in exchange for Ream's safety.

But that wasn't enough for Alexa.

I didn't know how Haven was treated, if she was abused or

forced to prostitute herself like Ream had been, but she'd been a prisoner. A prisoner for twelve years and that was something many couldn't come back from.

Deck had taken Haven aside and talked to her. I figured he was getting as much of the story as he could so he could keep us out of the police investigation on the house. I suspected Deck had something to do with the quick closure of the inquiry too. They would've found out how the fire started, yet it was deemed accidental.

What I couldn't figure was Haven's ability with a gun and that she was no longer a drug addict. Ream asked her outright, but that got him nowhere because Haven simply walked away.

I looked at Logan, Crisis, and Ream, who were talking quietly together, the lake behind them, the sun beaming down on their naked chests. Ream's hair was wet from swimming, and I felt the familiar warmth of love as I ran my gaze over him.

"What do you think they're talking about?" Emily asked.

"How sexy we are?" She snorted. "Or how much they love us and can't live without us."

"I think they're conspiring to get us sloshed tonight for drunk sex," Emily said.

Ream glanced over at me and winked. My heart skipped a beat, and I smiled. "Drunk sex is loud and the walls are paper thin in this place. I'm thinking lake sex at midnight. You can have it here." The cliff was a perfect spot, but Ream and I had it last night under the stars. Tonight I wanted lake sex, right after I kicked his ass at Monopoly. We went and bought a new board right after we all went go-karting. But this time I made sure he was never alone with the attendants.

Crisis kicked all our asses and surprisingly Kite came next. Guess he was better at live racing than gaming. Logan tied with Ream, although I think Ream did beat him by a fraction of a second. Emily and I ... well, we both decided to take it easy on the men. Kicking their butts in front of everyone, it was more fun watching them hack it out.

But Ream knew I threw the race.

He'd tossed me onto his shoulder and smacked my butt as we walked ahead of everyone back to the car. "You lost on purpose, baby."

He set me down against the car and leaned in. I wrapped my arms around his neck. "So then you owe me."

He raised his brows. "How so?"

I smiled.

"I don't recall making any wager." He nipped my neck.

I tilted my head to the side to give him better access then moaned as his tongue swirled over the sensitive place he nipped. "For saving you any embarrassment at losing to your girlfriend—"

"Fiancée," he growled then bit my neck—hard.

"Oww." I shoved back on his chest, but he was immoveable. "Okay, fiancée." We didn't have a date yet, and there was no rush. I'd been adamant at not even discussing it until after Logan and Emily's wedding in February. They wanted a winter wedding with a horse drawn sleigh to which Clifford was delegated. I think the damn horse was proud of being given a job.

"What do I owe you then, beautiful?"

He made his payment last night up on the cliff under the stars. Thin walls or not, I was certain they all heard me scream his name down at the cottage.

"Oh no." Emily grabbed my arm, jerking me from my thoughts.

"What?"

"Run."

"What?"

"Run!"

I glanced up and saw Ream and Logan running toward us. My eyes widened and Emily and I both bolted down the path. But neither of us were quick enough as we were hitched up by our men and carried kicking and laughing and screaming back up the hill.

"On three," Ream said.

"One," Logan counted.

Emily squealed. "Logan. Put me down. Don't you dare."

"Ream. No." I kicked and squirmed in his arms. His reaction was a chuckle.

"Fuck it. Go," Ream said.

Ream ran with me in his arms, Logan and Emily beside us as the boys jumped off the edge of the cliff and we plunged into the cool water at the same time.

I came up sputtering, Ream's arms still locked around me, and Logan and Emily were busy kissing then sinking beneath the surface of the water.

I heard a strange yelp from above and looked up just as Crisis flew over the edge of the cliff with Haven in his arms.

Holy shit.

"Fuck," Ream said, his arms tightening around me.

When they surfaced, Crisis was laughing his ass off and Haven clung to him for dear life. Shit, it was obvious she couldn't swim. Her eyes were wide and she was staring at Crisis like he was a lunatic. Well, maybe he was a little.

Ream was all revved up and ready to kick his ass, but I wrapped my legs around his hips and kissed him before he could start something with Crisis.

"Haven, babe. We are so doing that again." I looked up just as I caught the tiny quirk at the corner of her mouth. Crisis kept her locked to his side while he helped her to the edge of the lake, and before she could take off and hide like she always did, he grabbed her hand and pulled her along behind him.

Ream's eyes watched as the two disappeared up the path. His eyes narrowed and I could feel his shoulders tense beneath my hands. "She isn't dating that asshole."

I smiled. It wasn't like Ream would have a choice in anything when it came to Haven. She may be hurt and broken and driven inside herself, but the girl had shot three people point-blank, blew up a house, and survived twelve years as a prisoner.

Yeah, that girl was deciding her own fate.

I leaned against the kitchen counter and watched Ream from across the room. He was talking to Logan and chuckling at something he'd said. His grip on the beer bottle comfortable and relaxed—actually, everything about him was relaxed. Even more so now than ever was this complete confidence that rolled off him in waves.

I could hear him say something to Logan, and the husky deep sound vibrated with a familiar tone that felt like it was made just for me.

He was made just for me.

As if Ream knew I was thinking about him, he glanced at me and my heart leaped then started pounding as his eyes raked over my body. I cocked my hip and put my hand on it and lowered my gaze. Then I tilted my head slightly and my hair fell easily to the side making a veil across half my face. Slowly, I dragged my teeth over my lower lip.

I didn't have to look up to know that he was striding toward me. My body knew and it was heating up and lighting up with tingling, and these were good tingles. Actually, my symptoms had been behaving as of late. I'd even gained some of the weight back with the nutritionist's recommendations. I think Ream had something to do with it as well. I slept curled in his arms at night and woke to demanding kisses every morning.

There was an ease to us. A trust built after what had happened that had driven both of us into a place that not many relationships had. Logan and Emily had it—the ability to know what one another needed and giving it to them completely.

His smell hit me first and I breathed it in like a drug. Then his touch as his finger nudged beneath my chin and raised my head so I had to meet his eyes. Desire spread through me like wildfire in a heated blanket.

"You flirting with me, beautiful?"

His soft whispered tone was an orgasm in itself, and I held back my moan. He'd become even more cocky about his sexual prowess. He even let me go down on him once and the touching was slowly getting better. I think it was because his past was no longer hidden and he could finally begin to heal. "Is it working?"

His finger tightened on my chin. Then he leaned in and my breath hitched just before his mouth claimed mine. It was a hard, slow kiss, his tongue gliding across my teeth then seeking the familiar warmth of the velvet touch of my mouth. Claiming. Needing. Him telling me I was his.

I sagged into him and he wrapped his arm around my lower back, and with one sharp tug had me up against him, the hardness of his muscles pressing into me.

He groaned and deepened the kiss. "Kat."

I buried my hands into the short strands of his hair and pulled, needing him closer, wanting every part of him to be mine.

He was mine. Ream had been mine since the beginning, and it took us getting back to our beginning to find our way back to that.

"You going to fuck her right there on the kitchen counter, buddy?" Crisis's voice separated us.

I lifted my thigh onto Ream's hip, and he easily hitched me up so I could curl my legs around his waist. Then I looked over his shoulder at Crisis who stood beside Kite. "No, he's going to fuck me out on the beach. And then in the water, and maybe if I beg, he'll fuck me on the dock too."

Crisis rolled his eyes and groaned. Then I noticed his eyes go to the closed door and his smile faded. Haven had disappeared behind that door right after dinner.

I caught Emily's eye and she winked at me then took Logan's hand and stood on her tiptoes as she whispered into his ear. His expression never changed, but there was a slight tightening in his muscles. I just bet she'd just asked him to go to the cliff.

Ream nipped my ear and then his tongue slid over the sensitive spot. "You going to beg?"

"Baby, I'm going to do more than beg." I kissed the tip of his nose. "God, you're so lucky I gave you a second chance." He carried me to the sliding door, and I reached behind and slid it open for us. "Nite, everyone," I shouted over his shoulder.

Ream shut the door with the heel of his foot then his hands squeezed my ass. "I don't need second chances, Kitkat."

I ran my finger down his cheek then across to his lips where he grabbed it between his teeth then drew it in his mouth. "Bah, we're together because I gave you a second chance." I pulled my finger from his mouth and interlocked my fingers around his neck and hung my weight on him.

He adjusted his hold on me as we walked down the path to the water. "Never needed a second chance."

I laughed, rolling my eyes. "Sweetie, you needed a second chance. It was a dick move and you're lucky I took you back. I'm just super understanding and forgiving. I'm thinking I need some payback for being such an amazing chick."

The moonlight caught the glimmer of heated arrogance in his eyes, and I wiggled my pelvis into his waist.

"Second chances are for when you're done with the first. I wasn't done. I'll never be done. I don't need second chances, beautiful. Not with you. You're my first chance. And fuck if I love my first chance." He lowered to his knees on the grassy patch at the edge of the beach and had me flat on my back and my shirt ripped off before I could even come back with something. His first chance. His only chance. I reached up and cupped his cheek. "Ream?"

He finished taking his shirt off and tossed it somewhere behind me. "Yeah, baby?"

"I love our first chance too." His eyes smoldered and I continued, "And I'd have given you as many chances as you needed."

He groaned and then his mouth crushed mine and the weight of him came over me. My hands stroked, caressed, and touched every part of him as any control I had detonated into the evening air.

I clutched him to me, his cock pressed into my pelvis, his thighs straddling mine while his fierce kiss bruised my lips and took what I was more than willing to give.

"Please." I slipped my hand between us and tried to undo his pants. Needing. Wanting. Desperate to ease the ache that Ream ignited in me. "I need it in me now."

Ream pulled back, putting his palms on the grass on either side of my head. He stared at me for several seconds, and I breathed hard, feeling as if I would combust if he didn't kiss me, or fuck me, or do something.

"You need *me* in you."

"Yeah, that's what I said."

"No, you said *it*."

I reached up, curled my fingers into his hair, and yanked down. His arms gave way to the pressure and he was full on top of me again. "Semantics." I kissed him, my lips roaming over his, taking what was mine and knowing that whatever happened with me, that Ream would stand with me.

He'd been willing to sacrifice his life for mine. Just like he had for his sister, giving up his innocence in order to protect hers. I realized that when Ream loved, it was truly unconditional and it was what I needed all along. Him. His overprotectiveness. His determination. His understanding.

He rolled to the side, slid his pants off then ripped my panties and threw them over his shoulder. His finger slipped into my wetness and flicked across my clit.

My back arched. "Ream."

He kissed every part of me, taking his time, his hands caressing while his tongue tasted and his mouth worshiped. I writhed and begged him to put his cock inside me before he even got to between my legs.

Ream licked the wetness and then suckled hard, then soft and gentle. My body was a roller coaster of emotions, teetering on the edge then coming down again as he eased off.

Abruptly, he shoved two fingers inside me, and I moaned at the pain-pleasure of the sudden intrusion. He moved in and out while his thumb circled up higher causing my legs to open farther and my muscles to tighten. I lifted my butt off the ground, wanting more. Needing more.

"Fuck, you're beautiful," he said as his fingers continued to pump in and out of me while his other hand reached up and his finger stroked the side of my cheek where my scar was. It was a white line now and I could cover it up with makeup, but most of the time I didn't. It was part of me. I accepted it, just like I did my MS. And I had the support of Ream and my friends. I'd never face this alone, and I knew then that I didn't want to. Them knowing didn't make me weak, it made me stronger than ever.

He pulled his fingers from me and grabbed his cock and slid it between my legs. I planted my feet hard into the ground and lifted up just as he placed his cock at my opening. It pushed inside hard and deep, and I moaned, closing my eyes.

"Anxious?" Ream pulled his hips back a bit, and he slid out then tilted his pelvis and sunk deep again.

"Love you, baby." I curled my hand around his neck and brought his mouth to mine. That did it. Getting Ream to lose control took work, and I figured out what did it—sweetness. It won over my sass every time, so I used it to get what I needed. And what I needed was him fucking me.

He pushed into me hard, then slowly withdrew, and then shoved inside me again. Over and over until I panted and clenched at every part of him. He grabbed my thigh that I'd locked around his waist, fingers bruising my flesh as he thrust harder, faster, deeper.

"Oh God." I closed my eyes, my nails digging into his tatted forearms just below the inked butterflies. "Please. Ream."

"No. Wait," he growled. His pelvis rocked into me again and again, and I met his every movement, our bodies slick and slapping into one another, the sound echoing across the still water. He stopped moving and grabbed my hands and put them above my head.

Our fingers interlocked—just like we were. Like we'd always be.

The broken lock with the damaged key now fit together. We'd opened one another up, and it was beautiful.

He started moving again and lowered his head and kissed me. It was gentle and sweet, but filled with so much meaning. I submitted more of myself to him. Gave him all of me.

He thrust faster.

"Now," he murmured on my lips.

I let the feelings take me and my body succumbed to the climax and fell over the edge into a whirling tornado of ecstasy. Ream did several more hard thrusts, and then his mouth left mine. He tensed, his head back and jaw tight, eyes closed.

It took a few moments before Ream opened his eyes and met mine. Our hands were still locked and his cock still deep inside me. "No other. Ever."

I wasn't sure if he was saying that to me or telling me that I would have no other. It didn't really matter. Either way there would never be another. Ream was it for me.

We sat on the end of the dock, the full moon hitting the water so it looked like sparkling diamonds scattered across the surface. I sat between his legs, our feet swirling in the water while his head nuzzled my neck and his arm held me tight against him.

"So are you ever going to tell me who owns this place?"

"Mhmm," he murmured while his teeth nibbled the tip of my ear. "She's this hot sexy girl that adores me. I didn't tell you about her?"

"Ream," I smacked his thigh and he grabbed my hand and curled our fingers together.

He chuckled. "Well, she may have been sexy fifty years ago. Remember I told you about Urma?"

"The old woman who let you and Haven stay in her shed?"

He nodded. "She died a number of years ago. She must have seen something to do with the band and recognized me because her lawyer contacted me after she passed away. Urma left the cottage to me and Haven. The neighbor next door, she keeps an eye on it for me. She also stocks it when I bring my kidnapped women here." I laughed and he grinned. Ream may have called Haven his little angel, but it sounded like Urma had been both of theirs. "I came here after you were shot. I don't know … it always had this calming effect on me. Like Urma did. This place feels like her, simple and warm … safe. Her … that shed … it was safe. Didn't know her long, but she was like a mother, I guess. Like a mother should be. She cared." He caressed the side of my face with his thumb. "But now I have you. You're my safe, Kat."

I linked our fingers together and then pulled his hand to my mouth and kissed each finger. "There's nothing safe about me, Ream." No, I still had a battle to fight, one that would last the rest of my life, however long that was. But I wasn't alone. I didn't have to fight it by myself, and that made it so much easier to accept.

Ream squeezed my hand. "Baby, you're the safest place I've ever been. You're the only place I'll ever belong." He kissed my neck. "And you belong with me."

The End.

Dedication

This book is dedicated to all those suffering with Multiple Sclerosis. It is a complex disease that affects the CNS (Central Nervous System). It's unpredictable and the symptoms can vary immensely with each individual. An estimated 100,000 people are affected by this disease in Canada alone and over 2.3 million worldwide. This disease is usually diagnosed between the ages of fifteen and forty, but children have also been affected by MS. Many people with MS can and do live a productive life.

There is no cure.
But there is support. No one has to be alone.

http://www.overcomingmultiplesclerosis.org/

http://mssociety.ca

http://www.mayoclinic.org/diseases-conditions/multiple-sclerosis/basics/definition/con-20026689

A message from the Author

Hey you guys,
Thank you so much for reading "Overwhelmed by You." I hope
you enjoyed Kat and Ream's story. If you wouldn't mind helping
me out and leaving a review on the site where you purchased
Overwhelmed by You it would be much appreciated. Thank you!
All your support and love has been incredible. Truly, I'm floored.
So many new friends. I love chatting with each of you. So please,
come say hi on FB.
Cheers,
Nash xx

Acknowledgments

I wish I could name every individual I've had the pleasure to chat with on FB or through email or on GR. I wouldn't be here without you. Your amazing support, kind words, comments and the incredible reviews you've take the time to write … I seriously can't thank you enough. I love chatting with you and even though I haven't met most of you personally, I feel like I've made some great friends.

To Sarah, my emergency beta reader and my punching bag. When I'm freaking out over something you calmly put everything back into perspective … thank you.

To my editors Kristin, the Romantic editor and Max, The Polished Pen … this book breathes because of you both.

Kari from Cover to Cover designs, thank you for putting up with my constant emails when we are working on a cover. You see my vision and always gave me a kick ass cover. Love you.

Stacey, my wonderful formatter and Debra, The Book Enthusiast Promotions—you both 'bring it' every single time!

My beta reader Paula—WOW. I hope you realize you belong to me now!

Melissa, my pre-beta reader and my go to girl when I have plot issues or just … issues, lol. Love you missy. To my rockin' beta readers from SMI book club—Yaya…my personal stalker…and Midian, you girls saw things when I didn't … Love you!

Tia, damn I'm so lucky to have found you. You're jewelry is stunning and I love that the characters can come to life with your pieces. You are a remarkable woman!

To the bloggers I consider friends: G&J Totally Booked; Jessica

& Sarah Lovely Books; Kayla the Bibliophile and Sassy Sara. Thank you for all your love and support

To the amazing authors who I've had the pleasure to chat with and are truly stars with their words and their hearts...Penelope Ward, Pepper Winters, Nicola Hakin, Carmen Jenner, Lili St. Germain.

WOW...the bloggers. You girls are something else and I'm in awe of what you do. Thank you for your constant support, and for bringing books into the spotlight with your incredible devotion.

Elaine and Susan ... damn, I'm so lucky to have met beautiful warm women like you both.

To everyone in the Torn from You Book Club and my admins Michelle, Sarah and Jessica. Each of you have made me laugh and brought so much enjoyment to this long process of making my book come alive—thank you.

And to my agent Mark Gottlieb at Trident Media Group, thank you for all your support and your confidence in me. I'm excited to make this new journey with you.

Of course, as always, to my furry friends who give me unconditional love even when I'm in my writing cave. And to my ever supportive family—I love you.

Hugs and kisses to each of you.

What's Next

Nashoda Rose

Unyielding Series
"Perfect Chaos" (Unyielding #1) Georgie and Deck
"Perfect Ruin" (Unyielding #2) London and Kai
"Perfect ?" (Unyielding #3)

Tear Asunder Series (in no particular order)
"Untitled" (Tear Asunder #3) Crisis and Haven
"Untitled" (Tear Asunder #4)

Writing as Cindy Paterson (paranormal romance)

"Take" (Senses #4) Jasper and Max

Perfect Chaos (Unyielding #1)
by
Nashoda Rose

Prologue

I smoothed out the wrinkles on my bedspread then placed my stuffed brown bunny rabbit up against the white-and-pink flowered throw pillow. At sixteen, I was a little old for stuffed animals, but it had been a gift from my brother the first time he went away to Afghanistan with the military.

I straightened, then saw the sheet hanging down in the right corner and quickly tucked it back into the mattress. Perfect. I liked it … okay I was obsessed with being organized. Everything had its place, even me. I kept to the same bland colorless clothes, the same schedule, the same hair style. Why mess with what worked? My brother often teased me and said I should join the Canadian forces like him. I may like neat and tidy, but I hated fighting, blood, guns, and, unquestionably, any killing.

Connor knew that. He'd helped me bury my goldfish Goldie in the backyard when I was seven. Then the hamster Fiddlehead when I was ten. To this day there was a marked stone that Connor had made for him that was near the back fence. I could see it whenever I looked out the kitchen window.

I jerked as a car door slammed, which sounded as if it was in our driveway. The sun had just peaked over the horizon; it was too early for any visitors, plus it was Sunday and dad had the rule that he and mom sleep in. I always rose early wanting to get ahead of the day, another reason Connor said I'd excel in the military. Although, we both knew he'd never allow me anywhere near danger, which I was very content with. Danger to me was if my shampoo was missing and I had to use my brother's instead.

Connor wasn't due back for another month, that meant ... A sudden freeze hit my body, locking my limbs in place as I realized who might be in our driveway at six in the morning on a Sunday. My breath trapped in my throat as if clamped hands were strangling me.

No.

No. I shook my head back and forth. *Please don't knock.*

It was the newspaper boy. Early. He was an hour early today. In a second, I'd hear the clang as the newspaper bundle hit the metal screen door.

Eyes squeezed tightly shut, I waited for the familiar sound.

Nothing. I sucked in large amounts of air for my starved lungs.

Not him. Please, not him.

Connor.

Connor.

My heart thumped harder and harder in its cage and tears pooled in my eyes. I couldn't hear his footsteps, but I knew his black combat boots were walking up the stone path toward the house.

I can't lose him. Please.

Run.

Run and it won't be true.

But I couldn't move. My legs were locked in place as I waited for the nightmare to begin.

The knock.

Thump.

Thump.

Thump.

It was as if each thump was a punch to the stomach. No air. I couldn't breathe. I was silently screaming and nothing could stop the fear gripping my insides.

Please. No. I need him.

Silence.

I heard my parent's bedroom door open and the shuffling of feet down the hallway on the hardwood floors. The distinct click as the lock turned and then the front door opened followed by the screech of the screen door.

Silence.

It felt like hours as I stood in the middle of my room, afraid to look out the window and see the car I didn't want to see. Afraid to run. Afraid to move. Hoping I was still asleep and this was all a dream.

Yes, it was dream. I'd wake up any second. I'd call him today. I'd tell him how much I missed him and loved him. It had been weeks since we last spoke. I should've emailed him more often. Why hadn't I?

My mother's loud wail pierced the air, and my perfect world crashed to my feet. It was like I was being coiled up in the death grip of an anaconda and dragged under the water.

I fell to my knees, my arms wrapped around myself, and I rocked back and forth as my mother's cries became muffled as if she was being held up against something.

There were more footsteps. Not quiet and soft like my mom's. Not slow and lumbering like my dad's. Long, confident strides.

No. Go away. Just go away. It's not real.

The steps stopped outside my door, and then I heard the click as my door handle turned. It was opening up my soul and ripping out my heart.

I stopped rocking.

The door swung open.

I clamped my eyes shut not wanting to see him. Unable to face him. Face what he was here to tell me.

"Georgie."

His gruff tone I'd recognize anywhere. It scared me, always had. He scared me.

I sniffled as my nose dripped, and I felt the trickle of tears slip from the corners of my eyes.

"Look at me." If I ignored him, it would all go away. "Georgie."

It was the hint of softness in his voice when he said my name that had me open my eyes.

My gaze hit his legs first, the long, lean length covered in black cargo pants. There was a rip in the material just above his knee. Dirt. Smudges of dirt on his pants as if he'd come straight from whatever hell they'd been in.

They. In a second, the word *they* wouldn't exist anymore.

My gaze moved upward, hesitant, as if I my brain was fighting every step. His hands were curled into fists at his sides, his knuckles strong notches that had felt the harshness of pounding into another man. It was odd because his hands were clean, and yet I saw the dirt on his tatted arms and the … blood? Was it his blood or—

"Georgie."

The loud, abrupt sound of my name made me lurch and my gaze flew to his.

His jaw was tense. Eyes hard and cold—unemotional. He stared directly at me, not an ounce of compassion in his unyielding stare. But I saw other things. There beneath his stoic solidity … the torment, the pain, the darkness that was soon going to become my darkness.

I started shaking violently, and my throat tightened against the sobs that racked my body. "No." It was the only word I could get out.

Please no.

He stood and watched me tremble and cry on my knees in the middle of my room for several minutes before he said, "I couldn't save him."

His words cut into me with finality of the truth, and my breath hitched as more tears pooled and slipped from the confines of my eyelids. I tightened my arms around my body as if that would help the pain ease.

It didn't.

Nothing would.

Connor.

He was gone.

I'd never hear his teasing. Feel the touch of his hand ruffling my hair. Hear his voice calling me Georgie girl. He promised to come back.

Pain.

Hurt.

Devastation.

Georgie girl.

Chaos. My head screamed with chaos as Connor's image played across my mind. It was distorted and broken with bits of light being sucked apart by the darkness.

Destruction. I had to destroy. My perfect world was no longer. Nothing would ever be the same again. I'd never be the same again.

I scrambled to my feet and grabbed my duvet and tore it off the bed, the flowered throw pillow and bunny were tossed to the floor. A strange sound emerged from my throat as I dove for my dresser and swept my arm across the shiny neat surface—books, my jewelry box, and a vase crashed to the hardwood floor. I could hear glass shattering, and silver stud earrings, pearls, and rings scattered in every direction.

I didn't stop. I couldn't.

Destruction.

I grabbed my light off my nightstand and threw it across the room. The bulb made a loud pop as it hit the wall. I needed to destroy. Everything I'd made into a neat and tidy place was no longer. It was all gone. Nothing would be perfect again. My world had just burst open, and I was bleeding. It hurt. God, it hurt.

I tripped over my duvet as I went for the closet and fell to my knees. It didn't stop me ... the physical pain was nothing, almost welcoming to the emotional pain that was taking me apart piece by piece. I got up, then staggered to the closet and threw open the doors.

I wrenched my clothes off the hangers—the pretty, soft yellow dresses, white ones, black ones. Then the plain button-down blouses and the black pants. The empty hangers swung back and forth on the metal bar as every single piece of clothing was thrown to the floor.

When the closet was empty, I picked up whatever was in reach and began tearing. Buttons popped. Silk and nylon tore, sleeves ripped from the cores—like me. This was me being shredded apart.

Carelessly, I yanked and pulled at whatever my hands could get a hold of.

Rip.

Tear.

Ruin everything. Destroy.

I was breathing hard when I finished. Nothing was left alive. Just like me. I had nothing left except to run.

Run.

Run.

Run.

I ran for the door. I couldn't breathe. I had to get out of here. Away from this ruined perfect world. He was gone. Connor was gone.

My mind was whirling and frantic.

Escape.

I didn't even see him; my vision blurred from tears and anger and pain. He blocked the doorway, his tall lean frame preventing my path of escape.

I ran anyway, trying to dive past him.

He snagged me around the waist with one arm and my feet left the floor. I screamed and squirmed in his hold like a rag doll. He set me down directly in front of him, his hands latched onto my upper arms in a bruising grip.

"Georgie, look at me."

I kicked and yelled, trying to leave, but nothing would set me free. I knew I'd never be free again. My brother. My best friend. He was dead.

"Let me go. Let me go. Let me go."

Run. Get away.

"Look. At. Me."

This time his voice cut through my hysterical need to escape, and I stopped struggling, staring up at his unflinching eyes. How could he just stand there? He'd just destroyed my life, my family's life. And he was standing there looking at me with not an ounce of compassion.

"I hate you."

"You going to stand still?"

Chest heaving and heart pounding, I realized Deck had watched me destroy everything in my room. He never did anything to stop it. The one thing I did know about this man was that he was unbending. Connor always said Deck was the best team leader, because no matter what shit went down, Deck would never yield to anyone. He'd stand by his word no matter what, and I guessed that he wouldn't let me go until I bent to his will.

I stopped fighting.

He waited a second then released me. Then he reached into his back pocket and pulled out a small leather-bound book that had worn edges and a cracked spine. "He'd want you to have this."

I didn't move as I stared at what I knew was Connor's journal. Deck grabbed my wrist and shoved it in my hand. The abrupt hard surface hitting my palm.

Connor's name was written on the top in his familiar messy hand writing.

I nearly fell. Probably would've if Deck hadn't grabbed my arm. He guided me into my room, and I didn't object. All I did was stare down at the bound book. The last piece of my brother. It wasn't enough. It would never be enough.

I felt the softness of the mattress as Deck made me sit, and then the floor creaked as he started to walk away.

I looked up at the retreating figure. "I wish it was you, not him."

There was no reaction to my words, and really, I hadn't expected any. It just came out. And I did hate that Deck was here instead of Connor. I hated that he could walk back to his family and laugh and hold them and my brother couldn't.

He turned his head and met my eyes. For a second, I thought I witnessed remorse, but it was so quick that I could've imagined it or maybe I hoped to see it from my brother's best friend.

"Yeah." His whispered tone was barely audible as the door shut, and I listened to his steady booted steps walk away.

The front door opened, and the screen door screeched. Both shut.

I don't know why I did it, but I walked over to the window, parted the white sheer curtains and watched as he walked down the path. The tension in his back. The stiffness of his stride.

He stopped at the side of the car and stood still for a second. I couldn't see his face or what he was doing until he slammed both fists into the roof of the car; then his head dropped forward and his shoulders slouched.

My fingers curled around the delicate material of the curtains, and I didn't realize how hard until they ripped from the rod and fell to the floor leaving the window bare.

As if he'd heard it—but I knew that was impossible—Deck turned. Our eyes locked. It felt like he could see right into me with that direct gaze. I felt naked and vulnerable, unable to look away, trapped. He gave me these wounds. Wounds that would never heal. Deck was now part of the darkness inside me that I'd never escape from.

His nod was barely distinguishable before he broke the connection and opened the car door.

I watched his lean form curl into the driver's seat.

The engine came to life with a loud purr.

Life. Something Connor had lost.

I turned away just as I heard the squeal of the tires on the street.

My perfect world had just been thrown into utter destructive chaos.

About the Author

Nashoda Rose lives in Toronto with her assortment of pets. She writes contemporary romance with a splash of darkness, or maybe it's a tidal wave. Her novel "Torn from You" is the first in the Tear Asunder series. When she isn't writing, she can be found sitting in a field reading with her dog at her side while her horses graze nearby. She loves interacting with her readers on Facebook and chatting about her addiction—books.

"With You"

Sculpt is an illegal fighter.

He's also the lead singer of a local rock band.

No one knows his real name.

And from the moment I met him, he made me forget mine.

In order to convince Sculpt to give me self-defence lessons, I had to follow his one rule—no complaining or he'd walk. I didn't think it would be a problem. I could handle a few bruises. What I hadn't anticipated was landing on my back with Sculpt on top of me and my entire body burning up for him.

I tried to ignore it.

I failed of course. And having a hot, tattooed badass on top of me week after week, acting completely immune to what he was doing to my body—it was frustrating as hell, so I broke his rule—I complained.

Then he kissed me.

"Torn from You"

Love is like an avalanche. It hits hard, fast and without mercy.

At least it did for me when Sculpt, the lead singer of the rock band Tear Asunder knocked me off my feet. Literally, because he's also a fighter, illegally of course, and he taught me how to fight. He also taught me how to love and I fell hard for him. I mean the guy could do sweet, when he wasn't doing bossy, and I like sweet.

Then it all shattered.

Kidnapped.

Starved.

Beaten.

I was alone and fighting to survive.

When I heard Sculpt's voice, I thought he was there to save me.

I was wrong.

*Warning: This book contains very disturbing situations, graphic violence, strong language and sexual content. Over 18 years.

Books by Nashoda Rose

Seven Sixes (2016)

Tear Asunder Series
With You (free)
Torn from You
Overwhelmed by You
Shattered by You
Kept from You (2016)

Unyielding Series
Perfect Chaos
Perfect Ruin (December 2015)
Perfect Rage (February 2016)

Scars of the Wraith Series
Stygian
Take

Made in the USA
San Bernardino, CA
15 August 2017